Christmas on Nutcracker Court

Books by Judy Duarte

MULBERRY PARK

ENTERTAINING ANGELS

THE HOUSE ON SUGAR PLUM LANE

CHRISTMAS ON NUTCRACKER COURT

Published by Kensington Publishing Corporation

Christmas on Nutcracker Court

JUDY DUARTE

KENSINGTON BOOKS
www.kensingtonbooks.com

KENSINGTON BOOKS are published by

Kensington Publishing Corp.
119 West 40th Street
New York, NY 10018

All Kensington titles, imprints, and distributed lines are available at special quantity discounts for bulk purchases for sales promotion, premiums, fund-raising, educational, or institutional use.

Special book excerpts or customized printings can also be created to fit specific needs. For details, write or phone the office of the Kensington Special Sales Manager: Attn. Special Sales Department. Kensington Publishing Corp., 119 West 40th Street, New York, NY 10018. Phone: 1-800-221-2647.

Kensington and the K logo Reg. U.S. Pat. & TM Off.

ISBN-13: 978-0-7582-3895-5
ISBN-10: 0-7582-3895-9

First Kensington Trade Paperback Printing: October 2011
10 9 8 7 6 5 4 3 2 1

Printed in the United States of America

Christmas on Nutcracker Court

Chapter 1

"Hey! Wait up, Josh. You're walking too fast. Aren't you scared of snakes?"

Josh Westbrook turned to face Mikey, his eight-year-old brother. "It's too cold this time of year for rattlers to be out."

Mikey's eyes widened, and the lenses of his brand-new glasses made them look bigger than normal.

"Even on the Bushman Trail?" he asked.

"It's not like we're in darkest Africa or anything." Josh crossed his arms, trying to be patient and not having much luck.

They were just walking along one of the paths in the canyon that ran along the side of Mulberry Park. The Bushman Trail was only what some of the neighborhood kids called it.

Josh supposed it might be called other things, too. The canyon was a great place to play. And it was usually littered with aluminum cans and bottles a kid could take to the recycling center.

"Are you sure there aren't any snakes out here?" Mikey asked again, looking all scared.

"Yeah," Josh said. "I'm sure. We learned about it in school."

Mikey seemed to think about that for a minute, then said,

"Okay. But can you slow down a little? I've got a blister on my heel, and my foot hurts."

Josh glanced down at the faded Skechers that he'd outgrown a couple of years ago and his brother now wore. One dirty lace was broken, and the other was loose. "You better tie your shoes, Mikey."

"I will. But maybe we ought to go home now. If we get hurt or killed or something, Mom will find out that we left the yard. And then we'll be in big trouble."

Mikey was always stressing about stuff like that, and Josh couldn't help but roll his eyes. "She won't be mad at *you*. I'm the babysitter, and you're just doing what I told you, right?"

"I guess so. But she doesn't like it when we don't obey. And if something happens—"

Josh didn't let him finish. "What's going to happen? I'm here to protect you, aren't I? Besides, we're not going to get anywhere near those houses on Nutcracker Court."

Mikey used a dirty index finger to push his glasses back along the bridge of his nose. "Yeah, I know. But I got this really weird feeling like something bad is going to happen to us." He looked up and all around like the sky was going to open up and rain down snakes on them or something.

"Would you stop with that heebie-jeebie stuff, Mikey? I know you watched that dumb TV show about psychics, but that doesn't happen in real life."

Mikey scrunched his face as if he wasn't convinced, but at least he didn't argue anymore.

"So come on." Josh turned back to the path they'd been following through the brush and weeds. He didn't have to look over his shoulder to know that Mikey was right behind him. He could hear his footsteps.

To be honest, though, Josh wasn't all that sure about the psychic stuff. Maybe there were guys who knew things before they happened. It was also possible that God talked to people in dreams or gave them visions. But he'd never admit it to his little brother.

Mikey was a real wussy when it came to things like that, and Josh couldn't let him get all freaked out about something he had no control over.

Besides, there were a lot of other things they could worry about, like having to move out of their house before Christmas.

Their mom might not want them to know the truth, but Josh wasn't dumb. She never had enough money to pay the bills. Besides, Josh had answered the phone a couple of times when the landlord called, and the man let it slip that his mom was behind on the rent.

When he got the last call, it had worried him—a lot. So he'd prayed about it and asked God to do something—like letting him find a buried treasure or a briefcase full of money. But he hadn't found squat yet.

So now he was looking for the next best thing—empty cans and plastic bottles they could trade in for some cash.

"There's another one," Mikey said, pointing to an old beer can that had been scrunched. "I'll get it."

Before Josh could scan the area for more cans, he heard a bark, followed by a second one that seemed a little bit louder.

He supposed all dogs sounded alike, but he couldn't help looking up the slope to the fence that surrounded the house on Nutcracker Court that they tried to stay away from. Sometimes, when he and Mikey got too close to that backyard, a big, mean dog would bark like he was going to bust through the wood and eat them alive.

Actually, Josh wasn't totally sure that it wouldn't.

As the barking grew closer, fear splashed across Mikey's face. The lenses of his glasses magnified his eyes to almost twice their size, as he looked to Josh for direction. But Josh didn't know what to do, either.

Before he could even give it much thought, a big, ugly brown dog, with its tongue dangling out of its mouth, came loping through the weeds—straight at them!

Josh's heart nearly jumped right out of his chest.

"It's *him*," Mikey said, as he ducked behind Josh for protection.

Great. Josh wanted to run away himself, but he hadn't been lying when he told Mikey he'd take care of him. He just hadn't expected to have to stand up to a ferocious dog.

Before he could grab a stick or a rock, the dog slowed to a stop and plopped down on its haunches.

That was a good sign, wasn't it? Maybe the mutt was friendlier than they'd thought.

"Take it easy, boy. We're okay." Josh slowly reached out his hand, like he'd seen guys do on *Animal Planet,* and the dog lurched forward as though they'd been long-lost friends.

"Hey," Mikey said. "He's not so mean after all."

The goofy mutt gave Josh's hand a wet, sloppy lick.

"What kind of dog is he?" Mikey asked.

"Who knows? I've never seen one like him before." In fact, the wooly creature looked like the kind of dog a Yeti might have.

Josh patted the mongrel on the top of its head. "Maybe he only barked at us before because he wanted to play or something."

"Or else he wanted to escape his owner," Mikey added.

Josh wouldn't blame him for that. He'd only seen the guy once, but he'd been wearing a bathrobe at lunchtime. And his black hair had stuck up like he never combed it.

"Hey," Mikey said. "The dog's kind of ugly and has a mean bark, but he's really nice. Maybe we should take him home. We could tell Mom that we got her a watchdog for Christmas. He'd make a cool present."

A dog, even a big, ugly one, would be kind of cool to have, but a pet would mean one more mouth for her to feed, and that might only make things worse.

"I don't think so," Josh said, wishing things were different.

As the boys stroked the dog's long fur, dry leaves crunched and twigs snapped.

Josh looked up to see a barefoot man wearing light blue pajama bottoms and a white bathrobe that gaped open and revealed a broad, hairy chest. His frown was enough to scare Josh all over again.

"What do you think you're doing with my dog?" he asked.

Mikey eased closer to Josh. "We aren't doing anything, mister. Just petting him."

He had a *yeah, right* expression on his face. "Who let him out of the yard? The gate was wide open."

"We don't know," Josh said. "We weren't anywhere near your property."

"Well, somebody turned him loose. And they took off his collar."

Josh wondered if he could outrun the man. Maybe, but he had Mikey to think about. And with a blister on his foot and laces that never stayed tied, his kid brother would never be able to move fast enough.

"I've told you before to stay away from my house," the guy said, his tone sharp and angry. "And to quit harassing my dog."

"We didn't get anywhere near your yard." Josh tried to stand tall, act tough, and look older than his twelve years, but his voice came out a little wobbly. "And we weren't making any noise. Your dog just came running up to us. We thought he was going to bite us, and if he would have, our mom would sue you."

The man, whose dark hair was messed up just like before, narrowed his eyes and mumbled something about a crazy litigious society.

Josh had no idea what he was talking about, but that wasn't a surprise. The guy was clearly nuts. What kind of whack job slept during the day?

"What's your name?" the man asked, zeroing in on Josh. But maybe that was because Mikey had slipped almost completely behind him by this time.

Trying not to let the guy—or his little brother—know that

he was starting to shake in his shoes, he lifted his chin and told the truth. "Josh Westbrook."

"What's your telephone number?" the guy asked.

No way would Josh give him *that* information, but before he could clamp his mouth shut and cross his arms in defiance, Mikey rattled it off.

Josh wanted to clobber his kid brother. What had he been thinking?

The guy didn't write it down, though. Maybe he wouldn't remember it. But then again, that was probably just wishful thinking since it wasn't all that hard.

When they'd first moved into the house on Canyon Drive, his mom had asked for a number that would be easy for Mikey to remember.

Too bad they'd given her 555-1122.

The man pulled the tie from the loops on his robe and, using it as a leash, wrapped it around the dog's neck. "Come on, boy."

The dog only half-obeyed the guy. He kept trying to turn back and look at Josh and Mikey as though he wanted them to help him get away.

And who could blame him? Josh wouldn't want to go home with that man, either.

"Do you think he's going to call Mom?" Mikey asked.

"No," Josh said, even though he wasn't so sure about that.

When he got home, he was going to turn the ringer down on the telephone—unless the phone bill hadn't been paid, and it was shut off and not working already.

Their mom didn't need to deal with something like this. She was way too busy and stressed out for that.

And the fact was, Mikey wasn't the only one who needed Josh's protection.

The house had grown quiet, other than the clock ticking softly on the mantel, and although Carly Westbrook was ready to take a bath and soak in a hot tub before climbing into bed, she wanted to look over her bank statement one more time. In spite of her best efforts to make payments, the stack of bills seemed to be growing.

There was only so far she could stretch a hairdresser's monthly income, and it was time to face reality. Her financial condition was in dire straits, and she had to plan for a move.

But where would she go if she wanted to keep the boys in the same school? Mikey had been a poor reader, and in spite of getting him a library card during the summer and working with him each evening, it hadn't seemed to help much.

There'd been talk of putting him back into first grade, which she hated to do unless it was really necessary. He'd already repeated kindergarten once.

His teacher, Mrs. Hornkohl, who'd been giving him extra help during recess and after school, had suggested a visit to the eye doctor, which had been a real blessing. It turned out that Mikey had a vision problem that hadn't been detected, and his new glasses had made a remarkable difference.

Of course, that also had meant an additional expense that she hadn't counted on right before the holidays.

Carly blew out a sigh. It hadn't always been this tough to make ends meet, but after Derek left her, she just couldn't seem to stay on top of the bills no matter how hard she tried. And she kept getting pink notices that the power company was going to discontinue service if she didn't make a payment by a certain date.

In fact, after dinner this evening, while the boys were taking their baths, she'd tried to make a phone call to tell one of her clients that there'd been a cancellation and she could fit her in after all, but she'd found the line dead. At first, she'd been afraid that she'd lost service because she hadn't paid the bill. But then she'd noticed that the cord had been removed from the wall jack.

Thank goodness for that. But each month there was always an unexpected expense, like the new glasses and the optometrist bill.

Now, with an eviction process underway, she realized that a Christmas tree and presents for the boys were clearly out of the question this year.

Yet, worse than that, where would she and the kids go at the end of the month? To a motel? To a shelter?

She pushed the check register and bank statement to the side, clasped her hands together, then bowed her head.

Lord, I'm at my wit's end. I don't know what to do anymore. I need some debt relief—or a better-paying job at a salon that has a wealthier clientele. But I guess what I really need is a Christmas miracle.

She'd no more than said, "Amen," when the phone rang, and she nearly bolted from her chair. If this was the Christmas miracle she'd been asking for, God had moved a lot faster than she'd hoped.

But in spite of her faith, she was also a realist. There was no telling who was on the other end of the line or what they wanted.

"Mrs. Westbrook?" an unfamiliar male voice asked.

"Yes?"

"This is Max Tolliver."

The guy who lived on Nutcracker Court? A week ago, when the boys had mentioned a run-in with a grouchy man and his vicious dog, she'd driven by the house they'd described and had noted the name on the mailbox. She'd wanted to know more about him in case things ever escalated. In fact, she'd almost stopped in to talk to him that day, but had decided to keep driving.

"What can I do for you?" she asked.

"You can tell your boys to stay away from my house and property. They've been harassing me and my dog."

Her grip on the receiver tightened. "I'm not sure what you're talking about. How have they been bothering you?"

"They walk along the backside of my fence, which riles up my dog. And then he starts barking and howling. I work nights and sleep days, so you can understand why that's annoying. I've asked them to stay away, but they don't. And today they let the dog out. I had to go down to the canyon and bring him home."

Had Josh and Mikey been on the Bushman Trail again?

So much for the Christmas miracle she'd been praying for. She certainly didn't need this heaped on her.

She knew she shouldn't let Josh be in charge of his brother, but what could she do? Quit one of her jobs? Hire a sitter?

"I'm sorry that the boys have been bothering you, Mr. Tolliver. I'll talk to them and make sure it doesn't happen again."

"See that it doesn't."

She nearly let it go at that, but thought better of it. "They're sweet little boys, Mr. Tolliver. They don't mean any harm. I'm not sure how old you are, but surely you remember what it was like to be a child."

He chuffed, then said, "I'm not a mean old man, if that's what the boys told you. I don't have fangs or a dungeon in the basement filled with rats. I'm just a guy who appreciates his peace and quiet."

"I'll tell them to stay far away from your property, Mr. Tolliver. And as a side note, you won't have to worry about my sons much longer. We'll be moving within the next couple of weeks."

"Where are you going?" he asked.

She didn't respond. It really wasn't any of his business, but even if it had been, she didn't have a ready answer.

If God had a plan for her and the boys, He hadn't given her a clue as to what it was.

After phoning Mrs. Westbrook, Max Tolliver fixed himself a snack of microwave popcorn and a mug of hot coffee, then he settled back into his leather desk chair and tried to get back to work. He did his best writing at night, but as his fingers rested on the keyboard and he stared at the computer screen, his mind went blank.

For some reason, he couldn't seem to get back into the story he'd created.

What had possessed him to ask that woman where she and her family were moving? He really didn't care, as long as they left the neighborhood.

But the question had just rolled off his tongue, a leftover habit from his former job, he supposed. As a probation officer, he'd had to stay on top of the defendants who were on his caseload.

He didn't blame Mrs. Westbrook for ignoring his question, though. And he should be glad she didn't snap at him for even asking.

All that really mattered was that he would finally be able to have the peace and quiet he needed to get a few hours of uninterrupted sleep each day.

Now, focusing on the screen before him, he grabbed the mouse, scrolled up, and reread the paragraph he'd been working on before placing that telephone call.

Logan stood at the living room window, his breath fogging the glass as he peered at the driveway. He watched Priscilla throw a suitcase into the back of her black Toyota Prius. She was leaving, she'd told him earlier, heading back to the small Texas town that she'd once called home. And if her parting words rang true, she wasn't ever coming back.

But Logan Sinclair didn't need her.

He didn't need anyone.

Max's fingers were braced on the keyboard, itching to continue, to add a line or two more of introspection. He even closed his eyes and stroked the keys, hoping to get into Logan's head and let the character speak for himself.

But Logan Sinclair, the cynical cop who was up to his ears in trouble, wasn't talking, and Max had no idea why. Logan had certainly gotten himself into one heck of a mess without much help from the author who'd created him.

So what was the cop feeling now, as his wife backed out of the driveway and sped off, leaving him to face his enemies and the internal affairs department on his own?

Max wished he knew, but the character, who'd become so real to him over the past four hundred pages, suddenly seemed like a stranger.

And Max had no one to blame but Mrs. Westbrook.

Why'd he have to go and talk to her now? Why couldn't he have made that call before he'd started working this evening?

He should have known better. Interruptions to his writing process usually stopped him cold, which was why he found it easier to work at night and into the wee hours of the morning, when most of the world had gone to sleep.

Earlier this evening, after dinner, he'd put on a fresh pot of coffee, hoping a rush of caffeine would stimulate the muse. But even the hearty aroma of his favorite Kona blend hadn't done the trick.

The house was quiet, just the way he liked it. Yet, for some reason, the blasted *tick-tock-tick* of the clock on the mantel seemed to echo off the walls and play havoc with his ability to concentrate.

As Max glanced back at the blinking cursor that mocked him, he blew out a ragged sigh.

What if he'd actually been contracted to write this book and had a real deadline looming, rather than the self-imposed one he worked under now?

He'd given himself a year to write a novel, a dream he'd had since his teenage years. A dream that had continued to build until he hadn't been able to ignore it any longer.

Last January, when he'd been a probation officer, dealing with people who'd gotten themselves in legal trouble for one reason or another, his dream of writing the great American novel had grown too big for him to put off any longer. And fictitious Logan Sinclair, a rogue cop with a checkered past, had been on his mind more often than not. So he'd taken a leave of absence from the county and had given himself until the end of this year to finish the book.

Trouble was, he'd gone through the bulk of his savings and would have to either quit writing and go back to the "real job" or put his house on the market, risking it all for a dream that might never come true.

Of course, he had a solid proposal for a series of books featuring Logan Sinclair, but the last literary agent he'd queried had suggested that he complete the first book and then let him take a second look at it.

That response was the closest he'd ever come to having his dream validated by someone in the publishing business, so he'd dug in and started working. In the story, he'd just reached the part that would become the black moment and would lead to the climax and resolution.

But Priscilla Sinclair had really thrown a wrench into the machinery when she'd decided to leave her husband. Their heated argument, which had taken place a couple of pages back, had come out of the blue and exploded on the page while Max had been deep in the writing zone.

If the dialogue between Logan and Priscilla hadn't been so crisp, so real, Max might have considered deleting it and starting over. But their argument seemed reasonable, and so did her leaving.

He'd read about how this sort of thing happened to writers, how characters came alive and the story took off in a completely different direction than originally had been plotted. So while this didn't surprise him, it did back him into a corner.

Max blew out another sigh.

So why did Priscilla throw down the gauntlet at a time like

that? Poor Logan had enough on his plate and could really use some feminine support at this point. He certainly hadn't needed an ultimatum from her now.

Why didn't Logan just tell her, "Good riddance" and be done with it?

After going through a messy divorce of his own a little over a year ago, Max thought of all kinds of ways to end the scene.

Priscilla's car could blow a tire, and she could lose control and slam into a tree. The vehicle could explode upon impact. . . .

Okay, so he was a little angry with women these days, especially wives who left their husbands. And since he hadn't foreshadowed those kinds of problems in the Sinclairs' marriage before now, he'd have to come up with something else.

He tapped his index fingers on the J and F keys.

"So now what?" he asked himself.

Priscilla could realize that she'd made a terrible mistake by leaving the one man in the world who really loved her. Then she could make a U-turn, drive back home, and beg Logan to take her back.

But that was too cheesy for the book he was writing.

Hemingway, who'd been curled up beside the desk, began to stir and stretch his lanky body. The dog, which by all outward appearances was one part wolfhound and three parts mutt, had once been a stray in the neighborhood before becoming a pet.

Max liked to think that he'd merely sympathized with the overgrown pup and had taken him in, but he really hadn't had much of a choice in the matter. The crazy dog had plopped down on Max's front porch and stayed as if he'd had squatter's rights.

The dog yawned, then got to his wooly feet, padded to the entryway, scratched at the door, and whined.

Max really ought to let him out into the backyard, but the main entry was just a few steps away. So at night, it had become a lazy habit to let him pee in the front.

"Okay, okay," Max said, as he pushed back his desk chair, stood, and made his way to the entry. Then he opened the door and waited while Hemingway trotted down the steps, across the lawn, and over to the big elm in the center of the yard, where he liked to hike his leg.

Nutcracker Court was quiet this evening, but Max sensed he wasn't the only one outdoors. In the glow of a streetlight, he spotted a long-haired, bearded man standing near the curb in front of Helen Pritchard's darkened house.

Helen, a divorcée in her midfifties, had left early this morning to join her family on a three-week Mediterranean cruise. Max knew that because he was supposed to be watching the old Victorian while she was gone.

The lights were off, as they should be. But what was that guy doing out here at this time of night?

Before Max could quiz him, a woman with platinum-blond hair crossed Helen's lawn and joined the man on the sidewalk.

Max didn't like the thought of vagrants milling around the neighborhood, especially when most people were sleeping. He had half a notion to chase them off, but realized he wouldn't have to do it, once Hemingway noticed them.

But the dog seemed oblivious to the strangers and continued to sprinkle each bush in the front yard, marking his territory.

When Hemingway had made his rounds, he glanced out into the street, finally taking note of the couple.

Go get 'em, Max thought, expecting the dog to take off like a shot and make a big racket. But Hemingway merely loped toward the man and woman as if he'd just recognized long-lost friends.

"Hemingway!" Max called. "Get back here."

Clearly forgetting the hand that fed him, the dog joined the couple in the street.

Max grumbled under his breath, then made his way down the sidewalk and across Nutcracker Court. He didn't have to go far, because the shabby man met him halfway.

"How's it going?" the stranger asked, his blue eyes zeroing in on Max as though they'd met before.

"All right." Noting that the man's long gray coat was frayed and torn at the collar, Max returned his focus to the guy's bearded face. "Can I help you?"

"Actually . . ." The woman, who was wearing a light pink sweatshirt with HOME SWEET HOME embroidered on the front, smiled. "We'd like to help *you*."

"I don't need any work done around the house," Max said, figuring they were looking for odd jobs. "And if you need food or shelter, you might check out the Parkside Community Church. They have both a soup kitchen and an outreach program for those in need."

"My name's Jesse," the man said. "And this is Maggie."

Max merely nodded, his skeptical nature holding back any semblance of a smile.

"How's the book coming along?" Jesse asked.

Max tensed. How would this guy know he was a writer? If the living room blinds had been open, he might have thought the two had been spying on him.

Either way, Max chose not to answer his question and offered a prompt for the two strangers to move on. "It's a cold night to be out on the streets."

"Yes, it is. In fact, we're just heading for the bus stop." Jesse placed a hand on Maggie's shoulder. "Have a good evening. And merry Christmas to you and yours."

Max waited until they both disappeared into the shadows, then he grabbed Hemingway by the collar and led the dog home. As he did so, he glanced over his shoulder to take one last look at the couple to make sure they'd continued on their way.

Apparently so, he decided.

After more than fifteen years as a probation officer, Max usually had a second sense about troublemakers with lame excuses. And while he had half a notion to call the police and have those two checked out, he couldn't quite bring himself to do it.

Hopefully, that wasn't a big mistake.

Chapter 2

As dawn cast its morning light over Fairbrook, Susan Ferris carried a cup of honey-laced breakfast tea to her desk, took a seat, and started up the computer.

Less than a year ago, she used to sleep until nine or ten, but that was before Hank passed away. Now, try as she might, she could never seem to find a comfortable spot on that king-sized mattress. But she supposed that was to be expected after nearly twenty years of marriage.

When the beeps, blips, and groans finally stopped and the computer was up and running, she signed into her e-mail account, then waited until her in-box displayed the new messages.

There were only three this morning, but the one from Helen Pritchard jumped out at her.

That was odd. Helen, who lived on the other side of town, had left yesterday morning for a three-week vacation. And Susan had been the one to drop her off at the airport.

After landing at La Guardia, Helen planned to meet up with other family members and spend the night in Manhattan. Then they would board a cruise ship, cross the Atlantic, and visit Europe and the Mediterranean before flying home.

Even as late as yesterday morning, while the two friends shared a cup of tea before taking Helen's luggage out to the car, Helen had again asked if Susan wanted to go along. "I don't like the idea of you spending Christmas alone," she'd added. "It would do you good to join us."

The genuine concern had warmed Susan's heart. "You're a wonderful friend for thinking of me like that, but I'll be okay. Besides, it's a little late now, don't you think?"

"No, it's *not* too late. I have a private room on the ship that sleeps two, so you can easily purchase a ticket. And you already have a passport, which we can pick up on our way to the airport, along with a nightie and some undies. You can purchase anything else you need while we're in New York."

"You're forgetting that your plane leaves in less than three hours. And the flight is probably sold out."

"Wrong again." Helen's eyes lit up, and her lips stretched into a grin. "I checked last night. There are still plenty of seats left."

At that point, Susan had placed a hand on her friend's forearm and chuckled. "You're amazing—and such an orchestrator."

As usual, Helen had thought of everything.

"Don't tell me you can't afford it," Helen had countered as she'd tapped her index finger on one of the more colorful brochures she'd spread out on the kitchen table. "I know Hank left you in great financial shape. Please reconsider. It'll do you good to be away on your first holiday alone."

Susan found it tempting, of course, but she'd held her ground. Even if she was willing to run home, pack quickly, and ask Lynette or Rosa to look after her cat, the answer was still no.

But she wouldn't share the real reason for her refusal with Helen. If truth be told, she would have been a little uneasy around Helen's many relatives, especially when she'd always dreamed of having a family of her own someday. A dream that, sadly, seemed to have died with Hank.

At that very moment, just as if the cat had been able to

sense Susan's loneliness, it jumped on her lap and made a couple of circles before curling up in a big furry ball.

Snowflake was Susan's baby now. And while it wasn't quite the same as having a real child, she supposed a cuddly pet would have to do.

But enough of that. If she let those yearning thoughts creep up on her, she would fall into a big blue funk that would last most of the day. And with Christmas coming, it was going to be tough enough to stay upbeat. So she clicked on Helen's e-mail.

As the note opened, she saw that the other Diamond Lils had each been included and had received a copy, which wasn't surprising. The Lils, as the women in their weekly poker group often referred to themselves, had become close friends over the years.

In fact, it was the Lils who'd come together and helped Susan deal with Hank's loss last January. Rosa Alvarado, who attended Parkside Community Church, had practically handled the funeral arrangements single-handedly. And they'd all taken turns preparing meals and forcing Susan to eat.

So why had Helen e-mailed the group when they'd already said their good-byes on Thursday afternoon?

She'd also sent it last night, which meant she'd had to access the Internet from her hotel room in New York.

"Uh-oh," Susan said aloud, hoping it wasn't bad news.

Hi, Lils—
    I was in such a fog as I packed for my trip that I forgot to mention that my cousin, Mary-Margaret Di Angelo, will be house-sitting while I'm gone. And since Maggie doesn't know a soul in Fairbrook, I was hoping you would take her under your wing and make her feel welcome.
    I know I can count on you!
    Bon Voyage!
Helen

Susan sat back in her chair. Helen had never said anything about needing a house sitter. If she had, Susan would have volunteered.

Nor had she ever mentioned a cousin named Maggie.

Snowflake mewed and turned her head, as if she thought it was unusual, too.

But knowing Helen, she'd probably gotten a little scattered while packing, just as she'd said. So Susan typed in a quick reply.

> Don't worry about a thing. I'll stop by to check on Maggie this afternoon. You can count on me to make her feel welcome.
> Have a great trip!

Susan wasn't sure how the others would respond. Rosa was pretty busy these days.

Too busy, if you asked Susan. It seemed that her husband volunteered for every charitable organization in town, and poor Rosa did her best to keep up with him. Right now, they were knee-deep in the planning of Christmas Under the Stars, a holiday program held each December in Mulberry Park.

Lynette Tidball had more time on her hands, though, so maybe she would be able to join Susan at Helen's this afternoon.

Either way, she would make her mango-coconut cake to take as a welcome-to-Fairbrook gift for Maggie. She hadn't baked since last December, which wasn't surprising. She hadn't felt like doing a lot of things after Hank died.

But today, she actually looked forward to whipping up that cake batter and smelling it bake in the oven. People always raved about the taste and often asked her to give them the recipe, but there was no way she'd ever share it.

Her Aunt Pat had felt the same way. After Pat's death, Susan had the chore of packing up her belongings, keeping things that had sentimental value, and sending the rest to

Goodwill. But then she'd stumbled across her aunt's recipe box and realized she'd struck gold. So now the secret was hers.

When Susan had responded to all three of her e-mails, she returned to her bedroom and slipped her bare feet into the furry pink slippers Hank had given her two Christmases before last. They were getting old and frayed, but she just couldn't bring herself to throw them away.

After making her bed, she padded into the kitchen to check her pantry for the necessary ingredients and to make a list of what she'd need to purchase at the market. It would be nice to have something to focus on other than herself today, as well as her longing to find a husband to replace the one she'd lost.

Sometimes, while she was tossing and turning in that great big old bed, she would pray that the perfect man would come into her life and pull her out of the depression that seemed to plague her if she let it.

One Thursday afternoon, while playing poker at Helen's house, she'd told the Lils that she wanted to remarry and admitted that she'd like to meet that special someone sooner as opposed to later, hoping they'd step in as matchmakers.

But she hadn't told them her primary reason for finding a man—and quickly. Susan wanted to get pregnant before it was too late.

Most people probably assumed that either she or Hank had a fertility problem, but as far as she knew, neither of them did.

Hank had been a workaholic who'd spent his life trying to move up the corporate ladder. And Susan had learned to accept his drive for success and financial stability—just as he'd understood that she was a little dyslexic, that she had a lousy sense of direction, and that she sometimes overdrew the checking account.

Looking back, though, she now wondered if he'd been dragging his feet about having a child for a genetic reason.

Hank's younger brother was developmentally delayed and lived at Lydia's House, a residential home for the disabled in Fairbrook. It was a nice place, considering.

Hank's parents and his sister were pretty involved with the organization that funded the residence, and while Hank had made sizable donations each Christmas season, he rarely visited.

They'd never talked about it, but Susan wondered if Hank had been afraid that he might pass on whatever genes had caused Ronnie's problem to his son or daughter.

It really didn't matter, she supposed. About the time her biological clock had wound down and Hank had finally agreed to start their family, he'd died of a massive heart attack.

So here she was, on the far side of forty-one and sensing her days of motherhood were limited.

She'd prayed about it regularly, of course, and she hoped God would bless her with a new husband. But so far, she hadn't met any potential candidates.

Hopefully, she would meet the right man soon. Otherwise she feared it would be too late for her to conceive a baby. And Susan couldn't imagine living the rest of her life with only a cat to keep her company.

Carly stood in the small kitchen of the two-bedroom rented house, fixing lunches for Josh and Mikey. The boys had already eaten breakfast this morning—oatmeal, toast, and milk—and they were dressed for school. So she'd sent them both to the bathroom to brush their teeth, something she couldn't let them neglect.

Without dental insurance to cover the cost, cavities weren't in her budget. Of course, nothing unexpected was at this point.

Fortunately, she had a full schedule of appointments at Shear Magic today. And one of her best customers, Lynette Tidball, was coming in for highlights and a style. Lynette, a wealthy widow in her early thirties, was a decent tipper, which meant Carly would be able to stop at the market on the way home and pick up a few necessities that she'd been unable to purchase on her last grocery shopping trip.

"Josh!" she called. "The bus will be coming in a few minutes. It's time for you boys to go."

As her sons entered the kitchen, Josh slipped on the backpack he'd left near the table. "We're ready, Mom. But even if we weren't, the school isn't all that far from here. We can walk or take our bikes."

"Yes, but I'd feel much better if Mikey rode the bus." She glanced at the clock on the wall. "So don't dawdle, okay? You only have about five minutes."

Josh nodded, although his expression suggested that he wasn't all that happy about making sure his brother got to school safely. Fortunately, he didn't complain, which was a relief. She wasn't up for an argument this morning. And even if she was, she didn't like discussing some of her more serious concerns with her children.

Mikey was a little fearful these days, and Carly wasn't sure why. She had a feeling it had a lot to do with the divorce and her ex-husband's abandonment.

Okay, so she'd been the one to ask Derek to leave. But she'd also gotten tired of supporting his spending sprees, especially when he'd been unable or unwilling to hold a job.

What she hadn't expected was for him to walk out the door and never look back.

Maybe she ought to talk to Mikey's teacher about that. Mrs. Hornkohl had a heart for children. And she was also a single parent herself.

"Hey, Mom," Mikey said, as he stooped to pick up his backpack. "Can we have spaghetti for dinner tonight? We haven't had that in a long time."

Carly had tomato sauce, spices, and pasta in the pantry, but she would need to pick up some meat on her way home from work. She was careful what she put on her shopping list these days, but adding another half-pound of ground turkey meat shouldn't be a problem, especially with the extra tip money she'd be getting from Lynette.

"Sure," she said. "Spaghetti does sound good. I won't be here until after five, but it won't take long to fix."

"Cool," Josh said.

"Don't forget to call me as soon as you get home," Carly added. "And then you need to get your homework done."

"Even before we have a snack?" Mikey asked. "School makes us super hungry."

Carly smiled at her youngest son. "No, you can take time to eat a snack. But do me a favor, eat those granola bars in the pantry. I don't want them to go to waste."

After kissing them each good-bye and sending them on their way, Carly waited until she heard the front door open and close. Then she filled the sink with warm soapy water and washed the breakfast dishes.

Just as she was drying the saucepan she'd used to make oatmeal, her cell phone rang.

Hopefully, it was a client needing an appointment. She always tried to accommodate their schedules whenever possible, so she flipped open her cell and said, "Hello, this is Carly."

"I'm sorry to call you so early, but I have a two o'clock appointment for highlights, and I'm going to need to reschedule."

Carly's heart dropped. It was Lynette Tidball. And that left her with only two appointments this afternoon—and less tip money. So the spaghetti would have to wait for another day.

Still, she masked her disappointment the best she could. "Sure. When would you like to come in?"

"What do you have open for tomorrow or the next day?"

At least Lynette hadn't cancelled altogether. Carly blew out a little sigh and scanned her appointment book. "I can do it at ten o'clock tomorrow. Or one thirty on Wednesday."

"I'm not an early bird," Lynette said. "So Wednesday would work best for me."

"You've got it." Carly tried to sound upbeat, but she was getting so tired of taking one step forward only to slip and end up two steps behind.

"Thanks," Lynette said. "You're the best."

Carly certainly tried to be, but these days she felt second-rate.

Josh stood next to Mikey on the corner of Canyon and Park, wishing he could have ridden his bike to school and left Mikey here to wait with the other little kids.

Everyone else at this bus stop was in third grade or younger, so Josh was the oldest one here.

There were even a couple of moms who hung out with their kindergartners, so his little brother would be safe without him.

Too bad he couldn't just leave him. If Josh didn't have to look after Mikey, he could meet up with Tommy and Greg at the gas station and mini-mart near the school. Not that he had any money to buy junk, like his friends did, but it was cool to be with guys his own age.

Now he stood at the back of the line, waiting for Mr. Crenshaw, the bus driver, to show up.

"Oh, no." Mikey nudged Josh's arm and pointed down the street, where a big, wooly dog trudged up the side of the canyon and stepped onto the sidewalk.

It wasn't just any big, wooly dog, though. It was the one that belonged to the mean guy who lived on Nutcracker Court.

When the animal spotted them, it trotted down the sidewalk until it reached the bus stop. Then it plopped down on its haunches and started panting, its long pink tongue dangling out of its mouth.

The goofy mutt almost looked as though he was smiling and glad to have found a couple of friends.

"He must have gotten out again," Mikey said.

"Yeah, but he's wearing a collar this time." A blue one with a couple of metal tags hanging on it. Josh reached for them. One was a license. The other one was in the shape of a dog bone. It said his name was Hemingway and that he lived at 3186 Nutcracker Court.

Josh gave the dog's furry head and ears a scratch. "Who let you out *this* time, boy?"

Not that he expected an answer, but the dog's owner was really fussy about him staying in the yard, and Josh hoped that he and Mikey didn't get blamed again.

They probably would, though. So he slipped his hand under the collar and got a good hold of it.

"You get on the bus with everyone else and go to school," he told his brother. "I'm going to take the dog home."

"Don't do that, Josh. You'll get in big trouble."

The way Josh saw it, he was going to get in trouble either way. "I'll be okay. Don't worry."

"But you're going to miss the bus."

"If that happens, I'll just walk to school."

"But *Josh*—"

"I'll be fine." Josh tossed his brother a brave smile. "I'll see you on the playground after lunch."

Rather than taking another look at Mikey's face and risk seeing the worry splashed across it, Josh turned and led the dog to the path that cut through the canyon.

His plan was to put him back into his fenced yard without anyone being the wiser, then to walk down Nutcracker Court to Parkside Drive. The school was only a couple of blocks away from there.

Okay, so maybe Josh should have let the dumb mutt roam all over Fairbrook. What did he care?

Besides, if he got picked up by the dog catcher and hauled to the pound, he had a license. So they'd know who owned him and where he lived.

Of course, by taking him home, Josh would also get to

walk to school on his own today. And who knew? Maybe his friends would still be at the mini-mart.

"So you're Hemingway," he said, thinking it was a pretty dumb name for a dog. If the choice had been his, he would have called him something cool like Wolf or maybe even Yeti.

Still, he figured it would be a good idea to talk to the animal as if they were friends. It might make it a little easier to put him back in his yard.

Five minutes later, he and Hemingway were trudging up the slope to Nutcracker Court.

Josh's legs felt the strain of the uphill climb, and the dog half-pulled him to the grass on the other side. Then, as if knowing exactly where they were going, Hemingway headed toward the house where he lived.

This was the tricky part. Josh was going to have to open the gate and let the dog into the backyard without making any noise. He figured that wouldn't be a problem unless Hemingway gave him trouble.

Moments later, he stood before the gate—which was *closed.*

So how did the dog get out? Had he dug a hole under the fence?

If so, he was going to keep escaping until his owner found the hole and fixed it.

With one hand gripped tightly to the dog's collar, Josh stood on tiptoe and undid the latch with the other. Then he opened the gate and let the dog back in his yard.

Fortunately, the wooly beast obeyed.

Hey, Josh realized. *Beast* would have been another good name for him.

As Josh headed for the sidewalk, he brushed his hands on the denim fabric of his jeans. He was eager to put this chore behind him, but as he left the dog's front yard, he glanced at the mailbox in front of the yard. TOLLIVER was written on the side with faded black letters.

Was that the man's name? Or was it just left over from the last people who used to live there?

Oh, well. It didn't matter to Josh. He didn't plan on running into that guy ever again.

But as he stepped onto the sidewalk and turned toward Parkside Drive, he ran into someone who just might be a whole lot worse: Ross "the Boss" Shurlock, the meanest kid at Parkside Elementary.

Ross was bigger than most of the teachers, at least the women. And he weighed about two hundred pounds. At least, it felt that way when he sat on top of Josh on the playground during the third week of school.

All Josh had done was to stick up for Mikey when Ross had called him four eyes, but apparently, Ross didn't like other kids telling him to back off.

Ross had ended up getting detention that day. And he'd blamed Josh for ratting him out, but he hadn't. Mikey had told Mrs. Hornkohl, who'd then told the principal.

Some of the kids at school said Ross was a teenager already, which might be true. They also said that he was still in the sixth grade because he had to repeat kindergarten a couple of times.

Ross had to go to special classes for reading, too. One girl thought that was really sad, but Josh figured that a kid didn't need to be able to read if he was big and strong and good at kicking butts.

"Hey, Westbrook." Ross pushed his chest out like he was all big and tough. "What are you doing in my neighborhood?"

Josh hadn't known where Ross lived. And if he'd thought that his house was on Nutcracker Court, he would have had *two* big reasons to stay off this street.

"I'm not doing anything," Josh said. "Just taking a shortcut to school."

"Oh, yeah?" Ross, who had pimples on his face and even some black hairs growing on his chin, put his hands on his hips. "Says who?"

"The bell's going to ring pretty soon." Josh figured a reminder that there wasn't much time for a butt kicking would be a good idea.

But Ross didn't look like he cared about being tardy.

"I charge a toll to any kids who want to walk on this side of the canyon," he said. "But since we don't have a whole lot of time to make a deal on the price, why don't you just tell me how much you have on you."

Josh ran his hands along his empty pockets. "I don't have any money."

"That's too bad." Ross grabbed Josh by the shirt and gave it a hard twist until the fabric ripped.

Josh hoped his mom would think it was an old shirt. But getting in trouble with her tonight was the least of his problems right now.

Still, even though he was scared spitless, he tried to act like he wasn't. "Hey, Ross. Let loose."

"Not until you pay me. Empty your pockets."

If Josh had any money, he would gladly give it to the jerk just to be rid of him and on his way to school. But he didn't have any cash. So he reached into his pockets and turned them inside out. "See? You're out of luck today."

"No," Ross said, giving Josh a shove that knocked him to the concrete. "*You* are."

Then he kicked him, right in the face.

Josh grimaced in pain, but he didn't cry, even though his lip hurt like heck. His eyes got all teary, but he refused to yell for help.

As it turned out, he didn't have to.

Hemingway started barking like he wanted to break down the fence and eat up the bully who was messing with his new best friend. And moments later, the front door of his house swung open, and the grumpy man stepped out on the porch, looking just as mad and mean as ever.

Great. Now Josh was in double trouble. If he had a time machine, he'd wind it back to about ten minutes ago, and then he would have stayed with Mikey.

"Hey!" the man yelled. "Back off and get away from him!"

Ross took off running, leaving Josh to face the man alone.

He was really dead meat now, but he got to his feet and crossed his arms. He wanted to be brave, but his heart was pounding as though there were a hyperactive drummer and a rock band in his chest.

"What's going on here?" the man asked, his voice all mean and snarly.

"Nothing."

"Yeah, right. What were you two boys fighting about?"

Like Josh would tell *him*.

Even if the guy was a policeman or someone with any real authority, he still wouldn't tell. Ross might have run away just now, but that didn't mean he wouldn't still want to finish what he'd started later today or this week or this year.

So Josh gave a little shrug. "It was no big deal."

"So why did your friend rough you up?" Mr. Tolliver asked.

"He's not my *friend*."

Tolliver's eye twitched, but he continued to stare at Josh like a teacher who'd caught a guy cheating on a spelling test.

Finally, Tolliver crossed his own arms over his chest. "What are you doing on my street?"

"I returned your dog. He got out of your yard again. There must be a hole in your fence somewhere because the gate was closed. But I had nothing to do with it. I was just standing at the bus stop on Canyon when he came running up to me."

"I've already checked my backyard for holes, and the fence is secure. So how do you suppose he would have gotten out?"

Josh shrugged. "I don't know, mister. Maybe you just got a smart dog."

Tolliver scrunched his face, as though he found that hard

to believe, then he looked at Josh. "Your lip is bleeding. I've got tissues inside."

No way was Josh going into that guy's house—if that's what he had in mind.

"I'm okay." And to prove it, Josh lifted the torn neckline of his shirt and wiped his mouth. But dang, it hurt like heck when he did.

Tolliver, who was wearing sweatpants and no shirt, made his way toward Josh.

Uh-oh. Josh wondered what would happen if he just turned and walked away. It sure seemed like the best thing to do right now.

"Why was that kid giving you a hard time?" the guy asked.

Josh chuffed. "He gives *everyone* a hard time. He's a jerk."

Then Josh adjusted the straps of his backpack and started on his way.

He had no idea what time it was, but he figured his friends had already left for school. He just hoped Ross had done the same thing.

Running into that bully again was the last thing he wanted to do. But with the luck he'd been having this morning, who knew what the rest of his day would be like?

Chapter 3

As Max stood on the lawn, the morning dew chilled his bare feet. Yet rather than return to the house, he watched the Westbrook boy head down the street, his small shoulders slumped as if the backpack weighed a ton.

Max didn't think it was textbooks causing his sluggish steps or drooping head. It had to be the altercation that was burdening him.

For a moment, Max was tempted to follow behind and make sure that the bigger boy didn't pop out of the bushes and create more trouble. But how involved did he want to get?

Besides, the bully had taken off at a dead run and was probably in his seat at school by now.

Still, Max walked to the edge of the grass until the Westbrook boy turned left at the stop sign and disappeared from sight.

He really didn't believe the kid's story about returning Hemingway to the yard, but either way, he didn't like seeing big guys—no matter what the age—beating up on smaller ones. So in spite of the annoyance and having his sleep interrupted, he was glad he'd done his part.

Still, he couldn't help wondering if the parents had any idea where their kids were and what they'd been doing.

Probably not.

When Max had been a probation officer, he'd come into contact with a lot of people who might have been better citizens if their parents had kept a closer eye on them while they were growing up.

As he started back to the house—and back into bed—he heard a front door open and close. Looking over his shoulder, he spotted Grant Barrows on his front porch wearing a black sports jacket, a pale blue shirt, and a snazzy tie.

The self-employed neighbor who worked from home usually wore Hawaiian shirts, shorts, and flip-flops, so Max couldn't help commenting. "Wow. You sure clean up nice. Where are you going all decked out like that?"

Grant adjusted his tie. "To a job interview."

"No kidding?" Max made his way across the street, the grit and small rocks sharp on the bottoms of his feet until he reached Grant's concrete driveway. "What's the deal? Did you get tired of working at home these days?"

Grant shrugged. "Not really. But . . ." His hesitation suggested that he wasn't comfortable opening up to a neighbor.

"I'm sorry," Max said. "It's really none of my business. I was just curious, that's all."

"Yeah, well, with the economy what it is, I figure a little job security will go a long way."

Max knew what he meant. His own savings were dwindling, and without having a book contract within reach, he was uneasy about his decision to take a leave of absence from the county position he'd held for more than fifteen years.

Grant reached into his jacket pocket and pulled out his car keys. Then he pushed the button on the remote to unlock the door. "I haven't had a job interview since I graduated from college, so I'm a little more nervous than I'd like to admit."

"You shouldn't have any trouble impressing them."

"I hope you're right. But it's not just meeting with the company HR team that has me a little on edge. That part should be a breeze. It's just that . . . Well, bottom line? I both want and need this job."

If that was true, it was a shame. Grant had really been rolling in the self-made dough a year or so ago. He'd even poured a ton of cash into that massive renovation on the house. But it sure sounded as if he was having some serious financial trouble now. So if that was the case, there was no need to pry or to stir up any discomfort on his neighbor's part.

So Max said, "New clothes?"

Grant ran a hand down his silk tie. "Yeah. What do you think?"

That it must have cost a pretty penny, so maybe his financial picture wasn't all that bad. "Nice choice."

"Thanks. Hopefully it will impress the HR department. If I can get past that hurdle, I'll be invited back to meet some of the executives."

Since Grant seemed to have a healthy degree of self-confidence and some solid social skills, Max didn't see a problem with that. "I'm sure you'll knock 'em dead."

"I hope so, but I'm pushing fifty and haven't stepped into the corporate world for nearly twenty-five years. I just hope they can overlook all of that and see what I can bring to the table."

"I'm sure they will."

Grant shrugged a single shoulder. "If they don't, I'll have to come up with another option."

"What happened? I thought things were going well for you."

"They were, but thanks to a couple of bad investments . . ." Grant clucked his tongue. "Correction. They really weren't *bad* investments. They were just ill-fated."

"I don't understand."

Grant heaved a sigh. "I had an opportunity to make a big killing on two separate stock purchases. It wasn't a sure thing, of course, but I've always been a smart gambler. I did the research, and after realizing that the potential outweighed the risk, I bet the farm, hoping the stock would double or triple within a year."

"And it didn't?"

"A couple of months ago, an F5 tornado wiped out the major plant of one of the corporations. And about two weeks later, the chief financial officer of the other was arrested and convicted of embezzlement, which threw the firm into bankruptcy."

Ouch, Max thought. "I guess 'ill-fated' is a good word."

Grant slowly shook his head. "No one could have foreseen any of that, but it happened. And now I need to go back into the workforce."

"I'm sorry to hear that."

"Yeah, well . . . it happens." There was a beat of silence before Grant added, "I have to go. I want to arrive at the interview early."

"Good luck."

"Thanks." As Grant turned to reach for the door handle, Max glanced across the street and noticed a blond, middle-aged woman in Helen Pritchard's front yard—the same one he'd seen in the neighborhood last night, although the man was no longer with her.

She was standing near the hedge that separated Helen's property from his.

"Hey," Max said, stopping Grant. "Have you ever seen that woman before?" He nodded toward the blonde.

After checking her out, Grant said, "No. Who is she?"

"I'm not sure."

As she started toward them, Max got a better look at her in the daylight, noting that she wasn't anything remarkable. She was neither young nor old, tall nor short, slender nor overweight. Words like "ordinary" and "nondescript" came to mind.

As she reached the two men, Max said, "How's it going?"

"Great." When her sky-blue eyes sparked, a smile formed, lending an interesting appeal to her face.

Not that Max found her attractive or anything. He was just making a casual assessment of a stranger.

"Are you looking for someone?" he asked. If it was Helen, he wasn't going to mention that the woman was gone and that her house would be vacant for the next three weeks.

"No. I'm house-sitting for my cousin. She's on a cruise."

Max felt better knowing that she belonged in the neighborhood.

"My name is Mary-Margaret Di Angelo," she added, first reaching out her arm to Max, then to Grant. "But everyone calls me Maggie."

The men introduced themselves and shook her hand.

As Maggie scanned the exterior of Grant's house, Max assumed she was checking out the recent paint job, which had been part of the extensive renovations Grant had made. Most people made a fuss over the rich, green exterior with its red front door, black trim, and shutters.

Instead, she said, "I see that neither of you have put up your Christmas decorations yet. I'm going to take Helen's out of the attic this morning."

The folks who lived in the old Victorians on Nutcracker Court and Sugar Plum Lane always went overboard with lights and all the holiday paraphernalia. At times, it seemed a little over the top, with each home owner trying to outdo the others.

Even Jacob Kipper, whose wife was a cantor at the local synagogue, adorned his home with twinkly lights on the eaves, a battery-operated menorah in the window, and a HAPPY HANUKKAH sign on the front door.

The neighbors had been delighted by his cheery efforts, although Max suspected he'd only done it to keep everyone off his back.

But ever since Max and Karen had split, and she hadn't been around to fuss about it, he'd refused to join the others who took part in the silly custom. After all, without a wife or kids, why bother?

Besides, he'd never been one to bow to peer pressure. So he gave Maggie his standard answer. "No, I won't be dragging out the lights this year."

"That's too bad," she said.

He didn't think so. But he didn't have time to stand around and chat with a stranger who would probably end up accusing him of having a bah-humbug attitude.

Grant glanced at his wristwatch. "It was nice meeting you, but I've got to get out of here. Have a good day."

"You, too." Maggie smiled, those intensive eyes lighting up as she zeroed in on Grant.

Max had every reason to excuse himself at that point, too, but before he could move, a familiar bark sounded and grew louder.

Then, from out of nowhere, Hemingway came bounding across the street, his tongue dangling out of his mouth and flopping from side to side.

Max chuffed. How had he gotten out of the yard? Had the Westbrook boy been right? Had the dog found a way out on his own?

It didn't seem likely.

Assuming the dog had come looking for him, Max turned to face him. But Hemingway headed straight for Grant, as if noticing a friend and wanting to play.

"What a beautiful animal," Maggie said.

There wasn't anything beautiful about Hemingway. He was about as ugly as they came. But before Max could open his mouth to object, the dog jumped up, planting both front paws on Grant's new shirt and tie, smearing mud and dirt across the front of him.

A couple of swear words blasted out of Grant's mouth as he pushed the dog away.

"Oh, no," Maggie said. "Look what he did to your shirt."

Max grabbed Hemingway by the collar and held him back. "I'm so sorry about that."

Grant, clearly shell-shocked with surprise, merely glared at Max.

"If you'll let me have your shirt," Maggie said, "I can try to get the stain out for you."

The fabric might come clean, but Grant was going to have to change clothes completely, which meant he'd arrive at his appointment with very little time to spare.

To be honest, Max would have been angry, too.

Grant lifted his finger and shook it at Max. "That darn dog is becoming a public nuisance. He's been barking incessantly and using my lawn as a litter box whenever he gets out of your yard. And now this."

"Like I said, Grant. I'm really sorry. I'll buy you a new shirt and tie."

Grant rolled his eyes, then grumbled as he returned to his house.

Before Max could follow suit, Maggie bent over and gave Hemingway a scratch behind the ears.

What was she doing?

"Don't reward him for what he just did," Max said.

Maggie extended the scratch for a moment longer, then straightened. "He didn't mean any harm."

Max hated it when people humanized animals like that. "He's a dog. And he's out of control."

"He's like a child who just needs a little love. In fact, I think we're all like that."

Max had neither the patience nor the desire to continue this discussion with a stranger.

"Come on," he said, as he tugged at Hemingway's collar and led him home. "What am I going to do with you?"

When he glanced down at the delinquent animal, Hemingway looked up at him like a shaggy-haired kid.

But this four-legged kid didn't need love.

He needed obedience school—and someone with the time to take him.

*　　*　　*

While pinning up Ruth-Ann Draper's wet hair in rollers and listening to another weekly rendition of her granddaughter's divorce-related woes, Carly's cell phone vibrated in the front pocket of her smock.

"I'm so sorry, Ruth-Ann. I really need to get this." Feeling a little relieved to have an interruption and hoping to schedule another client, she answered without even checking the display to see who was calling. "This is Carly."

"Mrs. Westbrook, it's Margo Evans at Parkside Elementary. I'm afraid we have Joshua in the office this morning. And he appears to have been involved in a fight."

"He *appears* . . . ?" Couldn't he talk? A blast of adrenaline shot through Carly's veins as she tried to read between the lines.

"He has a split lip, a scrape on his chin, and a torn shirt," Mrs. Evans said, "but when he's quizzed about it, his responses are pretty evasive."

"Can you please hold on a moment, Mrs. Evans?" Carly set down the pink roller she'd been holding. "I need to find a quiet place to talk."

After covering the mouthpiece, she apologized again to Ruth-Ann and said, "I'm afraid I have to take this call. If you'll excuse me, I'll just be a minute." She offered her the latest *People* magazine and a smile of reassurance.

Once inside the break room, Carly returned her full attention to the school principal. "I'm sorry, Mrs. Evans. I don't understand. What's going on?"

"Joshua is sitting outside my office right now. He was more than five minutes late entering class this morning, so his teacher, who was working with another student at the back of the room, sent him to get a tardy slip. When the school admissions clerk noticed his injury and torn shirt, she asked him what happened, but he refused to explain. So she sent him to see me. Unfortunately, he won't tell me, either."

Why wouldn't Josh speak up? Was he afraid of getting into trouble? Was he trying to protect someone?

And why had he been late to class? He'd ridden the bus to school this morning, hadn't he?

Of course, after breakfast, he'd mentioned that he wanted to walk to school. But she'd insisted that he stay with . . .

Mikey.

Fear clawed at her chest. She tried to keep the panic from her voice as she asked, "Where's Mikey? The boys should have been together. Is he okay?"

"Yes, I've already checked into that. Michael is in class. And from what he told Mrs. Hornkohl, he rode the bus to school, but Joshua didn't."

Carly's heartbeat thudded in her ears. Josh had argued with her in the past. He'd also done his share of whining and complaining about looking after his brother or accepting responsibility. But up until now he'd always been compliant and had never rebelled or willfully disobeyed her.

Was this the sort of thing she had to look forward to when he became a teenager? Was this only the beginning?

She closed her eyes, trying to conjure an image of that sweet little baby who'd nursed at her breast, the toddler she'd cuddled in her arms—her firstborn son. Yet all she could see was the disappointment on his face when she'd told him he had to ride the bus this morning.

And now he was in some kind of trouble.

"I'll have to shuffle a few of my clients around," Carly said, "but I can probably be there within twenty minutes."

She'd ask one of the other stylists to finish rolling Ruth-Ann's hair and to put her under the dryer. Depending upon how long she would need to stay at the school, she'd probably have to ask someone to do the comb-out, too.

But her sons were—and always would be—her first priority.

"You don't need to leave work," Mrs. Evans said. "I know that you're a single mom and the sole support of the household. But I did want to notify you and let you know that Josh will have detention after school today. We'd like to keep him until four. Will that be a problem?"

"No, that's fine." Josh certainly deserved to be punished for disobeying and refusing to tell the truth when he was questioned. But what was she going to do with Mikey? He got out of class at two thirty, and her only option, at this point, was to pay the fee for him to stay for the YMCA day-care program.

Once again, there was another financial hit. If she could afford the cost in the first place, she would have registered her sons at the beginning of the school year.

"We'll take care of it from here," Mrs. Evans said.

But Carly had a second thought. "Can I speak to my son? Maybe he'll tell me what happened."

"Of course. I'll put him on the telephone."

As Carly waited to speak to Josh, she scanned the small break room where the stylists hung out when they were between clients. Right now she had it all to herself, which was a relief. She didn't like her coworkers knowing how tough things had been lately.

Moments later, Josh picked up the phone and uttered a sheepish, "Hello."

"What happened?" Carly asked him. "Why didn't you ride the bus this morning?"

Silence stretched across the line.

"Don't you dare ignore me, young man. I want to know what's going on. And I want to know *right* now."

"I was going to ride the bus, Mom. I was even waiting in line with Mikey when that man's dog got loose. It was wandering in the canyon. And when it started walking on the side of the road, I was afraid it would get hit by a car or something."

Carly rolled her eyes. "You left your brother alone to chase after a *dog*?"

"Don't worry. There were a couple of moms at the bus stop, so I knew Mikey would be safe without me."

"But it sounds as though *you* weren't safe. What happened after that?"

Silence again. The kind that made a mother suspect that a lie was brewing. Or that the truth was going to be a real struggle to tell.

So which was it?

Oh, no, she thought, as another possibility crossed her mind. Did he have a confrontation with Mr. Tolliver? Had it escalated?

Carly took a deep breath, then slowly let it out, hoping to regroup and tackle the questioning from another angle. "So did you take the dog home?"

"Yeah."

"Did the dog hurt you?"

"No, Hemingway's cool. He and I are becoming friends."

Maybe so, since their paths seemed to keep crossing. But Josh certainly wasn't a friend to the dog's owner.

"Did you have a run-in with Mr. Tolliver?" she asked.

"Kind of."

A cool chill fluttered down her spine. If the dog's owner had touched her son, if he'd hurt him, she'd . . . she'd . . . Well, she had half a notion to march up to his front door and let him have it. But that wouldn't solve anything.

She could, of course, call the police and report the incident.

Again, she wrestled with patience and composure, but she managed to ask, "What did that man do to you, honey?"

"Huh?"

"What happened when you returned the dog to Mr. Tolliver?"

"Nothing. I just put the dog inside the fence. And . . . and then I tripped and fell down and hurt my lip. That's all."

He was lying. She knew it as well as she knew her own name.

"Did that man threaten you?" she asked.

"Who?"

"Mr. Tolliver."

Another pause. Then he finally said, "Yeah. He told me to stay away from his yard."

Or what? "Did he say what he would do if you went back on his property?"

"Not exactly. I guess he'd yell at me. Or he'd tell you, and then I'd be in trouble."

The boy was already in trouble, and he wasn't making it easy for her to help him.

At times like this, she wished their father was still around to be a role model and to help Carly understand the male point of view. But she had to admit that even when he'd been a part of their lives, he hadn't been much help either way, so she was on her own with this one.

"We're going to talk about this again tonight," she said. "Now give the telephone to Mrs. Evans."

When the principal was back on the line, Carly told her what little she'd learned and what she'd gathered by connecting a few dots.

"Josh said that he fell down," Carly told Mrs. Evans. "But last night, the dog's owner called me to complain about the boys coming onto his property. It's possible that . . . Well, I'd hate to think that a grown man would hurt a child, but it does happen. And that might be why Josh isn't telling us the whole truth. It's possible that he's afraid of the man."

"Well, his shirt is torn," the principal added. "And it certainly looks as though someone might have grabbed it at the neckline and given it a hard twist."

Carly's stomach clenched up tight. "What legal options do I have if that man assaulted him?"

"I'm not sure. You'd have to talk to law enforcement officers, but I'd think that you could charge him with assault if he actually hurt your son." Mrs. Evans paused. "Do you know where he lives?"

"Yes, I do."

And on her lunch hour, Carly planned to stop by Mr. Tolliver's house. Then she would ask him the questions her son had refused to answer.

The doorbell rang, rousing Max from his sleep. He would have rolled over in bed and placed a pillow over his head, but whoever kept ringing that darn bell was annoying the dog, too.

And now, with Hemingway barking and howling up a storm, Max had no other choice but to get up and see who was at the door.

Grumbling, he kicked off the covers, rolled out of bed, and reached for his bathrobe. He slipped his arms into the sleeves without taking time to pull it together and tie the sash. Then he made his way downstairs.

"I'm coming!" he yelled, hoping that the blasted noise would stop—the ringing, the barking, the howling.

Oh, for Pete's sake. He'd been up until dawn again last night, trying to rewrite a scene that just wasn't coming together. Then, an hour after he'd finally turned in, Hemingway had whined and scratched at the door. So he'd put him in the backyard and had returned to bed. But around eight, the dog had put up a real fuss. And when Max had gone to see what was troubling him, he'd had to referee a couple of kids fighting in the street.

And now this . . .

He undoubtedly wore a scowl as he swung open the door, which didn't bother him in the least. But when he caught sight of an attractive brunette standing on the stoop, and he stared into the prettiest green eyes he'd ever seen and caught a whiff of floral perfume, his foul mood dissipated into the lightly scented air.

It was anyone's guess who she was or why she'd come to his house, but it didn't seem to matter one iota.

With her silky brown hair styled picture-perfect, and a slight flush on her cheeks, she was stunning.

And he was speechless.

Of course, if she were smiling instead of frowning, his brains and tongue might have deserted him for good.

She was, he realized, hot in every sense of the word—hot as in gorgeous and clearly hot under the collar.

"Can I help you?" he asked, thinking she'd come to the wrong house and was looking for one of his neighbors instead.

"Mr. Tolliver?"

"Yes." He pulled his robe together and reached for the sash that dangled along the side. After telling Hemingway to pipe down, he asked, "What seems to be the trouble?"

"I'm Carly Westbrook, Josh's mother."

Lucky kid, came to mind.

"And I want to know what happened this morning," she added.

"Maybe you should ask him."

She stiffened. "I did. And now I'm asking you."

"For one thing, your son woke me up."

"And so you assaulted him?"

"*What?*" Max tensed, and as his movement froze, the sash he'd been trying to tie around his waist slipped out of his fingers. "Are you crazy? Did your son tell you that I hurt him?"

Her demeanor softened a tad, but she continued to stand her ground. "No, he didn't actually say that, but he has a split lip and a torn shirt."

"Did he tell you anything about what happened?"

"Just that he brought your dog home. He's refusing to talk about his injuries. But I know that you don't want him on your property, and I know that he's afraid of you. So I thought I'd better get to the bottom of it."

"You're making an unwarranted leap in the wrong direction," Max said, both irritated at the woman and at himself for feeling even the least bit attracted to her.

"You didn't hurt him?" she asked.

Max crossed his arms over his mostly bare chest. "I may be a lot of things, Mrs. Westbrook, but I don't beat up on kids."

She didn't appear convinced. Instead, she crossed her own arms over her chest, causing the fabric of her pink blouse to pull taut against the buttonholes.

Forcing his gaze back to hers, Max said, "I can't vouch for the part about my dog getting out, but I saw a big kid beating up on your son this morning. When I came out on the porch to see what was causing the dog to make all the racket, I yelled and the bigger boy ran off."

Her arms loosened, then slowly dropped to her sides, and the tension left her face. "Do you know who the older boy is?"

"No, but he looked to be a couple of years older than your son and about forty pounds heavier."

"Does he live around here?" she asked.

"I have no idea. I work nights and sleep days." Max combed his hand through his hair. "At least, I *try* to sleep days."

She bit down on her bottom lip, then softened. "I'm sorry. It's just that I . . ."

Those spring-green eyes grew watery, but she managed to blink back the tears.

Max was grateful they hadn't overflowed and spilled down her cheeks. He'd never been patient when a woman started crying. He'd seen plenty of them do that when he'd been a probation officer, both female defendants or the wives and girlfriends of the men. And he'd learned to draw back and be tough. But as hardened—and skeptical—as he'd become on the job, he found himself really waffling now.

Finally, when she seemed to have pulled herself together, she blew out a weary breath. "I'm sorry for jumping to conclusions. I'm a single mother trying to raise two boys. And it hasn't been easy."

Max imagined it was difficult. His own mother had worked two jobs to support him and his brother.

"Josh has always been up front with me in the past, so I'm not used to him clamming up." She looked at him with those big green eyes again, drawing him into her troubles in spite of his resolve to mind his own business. "Do you have any idea why he wouldn't want to tell me about getting in a fight?"

"He might be afraid of repercussions from the older boy. And he might want to handle the problem on his own without hiding behind his mother's skirts. As little boys turn into big boys, they start drawing away from their moms."

That's what Max had done, and so had his brother.

As Mrs. Westbrook—Carly—looked up at him, her gaze clung to his as though he held all the answers. But that couldn't be further from the truth.

Rather than risk getting soft or any more involved than he was already, he circled the wagons around any compassion that swirled in his chest and slipped into probation-officer mode. "If I see that older boy around here again, I'll try to identify him for you. I don't like bullies."

She nodded. "Thank you. And again, I'm sorry for accusing you of hurting my son. It's just that . . ."

"You're a mother. And you care about your kids."

In spite of her earlier efforts, a single tear slipped down her cheek.

Aw, man. Don't do that, he wanted to tell her.

He probably ought to run through his mental Rolodex of social service organizations that might be able to help her, but he just stood there until she thanked him, then turned and walked away.

Instead of closing the door and retreating to the privacy of his home, he watched her get into her car, feeling a bit guilty and not at all sure why.

Chapter 4

As storm clouds rolled in from the northwest, shading the midday sun, Susan parked her car along the curb in front of Helen's house, a pale green Victorian with white trim.

Before leaving home, she'd carefully styled her hair and applied her makeup, something that had become a daily habit since Hank had passed away.

Not that she'd let herself go before. But these days she took extra care, especially when she was headed for Nutcracker Court. A couple of Helen's neighbors were eligible bachelors, and Susan wanted to be ready for a chance meeting with one or the other.

Both men were nice-looking and in the right age range, but more importantly, they each worked from home, which was an even bigger plus. Susan had once been married to a workaholic who'd spent most of his waking hours at the office, so she found a little detail like that to be especially appealing.

But that didn't mean she hadn't been happily married to Hank. They'd had their share of good times and had made some special memories.

Of course, there'd been the typical squabbles, slammed doors, and cold shoulders, too, but they'd loved each other and had been faithful to their vows.

And there was a lot to say for that.

Her only real complaint had been Hank's overwhelming drive to be the best at everything he did. That and the fact that he hadn't wanted to start a family until it was too late.

But Susan planned to remedy that—God willing. All she needed to do was find the right man. So the hunt was on.

Hunt? She scoffed at the poor word choice.

Just last Thursday, when she'd finally mentioned that she was interested in dating, Lynette had made a joke about Susan being on a manhunt. Susan had chuckled right along with her poker buddies, but the comment had rubbed her the wrong way.

It wasn't as though she was desperate and would throw herself at the first man to toss a smile her way. She was going to be very careful when it came to choosing a second husband.

In fact, she'd compiled a list of qualities she was looking for in a mate. And some of them were nonnegotiable, like honesty, financial security, a kind and loving heart, and the desire to father a child or two.

That was also why she wanted to get to know Max Tolliver and Grant Barrows a little better. She'd like to see if either of them was worth pursuing. And she wouldn't know that unless she had an opportunity to chat with them.

So, as she climbed out of her white Honda Civic, her thoughts weren't on Helen's cousin, Maggie. Instead, they were on the men who lived nearby.

There were some notable differences between the two, particularly in looks. Max had dark hair and an olive complexion, which suggested he had some Latin blood—Italian maybe, or Spanish. He was also tall and solid, with a build that suggested he worked out regularly.

On the other hand, Grant was several inches shorter, a little more slender, and as fair as Max was dark. His light brown hair appeared to be sun-streaked, even in the winter months. Whenever she spotted him out in his yard, she was reminded of a typical Southern California surfer, albeit one who was a little older than most. Of course, that could also be due to his wardrobe, which seemed to be limited to Hawaiian-style shirts, board shorts, and sandals.

Either way, she'd made up her mind to instigate a conversation with whichever man she spotted first.

As she slid out of the driver's seat and closed the door, she noticed that Max's blinds were drawn tight. She suspected that he might be asleep or hard at work on the novel he was writing. He was a bit of a recluse, she'd been told. But she loved books and thought it might be interesting to date an author.

Especially one with such soulful brown eyes—the pensive kind that weren't easy to read.

A couple of weeks ago, Max had been outside walking his dog when Susan had arrived to play poker. She'd offered him a shy smile, and when he'd smiled back, a little zing had rippled through her veins.

But since it didn't appear likely that she would run into him again this afternoon, she glanced over her shoulder at the house across the street, the home Grant Barrows had recently renovated. The project, which had included all new landscaping in the front and back, must have cost a small fortune, but from what Helen had said, the man was loaded.

Susan wasn't exactly sure what Grant did for a living, and neither was Helen, but they both agreed that he must be very successful.

After circling the car and opening up the passenger side, she removed the three-layer cake she'd made early this morning. Then she used her hip to shut the door.

She took a moment to admire her carefully frosted handiwork, knowing that it was sure to impress Helen's cousin, Maggie. And even Lynette, who was on a constant diet to maintain her Barbie-doll shape, wouldn't be able to resist a slice.

Before heading to the door, she took one last gander at

Max's house, hoping he'd open the shades or step out onto the porch. But no such luck.

Maybe on her next visit she would bring a double batch of homemade chocolate chip cookies and deliver a plate to each of the bachelors. An unexpected gift like that would be a great icebreaker and was sure to set off a conversation.

With a solid clever game plan simmering in her mind, she headed up Helen's walkway, her steps light, her heart hopeful. When she reached the stoop, she shifted the cake plate to one hand and rang the bell with the other.

Moments later, a fortysomething blonde opened the door wearing a pair of black slacks and a pale blue blouse.

"You must be Maggie," she told the woman. "My name is Susan. I'm a friend of Helen's—and one of the Diamond Lils."

Cousin Maggie broke into a smile that nearly lit the entry. And as her gaze lit upon the dessert in Susan's hands, her sky-blue eyes widened. "Oh, my. Would you look at that?"

"It's my mango-coconut cake. And you haven't seen anything yet. Wait until you actually take a bite."

"Please," Maggie said, opening up the screen door. "Come inside. I'll put on some water for tea. Or would you rather have coffee?"

"I'll have whatever you're having," Susan said.

"Then tea it is."

Minutes later, Susan was seated at the kitchen table, an antique made of oak. Maggie removed the pot of rhododendron that had been the centerpiece and replaced it with the mango-coconut cake.

"Helen mentioned that her friends, the Diamond Lils, might stop by," Maggie said, as she set the lush potted plant on the countertop. "And that you were dear friends."

"We've grown very close over the years," Susan said.

Maggie filled Helen's red teakettle with water, placed it on the stove, then turned on the flame. "Why do you call your-selves the Diamond Lils?"

Susan was a little surprised that Helen had mentioned them, but hadn't gone into detail. "I'm not sure who came up with the name first, but because of our weekly poker games, it seemed to fit. And it just stuck."

"Weekly poker games?" Maggie's movement stilled, and she cocked her head to the side. "Do you play for money?"

Was Maggie a prude about gambling and that sort of thing? If so, it seemed odd that Helen would ask the Dia-mond Lils to befriend her.

Either way, Susan wasn't going to lie. "Having a little wager on the table makes it a lot more fun. But we don't play for high stakes."

Maggie nodded, as though she understood. Then she re-moved two china cups and saucers from the cupboard and placed them on the table.

"In fact," Susan added, "each week, we save a portion of the kitty to use for something special."

Maggie's eyes brightened. "That's really nice. I'm sure there are a lot of worthwhile charities that can use some extra money, especially at this time of year."

"You're probably right," Susan said. "But we already have the fund earmarked for a trip to Laughlin. There's going to be a big poker tournament on the fifteenth of January that's part of a reality television show."

"What if you're not chosen to take part?"

"Oh, but we were. Helen sent in our application, and someone from the show came here a couple of weeks ago to interview us. And we're in." Susan tried to contain her ex-citement, but wasn't having much luck. "We're going to travel to Laughlin in style, too. Rosa's nephew works for a limousine company, and he's going to get us a special rate and drive us there. We'll stay at a nice hotel, eat at the best restaurants, see a couple of shows, and maybe even visit a spa."

They planned to play the slots, too, although Susan decided not to mention that.

"Wow," Maggie said, no longer giving off those anti-gambling vibes. "It sounds like a great trip."

"Doesn't it?" Susan burst into a smile. "We even ordered matching T-shirts for us to wear. They're red and have a sparkly decal on the front that says THE DIAMOND LILS."

As Maggie placed the sugar bowl, a jar of honey, and teaspoons on the table, Susan had a second thought and added, "In spite of our weekly games and the upcoming tournament, we're not big-time gamblers. We only play for an hour or so on Thursdays, then we end our afternoons by having dessert and socializing."

"The wrap-up part would be the most enjoyable to me," Maggie said, as she took a seat across from Susan. "I suppose that's because I've never really liked playing cards or board games."

"We'd be happy to give you some lessons. It really isn't hard to learn. And you might be surprised at how much you'd enjoy it."

"I don't know about that." Maggie tossed her a dimpled grin. "But I wouldn't mind fixing lunch for your group on Thursday and watching you play."

"That's a really nice offer. And I know that I'm not just speaking for myself when I say that we'd really appreciate it."

"Good, because I don't know anyone in Fairbrook yet, and it'll be a lonely three weeks if I just hole up in Helen's house—no matter how cozy it is."

"We're a great group. I'm sure you'll fit right in."

"I'm sure I will." Maggie pushed back her chair, stood, and went to the pantry. Then she opened the door and peered inside as if making a mental grocery list. "I make a great vegetarian lasagna. Do you think something like that would go over well?"

"I'm sure it will."

"Does anyone have food allergies?"

"Not that I know of, although Lynette is always dieting. But she rarely turns down anything tasty, so don't worry about her."

Maggie leaned against the kitchen counter and crossed her arms. "I'm looking forward to meeting the others. What are they like?"

"Actually, you may be surprised, but other than friendship, we have very little in common. To begin with, we're not the same age. Rosa Alvarado is sixty-two. Helen, as you know, is fifty-six. I'm forty-five, and Lynnette Tidball, who's only thirty-two, is the baby of the group." Susan studied the delicate pink rose and trellis pattern on Helen's china cup for a beat, then added, "Of course, Lynette used to be married to an older man, so she's probably more comfortable with our age differences than most women in their early thirties."

"Used to be married? What happened?"

"He passed away the summer before last."

Maggie seemed to think on that a bit, then asked, "How much older was he?"

"He was in his late fifties and nearly twice her age, but he *adored* her. And he was as rich as all get-out."

"Did she love him?"

"I know why you'd wonder about that, but I'm sure she did. For one thing, she hasn't remarried. And for a young woman, two years is a very long time to be alone."

It was a long time for a woman Susan's age to remain single, too, but she didn't mention that. Instead, she leaned back in her chair. "By the way, I invited both Lynette and Rosa to join us this afternoon, so you'll get to meet them and see for yourself."

"Should I put on a pot of coffee, too?" Maggie asked.

"Tea will be fine."

As Maggie returned to the cupboard and began removing two more cups and saucers from the shelf, Susan thought about the women who were no longer a part of their weekly poker group. They'd each brought something different to the table on Thursdays, and she'd been sad to see them go.

"There used to be sixteen of us," she said, not sure that it would matter to Maggie.

"What happened? Why did so many leave the group?"

"Oh, various reasons—disability, death, a new marriage, and a move out of state."

"That's too bad," Maggie said. "It's never easy to lose a friend."

"You're right." It hadn't been easy to lose a husband, either.

"Have you tried to find replacements?" Maggie asked.

"Yes, but we haven't had much luck. And now with Helen gone, there are only three of us—Rosa, Lynette, and me. So we probably won't be playing much poker."

"I'm sorry." Maggie placed a gentle hand on Susan's shoulder. "It sounds like it'll be a lonely Christmas season for you."

It would be especially lonely for Susan and Lynette. Rosa had a husband and children, so she'd never miss a beat. But rather than say anything that might result in sympathy or pity, Susan didn't comment.

After Maggie added tea service for Rosa and Lynette, she studied the mango-coconut cake. "That's so pretty, I'm going to hate cutting into it."

A surge of pride welled up inside, and Susan was glad she'd gone to all the trouble.

"Helen keeps a sterling-silver cake knife in her hutch," Susan said, pushing her chair away from the table. "I'll get it."

But before she could take two steps toward the formal dining room, the doorbell rang.

"That must be the others," Susan said. "I'll let them in."

Lynette Tidball stood on Helen's front stoop, her newly manicured hands lifted to protect the nails that had been polished a pretty shade of Christmas red, the tips trimmed with tiny stripes of green and white.

"Hey," Susan said, as she swung open the door and stepped aside to let Lynette in the house. "You're late. But your nails look good, as usual."

"I'm sorry," Lynette said. "There was an accident on Seaview Drive, and traffic was backed up for blocks."

"Was anyone hurt?"

"I think so. Paramedics were working on someone, but I couldn't tell if it was a man or woman."

As they crossed the living room and headed toward the kitchen, Susan said, "What did you do? Spend the morning at the salon?"

"No, just long enough for a manicure. I actually canceled my hair appointment so I could meet you here."

"Well, I'm glad you were able to shuffle things around. And for what it's worth, I like the longer length of your hair."

"Thanks," Lynette said. "But I'm ready for something different. What do you think about me adding highlights and shortening it a couple of inches?"

Susan laughed. "Honey, you're too funny. You'd look good if you dyed your hair purple and shaved it into a Mohawk style."

"Yeah, right."

Susan clicked her tongue. "What are we going to do with you, Lynnie? You always look as though you just stepped out of a fashion magazine, and you've got more money than the Rockefellers. Yet you don't seem to realize just how much you have going for you."

Lynette slowly shook her head, her mind flooding with thoughts, as well as an argument or two. Sure, she'd come a long way from a crummy childhood, but deep inside, she still felt like that geeky little girl from the other side of the tracks, the shy and awkward young woman who'd had crooked teeth and vision problems that had hampered her ability to read and learn in school.

Yet through some miracle of miracles, that mousy young woman with a slew of defects had somehow touched Peter Tidball's heart, become his wife, and entered his storybook world.

So wasn't it any wonder that she still had to pinch herself to make sure she wasn't dreaming about the way her life had turned out?

"Have you heard from Rosa?" Susan asked, as they headed for the kitchen. "Is she going to be able to join us?"

"I'm afraid not. She has another commitment. Apparently, she and her husband deliver meals to housebound seniors on Wednesdays."

Susan's steps slowed. "Since when? Is that a new project they've taken on?"

"Yes, I think so. It's so hard to keep up with all the volunteer work they do."

As they entered the kitchen, the teakettle began to whistle, and Helen's cousin removed it from the heat.

After Susan made the introductions, Maggie reached for a pot holder.

Lynette tried to spot a family resemblance in the middle-aged blonde, but couldn't see it right off. Helen's hair was a bright Irish red, although the color came from a bottle these days. And Maggie's was the color of pale moonbeams.

"Have a seat," Maggie said, as she carried the teakettle to the table.

As Lynette watched Helen's cousin pour hot water into the china cups, her gaze landed on the cake in the center of the table, and she turned to Susan. "Oh, my goodness. Did you make that?"

Susan smiled. "Everyone kept asking when I was going to whip up my mango-coconut recipe again, so I decided today was as good a day as any."

"I'm glad you did. That cake is to die for."

"With your sweet tooth, Lynnie, I'm surprised that you

don't take some baking classes and utilize that fancy oven of yours."

Lynette might have a state-of-the-art kitchen in her custom-built house, thanks to Peter's insistence, but she rarely used it. And for good reason.

But not one she wanted to share.

"Why should I go to the trouble of learning how to cook?" she asked Susan. "My best friends are all talented bakers and chefs. And they're more than willing to share the fruits of their culinary labors with me."

As Lynette reached for a tea bag—something herbal—Susan crossed her arms. "Every woman should know how to cook and bake, Lynnie, especially you. What if you get married again and your new husband doesn't want to eat all of his meals in restaurants?"

Lynette had certainly lucked out when she'd stumbled upon Peter, no doubt about it. But what were the chances that she'd find another man who was so gentle, kind, and generous? One who understood her quirks?

One who'd become the father figure she'd never had?

"I'm not looking for a husband," she reminded Susan. "But even if I was, I'd be as big as a barn if I spent too much time in my kitchen."

"Cut it out, Lynnie." Susan, who claimed to be about twenty pounds overweight, clicked her tongue. "You're the last one in the world who needs to diet."

Oh, yeah? Lynette had a natural inclination to eat her feelings, which was why, in high school, she'd weighed nearly two hundred pounds.

But as usual, she let the comment go. The Lils had no idea how difficult it was for her to maintain her weight—or how important it was for her not to slip back into self-destructive patterns.

So instead of letting the conversation continue, she scanned Helen's cheerful kitchen, with its bright yellow walls and white eyelet curtains. The room had provided a great backdrop for girl talk over the years. And in spite of being a little outdated, it had a cozy, down-home feel about it.

As Maggie placed dessert plates on the table, Susan said, "I'd better get that cake knife."

When she returned to the kitchen, she cut three generous slices for them to eat, then took a seat.

"Are you going to play poker with us on Thursday?" Lynette asked Maggie.

"I'm not really a gambler," Helen's cousin said.

Neither was Lynette. Even if her accountant insisted that Peter had left her financially secure, she had a deep-seated awareness that money was hard to come by, especially these days.

She still remembered how little she'd had while growing up—the hunger she'd felt some evenings when there'd been no dinner to be had, the uncertainty of where she'd spend the night. So she understood Maggie's concern.

To be honest, she sometimes had to force herself to cough up twenty dollars each week to buy into the poker game, but she was glad to be one of the Diamond Lils, and playing poker was a big part of who they were.

Besides, even if she never won a pot, the weekly investment was a lot cheaper than therapy.

"I'll put up the money for you the first time," Susan told Maggie. "So you don't have to worry about gambling."

Lynette didn't know why Susan didn't just drop it. Clearly, Maggie wasn't all that interested in playing, so Lynette added, "Poker is really secondary to us getting together on Thursdays."

And that was so true. Lynette had come to see the Lils as her sisters, mothers, and friends.

Maggie added a spoonful of honey to her tea, then gave it a quick stir. "I'm sure you're missing Helen and your Thursdays together. But may I make a suggestion?"

Susan, who'd taken the cake knife to the sink and was rinsing it off, glanced over her shoulder and said, "Please do."

"Why don't you do something different, something special while she's gone?"

Intrigued, Lynette sat up a little straighter. "Like what?"

"Like be a blessing to someone else, someone who's struggling and down and out."

Susan took her seat at the table. "Who do you have in mind?"

"Well, there are a lot of charitable organizations that need volunteers, as well as donations," Maggie said. "And it might give your group a whole new focus, at least during the holiday season."

"You're probably right," Susan said, as she opened a packet of Earl Grey and dropped the tea bag into her cup of water.

Lynette had to agree that the idea certainly had merit. While growing up, she'd benefited from various charitable organizations, as well as the church and school.

Susan glanced across the table at Lynette. "What do you think? Do you want to help the underprivileged this Christmas?"

"Are you talking about giving our time?" Lynette asked, knowing she had plenty of that.

"And money," Maggie said.

The little girl inside wanted to hang on tight to what she'd managed to accrue as an adult, so Lynette was pretty selective with the checks she wrote.

"It wouldn't have to be money," Susan said. "We can make Christmas cookies and deliver them to the soup kitchen."

"I'm not going to bake anything," Lynette said, "but I'd be happy to make the deliveries."

Then, on second thought, she probably should offer to help

Susan bake. The poor woman's dyslexia sometimes worked against her when reading a recipe.

Interestingly enough, Lynette thought, as she lifted her fork and dug into her slice of cake, Susan never screwed up that mango-coconut recipe.

Still there were other dishes and goodies, the recipes for which she hadn't committed to memory, that sometimes went awry.

Lynette wouldn't hurt Susan for the world, but once she'd made a salty batch of brownies that had made the Lils swear off chocolate for months.

Wouldn't it be awful to give a batch of cookies to the disadvantaged when the sugar and salt measurements had been transposed?

But as she opened her mouth and bit into the forkful of cake, and the moist and sweet tropical flavors blended in her mouth, she closed her eyes and savored the heavenly taste.

"Are you sure you can't spare even a little of your poker winnings for charity?" Maggie asked.

They probably could. They'd set aside a lot of money for that trip—more than they'd need. Lynette couldn't be sure, but she'd tried to keep a mental count of the total over the years and figured that they'd accumulated close to five thousand dollars, although Susan, who was the group treasurer, would know the exact amount.

Either way, Lynette would hate to see them blow the whole wad on the trip. So she said, "Maybe, after we get back from Laughlin, we can donate whatever is left."

Susan nodded in agreement.

As Maggie lifted her teacup, she glanced out the kitchen window for a moment or so, then she returned the cup to the saucer without taking a sip. "I understand how you feel, since you've been saving for so long. But my father once told me a story that changed my attitude about giving and doing for others. Would you mind if I shared it with you?"

Susan glanced at Lynette, then shrugged. "Go ahead. Let's hear it."

Maggie smiled and settled back into her seat. "A long time ago, a poor man named Adam was out seeking work so that he could support his widowed mother and his sister. The taxes were due on the run-down cabin they called home, and the pantry was growing bare.

"So Adam walked for hours along a country road and talked to several farmers, asking for work. But he couldn't find anyone willing to hire him."

Lynette glanced at Susan, who was studying Maggie with a furrowed brow and a quizzical look, clearly wondering where the woman was going with the story.

"Adam eventually grew worried," Maggie continued, "so he took a seat on a large stump that sat at the side of the road. Then he bowed his head and prayed for a miracle. When an hour had passed without any sign that his prayer had been answered, he got to his feet. He was prepared to return home empty-handed, when he spotted an old man approaching. The gray-haired man carried a large sack over his shoulder, and he was noticeably stooped by the weight of his burden.

"'What's the matter?' the old man asked. 'Lost your way?' Adam couldn't bring himself to ask for a handout, so he slowly shook his head. The man, his hair wispy and gray, his face craggy and weathered, tossed Adam a smile, then continued down the road.

"But Adam was unable to just sit and watch the old-timer labor under his load, so he caught up with him and offered to carry his sack for a spell.

"Together they walked another mile or two, and when they reached a fork in the road, the old man said, 'This is the end of the line for me.'

"Adam tried to hand over the sack, but the old man refused to take it. 'It's your burden now,' he said. 'I have no more use for it. My journey's at an end.'

"Adam watched the man take the path to the right, which was lined with trees, until he disappeared from sight.

"Stunned—and more than a little curious—Adam set the bag on the ground. When he loosened the strings that held it closed and peered inside, he found an old wooden box trimmed with aged leather and tarnished brass."

"What was in it?" Susan asked. "Was it the miracle he'd been praying for?"

Maggie smiled. "A handful of copper pennies."

"But pennies wouldn't go very far," Susan said. "What kind of miracle was that?"

Maggie's lips stretched into an even bigger smile, which brightened her face and put a spark in her eyes. "They were very special pennies."

"Magic ones?" Susan asked.

"Not in the way you might imagine, but they'd each been blessed." Maggie took a moment to sip her tea. "Like you, Adam knew the pennies wouldn't be enough to restock his family's pantry or pay the taxes that were due upon the house, but he carried the box home, thinking that the box might be old, but it was sturdy. He hoped someone might find it of value and buy it from him."

"Was the box an antique?" Lynette asked, making a guess and assuming that a moral to Maggie's story would be forthcoming.

But Helen's cousin didn't answer her question. Instead, she continued with the tale. "A few minutes later, Adam came across a young mother with a sick baby. The woman was crying because she had no money to buy medicine. Knowing that his pennies might help the woman, Adam was unable to walk away. So he opened the box. 'I don't have much money,' he said, but what I have is yours.'

"The young mother took the pennies he offered with tears in her eyes, thanked him repeatedly, and continued down the road. Adam, too, went on his way, but after traveling another mile or so, he ran into an elderly couple. They had a tale of woe, as well. They'd been turned out of the house in which they'd been living and had been forced to sleep in a field.

"Adam, who loved his mother and was grateful that he'd been able to provide shelter for her, sadly told the pair that he'd already given away all his money. When he opened the lid of the chest to show them that it was empty, there were a handful of nickels inside. He was more than a little surprised, to say the least, but he gave them to the couple.

"Several more times on his way home, Adam met someone who needed the coins more than he did. And each time he opened what should have been an empty chest, he found that they'd multiplied. Nickels were replaced by dimes, and dimes by quarters. By the time he got home, he had a handful of silver and could scarcely carry the load."

"That's a nice story," Susan said. "I guess your point is that we should share with others, and that we'll be blessed if we do."

"Not necessarily with money," Maggie said, "but you'll be blessed in ways you might never expect."

"We'll have to talk it over with Helen and Rosa," Susan said, "but maybe it would be in our best interest to make a few donations before we leave on that trip. We could certainly use a blessing before we go to Laughlin. It would be nice to have some heavenly luck during our poker tournament."

Lynette had a feeling that Susan had missed the point of the story. So she turned her gaze to Maggie, to check out her expression, only to see the woman was looking out the window again. But this time, she rolled her eyes and gave a little shrug, as if sharing her exasperation with someone outside.

Yet when Lynette looked through the window and into Helen's backyard, she didn't see anyone there.

Maggie was an odd one, that was for sure. But she was

Helen's cousin, and the Lils had been asked to keep her company. So it was the least they could do.

Lynette picked up her fork and finished off the rest of her cake.

But as she did, she couldn't help thinking about good deeds being rewarded with magic pennies.

Chapter 5

It was just after four when Carly picked up her sons from school and drove them home. And other than Mikey's comments about how much fun he had in the after-school program, the ride was quiet.

But that didn't mean Carly wasn't rehearsing the chat she planned to have with Josh as soon as she could get him alone.

After pulling into the drive, she shut off the ignition, but didn't get out of the car.

When both boys opened their doors, she told Josh to wait. "Mikey, you go ahead into the house. I want to talk to your brother before we go inside." Then she removed the keys from the ignition and handed them to her youngest son so he could let himself in.

Josh hung his head, but slid back into his seat.

When they were alone, Carly said, "I'm not buying the story that you fell down and hurt your lip."

Josh glanced at her, then looked away.

"I have a feeling you were involved in some kind of fight. And for some reason, you don't want me to know who else was involved or why."

Silence filled the car, and she watched an inner struggle cross his face, contorting his expression.

"Am I at least right about that?" she asked. "You fought with someone and don't want anyone to know who it was?"

Finally, he nodded. "If I tell on the kid, he'll get mad."

"Who is he?" she asked. "What's his name?"

Josh pursed his lips for a moment, then said, "He's just a kid."

"He sounds like a bully."

"I guess he is. And that's why I can't tell on him. If he finds out that I'm a snitch and a crybaby, he'll get even madder at me. And then things will be a whole lot worse."

"But Josh, if he's picking on you, he's probably doing it to others, too. We need to stop him from doing that."

"Yeah, well, some other kid and his mom can stop him. I don't want us to be dead heroes."

Carly gripped the steering wheel until her knuckles ached, then she let out an exasperated sigh. "I can't sit back and let someone bully you."

Josh opened his mouth to speak, then clamped his lips together.

"What am I going to do with you?" she asked.

"I don't know, Mom. But whatever you decide to do, at least I'll still be alive."

"Did that boy threaten to hurt you?" Carly asked.

"With him, it's not a threat. It's more like a promise. Besides, he already kicked my butt once. If it wasn't for that guy on Nutcracker Court chasing him off, I'd probably be dead already."

"Please," she said. "I can talk to Mrs. Evans and ask her to be discreet."

"You're both girls, Mom. You don't know what it's like to be a boy."

Carly wanted to scream, to cry, to shake her fist at someone, but if her son wasn't talking, she didn't know who to be angry with.

Where was a father—or an ex-husband—when you needed one?

But being envious of women who were married wasn't

going to get her anywhere. She was on her own and would have to come up with some way to handle the problem.

Finally, she leveled with him. "Listen, honey. I'm pedaling as fast as I can to hold this family together, and while I understand that you're still a child, you've got to help me."

Josh looked up at her as if she'd struck him across the face. "I *do* help you, Mom. A *lot*. I babysit Mikey every day, even when I'd rather go out and ride my bike or mess around with my friends. And I clean my room and put my clothes away. I do everything you ever ask me to do. I'm just not going to do this."

"Are you kidding?" she asked, knowing that he was dead serious. "You're not going to tell me that boy's name?"

Josh just shook his head. "Not if you poke me with a hundred needles or pour honey on me and tie me to an anthill."

Clearly, her usual form of discipline—time out and no dessert for supper—wasn't going to cause him to bend.

"Can I go now?" Josh asked.

"Yes, but I want you to go straight to your room and think about things."

"Yes, ma'am." Josh let himself out of the car and headed for the front door.

But Carly remained in the driver's seat, hanging on to the steering wheel as if it might help her control the mounting problems in her life.

On Wednesday morning, with the sidewalk still wet from last night's rain, Lynette entered Shear Magic, a small salon located across the street from Mulberry Park. She was running several minutes late for her ten o'clock appointment, so after wiping her feet on the mat at the door, she made her way to Carly's station, where the hairdresser was adding the finishing touches to the coiffure of a woman in her late seventies.

The soles of her new shoes clicked as she strode across the

blue tile flooring, her left foot making a slightly more pronounced sound than the right.

She wore a lift in her shoes these days to make her gait more even. Most people didn't notice, but it was something Lynette had lived with since she'd broken her leg as a child.

At the time she'd fallen down the stairs, she'd known that the injury to her leg had been serious. The pain had been excruciating, but her parents hadn't taken her to the doctor. Back then, she'd assumed they couldn't afford the medical bill. But as an adult, she realized it was probably because her father hadn't wanted anyone to ask for details about how she'd come to lose her balance since Child Protective Services had visited their house several times already.

Upon hearing Lynette's approach, Carly looked up from her work and smiled. "Hey there. How's it going?"

"Good. Do you want me to wait in the front?"

"No, I'm almost finished here." Carly pointed to one of the brown swivel chairs next to hers. "You can sit there. I'll be with you in just a minute."

Lynette glanced around the salon, which was empty today. "Where is everyone?"

"One's out sick, and the other took the afternoon off so she could go to the dentist." After shooting several blasts of hair spray to hold the older woman's gray curls in place, Carly said, "There you go, Joan."

"Thank you, honey." The older woman returned the mirror to Carly, then gripped the armrests with liver-spotted hands and began to rise. "I'll see you again next Wednesday at nine."

Carly helped Joan get to her feet. "Do you want me to call the van for you?"

"No, I'm going to meet a friend at the coffee shop next door." Then the elderly woman shuffled off without leaving a tip—or paying for the service.

Assuming she was a relative who'd received a freebie, Lynette asked, "Is that your grandma?"

"No, she's just a friend. She used to be my neighbor, but after her husband passed away, she moved into a local retirement home. On Wednesdays, the home provides a shuttle service for the residents so they can go to the market, the pharmacy, and the doctor or other appointments in town. It works out really well for her, but her funds are stretched pretty thin, so I don't charge her."

"That's nice of you."

Carly shrugged. "She used to bake sugar cookies for my boys each Christmas, so it's kind of my way of repaying her for the kindness."

Lynette thought about Maggie's story of the magic treasure box, but she didn't stew on it. Instead, she took a seat in the vacated swivel chair and watched in the mirror as Carly draped a blue striped cape around her and secured it at the back of her neck.

"Thanks again for rescheduling my appointment," Lynette said.

"No problem." As Carly gazed into the mirror and caught Lynette's eyes, she asked, "So what are we going to do today? Did you want highlights and a cut?"

"I'm ready for something new. What do you think about that?"

Carly lifted a light brown strand and studied its length and texture. "To be honest?"

Lynette nodded.

"I think the natural color is beautiful. It's a honey shade with a healthy shine. But I'd be happy to add highlights if you want me to."

Lynette studied her reflection, trying to see the beauty Carly had found.

Sure, whenever she looked into the mirror, she saw the same attractive image, but she was always a little taken aback by the stranger who peered back at her.

It had cost Peter a small fortune when he'd covered the cost of braces, contact lenses, a nose job, and breast implants, but his gifts had transformed a geeky twenty-year-old into the kind of wife he deserved—at least, outwardly. And while Lynette no longer bore much resemblance to the young woman she'd been before meeting Peter, she'd never really left her old self behind. So for that reason, whenever she looked into the mirror, it usually took a few moments for her to reconcile the two.

One of these days, she would probably begin to feel comfortable in her own skin, but in the meantime, she was up for a change. So she said, "Sure, let's add the highlights."

Nearly twenty minutes later, when Lynette's head was covered with pieces of folded foil and the bleaching solution had begun to process, Carly's telephone rang.

"Hold on," she told Lynette. "I'm going to put you under the hair dryer for a little while. But let me take this call, okay?"

"Sure." Lynette reached for a magazine that another customer had left near Carly's station. She had no intention of listening to her hairdresser's conversation, but she couldn't help tuning in when she picked up words like "I'm sorry" and "I can make a partial payment."

"Please," Carly told the caller, her voice hushed—but not enough for complete privacy. "I have kids, Jerry. Don't ask me to move before Christmas."

Lynette's stomach clenched as she realized what was happening. She'd overheard this kind of conversation in the past. But when she was a kid, her dad would usually pack up the family in the middle of the night and make them move before they were evicted. And unlike Carly, he hadn't seemed to care whether it was during a holiday or the night before a test at school.

She tried her best to study the glossy magazine pages and to appear to be deep in thought. She didn't want Carly to know she'd overheard anything or that she'd come to realize the hairdresser was having financial trouble.

Carly turned her back, stepped away, and lowered her

voice even further, yet Lynette could still make out some of her words.

"It's . . . my busiest . . . working . . . two salons."

She was implying that she was trying to raise the money. But she'd also just done an elderly woman's hair without charging her, clearly taking a financial hit out of the goodness of her heart.

"I'll . . . caught up . . . every penny."

Penny? Lynette was again reminded of Maggie's tale, although Carly's reality shot the moral of the story to smithereens.

So much for the magic treasure box. If the do-unto-others theme really worked, Carly wouldn't be struggling like this—especially at Christmas.

Just pondering Carly's plight sent Lynette's mind reeling back to the old days, when she'd worn shoes a size too small, when her birthday had come and gone without notice, let alone fanfare. And when she'd gone to bed with an empty stomach many a night.

Thank goodness those days were long behind her and she was able to provide for all her needs because of the trust fund Peter had set up for her.

She was, of course, tempted to loan Carly some money to see her through the holidays. But if she was struggling to pay her basic necessities now, how would she manage to do all of that in January and still be able to repay the debt?

A loan would become a gift, and even though Lynette's financial situation was solid these days, she couldn't very well give away what she had.

What if she lost it all and was forced to live in poverty again?

Of course, there were worse things than growing up poor—like waking to the sound of drunken parents yelling at each other until the neighbors called the police and trying to stay out of arm's reach on nights like that.

Still, she wanted to help Carly in some way. . . .

What the woman really needed was to meet and marry a nice, successful man who could support her, a man who would be kind to her children.

A man who would love her, just as Peter had loved Lynette. As the memory warmed her heart, a game plan began to unfold.

What if Lynette found a rich, older man who could provide for Carly and her sons? If she did, she could play matchmaker and set them up.

Carly was young and attractive, so that would make things easier—even if she did have children to add to the mix.

Okay then. Who did Lynette know that might fit the bill? These days, she didn't run in the same circles as she had when Peter was alive, but that was because his presence had ensured that she would fit in. So she'd have to give it some thought.

Of course, Helen lived next door to a couple of bachelors. Lynette wasn't sure if either or both of them were dating anyone—or if they liked kids. But she could certainly find out.

When Carly disconnected the line, her brow was furrowed. Worry weighed on her expression, yet she managed a smile. "I'm sorry about the interruption."

Lynette glanced up from the magazine she was pretending to read. "Excuse me?"

"I didn't mean to make you wait. Let's get you under some heat."

"All right." Lynette folded the magazine, using her finger to mark the page she hadn't read and had no intention of turning back to. Then she followed Carly to one of the dryers that lined the side wall.

"By the way," she said to the hairdresser. "Would you be interested in meeting a nice guy?"

"You've got to be kidding."

"Not at all. You're single, pretty, and have a good personality. And I have a feeling that you could really use a man in your life—especially in the evenings, after the kids go to bed."

Carly seemed to give the idea some thought, then slowly shook her head. "Honestly, I can't even think about dating, no matter how appealing it might be to have some adult companionship and to have access to a male perspective when it comes to dealing with my boys these days. My jobs and the kids keep me too busy. And even if I did have time for romance or a relationship, I'm afraid I've got too much excess baggage for a man to deal with."

If anyone had excess baggage, it had been Lynette when she'd first met Peter. But that hadn't stopped him, and now she was living on the right side of the tracks and had everything she'd ever wanted—except for the man who'd turned her life around.

"Would you at least be willing to meet a nice guy?" Lynette asked, as she took a seat under the dryer. "One who likes kids and who has a solid job and money in the bank?"

Again Carly paused, her hand resting on the dials that controlled the heat and the time. "It sounds as though you have someone in mind."

Well, not yet. Lynette still had some footwork to do and some men to check out. But she kept that little detail to herself and stretched the truth. "Yes, I do."

Carly seemed to ponder Lynette's little white lie—weakening maybe? Then she said, "But you're single, too. Why don't you go out with him?"

Because when Lynette left home at eighteen, she got caught up in a disastrous relationship with a sweet-talking high school dropout who turned out to be way too much like her father. Then, after watching a television documentary about the dynamics of domestic violence and the cycle of abuse, she'd realized that she was probably one of the women who would always be attracted to the wrong kind of man.

And while she watched her share of chick flicks and enjoyed an occasional romance novel, she didn't think that one of those happily-ever-afters was in the cards for her. So to make sure that history wouldn't repeat itself, she'd decided to date for security, rather than love.

And it had worked for her.

But instead of offering a confession, she tossed her hairdresser a breezy smile. "Because I'll never find another man like Peter, and even if I did, I'm not ready to date yet."

That seemed to appease Carly, who said, "I don't know, Lynette. I'm probably not ready yet, either."

Then she turned on the dryer, leaving Lynette to think about ways she could help make her hairdresser's life a little easier.

And her Christmas a little brighter.

On Wednesday evening, while Susan was adding chocolate chips to a triple batch of cookie dough to take to Helen's the next day, her phone rang.

She wiped her hands on a damp kitchen towel, then answered.

"Hi, Susan. How's everything going?" It was Barbie Lawson, her former sister-in-law.

"I'm fine. How about you?"

"Great."

"And your parents?" Susan asked.

"Dad's been having some trouble with his new blood pressure meds, but other than that, they're both well."

"I'm glad to hear it." Susan had spent a lot of time with Hank's family after the funeral, but as the grief began to lift, staying alone hadn't been so overwhelming. And she'd turned to the Lils for support. But she really needed to make an effort to see Stan and Donna Ferris soon.

"I called to invite you to the annual Christmas party at Lydia's House," Barbie said. "I know you've never gone with us before, but something tells me that was because Hank never felt comfortable there."

"He always blamed it on work," Susan said, "but you're probably right. I hadn't realized it at the time, but I've done some thinking about that lately."

"We'd love to include you this year, if you'd be okay with it."

Susan had never really given the annual Christmas party that much thought. She'd just gone along with Hank's decision to stay home.

"You'll be surprised at how much fun it is," Barbie said. "They have games, a gift exchange, and refreshments. Then Santa makes a showing."

Susan glanced at her nearly empty calendar, which hung on the wall near the phone. "I always get a little busy this time of year."

"I know what you mean. But the party at Lydia's House has become the highlight of the season for us, mostly because Ronnie gets so excited." Barbie paused a beat, then added, "All the kids do. It's so sweet."

The thought of children and Christmas had always tugged at Susan's heartstrings. But the "kids" Barbie was talking about were developmentally challenged adults and nothing like the ones she'd imagined opening presents under her tree.

Still, she'd never had any personal qualms about joining the Ferris family at Lydia's House. And Barbie was right. The decision to send a check instead of visiting in person had been Hank's decision. Yet she still felt a little apprehensive, and she wasn't sure why.

"This Christmas will probably be difficult for you," Barbie added. "But I think you'll really like the party. And you'll probably feel great on the way home. The kids begin decorating the place weeks before, and they're so excited to have their friends and families join in the fun. The holiday spirit is really contagious."

Barbie made it sound like something Susan might enjoy doing, although she still felt leery about committing.

"I really hope you'll go with us. Honestly, you'll probably find your attendance at the party a much bigger blessing to you than it is to the kids."

The word "blessing" brought Maggie's treasure chest story to mind, and Susan wondered if Barbie was right. Would she be glad she went? Would she really be blessed by it?

Deciding to give it a try in spite of her reservations, she asked, "What should I wear?"

"Something Christmas-y. Dad usually wears a battery-operated Santa Claus hat that lights up and a pair of green polka-dot suspenders."

Susan had a red silk vest with a Christmas tree appliqué on the front. And snowman earrings.

"What day did you say it was?" Susan asked.

"I don't think I did." Barbie chuckled. "It's at two o'clock on Christmas Eve and runs until about four. Are you free?"

Susan didn't even have to check the calendar. Other than her Thursdays with the Lils, she didn't have anything planned the entire month. "Sure, I'm free. I'll meet you there."

"I don't mind picking you up."

Agreeing to go was one thing, but Susan didn't want to ride with anyone. What if the party wasn't as much fun as Barbie seemed to think it was? And what if she wanted to cut out early?

"I've got another function to attend that day," she lied. "It really would be best if we drove separately."

"All right then. You won't be sorry. I promise."

Susan was already a little uneasy about the commitment, and after they said good-bye and the call ended, she tried to come up with a reason for it.

Maybe it was because she was subconsciously pulling away from her former in-laws so she would be free to marry another man and bond with his family. It made sense, although she feared it was more than that.

Either way, she wasn't going to contemplate it now. Instead, she went back to work on the cookies she planned to deliver to Max Tolliver and Grant Barrows tomorrow afternoon, sure they'd do the trick and at least open up some possibilities.

After all, she couldn't very well start thinking about wedding bells until she picked out her future husband.

Chapter 6

On Wednesday morning, while new storm clouds gathered overhead and threatened to rain on Fairbrook once again, Rosa Alvarado made her way across the soup kitchen to the industrial-size stove that had been donated by one of the wealthy members of Parkside Community Church.

The soup kitchen, a ministry that provided free meals to the homeless, and to low-income families and seniors, was located in a modular building at the back of the church grounds.

Normally, Rosa didn't help out on Wednesdays, but when Carlos, her husband, had heard that Dawn and Joe Randolph, the directors of the kitchen, were taking a family vacation, he volunteered to cover for them. So that, of course, meant that Rosa would be doing the cooking for the next six days straight.

Today she was making spaghetti, buttered green beans, and garlic bread. Dessert would be chocolate pound cake, which was already cooling on racks near the sink.

As she peered into the five-gallon pot of water she'd placed on the stove earlier, she saw that it was now boiling, so she added the pasta. Then she checked the meat, which was in another pan. The scent of tomatoes, basil, and garlic were coming together as the sauce simmered nicely, so she turned down the burner. But as she did so, she felt another hot flash coming on.

At sixty-two, she'd already gone through menopause, so having those annoying flushes start up again seemed odd—and unfair.

There could, of course, be something other than hormones causing them, but she hadn't gotten around to making an appointment to see the doctor yet. Her calendar was pretty full this month, so she wasn't sure when she'd find the time—certainly not in the next six days.

As the discomfort intensified, she fanned herself with a fluttery hand, which wasn't very effective, and sighed.

Earlier this morning, Pastor Craig had stopped by and turned on the heater, saying the weatherman was predicting both rain and hail by midafternoon.

Trouble was, the thermostat only read 71, yet it felt like an oven in here. If she'd been at home, she would have changed out of her winter clothes and into something summery. But since that wasn't an option, she considered going out on the back porch until she cooled off.

But even if she could blame those pesky hot flashes on age and hormones, she didn't know what was causing the occasional flutters and rumbles in her chest.

Nerves, she supposed, and good, old-fashioned stress.

Her hands had been a little shaky lately, especially this morning. But she'd also had three cups of coffee at breakfast, which probably explained why. She really ought to switch to drinking only decaf, but she'd sure been dragging lately, and without the caffeine, she'd probably be curled up in the corner right now, taking a nap.

"How's it going?" her husband of almost forty years asked as he slipped up behind her and peered over her shoulder and into the pan. "Need someone to taste the meat sauce for you?"

Rosa couldn't help but smile. Carlos loved her cooking, which was why he was about fifty pounds overweight. And since she did her best to prepare the meals and treats he enjoyed the most, she'd nearly gained the same amount.

Trouble was, she'd put on half of it over the past few months. But she blamed that on her bad knees, which made moving around difficult and exercise nearly impossible.

Carlos opened a drawer and pulled out a spoon, but before he could scoop up any sauce to taste, Pastor Craig entered the kitchen with a woman in her mid to late forties.

"Good news," the minister said. "I've got another volunteer to help you out while the Randolphs are in Hawaii."

Rosa and Carlos both turned to greet the woman, whom Craig referred to as Mary-Margaret Di Angelo.

After introductions were made all the way around, the blonde asked them to call her Maggie.

At that, Rosa cocked her head to the side, causing a drop of perspiration to dribble down her temple and onto her cheek. She swiped it away with the back of her hand and asked, "Are you related to Helen Pritchard?"

"Yes, I'm her cousin."

"I thought your name sounded familiar." Rosa wiped her damp hand on her apron before reaching out to greet Maggie with a handshake and a grin. "Helen's a friend of mine. She mentioned that you'd be house-sitting while she was gone. In fact, I was supposed to stop by with Lynette and Susan yesterday, but I wasn't able to join you."

"Oh, yes. You're *that* Rosa—and one of the Lils." Maggie's grip was warm and solid. "I'm glad we finally have a chance to meet."

Rosa was, too. "Are you planning to help us in the soup kitchen today?"

"I *can,*" Maggie said. "Do you need me?"

Rosa was about to say yes, when Carlos chimed in. "We've got things under control. But if you'd like to stay, we can probably find something for you to do."

If Rosa didn't love that man, she'd clobber him with the first kitchen utensil or appliance she could get her hands on. Carlos might have everything under control, but she was ready to drop in her tracks.

"Maggie," the associate minister said, "Carlos and Rosa deserve a special place in Heaven for all the charities they support both financially and with their time. If the church or the community has any kind of a need, you can count on the Alvarados to step up to the plate."

Carlos placed a hand on Rosa's shoulder and gave it an affectionate squeeze. "We do what we can, don't we, honey?"

"I'm not sure where they find the hours in a day," Pastor Craig added. "They also own the coffee shop on First Avenue, which is usually buzzing with customers."

"Actually," Carlos said, "our son runs it now. Rosa and I are pretty much retired these days."

That might be true, but thanks to Carlos and his insistence upon volunteering them both for every charity known to God and man, Rosa worked harder now than she ever had before.

Of course, she merely smiled in agreement. How did a wife complain about a good-hearted husband like Carlos? Or tell a man of God that she was too tuckered out to cook for thirty-five to forty hungry people, let alone to clean up afterward?

"You've both been a real blessing to Parkside Community Church," Pastor Craig said. "I don't know what we'd do without you."

Carlos stood tall, and his chest puffed out just a tad. "Thanks, Pastor. Rosa and I believe people should leave the world a little better than the way they found it."

He had a point, she supposed. But she was ready to let someone else volunteer for a while. What she wouldn't do to have a full day to herself.

Of course, she had that big weekend trip to Laughlin planned in January. She hadn't told Carlos yet, but he was going to have to get by without her while she was gone.

"Carlos," Pastor Craig said, "there's a leak in the men's room. Would you mind taking a look at it for me? I want to know if it's going to be an easy fix or if I should call a plumber to take care of it."

Carlos set the unused spoon on the counter, then followed Pastor Craig, leaving Maggie and Rosa alone.

Using the time without the men to her advantage, Rosa shifted her weight to ease the pressure on her bad knee and said, "I'd love to have your help today, unless you have other plans."

"The only thing I need to do is to stop by the market and pick up a few things. I'm making lunch tomorrow for the Lils. Will you be able to join us at Helen's?"

"I'm afraid not." Rosa tried to shake off her disappointment. "I've got to work here again tomorrow."

"Well, there's always next week," Maggie said.

"Yes, you're right. The Randolphs are returning on Wednesday, so as long as my husband doesn't line up something else for us to do, I'll be at Helen's next Thursday." Rosa chuckled, trying to make light of it, hoping she had.

"Doesn't your husband know that you already have a commitment that day?" Maggie asked.

"He should. I've been a Diamond Lil for almost ten years, but I've had to miss more poker games lately than I'd like to because he seems to think doing for others is more important than socializing with my friends." Rosa supposed his do-unto-others attitude was right, which was why she never complained.

The Lils often urged her to stand up to Carlos and refuse to help him on Thursdays, but she had reason to believe he needed the outlet his volunteerism provided him. Besides, he always chose good causes.

Rosa expected Helen's cousin to voice a similar thought. Instead Maggie said, "That's too bad."

"I really can't get mad at him for trying to help out those who are less fortunate than we are. It's not like he's asking me to do something selfish." The ache in Rosa's knee began to throb, and she stepped away from the stove. "Excuse me, but I've got to sit down for a minute."

"No problem. Is there something I can do to help?"

"Not at the moment. But as soon as the pasta is tender you can help me drain the water and add the spaghetti to the sauce." Rosa took a seat on the stool near the counter, stroked her knee, and slowly shook her head. "Boy, I'll tell you, old age is for the birds."

"Maybe you need a vacation," Maggie said.

"I'm sure I do." Again, she forced a chuckle, hoping Maggie didn't notice how hollow it sounded.

The first light drops of rain misted Josh's face, as he and Mikey walked along the Bushman Trail, their steps slowed down by the clumps of mud on the soles of their shoes.

The teachers had some kind of meeting this afternoon, so the kids had gotten out of school at noon.

"I hope we don't get in trouble," Mikey said. "You're supposed to be grounded."

"Mom said that I wasn't supposed to leave the house after we got home from school, and we haven't gotten home yet, have we?"

"No, but—"

"Whose fault is this anyway?" Josh asked, reminding his little brother why they hadn't gone straight home.

"I guess it's mine. I'm sorry, Josh. I didn't mean to leave that arrowhead out here."

"You shouldn't have had it in the first place. It was mine, not yours."

And Josh had a report on the Plains Indians due on Monday. He also had to get up in front of the whole class and show them his project, which he was still working on. But he couldn't finish it without that arrowhead.

"So where did you leave it?" he asked his brother.

"By the stream. On a flat rock."

Josh gritted his teeth and shook his head. He still had no idea why Mikey would bring that arrowhead down to the Bushman Trail, but that was a little kid for you—doing dumb things without thinking.

Coming down to the canyon before going home was kind of dumb, too, he supposed. If his mom found out, she wouldn't be happy about it. But the way Josh saw it, he had no other choice, other than to get a bad grade in social studies.

Besides, they weren't going very far—and they'd stick super close to the houses on Canyon Drive. No way would he risk running into Ross or getting near Mr. Tolliver's house. And once they got what they were looking for, they'd be home before their mom was the wiser.

Of course, their shoes were going to be a dead giveaway. But he had that all figured out. They would use the hose in the backyard to wash off most of the mud, then they'd throw their shoes in the washer and then the dryer before their mother even got off work.

"This is as far as we went the other day," Josh said, stopping in his tracks and turning to face his brother. "So where is it?"

"I *told* you. On a rock by the stream."

The stream ran along the entire bottom of the canyon and went all the way to the beach. It was also lined with rocks on both sides. So Josh rolled his eyes. "What kind of clue is that?"

"It's gotta be here somewhere. The rock was really flat on top, like a pancake. We probably already passed it. Come on, I'll find it." Retracing their steps, Mikey took the lead, which didn't happen very often. Josh figured he must have forgotten how scared he usually got when they came down here.

Or maybe he was finally growing up.

But ten minutes later, after passing the same old empty beer can about a hundred times, Mikey finally gave up. "Maybe someone found it. Or the rain washed it away."

Great. That was all Josh needed. He slapped his hands on his hips, ready to let Mikey know how mad he was, when he heard twigs snap and a series of thumps.

Turning to the sound, he spotted Hemingway loping toward them.

"Uh-oh," he said. "Guess who's loose again."

"Hey, boy." Mikey was the first to greet the dog, dropping to one knee and rubbing its wooly head. "How'd you get out this time?"

Who knew? But the way Josh saw it, Houdini was a better name for the mutt than Hemingway was.

"Do you think he's jumping over the fence?" Mikey asked.

"Maybe, but it's pretty high. I think a kangaroo would have a hard time getting over it."

Hemingway's tail wagged like crazy, and his back end started swinging back and forth with it.

"Look how happy he is to see us," Mikey said.

It sure seemed that way.

"I think he's getting out just because he wants to be with us," Mikey said.

That was possible. And, to be honest, Josh had to admit the goofy dog was kind of growing on him, too.

Mikey, whose glasses had slipped to the tip of his nose while he was stooped over and petting the dog, looked up at Josh. "Think we should take him back home so nothing happens to him?"

"No way." Josh was in enough trouble as it was. So that meant Hemingway was on his own while he was running loose. "I'm never going to take him home again."

The dog's owner was a grump, although Josh was a lot more scared of Ross than he was of Mr. Tolliver. "Come on, Mikey. We need to get out of here. We'll just have to forget that arrowhead for now."

"Okay." As Mikey turned to go, he looked to the right and cried out, "Hey, look! There it is!" Then he walked to the muddy edge of the swollen stream, where the arrowhead rested on a flat rock that was almost under water, thanks to the last rain. "I'll get it."

"Don't fall in," Josh said.

"I won't."

But just as Mikey leaned forward and reached for the arrowhead, his foot slipped. He probably wasn't going to fall in, and if he did, he knew how to swim, but Josh started after him anyway—just in case. Before he could get one step closer, Hemingway lurched forward and grabbed Mikey by the seat of his pants, just like he was Lassie or some kind of wonder dog. But then Hemingway slipped, too, bumping into Mikey and sending him headfirst into the rushing water.

It's not like the creek was all that deep; Mikey just had to stand up and he'd be okay. So Josh couldn't help but laugh when he thought about his little brother getting goosed by a dog and knocked into the water. Of course, they were in real trouble now, but some things were just plain funny.

Too bad they didn't have a camera with them. They could have sent it to *America's Funniest Home Videos* and made a ton of money—enough to solve all their family's problems.

But as Mikey stood up, sopping wet, he grinned from ear to ear and raised his fist up high in victory, just like he'd scored a winning touchdown in the last second of the game. "I still got it, Josh! I didn't let it go!"

The arrowhead?

That was great news, Josh thought. But now they had an even worse problem.

Mikey wasn't wearing his glasses anymore.

Carly's last appointment of the day called an hour earlier and canceled, saying she didn't like driving in the rain. So rather than stay at the salon and hope for a walk-in, she decided to call it a day before the upcoming storm hit with a vengeance.

She thought about stopping by the market on her way home, since a pot of homemade chicken vegetable soup sounded really good on a day like this and she'd need to pick up the ingredients. But she'd told Jerry Carlisle, her landlord, that she'd make a partial payment of the rent by the first of next week, so she was stuck making meals with whatever she had on hand.

And that meant they'd be dining on canned chili tonight.

By the time she reached the house, the wind had really kicked up, and the rain was coming down in a steady beat.

She could have called the boys to let them know she was going to be early, but decided to surprise them instead. During the winter months, it wasn't often that she got home before dark.

After parking the car in the garage, she entered the house through the laundry room, where the dryer was on. Whatever was inside was thumping and bumping as though the appliance was going to blow at any minute.

What in the world had the boys put in there?

She placed her purse and appointment book on top of the washer, then opened the dryer door. Inside, she found the clothes they'd been wearing this morning, as well as their shoes—all damp.

Apparently, they'd gotten wet on their way home from school.

She probably ought to be proud of them for trying to clean up after themselves, although she would've preferred that they waited for her.

After restarting the dryer, she grabbed her things. Then, hoping to keep the noise at a minimum, she shut the door to close off the laundry room from the rest of the house.

As she moved through the kitchen, she heard another noise coming from the bathroom. Her blow-dryer? Had the boys gotten so wet walking home from the bus stop that they'd needed to shower and wash their hair, too?

Unable to quell her curiosity, she strode to the hall, then opened the bathroom door, only to find her sons kneeling next to a great big, wooly dog.

And they were blow-drying its fur.

She wasn't sure who was more surprised, her or the boys. Even the mangy mutt looked up at her with guilty eyes.

"What in the world are you *doing?*" she asked.

"We . . ." Mikey bit his bottom lip, then looked at his brother as if wanting help with the explanation.

"It's a long story," Josh said, shutting off the blow-dryer.

"I've got plenty of time." Carly crossed her arms, thinking this had better be good—until her gaze traveled to the edge of the bathtub, where her favorite—and most *expensive*—shampoo bottle sat. Her jaw dropped, and she finally lost her cool. "Don't tell me you bathed that dog with my good stuff."

But the boys didn't need to say a word. The familiar floral scent, which she hadn't noticed until now, filled the room, even though it couldn't mask the smell of wet dog fur.

"I figured you wouldn't mind us cleaning him up when you found out why," Josh said.

Well, he'd figured *wrong*.

But before she could open her mouth, he added, "Hemingway saved Mikey's life. And we didn't think you'd want him to catch pneumonia and die because of it."

Mikey had been in danger? The annoyance in Carly's voice faded into the small confines of the bathroom, and her knees threatened to give out. "What happened?"

Her question had been pointed at Josh, but it was Mikey who responded first. "I lost Josh's arrowhead in the canyon the other day, and he needed it for his school project. So I went to find it for him, but I fell in the creek, and Hemingway grabbed me. So that's how we all got wet and muddy."

"Hemingway?" she asked.

"Mr. Tolliver's dog." Josh smiled at the critter and stroked its head. "At first we thought he was mean, but he's really cool. And he's even kind of cute, when you get used to looking at him."

Carly had no intention of getting used to him. In fact, she

was eager to get him out of the house as soon as possible, even if he was a hero.

"Actually," Mikey said, "it was kind of his fault that I fell in the water in the first place. He bumped into me."

Carly glanced at Josh, just in time to see him give his younger brother a frown. Had they embellished the dog's heroism?

"But he saved me," Mikey added. "I just wish he would have saved my glasses, too."

At that, Carly looked at her youngest son, just now realizing that his glasses were missing.

Under normal circumstances, she would have chalked it up as another inconvenient cost that parents dealt with on a regular basis, but she couldn't afford to buy another pair of glasses, especially this week.

And Mikey needed them for school.

What was she going to do?

"We tried to find them," Josh said. "That's how we got all wet. But when they fell in the water with Mikey, they must have floated all the way to the ocean."

Carly raked her hand through her hair as she sorted through the story they'd told her, but they seemed to have left out one important detail. "Why didn't you come straight home like you were supposed to?"

"It was my fault," Mikey said. "I was the one who lost the arrowhead. And Josh followed after me 'cause he's supposed to babysit me, remember?"

It was days like this that reminded her how badly she needed to hire a competent adult to look after the boys while she worked. But how was she supposed to pay that additional expense when she was going to be hard-pressed to pay even a part of the rent this month?

Oh, dear God. Is there ever going to be an end to all of this? Carly placed a hand over her forehead. *What am I going to do? How do I dig out of this hole?*

Yet she didn't expect an answer. She'd been praying for all

that she was worth lately, asking that God would send an angel to watch over the boys while she was at work and to make sure they stayed out of trouble. She'd also asked that her money troubles would ease up, and that she would be able to create a happy home for her sons. But so far, her prayers seemed to have gotten trapped in the ozone.

Right now, she'd appreciate having another adult to turn to, someone to wrap his arms around her and assure her that they would both sit back and laugh about all of this one day.

But how many eligible bachelors wanted to become stepfathers and take on a ready-made family?

Not many, she suspected.

Lynette might think she'd found the perfect guy for Carly, but she was wrong. What man in his right mind would choose Carly when he could just as easily have someone as pretty—and as unencumbered—as Lynette?

Carly closed her eyes, then took a deep breath and slowly let it go. "Okay, boys. I want you both to take a shower. Then put on your pajamas."

"But it's not even night yet," Josh said.

"I don't care what time it is," she snapped. "Get ready for bed, then clean up this mess."

"But what about Hemingway?" Mikey asked. "Where should we put him?"

"Outside."

"But it's raining. And we already gave him a bath. You can't send him out where he'll get dirty and wet."

She was speechless for a couple of beats, then an idea struck. As she turned toward the door, where her bathrobe hung, she reached for the sash and pulled it through the loops. Then she slipped it through the dog's collar, using it as a makeshift leash.

"What are you doing?" Josh asked.

"Don't worry about that. You do as I say. I'll be back in a few minutes."

"Where are you going?" he asked.

She tugged on the sash, drawing the dog through the doorway. "I'm going to drive him home."

"That's really cool of you, Mom."

Carly glanced at her oldest son, saw him smiling. But she didn't respond to his praise.

He might think she was being a good mother and an animal lover, but Mikey needed new glasses, and Max Tolliver's dog was responsible.

Chapter 7

As the rain pelted the window and a fire blazed warm in the hearth, Max paced the length of the living room floor, from the computer desk to the front door and back again.

Earlier, he'd been hard at work, his mind locked on his manuscript, while Hemingway roamed the yard. But then a streak of lightning lit the room, and a roar of thunder shook the walls, jerking Max back to reality.

The dog hated thunderstorms, so Max had gone to let him in. The silence—no howling, crying, or scratching claws upon the door—had been his first clue that something was amiss.

As he opened the door and stepped out onto the porch, the only sound that met him was the storm—the wind raking through the trees, the raindrops pounding the rooftop and pouring on the ground.

"Hemingway!" he'd shouted several times. He'd whistled, too, but the dog hadn't come running.

The gate had been closed, so he had no idea how he'd gotten out. But at that point, it hadn't really mattered.

So he'd taken the car and searched the neighborhood, going as far as to circle Mulberry Park and to check out Canyon Drive, but the dog was nowhere to be found.

Hemingway didn't have much street sense. In fact, there were times when Max didn't think he had any sense at all.

He tried to tell himself that he would come home eventually. And that animals were accustomed to being outdoors, even in bad weather. But that didn't make him feel any better about knowing that Hemingway was on the loose.

As pesky as that dog could sometimes be, and as often as Max had threatened to take him to the pound, you'd think that he could shake off the uneasiness. But he couldn't seem to do that.

It was well after five o'clock now, so he didn't expect anyone at the animal shelter to answer the phone. Still, they had to have some kind of emergency crew, didn't they? Someone available to pick up strays and protect them from the storm?

He started for the telephone, but when the doorbell rang, he came to a stop. He didn't get much company, especially since he'd been keeping to himself lately. But Hemingway had a license and an identity tag with his name and address. Maybe someone had found him.

He crossed the living room floor and opened the door, where he found the dog waiting, tail wagging, butt swinging back and forth. But it wasn't Hemingway's presence that surprised him the most, it was the woman who'd brought him home.

Carly Westbrook stood on his stoop, her brown hair damp, her mascara smudged—yet just as attractive as the first time he'd seen her. Maybe more so, he thought, a grin tugging at his lips.

In her hand, she held a ribbon of blue linen, which was tied to Hemingway's red collar.

Before he could thank her for coming out in the rain to bring his dog home, Hemingway lunged inside, nearly dragging the poor woman along with him.

Max's gaze flicked from the crazy mutt to the pretty brunette and back again.

"Thanks for bringing him home," he finally said. "Where did you find him?"

"In my bathroom."

Max cocked his head. "How did he get in there?"

"My boys gave him a bath."

Her answer only provoked more questions, like how the dog got to her house in the first place. But rather than quiz her further, Max opened the door wider and stepped aside. "Please, come in out of the rain and cold."

She seemed to hesitate for a moment, then complied. But she didn't do more than cross the threshold.

"Can I get you something to drink? Something warm, like coffee maybe?"

"No, I can't stay. I've got to get back to the boys." Yet she stood there, in the foyer. Waiting for something, it seemed.

A reward, maybe?

Her clothing—brown slacks, white blouse, and black jacket—were rain-splattered. And her cheeks were flushed, although he wasn't sure if that was from embarrassment due to the awkward situation or from the cold.

"So how did my dog end up at your house?" he finally asked.

"He and my boys were in the canyon. And when Mikey—Michael—was reaching into the water for something, your dog knocked him in."

Max tensed. "Is your son okay?"

"Yes. Apparently, your dog also pulled him back to shore."

Hemingway? A clumsy hero?

Max couldn't help but smile as he glanced down at the lovable mutt who was sitting on his haunches, his tongue lolling out of his mouth.

His fur had a glossy sheen this evening, and he looked better than he did after the time Max had taken him to the groomers.

"Your kids gave him a bath?" he asked.

"With my best shampoo."

Max caught the hint of spring flowers and smiled again. "He smells great. You've got good taste in bath products."

He'd only been trying to make light of it all—Hemingway

getting out, the kids giving him a bath, their pretty mother bringing the dog home in the rain.

But as she clutched her purse tightly to her side and frowned, it was apparent that she didn't find it funny. "My son lost his glasses in the creek."

"I'm sorry to hear that."

"They were expensive, and I can't afford to replace them right now."

Uh-oh. Was she expecting him to pay for them? Was that what this awkward moment was all about?

Max took a defensive stance. "How did the dog get out of my yard?"

"I have no idea, but he keeps ending up with my boys."

He couldn't argue that point, but neither could he help but suspect that her kids had a part in his dog's escape. But rather than accuse them without any solid evidence, he softened the blow. "Maybe they're trying to adopt him."

She crossed her arms. "I've told the boys to stay away from your property and your dog. And they insist that they have."

Maybe so, but Max knew something about human nature, and confessions didn't come easy for most people. "Have you considered that they might be lying to you?"

"I suppose they could be, but I believe them. So I'd have to say it's probably the other way around. Your dog is trying to adopt my kids."

"Do they need adopting?"

She bristled, clearly taking offense at his remark. And to be honest, he wasn't entirely sure why he'd said it, why he'd implied that she might not be watching them closely enough. It was possible, he supposed, but he had no way of knowing that was the case.

"I love my kids," she said. "And I try to keep close tabs on them, but I'm also pedaling as fast as I can, trying to stay on top of the creditors and my landlord. Christmas is coming, and I'm not even going to be able to afford a tree."

He was sorry to hear that, but what did she expect him to do or to say? He wasn't the one who'd left her in a lurch.

"I'm a hairdresser," she added. "And I've been working six days a week. Sometimes I stay late at the salon, hoping to pick up the walk-in clientele. As a result, the boys are left to fend for themselves, which is a huge worry for me. But I can't see any way around it right now, especially this month."

It was more than Max wanted to know, more than he needed to know. And he wondered if, after she went home and thought about it, she'd feel sorry about dumping all of that on him.

He was usually good at reading people, although he wasn't at all sure about her. He had a hunch that she was even less sure about him, and that's usually the way he liked it. But something about this whole thing made him uneasy and left him a little unbalanced.

"I'm sorry for venting," she said. "And it kills me to have to come here and ask you to pay for my son's glasses."

Max bristled. So that's why she went to the trouble of bringing Hemingway home. To ask him for money. Well, he was financially strapped, too. And he didn't like being backed into a corner.

"Didn't my dog pull your son out of the creek?" he asked.

She nodded.

"Then, if that's the case, the cost of the glasses should be on you."

"But your dog caused Michael to fall into the water in the first place. And my son needs those glasses." Her eyes—a pretty shade of green in the lamplight—welled with tears.

Aw, man. Don't do that, lady.

Max knew that crying was often a ploy, and that she could be playing him for a fool, but that didn't stop sympathy from chipping away at his resolve until he turned and strode for his desk to get his checkbook, which he kept in the top drawer.

Annoyed by his weakness and grumbling under his breath,

he grabbed a pen. On the PAY TO THE ORDER OF line, he wrote "Carly Westbrook," then made it out for one hundred dollars and signed the darn thing.

Yet he held his ground as he tore out the check and handed it to her. "I won't pay to replace his glasses. But here's a reward for finding my dog."

As she took it from him, her hand trembled slightly. She bit her bottom lip, and when she gazed at him, one of the tears welling in her eyes overflowed and slid down her cheek. "Thank you."

As she turned to go back out into the rain, he found himself stopping her. "I've got an umbrella you can use."

"That's okay," she said. "I don't mind getting wet."

That might be true, but he figured the real reason she turned down his offer was because she didn't want to feel beholden to him, and he couldn't blame her for that.

Somehow, thanks to his dog and a couple of disobedient kids, they'd ended up in some kind of neighborly cold war, which was a shame.

As feisty as he could be at times, as quick as he was with a snappy retort, he didn't feel like fighting with a beautiful single mother who was prone to tears.

Especially since he found her far more attractive than he ought to.

He opened the door for her, then watched as she ducked out into the rain. When she'd gotten safely into her car and started the engine, he turned to the dog. "What am I going to do with you?"

Hemingway cocked his furry head to the side, clearly clueless.

But the dumb dog wasn't any more perplexed than Max.

On Thursday morning, just before noon, Lynette was the first to arrive at Helen's house. After parking at the curb and shutting off the ignition, she scanned the neighborhood, hoping to see one of the bachelors out and about.

She wasn't too hopeful until she spotted Grant Barrows leaving his house. He was wearing a dark sports jacket and tie today, which was unusual for a laid-back guy like him.

Since she would need an excuse to approach him, she decided that making a comment about his appearance would work as well as anything. So she slid out of the driver's seat, grabbed her purse, then locked the car and strolled toward Grant.

"Don't you look nice," she said.

"Thanks."

"Going to a wedding?" She cast him a playful grin, doubting that was the case.

He lobbed a boyish smile right back at her. "Actually, I've got a job interview."

Lynette could have sworn that Helen said he worked at home, but she could be wrong. Either way, she wasn't mistaken about him being wealthy. She didn't forget details like that. So, determined to set him up with Carly, she dropped her keys into her purse and approached him, hoping he had time to chat for a minute or two.

"Nice tie," she said, checking out the stylish but conservative blue and gray print.

"You like it?" He glanced down the front of him, then smoothed his hand over the length of the silk.

"I certainly do." She'd always found Grant attractive, even in shorts and flip-flops. But she'd had no idea how sharp he would look when he dressed up.

If she was interested in him herself, she wouldn't have been so bold as to approach him, but she was doing this for Carly, so it was easy to be outgoing for a change.

So how did she go about setting them up? She'd never been a matchmaker before. As her gaze lifted to his handsome face and those expressive brown eyes, she noticed the way the sun highlighted the gold strands in his hair, and an idea struck.

She tipped her head slightly and pretended to check out his

hair, thinking that the longer length really suited the casual, Tommy Bahama style he usually wore, but keeping that thought to herself.

"What's the matter?" he asked, furrowing his brow. He lifted his hand and ran it across his head as if checking to see if maybe he'd suddenly sprouted a cowlick.

"Nothing. It's just that . . ." She nibbled on her bottom lip. "Maybe it's the jacket and tie, but your hair seems a little long."

He flinched slightly, as if he might be as insecure as she was—which was a wild assumption. No one was as self-conscious as Lynette, especially a man like him.

"Do you think I need a haircut?" he asked.

No, not at all. Not even when he was all spiffed up in a jacket and tie, but if she wanted to set him up with a hair-dresser, well . . .

"Maybe just a trim," she said. "Who normally styles it for you?"

"Whoever's available at the Clip Joint down on Third Avenue. I'm usually a walk-in client. And only when it starts to curl at the collar."

"Can I make a suggestion?"

"Sure." He crossed his arms over his chest, bracing himself, it seemed.

She probably shouldn't have implied that there was something wrong with his appearance, especially before an interview, but at this point, she wasn't sure how to reel in her comment, so she continued what she'd started.

"Why don't you make an appointment with Carly down at Shear Magic? She's a great hairstylist and reasonably priced—although the cost probably isn't a factor for you." Lynette smiled and gave a little shrug. "She's also a good friend, and since she's trying to build up a clientele, I've been sending people her way."

Grant slid a gaze over her, just as she'd done to him, which set off a nervous flutter in her stomach, something that always happened when a man, especially one who was attractive, studied her.

She never knew quite how to deal with that sort of thing, so it stymied her a bit.

"Your friend is lucky to have you as her PR person," Grant said.

Shaking off the momentary insecurity, Lynette managed to veer back on track. "I'm sure you don't care about highlights, especially since yours are natural. But Carly styled my hair the other day. What do you think?"

"Very nice." This time his smile broadened, revealing a pair of dimples that Carly might find appealing.

Lynette certainly did.

Nevertheless, she opened her purse and reached inside. "I just so happen to have one of her cards."

Unfortunately, she'd tucked them in some little nook or pocket, so it took several seconds of digging around to find the little stack she'd been looking for. Then she handed one to Grant.

He took the card from her, gave it a quick once-over, then glanced at his wristwatch and sobered. "I'm afraid I have to go or I'll be late."

"I hope I didn't take up too much of your time."

"No problem, Lynette. Maybe we can talk more later, after you ladies play poker."

"Sure," she said, not bothering to tell him they'd only be eating lunch today. While he was gone, she would have to call Carly and see what times she had available to give Grant a haircut.

So far, everything seemed to be working out nicely.

As Lynette started back to Helen's house, she took one last glance at Grant, only to find that he'd paused at his car door and was looking at her. The intensity of his gaze caught her off guard, and she tried to read his expression. Interest? Curiosity? Suspicion?

She didn't have a clue, and not knowing what he was thinking stirred up the butterflies in her stomach again.

If she hadn't been determined to find a financially secure man for Carly, she might have gotten cold feet about approaching Grant again, but as it was, she'd do whatever she could to see that the potential couple had a chance to meet.

So she waved good-bye as if she hadn't noticed anything unusual and turned toward Helen's house, just as Susan was arriving.

Eager to break free and to shake the flutters, she raised her hand and gave her friend a wave. But Susan didn't seem to notice.

As Susan parked in front of Helen's house, she was still stewing over her most recent conversation with Hank's sister.

Barbie's call had ended ten minutes ago, but Susan was growing more and more bothered by it. It wasn't so much the call that made her uneasy, it was what she'd agreed to do. And now she was trying to figure out a way to get out of attending that holiday party at Lydia's House altogether.

Fortunately, as she parked her car on Nutcracker Court, she spotted Lynette talking to Grant Barrows, and her mood lifted.

She'd asked her friends to be on the lookout for an eligible bachelor who might be interested in dating her, and since it appeared that Lynette was already on it, a thrill shot right through her.

Smiling to herself, she shut off the ignition. But before she could reach for the plate of cookies she'd made for Grant, she saw him climb into his car and back out of his driveway.

She hadn't gotten a real good look at him, since he was standing on the other side of his car, but he appeared to be dressed up and to have combed his hair differently.

He was usually home on Thursday afternoons, so she couldn't help wondering where he was going.

As the women came together, Lynette zeroed right in on the goodies she'd brought. "I love chocolate chip cookies. Are they homemade?"

"They sure are. Hank's mother gave me the recipe years ago and told me it was a surefire way to put a smile on any man's face. And I have to say, it worked like a charm, even when I accidentally overdrew the checking account and Hank was fit to be tied."

"Magic cookies, huh?"

Susan laughed. "It sure seemed like that at times. After eating a couple of these, fresh from the oven, Hank's foul mood would usually turn to sweet within ten minutes. So I memorized the recipe, right down to the real-churned butter and the brand of chocolate chips to use."

"Smart lady."

Susan liked to think so. And that's why she'd made these cookies today. She hoped they would have the same "magical" effect on Grant and Max.

As the women walked along the sidewalk to Helen's door, Susan said, "I saw you talking to Grant. Where was he going all dressed up like that?"

"To a job interview."

"Oh?" Susan's steps slowed. "I thought he worked at home."

"Me, too."

Susan waited for Lynette to offer more info, but she didn't, which left her more curious than ever.

"So what else did he have to say?" she asked.

"Not much. We just talked for a minute or two."

Susan hated to pressure her friend for more details, especially if there weren't any to be had. So she let the subject drop for now. Her biological clock might be ticking, but some things shouldn't be rushed.

Once they reached the door, Lynette said, "You've got your hands full. Let me get the bell."

Moments later, Maggie welcomed them into the house, where they were met with the warm, tantalizing aroma of tomatoes, basil, and oregano.

"Something sure smells good," Lynette said. "I'm glad I came hungry. Did you make the vegetable lasagna you told us about?"

"I sure did." Maggie's smile lit her eyes and made her rather ordinary face look radiant—and almost pretty. "I made Caesar salad, too."

Susan lifted the plate of cookies in her hands. "And I brought dessert."

"Just looking at them makes my mouth water," Maggie said, as she led them into the kitchen, where the table was already set for three.

"It's too bad Rosa has to work at the soup kitchen." The comment tumbled out of Susan's mouth before she gave it any thought, and since Maggie seemed to be a champion for doing unto others and volunteerism, she decided she'd better clarify. "I mean it's great that Rosa is helping out. I probably should be, too. It's just a shame that she can't join us. Lynette and I really miss her."

"I'm sure you do." Maggie took the cookies from Susan and set them on the counter. "Why don't you pull out a chair and have a seat. I'll pour us some iced tea."

The table, which had a small pot of violets as a centerpiece, had been set with Helen's best linen and china.

The Lils had shared many a meal together, most of them potluck. And while Helen was a wonderful hostess, Maggie certainly knew how to make someone feel like a special guest.

"It was so nice of you to make lunch for us," Lynette said.

Susan quickly chimed in with her thanks, as well.

"You're more than welcome," Maggie said, as she began filling the plates and setting them on the table.

Within minutes, they were all seated and enjoying one of the tastiest meals they'd had in a long time.

"You're a great cook," Susan said, "and a wonderful hostess."

Helen's cousin smiled. "Thanks. I enjoy sharing meals with my friends."

"I do, too." Lynette placed a spoonful of sugar in her glass of iced tea and gave it a stir. "It's really too bad that Rosa had to miss this. For once it would be nice if she could kick back and enjoy a meal. She's usually the one cooking and waiting on everyone else."

"Did I mention that I got the chance to meet her yesterday?" Maggie asked.

"No, you didn't." Lynette set down her spoon, then picked up her glass. "Where did you see her?"

"At the soup kitchen. I stopped by to see if I could volunteer my time, and Pastor Craig introduced us." Maggie stuck her fork into her salad and speared a piece of romaine. "She's very nice, but she appeared to be a little worn and frazzled yesterday."

"I'm not surprised." Susan leaned back in her chair. "She's been really busy lately, and at her age, she really shouldn't push so hard. I've been meaning to stop in and check on her."

"She also seemed a little flushed and out of breath," Maggie added. "I'm sure she could use some help in the kitchen, if either of you can find the time."

"I know her husband means well," Lynette said, "but you know what they say—charity begins at home."

Susan wondered if Maggie would agree. She seemed to have a soft heart about giving and doing for others. At least, she'd made Susan feel a little guilty about hanging on to their poker winnings and spending it on the tournament in Laughlin. Maybe an hour or two spent volunteering at the soup kitchen would lessen those feelings. It was something to think about.

Not that that Susan was selfish or greedy. She was concerned about the disadvantaged. You could even ask her accountant. She and Hank always had charitable donations to write off on their taxes.

Of course, after that phone call with Barbie, she wondered if she might be more selfish than she'd thought.

"What's the matter?" Maggie asked. "Is something wrong?"

Susan glanced up, realizing that the hostess had been addressing her. "I'm sorry. I didn't mean to be rude. I was just thinking about something."

"Something burdensome?" Maggie asked.

Yes, but she didn't think it was a good idea to share it here, especially in front of Maggie. So she managed a smile. "It's really nothing important."

Lynette seemed to take her at her word and kept eating, but not Maggie. "If it's bothering you, maybe we can help."

"It's no big deal. It's just that . . . Well, Barbie, my sister-in-law, called me earlier this morning."

"I thought you got along well with Hank's family," Lynette said between bites.

"I did. I *do*! In fact, Barbie asked me to join her and her parents at the annual holiday party at Lydia's House, and I agreed to attend." Susan knew that Lynette would understand. But what about Maggie?

"Are you uneasy about celebrating Christmas with Hank's family?" Lynette asked.

"It'll be tough," Susan admitted. "This will be the first year without him. But it's not that. It's just that I've never really been to Lydia's House. And I'm not sure if I'll feel comfortable there."

There. She'd said it. She looked down at her plate, focusing on a piece of zucchini covered with ricotta cheese and marinara. She ought to spear it with her fork and shove it into her mouth, which would make it impolite to speak if Maggie or Lynette quizzed her further.

Should she have to explain what Lydia's House was? Or would Maggie already know? The woman seemed to be so charity-minded that it might not need an explanation.

"So why did you agree to go?" Lynette asked.

"Because . . . Well, I never understood why Hank refused to go in the past, and I always thought that he should. But I figured he had his reasons." Susan fingered the edge of her napkin. "I think I can handle one afternoon as a guest. But when Barbie called today, she asked me to be in charge of the cookie decorating table and to help her with the games."

"And that bothers you?" Lynette asked.

"To be honest, I'm not sure what to say or how to act with them. It's . . . well, it's out of my comfort zone, I guess."

"Why?" Maggie asked. "They're just like you in a lot of ways, vulnerable, loving, kind. They laugh when they're happy and cry when they're hurt."

"I'm sure you're right." Susan offered the woman a smile, but didn't think she'd understand.

But the truth was, she'd come to believe that Hank had been afraid to have a child because they might have one like his brother, Ronnie. And since Susan was no longer able to have Hank's baby, that fear shouldn't concern her.

Yet it did. She was getting older, and the odds of having a child with a genetic defect of some kind were higher for her.

And being at Lydia's House was going to give faces to her fears.

Chapter 8

Rosa had no more than cleaned the soup kitchen and driven home, when she was faced with fixing dinner—and not just for her and Carlos. She'd volunteered to make an extra chicken casserole to deliver to the Dawsons, a couple who belonged to their small group at church.

Rosa and Carlos had grown close to Sam and Claire over the past year. And since Claire had just given birth to a new baby girl and was in the hospital, Rosa had volunteered to make dinner for Sam and their daughters, eleven-year-old Analisa and Emalee, who was almost two.

Fortunately, Rosa had cooked the chicken this morning, so now all she had to do was add some chopped vegetables, rice, and broth.

Her knees and her back ached like crazy, though, so she was going to have to take some painkillers if she wanted to get the job done. She'd just have to tell Carlos that he needed to deliver the meal this evening by himself. She was going to lie down as soon as she got it in the oven. But at least her only obligation was dinner. She'd managed to get out of looking after the children while Claire was in the hospital—but just barely.

Several weeks ago, while their small group had been having refreshments, Carlos had told the Dawsons that he and Rosa would be happy to watch the older girls when Claire went into labor. Rosa had nearly choked on the brownie she'd been eating. But she'd been spared when Gail Jamison—bless her heart—had volunteered at the same time.

"I'd love to have the girls," Rosa had quickly chimed in, "but I'll bet they'd be happier with Gail."

And that was a fact. Gail looked after her three-year-old grandson while her daughter worked, so she had plenty of toys and a child-friendly house and yard.

Claire had agreed, thankfully, and Rosa had breathed a sigh of relief. Not that she didn't love children, but with her bad knees, she'd never be able to keep up with a two-year-old. She'd hated to embarrass her husband by admitting in front of the group that his offer to handle the childcare would be too much for her.

What was she going to do with Carlos? If that man got wind of any kind of need in the church or the community, he nearly broke his neck trying to take care of it himself.

Rosa knew she'd probably never get Carlos to slow down when it came to his charity work, but hopefully he'd start consulting her before volunteering her time or services.

It was Rosa, however, who'd offered to fix dinner for the Dawsons tonight, so she couldn't complain about that.

As she greased the baking dishes, she realized that she probably ought to touch base with Sam and let him know when he could expect the evening meal to arrive. So she washed her hands, then went to the built-in desk near the kitchen nook, where she opened the address book and looked under the Ds. When she spotted Sam and Claire's name, she called their number.

Sam answered on the third ring.

Rosa didn't bother introducing herself since she knew Sam would recognize her voice. "Hi, Sam. How's everyone doing today?"

"We're great. The baby was a couple of weeks early, so she's a lot smaller than Emalee was. But the doctor's not concerned."

"Good. And Claire?"

"She's missing the older girls and eager to come home."

"I remember feeling that way." Rosa and Carlos had three children, although they were all grown and gone now.

Goodness, if truth be told, she still felt that way. Their oldest, Susanna, was the only one of the kids with a family, but they lived in Colorado. They usually came to Fairbrook for the major holidays, although that wasn't going to happen this Christmas. Susana's husband lost his job three months ago, and they couldn't afford to make the trip.

Christmas wouldn't be the same without any children in the house, but there wasn't much Rosa could do about it. She and Carlos were strapped this year, too.

"I'm making a chicken casserole for your dinner this evening," Rosa told Sam. "Carlos will bring it to you when he gets home from the church. He's changing out the lights in the choir room."

"Claire and I sure appreciate your kindness."

"You're more than welcome."

They said good-bye, and Rosa hung up the phone. As she turned to the stove, a wave of dizziness struck, and she grabbed the counter to steady herself.

It didn't last very long, thank goodness, but she still took a moment to sit down at the kitchen table until it was gone.

She wasn't sure what it meant—if anything. But she probably ought to make an appointment with Dr. Kipper. She glanced at the clock on the oven door and saw that it was nearing five. She'd have to call now, since the office would be closing soon. But quite frankly, she didn't dare get up just yet. She needed a few more minutes to rest.

About the time she began to coax herself to stand and drag herself over to the desk so she could make the call, Carlos came in.

"How's it going, honey? Is the meal for the Dawsons about ready?"

"It will be."

He paused for a moment and studied her. "Are you okay? You look a little pale."

"I'm sure it's nothing. I'm just tired. But you're going to have to deliver the casserole to Sam's house. My knees are killing me."

"No problem. After dinner, maybe you should take some aspirin and get off your feet."

She planned to.

"By the way," he said, "the Christmas Under the Stars committee is meeting again tomorrow evening at the church. I told them we'd bring the refreshments."

There he went again. The man was a saint, but sometimes Rosa thought he was going to be the death of her.

"Would you mind if I picked up something from the bakery?" she asked.

"I guess not. Why? Don't you want to make cookies or something?"

"I'm not going to have time to do it myself. The soup kitchen is keeping me pretty busy."

"I guess you're right," he said. "Do whatever you have to do."

As Carlos opened the fridge, probably trying to find a snack to hold him over until dinner, Rosa glanced at the clock. It was 4:59. Apparently, she wouldn't have time to call Dr. Kipper's office before his staff left for the day, which was too bad.

She had even less time to be sick.

Max had big plans for Friday, but he'd worked late the night before and didn't roll out of bed until after one o'clock in the afternoon. He'd hoped to wake up earlier, but since he hadn't gone so far as to set the alarm, he wasn't going to beat himself up for lagging.

Once his bare feet hit the cold floor, the first thing he did was to let Hemingway out in the backyard. Then he took a shower and dressed warmly. The television weatherman had predicted that San Diego County was in for a cold spell, and Max had no idea how long he'd have to stay outside.

With that out of the way, he stopped in the kitchen, fixed a pot of coffee, and poured himself a cup. Then he grabbed a banana to tide him over and headed out the front door.

He kept a couple of chairs on the porch, although he never used them. So he snagged one of them now and carried it to the lawn. After taking a moment to find the perfect spot, he chose a place that provided a view of the gate and the south side of his fence. Then he took a seat.

If he had to camp out all day long, he was determined to find out how his dog was getting out of the yard.

As he settled into his seat, he realized that he should have brought out some of his manuscript pages so he could do some editing while he was sitting here. That way, if he had to wait too long, he'd put his time to good use.

For once, he hoped to see those Westbrook kids on Nut-cracker Court. If they were the ones who kept letting his dog out—or encouraging Hemingway to escape somehow—Max wanted to catch them in the act.

He sat there for an hour or so, then decided he needed more than a banana to keep him going. So he went inside for something to eat.

While he was fixing a ham sandwich, he peered out the kitchen window and spotted Hemingway sitting on his haunches near the gate. The dog whimpered a couple of times, then wagged his tail and got to his feet as if someone was there. Then, almost like magic, the gate swung open and the crazy mutt took off.

Oh, for Pete's sake. The minute Max had left his post . . .

Swearing under his breath, he rushed out the front door, down the steps, and into the yard. It had only been a matter of seconds, but the gate was wide open.

And Hemingway was long gone.

Max looked to his right and his left, but didn't see any of

the kids. He did, however, spot the woman who was house-sitting for Helen, walking down the sidewalk.

"Hey, Maggie," he called. "Did you see my dog?"

"Actually, he just ran out of your yard, leaped over the hedge, and took off. It looked as though he might have been heading for the canyon."

Good. At least he had a witness to the crime. "Who was with him?"

"No one. He ran off by himself."

"Then who opened the gate?"

Maggie drew to a stop. "I'm afraid I can't answer that."

Why not? For a moment, he wondered if she could have been the culprit, but she was coming from the wrong direction, and he doubted that she could have gotten that far away without being out of breath. So he didn't ask.

Still, that gate couldn't have opened by itself.

"You know," Maggie said, shoving her hands in the pockets of her jacket. "Your dog would be much happier if he had kids to play with on a regular basis."

Annoyed by the woman's interference, Max crossed his arms over his chest. "And how would you know that?"

"He told me."

The woman was clearly nuts. But then again, Max supposed he shouldn't talk. What kind of fool hid out in the yard to spy on a dog?

He raked a hand through his hair. Now what did he do? Chase after the dog? Or say good riddance to the mutt?

"He really loves those kids," Maggie added.

"What kids?"

"The two boys. I think he called them Joshua and Michael."

"*He?*" Max wasn't following her.

"Hemingway, although he'd rather be called Butch."

In spite of knowing he ought to end the conversation right here and now, he found himself saying, "*Excuse me?*"

"Butch is what his old family used to call him," Maggie added.

"What are you talking about?"

She cocked her head to the side as though he was the one who'd lost touch with reality. "Weren't we talking about your dog?"

Max nodded, although the urge to go inside and leave the crazy woman on her own was growing stronger by the second. He'd wasted way too much time on this conversation already.

"Hemingway would rather be called Butch. That's what his name was before he came to live with you."

Max had no idea where Hemingway had come from. He'd just showed up one day, sat on the porch, and settled in—like a four-legged squatter.

So how had Maggie known that? It wasn't like it was public knowledge.

"What are you?" he finally asked her. "A dog whisperer?"

"I suppose you could say that."

There weren't many people who were more skeptical than Max, but he had to admit he was curious about Maggie's claims.

"So what happened?" he asked. "Why isn't the dog living with that family?"

"The parents divorced and had to sell the house. Since the mother and kids had to move into an apartment, they couldn't keep Butch. So the father took him and moved to Fairbrook."

"So where's the father now?" Max asked, playing Maggie's game. To be honest, he was a storyteller, too. And he could appreciate a good yarn when he heard one. "Why isn't the dog with him?"

"Butch—or rather, Hemingway—didn't like the guy very much and blamed him for the breakup. He thought you'd be a lot nicer, so he decided to hang out here, hoping you'd let him stay. And you did."

Max wasn't putting any stock in her story, although he had to admit that Maggie would have no way of knowing Hemingway had arrived one day out of the blue.

Who was to say if she was crazy or not? He'd heard that some people had a way with animals, even if he didn't believe that they could actually carry on two-way conversations.

"I'd planned to have him neutered," Max said. "So maybe that will help."

"Oh, poor Butch," Maggie said. "He's not going to like that."

Max didn't think he would, but he was only a dog, for Pete's sake. And it was something Max shouldn't have put off. Hopefully, Hemingway wasn't impregnating every female pooch in town.

Maggie scanned his yard and house. "I see that you haven't put up your Christmas lights yet."

"I'm not in the mood for all the neighborhood holiday hoopla, so I won't be decorating this year." If truth be told, he couldn't see himself doing it next year, either.

Max hadn't felt like celebrating since Karen had left him for Jack, a man he'd once thought of as a friend.

"It's too bad you don't have children," Maggie said. "Christmas would be a lot more fun for you this year. And your dog would be a whole lot happier."

"Well, I can't very well go out and adopt a few kids just because Hemingway—or should I say *Butch*?—isn't content to stay home and hang out with me."

Actually, when he and Karen had first gotten married, he'd wanted kids, but she hadn't. He figured she'd change her mind eventually, but by the time having a baby and starting a family had become important to him, she'd moved on.

So it was just as well that there weren't any kids in the mix. It would have made the divorce process a lot tougher to deal with.

"It was her loss," Maggie said.

He hadn't said anything out loud, so he had no idea what she was talking about. "Whose loss would that be?"

"Your ex-wife's. She made a mistake when she left you, although she hasn't realized that yet. But she won't come back."

This was too weird, he thought, even though Maggie's words had a balming effect on his wounded pride. But she was clearly a couple of cracked eggs short of a dozen, so he needed to cut their conversation short and go inside, where he could slip back into a fictional tale that would be a more productive use of his time.

"You know," Maggie said, "some people who are lonely during the holiday season find that it's a good idea if they go through the motions anyway. And most of them are happier when they focus on others rather than themselves."

"Maybe, but sometimes people prefer being left alone," he said.

"Do they really?"

Before he could respond or excuse himself, she turned and walked away, leaving him standing on the lawn like a scarecrow in a withered cornfield, the chill of the air and dead leaves crackling in the breeze.

Susan hadn't known what to expect when she'd entered the soup kitchen, so she'd been nervous when she'd arrived this morning. But her initial uneasiness hadn't lasted long. Everyone she'd met so far had been kind and friendly, and before long, she'd settled right in.

She was glad she'd decided to offer Rosa a hand. Of course, she hadn't realized just how much work it was to feed forty or fifty hungry people. From the moment she'd entered the door, she'd been given a job—and she'd stayed busy.

Her first task had been peeling potatoes while Rosa prepared the main dish and vegetables. They'd continued to work together for more than an hour, but when the first people had begun to arrive, they'd split up, with Susan going into the dining room to start serving meals.

Susan had expected to see a lot of riffraff, but she'd been wrong. Sure, there'd been several men who'd worn dirty, ragged clothing and appeared to be living on the streets, but they'd been both polite and appreciative. Several of the other "guests," as Carlos called them, were senior citizens on fixed incomes. And a few of those were veterans, if the military-style hats with American Legion and VFW patches were any clue.

One of the first to arrive had been a mother with two school-age children. The woman, a brunette Carlos had called Joanie, had worn a threadbare sweater that was no match to the wintry chill outdoors. Susan had been tempted to hand over her own jacket to her, but she hadn't known how to do it without embarrassing the woman.

The children, a boy who was about nine or ten and a girl who was a couple years younger, stuck close to their mother's side, their eyes bright yet apprehensive.

Susan had been drawn to them, but for some reason, once she'd said hello and served their plates, she'd remained at her post and kept her mind on her work.

She wasn't sure why she'd felt so awkward around the small family, and after they'd taken seats, she wished she would have done or said more.

When she'd seen Carlos discreetly slip Joanie some cash, along with an invitation to attend Christmas Under the Stars in Mulberry Park next week, she'd been relieved. Yet even after the small family left, they'd remained on her mind—and on her heart.

During a lull, Susan asked Rosa, "Does Joanie come here often?"

"Not every day."

Susan glanced at the clock on the wall, noting the time.

"Did school get out early today? Or has Christmas break already started?"

"Joanie's kids are in a special program. On Mondays and Fridays they get out of class around eleven, and Joanie brings them here for lunch. Afterward, they attend some kind of family counseling session sponsored by the local battered women's shelter."

It didn't take Susan long to read between the lines. "Do they live at the shelter?"

"Not anymore. They're in a transitional living situation now."

"Is Joanie able to work?"

"She has a job, but it's only part-time. Her hours were cut, so even with help, they're struggling. Of course, everyone here has one problem or another."

Susan scanned the room, realizing that all of the "guests" had sad stories to tell. And that Carlos probably knew them all. As he made the rounds, he would chat for a while with the various groups who sat together or take a seat next to one who sat alone.

But there was plenty of work to be done in the kitchen, particularly the cleanup, so Susan couldn't help voicing her annoyance to Rosa. "You know, there are more productive things he could be doing right now."

Taking out the trash came to mind, and so did washing some of the dirty pots and pans piled up in the sink and on the counters.

"His job is to make each of the guests feel welcome. I'd do it myself, but Carlos is a lot more outgoing than I am." Rosa shifted her weight to one leg. "We seem to be having a lull right now, so I'll go back into the kitchen and start cleaning up."

"I've got a better idea," Susan said. "I'll wash the pots and pans while you use the slow time to get off your feet for a while."

"No, you stay here. It's easier if I work in the kitchen. I know where everything belongs."

As Rosa turned to go, Susan made a quick scan of the dining room, with its long, rectangular tables providing seating for the nearly twenty people who'd come to eat. At the rear, near the restrooms, two bulletin boards trimmed with a Frosty-the-Snowman border displayed flyers that advertised the community clinic, various hotlines, as well as benefits and opportunities in the area.

The soup kitchen, Susan realized, did more than feed the hungry. And since she considered Parkside Community her home church, even though she rarely attended Sunday services herself, she couldn't help feeling proud—and a part of—what they were doing.

As the front door swung open again, she glanced up to see Maggie enter the room. She hung up her jacket on one of the hooks by the door, then made her way to the buffet line. "I'm sorry I'm late. I meant to get here sooner, but something came up. I'll need to wash my hands, but what can I do to help?"

Before Susan could suggest that she assist with the cleanup— or better yet, give Rosa a break completely—the door opened again, and a family of five entered.

"Oh, good," Maggie whispered to Susan, "they're back."

"Who are they?"

"The man's name is Dave. He's been out of work for two months, and his wife, Marie, is battling breast cancer."

How sad, Susan thought, but she tried her best to put on a happy face and give them a welcoming smile.

As Susan filled the family's plates, and Maggie went to the restroom to wash her hands, a middle-aged man entered the dining room wearing a frayed dark jacket and dirty pants. His shoulders slumped when he walked, as if he was weary from carrying a load he'd yet to check in at the door.

"Hey, Jerry," Carlos called out. "It's good to see you,

buddy. How're you feeling? Did you finally get rid of that sinus infection?"

The ragged man smiled, and his shoulders seemed to straighten a bit. "It's better, Carlos. That doctor down at the free clinic prescribed some medication, and it worked like a charm."

"Glad to hear it."

Susan was beginning to see that Rosa had been right. Carlos had a way of making the guests feel important. He treated them as though he were the owner of a mom-and-pop-style diner, and they were friends and patrons, rather than people in line for a handout.

Jerry had no more than reached the buffet line, when Carlos called out, "I almost forgot to give you this."

"What's that?"

Carlos crossed the room, reached into his pocket, and pulled out a plastic baggie filled with chunky brown pellets. "I've got some treats for you."

What in the world was he doing? Giving dog food to a man who was down on his luck?

"How's ol' Rex doing?" Carlos asked.

"Just fine." Jerry took the bag and placed it in his jacket pocket. Then he nodded toward the door. "He's waiting outside for me. I got him tied to my cart."

The homeless man had a dog when he couldn't even support himself?

As the door swung open and shut again, Susan looked to the entrance, where an elderly couple made their way inside. Even bundled up in a bulky jacket, the man appeared short and frail. The stooped and gray woman, whom Susan assumed was his wife, walked with a cane.

After hanging their outerwear near the door, they shuffled toward the buffet line.

Susan offered them a friendly smile, just as she'd seen Carlos do.

"Good afternoon," she said. "My name is Susan."

"I'm Stanley Grainger, and this is my wife, Edna."

"It's nice to meet you. Can I get you some meat loaf and mashed potatoes?"

"Yes," Edna said. "Please."

"Green beans, too?" Susan asked.

They both nodded.

After filling their plates, Susan pointed to the table to the left of her. "There's coffee and punch to choose from. The glasses and cups are right there. But if you'd like to take your plates and find a place to sit, I'd be happy to get your drinks and bring them to you."

"That would be nice." Edna smiled, softening the craggy lines on her face. "Thank you, Susan."

"My pleasure. What can I get you to drink?"

"Punch for me," Edna said. "I've been told to cut back on caffeine. But my husband would like coffee—black, with a little sugar."

Stan placed a liver-spotted hand on his wife's back. "There are a couple of seats at the front table, honey. Let's take those so you don't have to walk too far."

It was heartwarming to see the affection the elderly couple shared for each other. And Susan wondered if she and Hank would have grown close like that, if he'd lived and they'd been in their golden years.

She'd like to think that they would have.

After delivering Stan and Edna's drinks, Susan took a moment to chat with the couple, just as she'd seen Carlos doing with the other guests.

"Is it getting any warmer outside?" she asked.

The old man shook his head. "Not really. Our car isn't running, so we almost didn't come today. But fortunately, our neighbor was able to give us a ride."

"He's a nice young man," Edna added. "He lost his wife in a car accident nearly a year ago, but he's a good father and is trying to make the best of things this Christmas. Stan and I would like to help, but there's not much we can do. I did knit the girl a muffler and mittens with scraps of yarn I had."

Susan wasn't sure if a child living in a coastal community in Southern California would appreciate snow wear, but she didn't want to put a damper on the spirit in which the gift had been made, so she said, "That's really sweet of you. And it's great that you have a nice neighbor. I'm glad he was able to give you a ride today."

"So are we." Edna picked up her paper napkin and placed it in her lap.

"By the way," Susan told the couple. "We have apple cobbler for dessert today. Just give me a wave when you're ready for a serving, and I'll bring it to you."

Edna reached out and patted Susan's hand. "You folks sure are good to us."

The sincerity in her gaze mocked the frailty of her hand as her fingers pressed gently on Susan's wrist, warming her from the inside out. Susan hadn't been touched like that, with so much feeling, in years. "You're more than welcome, Edna."

Twenty minutes later, as Stan went to throw away their paper plates and trash, Edna slowly got to her feet and reached for her cane.

Knowing that Maggie could handle what little traffic they had at the buffet line, Susan left her station and went to open the door for the elderly couple. "Let me get that for you."

"Thank you," Stan said.

As the elderly couple shuffled outside, Susan couldn't help noting a grocery cart loaded down with odds and ends and covered with a blue vinyl tarp. A short-haired shepherd-mix with a dirty red collar was tethered to the side with a frayed piece of rope.

Poor little mutt, she thought, as she gazed upon him and spotted the gray hair around its snout. He was old and homeless, too—a tough life, even for a dog. No wonder Carlos had given Jerry those treats for ol' Rex.

She had to admit that it was certainly nice—all that he and Rosa were doing. She wondered if Hank would have ever given of himself like that to make life easier on the disadvantaged.

Probably not. He really wasn't like Carlos, whom she'd begun to think of as a good man.

The next time Susan married, she would have to find a man like Carlos, a man who was willing to put others ahead of himself.

"There he is," Stan said, pointing to a silver Jeep Grand Cherokee that had just pulled into a parking space in front.

The driver must be the neighbor they'd mentioned earlier, the widower facing his first Christmas without his wife. Of course, he wasn't actually alone; he had a daughter.

Susan studied the redheaded girl in the passenger seat, who wore her hair in pigtails. As Edna neared the car, the child jumped out of her seat and offered it to the old woman.

For some reason, Susan continued to stand in the doorway until the elderly couple had climbed into the vehicle and the driver began backing out of the parking lot. Then she lifted her hand and wiggled her fingers in a wave.

When Stan and Edna were as good as gone, she took one last look at poor ol' Rex, then returned to her post at the buffet line and stood next to Maggie.

Lowering her voice to a discreet whisper, she said, "I know there are a lot of people who are hungry and needy in this world, but I've got to tell you, Maggie, I can't help feeling sorry for Jerry's dog."

"Why is that?"

"Well, the man can't even support himself, yet he has a pet. It just doesn't seem fair to the animal."

"Actually, Jerry found Rex in a parking lot behind the bowling alley. He'd been hit by a car and left for dead. But Jerry nursed him back to health, and they've been inseparable ever since."

"Oh, really?"

"Everyone deserves to love and be loved," Maggie said.

Susan hoped she was right.

Because she was beginning to wonder if she'd ever loved or been loved at all.

Chapter 9

Assuming the dog would eventually find its way home, Max spent the afternoon working on his manuscript. But even though the wind had caused the tree branches to scratch against the windowpanes, and it seemed to be growing darker and colder outside by the minute, Hemingway still hadn't returned.

It served the dumb mutt right to get lost, Max decided. Yet in spite of his best effort to focus on the story he was writing, he wasn't having much luck. So he'd gone outside and walked up and down the street, calling Hemingway to no avail.

He'd finally returned to the house, grumbling all the while that the dog deserved whatever happened. Yet he couldn't quite seem to put his worries behind him.

An hour later, he was back on the front porch, whistling again.

"Hemingway!" Max hollered one last time, hoping the mutt hadn't been picked up by the dog catcher and taken to the pound.

Of course, if that's what had happened to him, at least he'd be safe until morning.

The wind had kicked up with a chill that would do the North Pole proud. Okay, so that was just a Southern California native's opinion on an unseasonably cool winter day, but it was brisk enough to require a jacket and shoes.

At the sound of an approaching vehicle, Max looked down the street and saw Grant Barrows returning home. As his neighbor got out of his car, wearing sweats and carrying a gym bag, Max crossed the street to ask if he'd seen Hemingway.

He braced himself for a snappy retort, though. Grant wasn't a fan of the dog and might actually be glad he was gone. In fact, he might have even been annoyed enough to call animal control and turn him in.

Max decided to make a little neighborly chitchat first, then ask him about Hemingway in a roundabout way. "Hey," he said upon his approach, "how's it going, Grant?"

"All right."

"I've been meaning to ask. How did your interview go the other day?"

"Which one? I've had three so far, but I haven't heard anything positive yet." Grant closed his car door. "Something tells me no one's going to make any hiring decisions until after the holidays and the beginning of the year."

"That's a possibility."

They stood there for a moment, Max's big question looming in the night. Finally, he said, "By the way, my dog got out again this morning, and he hasn't come home yet. I don't suppose you've seen him."

"No, I haven't." Grant leaned against his vehicle. "It's a bad night for him to be roaming the streets."

"Yeah, that's what I'm thinking." Max shrugged. "I know he's been a nuisance lately, and I'm really sorry about that. I've been doing everything I can to find out how he's getting out of the yard."

Max waited for a response, maybe even a reminder that he owed Grant a new dress shirt for the one Hemingway had stained the other day.

Instead, Grant said, "I've always believed there was something to the old adage about turning something loose. If it doesn't come back, it was never yours in the first place."

Maggie's words came to mind, and Max couldn't help wondering if there was some truth to it all—the old adage *and* her comment. Maybe Hemingway was out looking for his old owners.

In truth, though, Max really thought all that dog whisperer crap was a crock.

"He'd probably be happier if he lived with a family," Grant added. "Don't you think? He'd have children to keep him busy and leave him too tired to jump the fence and create havoc in the neighborhood."

Max didn't think Hemingway had been going over the fence, but that didn't really matter. Grant had a point, and he couldn't help considering the fact that—no matter how far-out the possibility—the dog might be missing the kids he used to live with.

But that didn't mean Max was buying in to Maggie's tale. Dogs didn't communicate telepathically with people—even crackpots.

"Hey," Grant said, "I've got a question for you."

"What's that?"

"Do you know Lynette? Helen's pretty, blond friend?"

"Just by name and sight. I really haven't talked to her, why?"

"I just wondered what her story was."

"I have no idea. Maybe you ought to ask Helen when she gets home. Or even Maggie, her house sitter."

"I'll probably wait. Maggie seems a little . . ."

"Off?" Max supplied. That had been his take, too.

"I don't know." Grant paused, as if giving it some thought. "I'm not really sure what I mean."

"I had the same feeling. What makes you think she's a little . . ." He wanted to say "whacky," but ended his sentence with "odd" instead.

"I'm not saying that I think she's crazy. It's just that she has a way about . . . Well, knowing things."

At that, Max couldn't help perking up. "Like what things?"

"She seemed to know something about the last interview I had. And there's really no way she could have."

"What did she say?"

Grant glanced down at the ground, then back up again. "The HR person asked me if I had a family, and when I said no, he acted a little . . . Well, like he was sorry to hear it. And then, after I got home, Maggie brought over a plate of cookies that one of Helen's friends had made. And while she was here, she told me not to feel badly about the interview, that the company was very family-oriented, and that something better would come around."

"She mentioned that just out of the blue?"

"Yeah, and I'm not sure how she even knew about the interview, unless Lynette told her."

"You're right. It's a little weird." Grant glanced across the street, at Max's house. "Do you get a lot of grief about not decorating for Christmas?"

"Some, but I just ignore it. Why?"

"This morning, Maggie came by and volunteered to help me put up lights."

"She mentioned something to me about my lack of decorations, too," Max said, "but I told her I wasn't in the holiday spirit this year."

"It's not that I'm a Grinch, but as far as I'm concerned, December twenty-fifth is just another day. I'll probably buy a wreath and stick it on the door, though. Maybe then Maggie and some of the other neighbors will stay off my back."

Max crossed his arms and nodded. "That's one of the nice things about working nights and sleeping days. The neighbors don't see much of me, so they can't put a lot of pressure on me to conform."

Grant smiled. "If I get any kind of a job offer for a night shift, I'll keep that positive point in mind."

"Well," Max said, "it's getting cold out here. I think I'll head back inside where it's warm."

"Good luck finding your dog."

"Thanks. But you might be right. If he's happy living with me, he shouldn't have the need to roam."

With nothing more to add, Max told his neighbor good night, then returned to his house. About the time he was climbing the porch steps, he heard a whimper, followed by a little bark.

Max turned around. *"Hemingway?"*

The dog barked again, this time louder.

"Where've you been?" Max called to the night shadows. "Come on over here."

Hemingway hobbled into view, holding up his left rear paw.

"What happened, buddy?"

The dog slowed to a stop in front of Max, then plopped down in a half sit/half squat.

Max stooped to get a better look at the bad leg, but with only the yellow glow of the porch light, it was impossible to determine what was wrong. Still, he reached for the rear paw and examined it the best he could.

Just as he skimmed his fingers across something hard and sharp, the dog flinched and cried.

What was it? A thorn? A piece of glass?

"Were you in the canyon again?" he asked.

There wasn't a response, of course. But if Max actually thought Maggie had any dog whispering talent, he'd take the dog to her and have her ask him.

Instead, he bent over, wrapped his arms around Hemingway's chest, and carried him into the house, where a fire blazed softly in the hearth and the lamplight lit the room. Once inside, he set the dog down on the carpet and proceeded to examine the leg.

Sure enough, he found a thorn stuck between the pads of his paw and carefully removed it. When he was done, Hemingway began to lick the wound.

"Maybe that'll teach you for running off," Max said.

The dog merely looked up from what he was doing, then rested his head on his front legs.

All right. So Max had been worried about the crazy mutt. Why not admit it?

"Hey, Hemingway," he said. "I'm glad you're back."

The dog's response was a swish of the tail and a noise that came out like a half whine/half groan.

Max couldn't blame the four-legged wanderer for being wiped out and wanting to snooze, he supposed. Who knew where he'd been or what he'd been up to.

Still, on a whim, Max said, "Hey, Butch."

The dog looked up, his eyes wide and alert, then he gave a little bark before getting to his feet. As he hobbled over to where Max was sitting, his tail wagged to beat the band.

No way was that dog's name Butch.

Yet Max couldn't help wondering if Maggie really did have a gift, or if she and the dog were somehow in cahoots and playing a trick on him.

It was after nine o'clock that evening when Rosa and Carlos arrived at their 1970s-style tract home in Serena Vista, a tired, old subdivision located on the east side of Fairbrook.

As usual, Carlos parked in the driveway, rather than in the garage, which had accumulated so much junk over the years that even one of their vehicles no longer fit inside.

Rosa wished she could say that she loved this house or the neighborhood, but that was no longer the case. And she feared a remodel or some renovations wouldn't change that.

She took a moment to study the cream-colored stucco with its cracked and peeling brown trim, thinking it needed new paint, something bright and cheery. In fact, the four-bedroom house needed a lot of things: new curtains, new furniture, new appliances. Even a new family.

Now that the kids were grown and gone, the spacious old home was much too large for a retired couple suffering from the first pangs of arthritis. And with all the community work Carlos had committed to, he found very little time to keep up the yard the way he once did.

In the past, Rosa would have tried to help with that, but at her age, there was no way she could take on mowing and edging the lawn, too. Goodness, she had trouble keeping the inside as clean as she used to, even when she'd had small children underfoot.

Rosa, like both her mother and her *abuelita,* believed that a floor wasn't really clean unless someone got on their hands and knees to mop it—something she could no longer do.

Not that the house was a mess; she kept it picked up. She also made sure that the bathrooms were clean and the dishes washed and put away. But she always seemed to spot something that needed to be done, something that wasn't up to her usual standards.

Now, as she and Carlos got out of the car, she brought up a conversation they'd had several times already. "I really wish you'd reconsider talking to a real estate agent, honey."

"I told you before. I *don't* want to sell the house. We have memories here. This is where we raised our kids, it's where they call home. And even if that weren't the case, the mortgage is just about paid off."

"But it's too big for us. We don't need all the space—or the extra work it requires. Besides, those new condos on Ocean-view Drive are really nice. I think one of them would suit us a whole lot better."

"How do you figure?" Carlos stopped in the middle of the sidewalk, turned to face her, and folded his arms over his barrel chest. "We'd have those homeowner's fees to pay. And even if we poured all the money from the sale of this house into the new one, we'd still have to take a loan out at the bank. Those condos are really overpriced."

Some of them also provided an ocean view and a lovely, restful sea breeze that could really pick up a woman's spirit. But she doubted he would care about that.

Crossing her own arms, she said, "But if we moved to a condo, you wouldn't have any yard work to do or any repairs to make. Everything would be new and under warranty."

Carlos merely grunted, which was what he usually did when he didn't like the direction their conversation was going. Then he uncrossed his arms, turned, and headed for the door.

She followed behind, watching as he pulled out his key and inserted it into the lock, jiggling it a little so it would slip into place and work properly.

Once inside, he turned on the light.

Yet it still didn't feel like home to Rosa. All she could see were the tired walls begging for a fresh coat of paint and the old shag carpet with matted-down traffic areas.

And for some reason, she just couldn't seem to let the subject drop.

"I know you don't like changes, and making a move like that is a big one, but really, Carlos, I'm just trying to look out for you."

"How's that?"

"You're overdoing it, honey. You're not as young as you used to be. And neither am I. It's time we really retired, but it seems as though we're working harder now than ever."

He shed his jacket and hung it on the hook near the door. Then he offered her a weary smile. "When something happens to me, you can sell the house and do anything you want. You won't be locked into that condominium with all your cash tied up in equity."

There he went again, implying that he didn't have long to live. "What makes you think you'll be the first to go?"

He grunted again.

Rosa knew he'd made up his mind and that he probably wouldn't budge.

What had happened to that handsome young man who'd asked Daddy for her hand in marriage, the man who'd sworn he'd do everything to make her happy? The guy who'd actually done just that until about five years ago?

She had no idea how he'd morphed into an old man hellbent on helping as many people as he could before he dropped in his tracks. Or, more likely, before *she* did. But she knew when she was barking up the wrong tree. So she placed her purse on the bottom step of the stairs, then started the long, painful climb to the bedroom.

"Just think," he said, as he followed her up to their room. "You can take as many cruises as you want to when I'm gone."

She stopped and turned to face him. Then she lifted her finger and pointed it at him in a downward direction, thanks to the extra height two stair steps gave her. "Listen here, Carlos. I'm not going on a cruise without you."

He smiled, resembling that young man she'd fallen in love with nearly forty years ago. Then he reached up and cupped her cheek. "Okay, who knows? Maybe we can take a cruise together, but I have some things I need to do first."

"Like what?"

"Just *things*."

He could be so cryptic when he wanted to. So she let out a sigh, clicked her tongue, and threw up her hands in submission. Then she turned and continued her climb upstairs.

When she reached the landing, and he was only a step behind her, she gave it one last shot and said, "Did you ever take a look at that brochure I showed you?"

"The one that advertised the Caribbean cruise you wanted to take?" He smiled. "Yes, I did. And it looks nice, honey, but it's pretty expensive."

And he'd probably rather spend their money on charity or give it to the church.

Goodness. Did that make her selfish? She hoped not. A lot of people believed in tithing 10 percent, but Carlos gave above and beyond that.

Was there something wrong with her wanting them to spend a little of their savings on themselves? Couldn't they consider it an investment in their marriage?

Rosa blew out another sigh, one that was wearier than the last, then entered the bedroom and turned down the quilt.

"I'm getting tired," she told him. "And I'm not so sure how much time I have left, either. I'd like to make the best of it. Wouldn't you?"

"So which is it you want to have the most?" he asked. "A new condo or a cruise? You can't have it all."

The way he looked at her, with his hands on his hips and his head cocked to the side as though she were a spoiled, errant child, made her feel like a whining nag, and the feeling didn't sit well with her. So she let the subject drop—for now, anyway.

While he undressed, she took her flannel nightgown into the bathroom, brushed her teeth, and got ready for bed.

When she returned to their room, Carlos was standing by the nightstand in his Jockey shorts. His back was to her, and he was running his hand up and down the length of his left arm.

"What's the matter?" she asked.

"Nothing."

"Is your arm bothering you?"

"A little bit. It's probably just some tendinitis. It happens sometimes."

"Maybe you ought to see a doctor."

"I might do that." He gave her a no-worries smile, then padded into the bathroom.

While he was gone, she climbed under the covers and reached for the pillow she tucked between her knees at night, something that seemed to help ease the aches and pains she usually woke up having in the morning.

Moments later, Carlos returned carrying a glass of water and a bottle of antacids. He placed them both on the nightstand next to his side of the bed.

"Is your stomach bothering you?" she asked.

"Yeah. I've got some heartburn. I think you were right. Eating that chili cheeseburger wasn't a good idea."

He'd insisted upon having fast food for dinner tonight, which had been a relief in one sense. It had saved her from cooking dinner and cleaning up the kitchen when she was already exhausted. But he should have chosen that grilled chicken burger on a wheat bun, like she'd suggested.

She clicked her tongue. Sometimes Carlos could be *so* set in his ways.

He turned off the light, then joined her in bed. Instead of cuddling, like they used to do in the early years, he rolled to the side, letting his back face her.

While the clock on the bureau *tick-tocked* louder than she remembered it ever doing before, she did her best to block out the annoying sound, as well as the thoughts that tumbled through her brain.

But she couldn't seem to quell the resentment that had begun to root in her heart.

Carly had turned out the lights and climbed into bed, just as Mikey started coughing again. She'd noticed his cold symptoms at dinner this evening, and they seemed to be getting worse. So she threw off the covers and went into the room the boys shared, since Mikey had fewer nightmares when he slept near his brother.

She didn't normally go to bed while the kids were still awake, but she hadn't gotten much sleep the night before. Too much to stress about, she supposed.

When she entered the room, Josh was sitting on the floor near the toy box, thumbing through a *National Geographic*

Kids magazine, a subscription Sharon Garvey had paid for before she'd moved away.

Carly missed her neighbor and friend at times like this—when she was out of children's cold medication and needed to make an evening run to purchase some. One call to Sharon, and Carly would have someone to look after the boys for a couple of minutes.

But she no longer had that option.

Mikey, who was curled up in bed already, sat up and grimaced. "My throat hurts, Mommy."

Carly crossed the room and took a seat on the edge of his mattress, then she placed a hand on his forehead. He didn't feel particularly warm, but that didn't mean anything. The child clearly wasn't feeling well.

"Can I sleep on the sofa?" Josh asked. "I don't want Mikey to get me sick."

"No, you stay in the room. Mikey can sleep with me."

"Can I bring my teddy, too?" her youngest son asked.

"Yes. You can go now, but you'll need to wait for me a few minutes. I need to run to the store and pick up something for your cough." The pharmacy was probably closed by now, but the market stayed open until eleven.

"But don't buy any of the red stuff," Mikey said, as he threw off the covers and climbed out of his bed. "I hate that one."

"I'll see what I can do." Carly glanced at Josh, who was still thumbing through the magazine. "I'm going to have to leave for a few minutes. Will you watch your brother? It won't take me very long."

"Sure." Clearly focused on a colorful photo of tree frogs, he didn't look up.

"And if anyone calls . . ." she began.

"I know the rules. You're taking a shower. If they give me their phone number, you'll call them as soon as you get dried off."

"Good."

After Mikey left the room, Carly watched her oldest son for a moment, taking note of how much he'd grown and being both pleased by his maturity and uneasy at the thought of all the changes the teen years were sure to bring.

But she didn't have time for maternal musing. "I'll have my cell phone with me, Josh. And it's fully charged. Call me if you have any trouble whatsoever. I'm only a few blocks away."

"Got it." He finally looked up and caught her eye. "Don't worry about us. Just go do what you have to do."

"I'll lock the door when I leave, but bolt it after I go, okay?"

He frowned, clearly miffed by her instructions. "Come on, Mom. I know the routine. I'm not a kid anymore, okay?"

No, it wasn't okay. He was in that in-between stage, neither child nor teenager. And she wasn't sure what effect his age was having on their mother/son relationship.

"I love you," she added, leaving all her other concerns behind.

"I know."

What? No "I love you" back?

She told herself that he was growing older, that kissing his mother good-bye and saying "I love you" was probably too mushy for him. But that didn't mean it didn't worry her to think his feelings for her were changing, too.

Again, she shook off her concern—or at least she tried to—and went back to her room, where she slipped out of her pajamas, threw on the clothes she'd been wearing earlier, and put on a pair of sneakers.

Next she grabbed her jacket and purse, taking a moment to count her cash. Convinced that she had enough money to make the purchase without using the credit card that was already stretched to the max, she left the house, making sure the door was locked.

Once in her car, she made the quick drive to the market.

She didn't like leaving the kids alone during the day, but she hated doing so in the evening, when any number of things could go wrong. Still, the store was only a couple of blocks away.

And she would hurry back.

Chapter 10

With a little arm twisting, Chuck Lassiter had spilled his guts, but Logan wasn't any closer to an arrest.

So he'd met his partner for a drink at Rayburn's, a trendy bar near the marina, where they discussed the case for an hour or so. Then they'd spent the rest of the time shooting the breeze and having a few laughs. Logan probably ought to call home, but Priscilla knew his job came first.

It was almost nine when he finally called it a day, but what else was new? He rarely returned home before dark.

Upon entering the living room, he'd expected to catch a whiff of whatever Priscilla had made for dinner and was keeping warm in the oven for him.

Instead, he spotted her suitcase near the fireplace.

"Baby?" he called.

She didn't respond, but when she entered the room, he nodded toward her bag. "What's that?"

"I'm leaving, Logan."

She'd made it sound like it was for good.

"Where are you going?" he asked.

"Home. To Texas."

There hadn't been anything for her in that Podunk town, at least, that's what she'd told him when they'd met three years ago.

*The question rolled off his tongue before he could stop it.
"When are you coming back?"*

"I'm not."

*Her words held a chill and a finality that he'd never heard
before, and his gut clenched at the thought that she might
mean what she said.*

*But Logan didn't like being backed into a corner. So, he
shrugged. "Suit yourself."*

Max reread the beginning of the scene that had almost
written itself. He hadn't planned for it to unfold like that. Up
until this point, Priscilla had only had a walk-on part in his
novel. But while he'd sat at the keyboard, typing out the
pages, the dialogue had just taken off.

And that was the problem. He hadn't expected Priscilla to
walk out on Logan, although he liked the way her departure
had left his protagonist a little unbalanced. That would come
in handy during the next scene. But Max didn't know where
to go from here.

Something was out of whack, although he couldn't figure
out what it was. Then again, maybe it wasn't.

Either way, Max seemed to be suffering from a little
writer's block tonight. He also had a nagging headache, a
byproduct of scrunching his shoulders for hours on end and
stressing about a scene that wouldn't play out. But there wasn't
any need to beat himself up about something out of his control.

Maybe a change of activity would help—not to mention a
couple of aspirin.

He pushed back his desk chair, got to his feet, and went
into the bathroom, where he opened the medicine cabinet.
He shuffled around the Band-Aids, toothpaste, dental floss,
and his extra razor cartridges.

Where in the world was the aspirin? He could have sworn
he had a bottle in here somewhere. But apparently he didn't.

After closing the mirrored door a little harder than necessary, he went into the kitchen. Sometimes a snack or a bite to eat helped, but it wasn't a bowl of chili or something hearty he was craving. He wanted something sweet.

Trouble was, when he opened up the pantry, he found it miserably empty.

Okay, so he had plenty of stuff inside—canned goods mostly, a can of coffee, a jar of gherkins, a new bottle of Tabasco, various condiments . . . But there wasn't anything in there that he wanted to munch on this evening.

Sometimes eating junk food helped him deal with a temporary case of writer's block. Not that he was blocked, exactly. It was just that something was off, and since he couldn't figure out what wasn't working, he couldn't very well fix it. So that made it impossible for him to go on.

He reached for a bag of half-eaten Cheetos he'd left on the middle shelf a while back, opened it up, and popped one into his mouth. Instead of the cheesy crunch he'd been expecting, his teeth bit into gummy, bland air. He guessed they'd been in there longer than he'd remembered.

Next to the Cheetos he spotted a package of raw almonds, but he left it on the shelf. That wasn't going to do the trick tonight—too healthy.

It seemed as though his pantry could compete with Old Mother Hubbard's cupboard this evening. And her financial outlook was probably better than his at this moment, too. If he didn't score ink soon, he'd be back working nine-to-five at the probation department.

He couldn't very well complain about that, though. It was a solid job with great benefits. Besides, he was good at what he did. He could spot a liar a mile away or sense a violation in the works. But somewhere along the line, it had become . . . well, just a job, and he'd wanted something new and different.

Actually, he'd needed it. And a book contract with a major New York publisher would certainly fill the bill. Besides, he'd put too much time into this manuscript to call it quits now.

He kneaded his temples, then rolled his head from side to side, hoping it would make the ache go away. Then he crossed the room and swung open the refrigerator door.

There wasn't much in there, either—particularly milk, which he was going to need in the morning. Of course, he wasn't about to make this a full-on shopping trip at this time of night, but a run to the market was in order.

"You wait here," he told Hemingway, who was snoozing by the hearth and didn't seem to give a squat either way. "I'll be back before you can say Purina Puppy Chow."

Five minutes later, Max entered the supermarket on the corner of Park and First Street. He'd made out a grocery list while he'd been in the parking lot, which he didn't do very often, but he was actually out of quite a few things.

So he grabbed a cart and started down the aisles, heading straight for the section that provided his favorite junk food. Then he went in search of the other items he needed, as well as some he didn't.

Okay, so he was an impulse shopper.

He moved up one aisle and down the next, stopping when he came to the breakfast cereal. He probably ought to choose something healthy, with plenty of bran and fiber, but he opted for sweet and tasty instead. He wasn't in the mood for health food this week.

Next he headed for the pet supplies, thinking he'd get Hemingway a different brand of food than the stuff he had at home—maybe something canned, moist, and meaty, rather than dry.

Would that make the mutt happier and more content? And more likely to stay in the yard and not run off?

If the gourmet dog chow didn't work, then maybe Max should turn Hemingway in to the pound himself. After all, if he wasn't happy living with a single guy like him and pre-ferred a family, then so be it.

Max had copped a similar attitude when his wife had told

him that she wasn't happy being married to him and that she was leaving.

He could have groveled, he supposed, but that wouldn't have helped. Instead, he'd stood by and watched her move out. And two weeks later, he'd found out she was dating a guy he'd once played golf with, a guy he'd thought of as a friend.

She'd told him that the new relationship had started after their split, but Max hadn't believed her. And he'd pretended that he didn't care either way.

It was weird, though. For some reason, he was doing more to save the relationship with his dog than he'd been willing to put into his marriage. But that was probably because he hadn't been so happy, either.

Grabbing two cans of the most expensive dog food he could find, Max put them in the cart, then continued to the area of the store where he could find the aspirin. His headache had eased once he'd gone out into the night air, but it wasn't completely gone.

As he turned down the pharmaceutical aisle, he nearly froze in his tracks when he saw Carly Westbrook scanning the shelves. She had on a pair of running shoes, black slacks, and a dark jacket, nothing very stylish. And she wasn't wearing any makeup to speak of. Still she was an attractive woman, the kind who could make a man block traffic in a grocery store by parking himself in an aisle just to look at her.

He continued to study her a moment, the way she furrowed her brow and nibbled on her bottom lip. The way those glossy, chocolate-colored strands curled softly around her shoulders. She hadn't run a comb through her hair in a while, but it didn't seem to matter.

Finally, Max cleared his voice and said, "Fancy meeting you here."

She looked up, and when recognition crossed her face, her cheeks flushed and her lips parted. "Oh. Hi."

He couldn't expect more than that from her, he supposed. Not after that last awkward confrontation they'd had. But he wasn't ready to move on just yet, so he asked, "Did you get your boy's new glasses?"

"I . . . uh . . . placed an order, but they won't be in for a week or two." She smoothed her hair with her hand, as though she knew she'd left home in a hurry and wished she hadn't. Or maybe it had just been a nervous gesture on her part. Max had probably been the last man in the world she'd expected to see tonight.

He certainly hadn't expected to see her here, either.

She bit down on her bottom lip, in a move that was actually kind of cute—and more alluring than it should be. Then she said, "I'm sorry for . . . the other night."

Did she mean that she was sorry for jumping to conclusions, blaming his dog for an innocent mishap, and demanding that he pay for her son's glasses?

Part of him wanted to pop off with a snappy retort, something snide or cynical, but he couldn't quite bring himself to do so. For some reason the pretty single mom had a way of disarming his spiteful side.

For lack of anything better to start a conversation, he found himself asking, "Are you ready for Christmas yet?"

It was a lame thing to bring up, especially coming from a guy who'd grown tired of hearing that particular question repeated ad nauseam and whose own answer was always the same.

"There's not much to get ready for this year," she said. "I plan to pick up a couple of small gifts for the boys at the dollar store, but like I said the other night, we won't be having a tree." She shrugged, then straightened her shoulders and shoved her hands in her jacket pockets. "But that doesn't mean we won't try to make the day special. We'll go to church in the morning, have frozen turkey potpies for dinner, and read the Christmas story before opening packages."

"I'm sure your sons will enjoy that."

"I hope you're right. Mikey will, I know. But Josh . . ." She paused, and he watched as uncertainty clouded her brow. She tried to break free of it, but even when she gave another shrug, he could see that worry still weighed heavy in her eyes. "I'm not so sure what to expect from him these days."

"Has that bully been bothering him again?"

She stiffened, and when she caught his eye, her gaze snaked around his with a death grip. "Do you think that could be the problem? Could he be terrorized by that bully? I'd thought it was just something he was going through, like the aging process or male hormones or something. But if he's feeling frightened or threatened . . . Well, I'd better call the school and see what I can do to stop it."

Max had no way of knowing what was going on with her son, and while he wasn't about to assume that he did, he hated to see her worry. "I'm sure it's nothing to stress about. He's probably just trying to exert his independence. There comes a time in a boy's life when he doesn't want his mother to know everything he's thinking."

"I hope you're right."

So did Max.

"Well," she said, removing her hands from her pockets and probably intending to go on her way. "Thanks for sharing the male perspective. I'm afraid I'm lost when it comes to things like that. I was a real girly-girl growing up."

Weren't most women?

She must have read the curiosity in his eyes, the interest, because she said, "Oh, you know. I liked to play with my dolls, and I loved wearing dresses and shopping for new party shoes."

A smile stretched across his face. Even tonight, when she'd clearly dashed off to the store without giving her appearance any thought, she still had a distinctly feminine aura, and he couldn't help wondering what she'd look like if she was going to a party and wearing a fancy dress and heels.

"In fact," she added, "as far as my friends and I were concerned, we thought all boys had cooties."

Those were the little girls who were fun to chase in school, whether a boy's threat was a toad in his hand or puckered lips.

"So I take it you didn't have any brothers," he said.

"No, and my dad died when I was twelve."

"Where's the boys' father?" he asked.

"I haven't seen him or heard from him in years. So he's not going to be any help at all."

Max assumed she wasn't getting any financial support from the guy, either, which was too bad. It had to be a lousy situation for her, especially at this time of year.

He wondered if she was as angry and distrustful of men as he was with women—something he really didn't like admitting. It was easier to stay in his writing cave and to take out his frustration on any female he came across, even one who was fictional.

Maybe that's why he couldn't seem to work through the Priscilla/Logan issue.

Carly, who had no grocery cart at all, scanned the inside of his and smiled. "Froot Loops? Macaroni and cheese? Chips, candy . . . ?"

He shrugged. "What can I say? I guess I'm just a kid at heart."

At that, she almost laughed. "You could have fooled me."

Yeah, well, there were some things he concealed pretty well. But he returned her chuckle with a smile.

"All you need is some ice cream to go with those cookies," she added.

"I haven't gone down the freezer aisle yet, but that's next on my list."

He wondered what she thought about his shopping habits. He supposed he couldn't blame her for making assumptions. The truth was, he'd been raised in a strict household, and no one had ever asked him what he'd wanted to eat, or where he'd like to go, or what he'd like to watch on television. So now that he was an adult and could do whatever he pleased, he tended to be a little self-centered.

"So where's *your* cart?" he asked.

"I only came for some cold medicine." She glanced at her wristwatch, which was perched on a delicate wrist. She had pretty hands, too, he noticed, with medium-length nails that had been neatly manicured.

When she looked back up at him, she said, "I'm afraid I have to run. I have a sick child at home and don't like leaving the boys alone this late at night."

"Which one's sick?"

"Mikey. The little one."

"I'm sorry to hear that." And he was. But he was also glad he'd run into her this evening, and he wasn't quite ready for her to leave. "Do you trust the older boy to look after his brother?"

"Yes, but it's getting late."

When it came to kids being home alone, Max supposed she was right. But he still couldn't help wanting to keep her here just a moment longer.

"How do the boys get along?" he asked.

"For the most part, great. Josh is really good with Mikey, although he complains once in a while about being left in charge. I've tried to talk to him about it, but he's a lot more introspective than he's ever been before. So I'm really not sure what he's thinking. And that bothers me."

"It's hard for some boys to confide in a woman," he said, "especially a mother."

"I guess." She reached for a small box on the shelf, then gave another half shrug. "It's also difficult not having a man to talk to about it." Her cheeks flushed, and she momentarily broke eye contact before regaining it. "I mean his father. You know?"

Yeah, he knew. If he and his ex were still married, he might have asked her to read over his manuscript and get her take on what was wrong, what was missing. But Karen didn't know anything about the writing process. And she'd never been very supportive of his dream anyway.

As Carly turned and reached for another box on the shelf, turning it to read the label, an idea struck. A wild one, granted, but it was the best thing either of them had going right now.

"I know a way we could help each other out."

She wrinkled her brow. "How's that?"

"You'd like a man's perspective on raising sons, and I'd like a woman's perspective on a problem I have, too. So maybe we could do a trade-off."

He figured she was going to blow him off, but she surprised him. "I wouldn't mind picking your brain and sharing my opinion with you, but I don't have time now. I have to get home."

"I realize that. But how about coffee one of these days? Or maybe even lunch—my treat, of course. I'd really like your opinion about something."

"What's the matter? Are you having trouble with a woman?"

"No," he said, not wanting to tell her he'd had plenty of those kinds of problems last year. But he couldn't lie, either. "Actually, once my divorce was final, my female troubles were over."

"You're lucky. I think a divorce just leaves a person with a whole new set of problems."

She might be right, but he didn't want to think about that, so he asked, "What do you have planned for Monday?"

"It's a light day for me at the salon. I used to take it off, but . . . Well, the holidays are a busy time and I can use the money."

He'd figured as much. "So what time can you meet?"

"How about one o'clock?"

"Great. Where?"

"Someplace close to Shear Magic, where I work."

That narrowed down the choices. "There's a little bistro

not far from the florist on Parkside Drive. What do you think about that?"

"Sounds good, but I really need to go now."

"Okay. I'll see you then."

She nodded, made a final decision on the medicine, putting the other back on the shelf, then hurried off toward the checkout lanes.

It was only a meeting, Max reminded himself, a sharing of perspectives. Yet for some reason, it felt a little bit like a date.

Carly paid for the medication, using her credit card, which she hated to do, but she didn't have quite enough cash on her this evening, so her options were limited.

After seeing Max's cart, which was filled with all kinds of goodies her boys would have loved, she'd been tempted to buy them a treat, too, and surprise them. But the sorry fact was, Mikey's medication had been the only extra she could afford tonight.

Besides, she told herself, it was getting too late for a bed-time snack.

Once she'd checked out, she hurried to the car and drove home. Yet on the way, she couldn't help thinking about Max Tolliver. As much as she wanted to consider him a villain, there was something decent about him, something nice.

And he wasn't bad to look at, either. At least, when he smiled and those caramel brown eyes lit up.

She couldn't believe she actually agreed to have lunch with him, though. And she wondered what kind of problem he had that needed a woman's perspective. She supposed she'd find out soon enough.

Still, as unexpected as his "idea" had been, how unlikely it was that they might be able to help each other out, she was actually looking forward to having lunch with him.

Sure, she wanted to discuss Josh and whatever was going on with him right now. But she was also looking forward to meeting with Max because it had been ages since she'd sat across a restaurant table from a handsome man who was buying her lunch.

It seemed to have all the makings of a casual first date, although she knew that it wasn't. She and Max were unlikely friends, let alone potential mates, so there was no need to worry about that.

Moments later, she arrived at the house and parked in the garage. Then she let herself in through the kitchen.

"I'm home," she called.

No answer.

She glanced at the clock on the microwave, noting that she'd only been gone fifteen minutes—maybe seventeen or eighteen. "Josh? Where are you?"

"In here."

She followed his voice to the living room, where he sat on the sofa. "Thanks for holding down the fort."

"No problem."

"What would I do without you?" she asked, not expecting an answer to what she'd meant as a compliment.

"I don't know." He looked up at her with eyes the same color as his father's and a brow that furrowed in much the same manner. "I guess you'd really have problems."

It hadn't been the answer she'd been expecting, but the truth struck her hard.

So with that in mind, as well as Mikey's cough, she probably wouldn't be getting much sleep tonight, either.

When lunch had ended on Thursday afternoon, Lynette had hung out long enough to help Maggie with the dishes, hoping to see Grant after he returned from his job interview, but it hadn't panned out that way. She'd made several excuses to go into Helen's living room so she could sneak a peek out the window, but Grant had yet to return.

Susan had waited around, too, since she'd made a plate of cookies to give to either Grant or Max. Lynette hadn't realized that Susan knew any of Helen's neighbors that well, but she'd never been very observant.

Eventually, Susan had given the cookies to Maggie, asking her to deliver them to whichever man she happened to see first, although they'd all agreed that it was more likely to be Grant, since Max seemed to be a recluse.

"Maybe it's best if you give the cookies to Grant," Susan had finally said. "He seems like the kind of guy who would enjoy something sweet and chewy. He's got those darling boyish dimples when he smiles, and something tells me he's a real kid at heart."

Maggie had chuckled at that. "It's funny to think of men in their forties as boyish and cute."

"All right," Susan had admitted. "Grant is a drop-dead-gorgeous grown-up. He's also a little laid-back and casual, which makes him appealing."

"I'll agree with that," Lynette had said, "but Max isn't bad looking. He could certainly compete with Grant in the gorgeous department if he'd smile more."

"I couldn't agree more," Maggie had said, "which is why I'm working on that."

"On what?" Lynette had added. "Making him smile more?"

Maggie had nodded, although she hadn't mentioned just how she planned to go about it.

Lynette might have asked her at that point, but she was more interested in Grant. Of the two men, she thought he might have the most money, be the best looking, and be more of the kind of guy who'd enjoy having a couple of boys around. So he'd probably be the better match for Carly.

"Maggie," Susan had said, "are you interested in Max?"

"In what way?"

"Well, romantically, I suppose." Susan had seemed to be a little concerned by that and added, "Would you go out with him if he asked you on a date?"

"Oh, no," Maggie had said. "I won't be in town long enough for that sort of thing."

At that, Susan had grinned and handed over the cookies to Maggie. "Give these to whoever you think would appreciate them most."

Then she'd thanked Maggie again for lunch, said good-bye, and left.

Lynette had figured that she would give them to Grant for Susan when she talked to him about scheduling his haircut, something that would have worked out great, if the man—boyish or not—would have come home.

Apparently, his interview had been going well. She'd hoped so, since it had seemed important to him. But since she hadn't been able to wait forever, she'd gone home that day.

In the meantime, Lynette had talked to Carly on the telephone and had learned that there were plenty of times Grant could get a haircut. So she'd taken the first available appointment for him, which was Monday at twelve thirty.

However, she hated to cancel on Carly at the last minute, which she'd already done recently. So on Friday afternoon, she made up a reason to visit Maggie, hoping she would run into Grant, as well.

And if she didn't see him outside? Then she would just walk up to his front door and ring the bell. After all, if she was going to be a successful matchmaker, she needed to learn more about the man so she could sing his praises to Carly—and vice versa.

Now, after she climbed out of the car and locked the door, she hurried up to the entrance of the Petal Pusher, a little nursery and gardening store on the outskirts of town.

It wasn't nearly as cold today as it had been yesterday, so she wore her black leggings and a beige top and sweater. That was one of the things she liked about Southern California winters, they could be unpredictable, although usually mild.

After purchasing a lush plant to give Maggie in appreciation for having her and Susan for lunch yesterday, she returned to her vehicle and drove to Nutcracker Court.

As she neared Helen's house, she spotted Grant trimming his hedge, something she decided was Fate at work. So after parking, she removed the plant from the passenger seat, got out of the car, and made her way to his yard.

He was wearing a light blue Hawaiian shirt and a pair of jeans. A hank of his sun-streaked hair had fallen on his forehead as he bent over his work.

If things fell into place the way Lynette hoped they would, Carly would be a very lucky lady.

Lynette had been lucky, too. But while Hank had been a blessing and a wonderful man in so many ways, Lynette might have loved him in a husbandly rather than brotherly fashion if he'd looked a little more like Grant Barrows and a little less like a stylish and contemporary version of Old Saint Nick.

Still, she wasn't looking for another husband. If she were on the prowl, it would be a real plus if the guy was not only wealthy, kind, and generous, but young and handsome, too.

As Grant heard her approach, he looked up from his yard work and smiled. "Is that for me?"

"The plant?" She laughed. "No, it's for Maggie. But when I saw you out here, I thought I'd ask how your interview went."

"As well as could be expected, I guess."

She wasn't sure if that was good or bad, so she let it go. "I wanted to tell you that I talked to Carly, the hairstylist I was telling you about. And she's got an opening on Monday afternoon at twelve thirty. I told her to pencil you in. Will that work for you?"

"Sure," he said. "Why not."

Lynette brightened. "I can meet you there and introduce you two."

"Sounds good," he said. "Maybe we can get a bite to eat afterward."

"Good idea. I'll ask Carly if she's free to join us."

"*Carly?*"

Lynette nodded. "She's single. And she's also very attractive. I think you'll like her."

Grant's smile dimmed. "I thought she was looking for new clients. Sounds like she's looking for more than that."

"Oh, no." Lynette hadn't meant to be so obvious and tried to backpedal. "Carly is career-focused right now. Of course, once you see her, you might be tempted to ask her out. And it would probably do her a world of good if she spent some time away from the salon for a change."

Grant seemed to think on that for the longest time. Finally, his gaze locked in on hers, threatening to turn her inside out, if she'd let him, and asked, "Is Carly as pretty as you?"

A bevy of butterflies took flight in Lynette's tummy, and she struggled to make sense of it. Compliments always did that to her. But then again, so did young and handsome men who were the least bit friendly. But she shook it off.

"Carly is much prettier than I could ever hope to be." And that was true since the brunette's beauty was natural and not paid for. "In fact, she makes me look like Secondhand Rose."

"Oh, yeah?" He seemed skeptical, which left her a little unbalanced. But not because she feared he would be disappointed when he saw Carly face-to-face.

Still, Lynette nodded, grateful that Grant got the hint and that the butterflies had begun to subside.

"Okay," he said. "I'll get my hair cut on Monday. And we'll take it from there—that is, if Carly's interested."

Lynette felt as though she'd scored one for the home team. "I'm sure she will be."

How could she not? Grant was a hunk—and financially secure to boot.

Pleased that she'd pulled off what she'd planned, she

tossed Grant one of her biggest, brightest smiles, one that showed off the pretty veneers Hank had purchased during their engagement.

"I'll meet you at Shear Magic on Tuesday at twelve thirty," Grant said.

"Great."

But for some reason, his agreement only stirred up those butterflies all over again.

Chapter 11

On Monday morning, during a lull between clients, Carly used her free time to snack on a granola bar she'd brought from home and to ponder an upcoming problem.

The kids would be getting out of school for Christmas vacation at the end of the week, and she wasn't sure what she'd do with them while she worked. Sharon had watched them last year as a favor, which had been a real blessing, but that was no longer an option.

Hiring a sitter was out of the question, of course, but she might be able to find another mother who was willing to work out a trade, such as two weeks of childcare for free haircuts and salon services.

Too bad she couldn't think of another mom who didn't work outside the home.

So it looked like Josh would have to watch Mikey during the school break, although she hated to have to rely on him. He was feeling put upon by all that she asked of him lately, and while she didn't think she was wrong to do so, she hated to see him grow any more resentful than he already was.

Maybe Max Tolliver would have some suggestions for her when they had lunch today. She certainly hoped so.

As she popped the last of the granola bar into her mouth, she glanced at the clock on the break room wall: 12:26.

Lynette's friend would be coming in for a haircut soon.

After that, Carly would meet Max at the bistro down the street. It was a nice place and not terribly expensive, although she rarely ate there anymore.

Since Max had been the one to invite her to lunch, she assumed he would pick up the tab. Still, just to be on the safe side, she would only order a cup of soup—something that she could afford if they ended up going Dutch treat.

She wasn't sure what had possessed her to agree to meet with Max, though. Her past contacts with him gave her no reason to believe he was good with kids or that he was the least bit understanding—or paternal. But he'd shown a softer side lately, so who knew what he'd have to say?

Of course, he would be asking for her opinion about something, too. She was curious about the problem he had that warranted some advice from a female perspective.

He'd said that he was divorced and implied that he wasn't having any romantic troubles. Maybe he had an issue with a neighbor. Carly could see how someone who was short-tempered and cranky, as Max seemed to be, might set someone else off. She'd certainly been annoyed at both his tone and his attitude during their initial conversations.

She had, of course, seen him in a different light lately. Not that she liked him a whole lot better, but she no longer saw him as an ogre.

He also had nice eyes—when they revealed a little compassion, tolerance, and sympathy.

"Hey," a woman called from the doorway. "There you are."

Carly looked up to see Lynette peering into the break room and smiled. "Did you bring your friend?"

"No, I thought I'd meet him here and hang out while you cut his hair."

"Cool." Carly brushed her fingers across her lips, feeling for crumbs and not finding any.

"Why don't you put on a little lipstick before you meet him," Lynette said.

A little taken aback by the suggestion, Carly glanced in the mirror that hung near the door. Her hair and everything else appeared to be in place—even a remaining tinge of the Pink Grapefruit gloss she'd applied earlier this morning.

"I'm sorry," Lynette said. "I didn't mean to imply there was anything wrong. You look great—as usual. It's just that Grant is a bachelor. He's also single, wealthy, and looking for a nice woman."

Uh-oh. So this wasn't just another hair appointment. Before Carly had gotten married, people were always trying to set her up with guys, not that she'd needed much help.

"What is this?" Carly asked. "A setup?"

"Only if you want it to be."

"I'm not looking for a boyfriend."

Lynette smiled. "Sometimes the best romances spark when people aren't looking."

"You might be right, and Grant might be a nice guy, but I have very little to offer anyone right now, other than a couple of kids and more bills than I can afford to pay."

"I think you'd be surprised."

About that time, Trevor, who was handling the front desk while Twyla was at lunch, poked his head in the door. "Carly, your twelve-thirty is here."

"Oh, good," Lynette said. "Come on, I'll introduce you."

Carly took one last look in the mirror, but not to check her appearance. She was actually looking for a sympathetic face, someone who would agree that the last thing in the world she needed right now was romance.

Sure enough, the woman gazing back at her was rolling her eyes at the idea, too.

Nevertheless, Carly headed to the front of the salon, where she would meet her would-be suitor, her heels clicking across the tile floor with skepticism and irritation.

What made some people think that a single woman couldn't be happy without a man?

Not that Carly was actually happy these days, but her mood could easily be lifted by finding a winning lottery ticket, receiving an unexpected inheritance, or being able to schedule a series of free family counseling sessions.

As Carly followed Lynette to the front of the shop, she noticed the blonde had an optimistic spring in her step, which was more than a little annoying. She wished she could feign a headache, ask one of the other stylists to cut Grant's hair, and go home sick.

If the guy was all that special, why didn't Lynette want him?

Upon nearing the reception desk, Carly spotted a man who was about the right age—in his early forties. He wasn't tall, maybe an inch or two under six feet, but with that surfer-boy hair and a striking smile, he was definitely a sight to behold.

He was dressed casually in black jeans and a white-cotton shirt, open at the collar, rolled at the cuffs.

When Lynette welcomed the man with a hug, there was little doubt as to who he was.

He was also just another client, Carly told herself, as she reached out and introduced herself.

His hand gripped hers, enveloping her in warmth and strength—and making her wonder if having a male companion might not be a bad idea after all.

She drew her fingers from his, then said, "Please, have a seat."

When he sat in her chair and caught her gaze in the mirror, she nearly lost her professional edge, but she got it back again.

"How much would you like taken off?" she asked.

Grant glanced at Lynette and grinned, then he returned his focus to the mirror—and to Carly. "I'm afraid you'll have to ask my friend. She's the one who seems to think I need a haircut."

"And you don't?" Carly wondered if Lynette had coerced the guy into making the appointment. It sure seemed that way.

"Actually," Grant said, "I don't mind the length, but it could stand a trim."

"Then that's what we'll do." She took him to the shampoo bowl, reclined the back of the seat, then proceeded to wet and lather his hair.

"I didn't expect this," he said. "If your haircuts are as good as your head massages, you've got yourself another regular customer."

Carly smiled as she rinsed off the suds. "Thanks. I try to take good care of my clients."

Twenty minutes later, Grant's hair was cut, styled, and blow-dried.

"There you go," Carly said, as she handed him a mirror, then swung his chair around so he could get a glimpse of the backside of his head. "What do you think?"

"It looks great." He offered her a heart-stroking smile, then turned to Lynette, who was grinning in agreement.

"Then you're good to go." Carly, glad to know she'd pleased them both, stepped back.

"Have you eaten yet?" Lynette asked. "If you can take a break, I thought it might be nice to walk to the bistro down the street. It would be my treat."

"I'm sorry." Carly glanced at the small clock in her station. "I already have plans for lunch."

"Okay. Maybe next time." Lynette smiled.

As Grant got to his feet, Lynette scrunched her nose and nodded in Carly's direction. Apparently catching the gist of Lynette's nonverbal communication, Grant turned to Carly and smiled. "Can I ask you something?"

She hoped he was going to suggest that she take a little more off the sides or the back, but she had a feeling he was going to ask something else. Surely, he wouldn't ask her out.

"Go ahead." She offered up a smile and hoped her skittish nerves didn't reveal themselves in her voice or her expression.

"Would you like to have dinner with me on Saturday night?"

She should have expected a question like that, since Lynette had clearly been matchmaking, but it still took her a little by surprise.

Carly hadn't had a date in years—certainly not since she'd gotten married.

Grant seemed nice enough, though, and he was certainly attractive. Yet even if she wanted to go out with him, she had no one she could ask to stay with the boys. Besides, she was away from them too often as it was. "I . . . uh, I'd like to, Grant, but I have two kids, and I may not be able to find a sitter."

"If you can't," Lynette said, "I like kids. And I'm not doing anything on Saturday night. I'll watch them for you."

Was Lynette that intent upon setting up her hairstylist and her friend? Carly wasn't sure if she should be happy about that or not, but the offer did strike another possibility she hadn't considered.

Was there a chance Lynette might want to help out with child care over Christmas vacation?

For a moment, Carly completely forgot that there was still a question hanging in the air like a wind-damaged kite. That is, until she looked at Grant.

Expressive eyes, the color of a summer sky, and a playful smile, made it difficult to turn him down, even though that's what she needed to do.

Still, before she could offer an excuse—and she had a full list of them she could rattle off—she found herself saying, "All right, if Lynette is serious about babysitting, I'll go out with you on Saturday night."

Yet once the words had rolled off her tongue, she wondered how she was going to take them back.

* * *

Max couldn't find a place to park in front of the bistro, and by the time he found one a few spaces away from the entrance to Shear Magic, he was more than five minutes late. But that couldn't be helped.

As he'd gotten ready to leave the house, he'd glanced out in the backyard and noticed that Hemingway was gone again. If the dog had been looking for the kids, as Maggie had suggested he was doing when he escaped, the laugh was on both of them. School was in session, and there weren't any potential playmates roaming the neighborhood.

Still, Max had gone through the motions, calling the dog's name and checking the gate—which had been closed.

On a whim, and wondering how Hemingway had gotten out this time, he'd searched the yard carefully, looking for holes under the fence that he could have missed.

While looking behind a bush that needed pruning in the worst way, he found Hemingway snoozing.

"Hey," Max had said, "what are you doing under there?"

The mutt looked up, but didn't raise his head very far from the front paws on which he'd been resting his chin.

"I'm taking off for a while. See if you can stay out of trouble, okay?"

Hemingway didn't appear to be going anywhere, so Max had returned to the house and grabbed his car keys. Then he'd driven to the salon.

He'd no more than approached the front door of the shop, where bright red letters announced WALK-INS WELCOME, when his neighbor, Grant Barrows, walked out.

Grant's hair, which was usually a lot longer than Max would have ever worn his, had been cut and styled. When he noticed Max, he gave a quick nod of his chin in greeting. "Hey, how's it going?"

"Not bad."

"You're out and about early today," Grant said.

Max didn't see the need to explain what he was up to or

why. He just lifted the briefcase he held and said, "Business meeting."

They stood like that for a moment, both a little surprised to see each other anywhere other than Nutcracker Court.

"Nice haircut," Max said.

"Thanks." Grant nodded toward the salon. "The stylist was Carly."

"Oh, yeah?" How was that for a coincidence? "Have you been going to her long?"

"No, this was my first visit."

"She did a good job."

Grant chuckled. "I think so, too, but even if she'd whacked it all off, I'd probably make another appointment. She's a real sweetheart and nice to look at, too."

Max, who kept things close to the vest, wasn't about to admit that he had a lunch date with that same sweetheart of a stylist. Okay, so their meeting wasn't actually a date.

Before either man could continue, Lynette, the young blonde who played poker with the Diamond Lils at Helen's house, came out of the shop.

She winked at Grant and said hello to Max.

Another coincidence? Before Max could come to a conclusion, she said, "I've gotta run. I'll see you guys later." Then she struck off down the street, swaying her denim-clad hips.

Grant must have noticed the question in Max's eyes because he said, "Lynette's been trying to set me up with Carly, her hairdresser."

"Oh, yeah?" The news had an unsettling effect, although Max had no idea why. Maybe because he felt a little protective of Carly and her kids, and he didn't think Grant was the kind of guy she needed.

"Actually," Grant said, as he looked down the street, "when Lynette first approached me about making an appointment with her hairstylist, I thought she was hitting on me. But she threw me a curve when she said I'd really like Carly."

Max could see how that might come out of the blue. In his mind, Grant and Lynette made a better match.

"To be honest," Grant added, "I was a little disappointed at first, but then I met Carly, and she's a knockout."

Max had noticed. And he couldn't fault Grant for thinking so, too.

"I hear she's got a couple of kids," he found himself throwing out there, although he wasn't entirely sure why he had. To inject a dose of reality, he supposed, and maybe put a damper on a possible romance that might crash and burn eventually.

"Yeah, well, it's only dinner on Saturday night. It's not like I'm expecting anything to develop between us. But who knows?"

Well, Max knew—or at least, he had plenty of doubts about things working out between those two. One time, when he and Grant had been shooting the breeze, Grant had mentioned loving the bachelor life. And Carly, with her ready-made family, was sure to end those beach-boy days and hot-tub nights.

"Good luck," Max said, being a little more sarcastic than sincere.

"Thanks, but I'm not sure I even want to be lucky. Either way, Carly's the kind of woman a man wouldn't mind looking at from across the table or spending the evening with, so no matter what happens, a dinner date isn't going to be a waste of time."

Max would be looking across the table at her in a few short minutes. And he didn't think it would be a waste of his time, either.

After Grant left, Max had been tempted to enter the salon, find Carly, and ask if he should wait until they could leave together, but he'd told her he would meet her at the restaurant and decided to stick with the game plan.

When he entered the California Bistro, a trendy little eatery just down the street, he approached the matronly hostess.

"Just one for lunch?" she asked.

"No, I'm waiting for a lady. There's going to be two of us."

The hostess reached for a couple of menus. "Would you like me to seat you now? Or would you rather wait for your friend?"

He was just about to say that he wasn't in any rush to be seated when Carly entered the diner wearing a breezy smile.

"Hi," she said. "I'm sorry I'm late."

"No problem. I just walked in."

Even though the hostess was prepared to lead them to their table, Max couldn't help sketching an appreciative gaze over Carly, making note of sable brown hair that cloaked her shoulders, a pair of blue-green eyes highlighted by long dark lashes, a pretty mouth with a fresh application of pink lipstick.

She smiled again, and his pulse spiked.

You'd think that this was a real date and not just a neighborly favor of one lost soul helping out another.

The hostess took them to a quiet table for two, which bore a white linen covering and a black ceramic bud vase holding a single red rose.

As the hostess pulled out a chair for Carly, Max took the seat across from her.

"I'll leave these with you," the hostess said, handing them menus before she returned to the front of the restaurant.

"Thanks for meeting me," Max said. "How long do you have?"

She glanced at her watch. "I had an hour, but we're down to fifty-three minutes now. I had a phone call I needed to return."

"Then I'll talk fast." He shot her a casual smile, and when

she returned it, he couldn't help feeling a little like a nerdy tenth-grader who'd just gotten introduced to a varsity cheerleader.

Had Grant felt the same way earlier?

"I'm not sure how much I can help you," Carly said, "especially since I don't know what your problem is."

"Actually, it's a fictional problem."

She stiffened and furrowed her brow. "You mean you only made up an excuse to meet me for lunch?"

"No, I didn't do *that*." Apparently she didn't know that he was an author—or at least, a wannabe at this point. "It's a *real* fictional problem. I'm writing a novel, and it seems that I've written myself into a corner. So I was hoping to get a woman's perspective on a scene that's not working."

"I had no idea that you were an author. Do you have a pen name?"

He couldn't count how many times that happened. Whenever he mentioned writing a book, people just assumed he was already published with hardbound novels on the shelves.

"I haven't sold the manuscript yet," he admitted, "but I've gotten some positive feedback from an agent and would like to get the full manuscript back to him before his office closes for Christmas and New Year's, but I'm at a crossroads. I need to either cut a character completely out of the story, which is what I probably ought to do. Or . . . Well, this might sound weird to someone who doesn't write, but the characters seem to have taken this story and run away with it."

"That's interesting." She leaned forward, resting her forearms on the table. "A runaway plot?"

"Not exactly. The action works well, and I like what's happening so far, but my protagonist's wife just dropped a bomb on him, and . . . Well, that's where I was hoping you'd come in and tell me what I'm missing."

She merely looked at him, as if not knowing what to say, what to do.

"I . . . uh . . ." He reached for the briefcase he'd left on the floor next to his seat. "I brought a scene for you to read—that is, if you don't mind."

She didn't say no, so he flipped open the briefcase, pulled out his pages, and handed them to her.

"I'm not sure how helpful I'll be," she said, taking them from him. "What kind of a book is it?"

"A men's action-adventure novel, I guess. It's got some suspense . . ."

"Blood, guns, guts?"

"A little bad language, too. Would you be opposed to reading it?"

"No, but all I can do is give you a reader's perspective."

And that's just what he wanted—a female reader—although he wasn't sure that his book would appeal to most women.

She glanced at the pages he'd given her—about ten, double-spaced—then started reading.

In the meantime, the busboy brought them water with lemon slices, as well as a basket of bread. Max thanked him, but Carly seemed oblivious to those around her. That was, he decided, a good sign. She was pulled right into the story.

It took all he had not to get up, circle the table, and read over her shoulder. But he bided his time, taking a sip of water, reaching for a slice of bread, and trying to pretend as though he could actually look at the menu and make a choice.

When the waiter came by to take their orders, Max waved him off. "Just a minute," he mouthed to the guy.

Finally, when Max didn't think he could take the suspense any longer, Carly looked up from the pages.

"Logan's a jerk," she said. "Is he the bad guy?"

Was she kidding?

Of course, she only had ten pages that were taken from the last third of the book, so he cut her some slack. "No, he's not the villain. He's the protagonist. He's sharp, and he doesn't take any crap from anyone."

Carly sat back in her seat. "Yeah, well now his wife isn't taking any crap from him."

She had a point, he supposed. And it looked as though she'd hit the same wall he had. Of course, she didn't have a synopsis to go by and had no idea how he'd planned to wrap things up.

"So now what?" he asked. "Logan can't chase after her."

"Why can't he?"

"Because he's tough. And he's not the kind of man who would beg a woman to stay."

At that moment, the waiter eased closer again, and Max nodded.

"We'd better order," Max said. "Or you won't have a chance to eat."

"Can I answer any questions for you?" the waiter asked. "Or do you already know what you'd like to eat?"

Carly said, "I'll take the tortilla soup."

Max wanted something heartier than that. "What's your special?"

"Fish tacos," the waiter said.

"Great. I'll have that."

The guy nodded, then took off, leaving them alone again.

"Okay," Max said. "Here's what I'm thinking. Maybe I need to kill off Priscilla. Or do you think it would be best to eliminate her character completely?"

"You can't do *that*."

"Why can't I?"

"Because I like her. And I felt myself cheering for her when she left him."

Oh, brother. Maybe asking Carly to read the scene had been a bad idea.

"You're just saying that because you're a woman," Max said. "And if I do what you're suggesting, I'd turn a men's action/adventure novel into a romance."

"I'm not telling you to do anything. It's your book, but I think there needs to be some emotion here on Logan's part.

How was he feeling when she walked out? Did he feel crushed, betrayed, guilty, what?"

"That's the problem," Max said. "I don't know what he's feeling. And I don't have a clue why I even let him be married in the first place. He'd make a much better bachelor."

"Well, there you go." Carly set his pages on an empty part of the table, leaned back in her seat, and crossed her arms. "Why did they get married? What did Priscilla see in him? Why did they fall in love?"

"I don't know." The comment came out a little snarkier than it should have, but he couldn't help it. "And who said anything about love? Maybe they were just sexually attracted to each other and found marriage convenient."

"That's your problem," she said, as if she had some kind of literary degree. "You're afraid of having any emotion in your book."

"I've got emotion—fear, anxiety, anger."

"But not love."

"This is *not* a romance."

"I'm not saying that you need to have a happily-ever-after ending. They can actually divorce, if you want them to. But he's got to feel something about the loss of his wife, about the failure of his marriage. And until you get a handle on that, I don't think you're going to sell it to anyone—an agent, an editor, or a reader."

Max chuffed. "Maybe I should just eliminate her character completely. Maybe Logan is a dyed-in-the-wool bachelor. Or maybe his first love cheated on him, so he's sworn off women for good."

"It's your book, but as a reader, I think cutting Priscilla is a big mistake."

She might be a reader, but she was also a female. What would a man say?

Still, Max could hardly complain about an opinion he'd asked to hear. And he'd wanted a female perspective.

Carly leaned forward and placed her elbows on the table.

"Listen, Max. You're a good writer. But just because Logan has trouble dealing with his feelings doesn't mean you have to cut out the one person in the world who will make him look deep within himself."

"What are you? A closet novelist?"

"No, I just love to read. And English was my favorite subject in school. If I'd gone to college, instead of getting married, I might have ended up teaching literature at Fairbrook High."

Before he could respond, the waiter brought their food.

Carly thanked the guy.

Max did, too, but as he reached for a fish taco and took a bite, he noticed that Carly bowed her head and said a silent prayer.

He hadn't realized she was one of those religious types. Of course, she hadn't preached at him or anything.

Still, what she'd said about Priscilla making Logan reach deep inside of himself made Max wonder if Carly might be a little more helpful than he'd thought.

What if she read the entire manuscript—or at least, everything leading up until this scene? Would she feel differently about Priscilla?

He took a second bite of his taco, then while he was chewing and swallowing, decided to go for it. "I don't suppose you'd want to take a look at all of it, would you?"

"Your book?"

"I could e-mail it to you. Or if you'd rather have a hard copy, I could print it out and deliver it to you."

She merely looked at him from across the table, her spoon lifted and full of soup.

"Of course, I'd pay you," he added. "I wouldn't ask you to spend your time reading and critiquing for free."

She lowered her spoon without taking a bite. "You know, if things weren't so tough for me financially right now, I'd tell you that I'd do it as a favor—and for fun."

Money talked, he decided. Didn't it always? But he found himself grinning and feeling somewhat relieved.

"Would two hundred dollars help?" he asked. "You wouldn't need to do a full-on line edit or anything. Just read the first three hundred pages and tell me what you think."

"About Priscilla?"

Mostly, yes. He thought the other characters were spot-on. But he said, "Just let me know how you feel about the story—the characters, the conflict, the plot, or whatever."

"Okay. I can do that. And an extra two hundred dollars would help a lot."

"Great. Thanks."

"But you'd better snail mail it to me or drop it off at the house. I had to eliminate my Internet server."

"No problem. I'll get it to you." He picked up his fork, then realized she'd done more than he'd asked her to do, and now he owed her one.

"So what's going on with Josh?" he asked.

She swallowed, then picked up her napkin and blotted her lips. For some reason, just watching her and waiting for her to speak kicked up his pulse rate a notch.

"I'm not sure," she said. "He's been so introspective lately. And he's resentful that I depend on him to help out in so many ways. But things are really tight these days. I really shouldn't have rented the house we're in, but I was determined to raise the kids in a nice neighborhood and to make sure they attended a good school. And that's why I'm having so much trouble now. I'm overextended."

"Because of the rent?"

"And a few other unexpected expenses over the past few months. I probably should have rented one of the apartments on the other side of town. The utility bills would have been a lot less." She inhaled, then blew out a troubled sigh. "But then the boys wouldn't have had a yard to play in."

"So why don't you move?"

"I'm afraid I'm going to have to. I'm embarrassed to admit this, but I fell behind on the rent, and I'm not sure how long I can convince my landlord not to start the eviction process—if he hasn't already."

"A lot of kids have to grow up in apartments," Max said, thinking she shouldn't have gotten a place she couldn't afford. But she seemed to know that now, so there was no reason to make her feel worse.

She reached for a slice of bread. "You're right. When my dad died, my mother and I had to live in an apartment for a couple of years. It really wasn't so bad. We had nice neighbors, and we were happy."

"Kids are pretty adaptable. They usually make friends anywhere."

"That's true. I stayed indoors a lot, though. So I didn't have many friends in the complex to lead me astray."

"Why'd you stay inside?"

"I did my homework, cooked dinner for my mom, and spent my free time reading. But most boys would rather play outside if they had a chance, wouldn't they?"

Max hadn't thought about his boyhood in ages, but if he'd grown up on Nutcracker Court, he would have spent all of his free time down in the canyon. But that didn't mean he wouldn't have made the best of living in an apartment complex. "Like I said, kids will find out how to have fun no matter where they are."

"I hope so."

They returned to their respective meals for a while, then she looked up and wrapped her gaze around his, nearly choking the breath out of him. "I really wish I could afford day care. I hate that Josh has to look out for his brother—and that I don't get home until after dark sometimes."

"If you moved into an apartment, would you be able to afford the cost of a sitter?"

"Maybe. When we first moved into the house, I lucked out. There was an older woman who lived next door to us, and she really took a liking to the boys. She didn't have children, and she used to dote on them and do grandmotherly things."

Max didn't know any of his grandparents. "What kind of things did she do?"

"She used to make them cookies and color with Mikey. She'd play board games with them, too." Carly shrugged, breaking eye contact for a moment. "I miss her. She was a special lady. And Josh was a lot happier back then."

"What happened? Why isn't she helping out now?"

"She lost her husband about six months ago and moved in with her sister to make ends meet." Carly shrugged a single shoulder, then gave him a wistful smile. "It would be nice to find someone else to at least watch Mikey. That way Josh could have some time to himself."

It seemed reasonable, so Max didn't comment. Yet even his silence seemed to speak to her.

"*What?*" she asked.

"I didn't say anything."

"You didn't have to. But I know you were thinking something."

She might be attractive, but she was still a typical woman—always trying to read into everything.

"Do you think Josh should have more time to himself?" she asked.

"How old is he?"

"He'll be thirteen next March."

Max didn't know what to tell her. A lot of kids had adult responsibilities and played active roles in their family. And the way he saw it, the kids were all the better for it.

It was clear that Carly was really struggling, though. And not just financially. Raising boys must be tough for a single mother, and he sympathized. But there wasn't much he could do about it. He certainly couldn't offer to babysit whenever she worked.

When would he write? The noise and commotion alone would drive him up a wall.

He took another bite of his taco, filling his mouth so he wouldn't say—or *offer*—anything stupid. Yet as he chewed, he realized he owed her something more, although he wasn't sure what.

"I could talk to your son," he finally said. "Maybe he'll tell me what's bothering him."

She looked up, and hope sparked in her eyes, making the green even brighter. "I'd really appreciate it if you would. Maybe I could fix dinner for you one evening this week, and you could come over and talk to him at our house. You can even bring your dog. The boys have really taken a liking to him."

His first impulse was to decline dinner. Max never had been very family oriented. He was a lot like Logan in that way.

Maybe that was why he understood his protagonist so well. But if Carly was going to read his manuscript and offer some suggestions, then it wouldn't hurt for him to bend just a little.

Max owed her that much.

At least, that was the excuse he gave himself for accepting her invitation to have dinner with her and the kids on Thursday night.

Chapter 12

It was Thursday again, and Susan was on her way to Nutcracker Court to meet the Lils and Maggie for coffee, but she wasn't going empty-handed.

This time, however, she wasn't taking food, like she'd done on Tuesday, when one of her neighbors had given her a homemade fruitcake. Since Susan had never really liked that particular holiday goodie—and wouldn't be able to eat the whole thing by herself, even if she had—she'd taken it to Grant.

He'd been a little surprised by her unexpected visit, but he'd smiled, taken the cake, and thanked her.

Now she was back, bearing yet another gift—this one was a lot more practical for a busy man like him.

While out shopping yesterday, she'd found a darling little snowman he could put in his front yard. It had the sweetest little face, and when it was turned on, it lit up and waved at passersby.

She'd also picked up a lush poinsettia plant for his front porch, although she'd left it in her car since she couldn't carry everything at once. Hopefully, he wouldn't think it was presumptuous of her to give them to him, and if he insisted upon paying for it, so be it. But either way, he really needed a little holiday cheer.

Before leaving her house, she'd put on her nicest pair of

black slacks, a cream-colored turtleneck sweater, and topped it off with a red Christmas vest. Then she'd carefully applied her makeup and sprayed on a dab of her favorite perfume.

And now here she was, standing on Grant's stoop, ringing his bell.

When he answered the door, he was barefoot and wearing a wet suit, as if he was just going to pack up his surfboard and head to the beach, which she thought was rather odd on a chilly day like this. Yet even more amazing was the way the black, rubbery material molded over every perfect muscle in his body, reminding her that he was much more than a pretty face.

As he glanced at the life-sized snowman made of lights and tubing, his jaw dropped a little more, and she wasn't sure who was more surprised to see the other—him or her.

"I hope you don't mind," she said, "but I saw this cute little guy and thought he'd look great on your lawn for the Christmas season. So I picked it up for you—as a gift."

"That was thoughtful, but I hate to have you spending your money on something I probably won't use. Maybe you should put it on your lawn instead."

She laughed. "Actually, I found it at a buy-one-get-one-free sale, so I picked up two. So yours didn't cost a dime."

If she hadn't been holding on to the snowman with both hands, she would have put one behind her back and crossed her fingers to ward off any bad luck from stretching the truth, since there hadn't been any such sale, and she'd actually paid almost thirty dollars for it.

"Why me?" he asked.

Because she wanted him to notice her and to realize how nice it would be to have a woman in his life who would look out for him. But she wasn't about to admit that.

Instead, she smiled. "I know how busy you must be at this time of the year, and I wanted to make it easy on you. Besides, everyone else on this street has already decorated their houses."

"Max hasn't."

Her mother would have said, "If Max jumped off a cliff, would you do it, too?" And for some silly reason—a rush of girlish excitement, probably—she found herself repeating the question to Grant.

"That's not the same thing," he said.

"No, it isn't. I'm sorry, I couldn't help teasing a little." She extended her arms, handing him the snowman. "Please take it."

"I'm really not big on holiday decorations," he said, "or splurging on energy bills."

"You don't have to worry about that. It's battery-operated."

Silence stretched between them, then he relented and took the snowman from her. "Thank you. I guess it'll keep the neighbors from complaining."

His appreciation warmed her heart, and she hoped that they were becoming . . . Well, becoming friends would be a nice start.

She thought she detected a slight smile on his face, as he placed the snowman inside his house, and it pleased her to know that her gift had been so well received. In fact, she'd forgotten to mention the poinsettia that was still in her car.

But maybe it was best if she gave the plant to Max instead. It wouldn't hurt to become friends with him, too.

Of course, Max was probably sleeping or holed up in his office, so he might not answer the door, but she could always leave it on his porch. If she let Maggie know what she'd done, he'd eventually find out who'd been thinking of him.

After Grant thanked Susan again and shut the door, she headed for her car to get the plant, just as Lynette arrived.

So she left the plant right where it was and greeted her friend.

"Don't you look nice," Lynette said, as she closed her car door. "Is that a new vest?"

"No, I've had it a couple of years."

"Well, it's really cute." Lynette smiled, then asked, "Did I see you coming from Grant's house?"

"Yes, you did. I gave him a Christmas decoration he could use in his front yard."

"Did he take it?"

"Yes, although, for a moment, I thought he was going to refuse it." Susan couldn't help grinning as she imagined her gift being put to use. "It's so cute. It lights up and waves at passersby."

"That doesn't seem like the kind of thing a bachelor would want in his yard, but then again, maybe he's thinking about children and family this time of year."

"Do you think?" Susan brightened. She certainly hoped that was true. And if it was, it was a good sign.

Before they could make their way to Helen's front door, Rosa pulled up and parked behind Lynette.

"Oh, good," Susan said. "I'm so glad she could make it. We don't see her very much anymore. Maybe, now that there are four of us, we can talk Maggie into joining us for a few hands of poker."

"That would be fun."

Susan and Lynette waited for Rosa to get out of the car, and when she did, they headed up the sidewalk together.

"We're so happy to see you," Lynette told Rosa. "It's not the same when you're not here. It's nice that Carlos let you come today."

Rosa, who moved with a limp, slowed her steps. "Actually, I told him not to make any more plans for me on Thursdays."

"That's great." Susan and the other Lils had been worried about her for the past several months. "I'm so proud of you."

"In fact," Rosa said, as they neared Helen's porch, "Carlos and I had words earlier this morning. I've always been pretty passive, but ever since the other night, when we got home from a meeting at the church, I started speaking my own mind."

"I'm glad to hear you're finally standing up to him for a change." The minute Susan's response left her lips, she regretted them. "I'm sorry, Rosa. I didn't mean for it to sound that way. It's not that I think Carlos controls your every move, it's just that—"

"I know what you mean." Rosa, who was the first to reach the door, rang the bell. "We had a little disagreement about that Laughlin trip over breakfast. He thought that three or four days was entirely too long for me to be away, but I told him under no uncertain terms that I was going with my friends and would stay for the duration of the trip. Then I blocked out that weekend on his calendar, just to be sure he didn't plan anything for me."

Maggie opened the door and, with a smile that lit her intensive blue eyes, welcomed them into the house.

As Susan stepped into the cozy living room, with the familiar furniture and the Pritchard family photos adorning the mantel, Susan was reminded of the one Lil who was still missing.

"Have you heard from Helen?" she asked Maggie.

"No, I haven't. I'm sure she's having too much fun to contact any of us."

"Hopefully, she'll find time to send an e-mail," Lynette said. "I hear those phone calls from the cruise ship can be very expensive."

Lynette, who'd been left way more money than she knew what to do with, could be frugal to a fault, but Susan wouldn't hold that against her.

As Maggie led them into the kitchen, the aroma of fresh-perked coffee grew stronger until it filled the air. And Susan, for one, was looking forward to chatting over a cup of java with her closest friends—and with Maggie, of course.

Ten minutes later, they were seated around the kitchen

table, sipping coffee and eating slices of pumpkin bread Maggie had baked earlier that morning.

"Have any of you decided how you're going to use your money to bless someone else this Christmas?" Maggie asked.

"We're not planning to spend very much of it," Lynette reminded her.

"We're still going to Laughlin," Rosa added. "I've already put my foot down with Carlos, which I rarely do. So I'd hate to have to back down. . . ."

Susan reached over and patted Rosa's hand. "You're not going to have to give in to him. We've already committed to that trip."

"It's not that we can't spare a little money, though." Lynette cut another piece of pumpkin bread with her fork. "We probably have five thousand dollars or more saved, which is more than we're going to need."

"Oh, it's not that much," Susan said, as she reached for her oversized purse, glad she'd thought to bring the money with her today, and dug out the yellow manila envelope that held the cash they'd been setting aside for the past two years. "If you wait a minute, I can tell you the exact amount."

Susan ran her finger down the front of the bulging package, where she'd listed dates, amounts, and a running total, until she found the bottom line. "Here it is. We have two thousand, six hundred, and forty-four dollars."

"That can't be right." Lynette reached for the envelope, almost snatching it out of Susan's hands. "Let me see that list."

"What's the matter?" Susan asked her. "Don't you *trust* me?"

"Of course, I do. You're as honest as Abe Lincoln himself, which is why we let you hold on to the money in the first place. But remember that day you had your checking account all screwed up and needed me to help you figure out what went wrong?" Lynette smiled, as if trying to soften her words. "You have a tendency to transpose the numbers, Suze."

The truth and the patronizing way in which Lynette had said it, struck a hard blow, reminding Susan of the dyslexia she'd battled all of her life—the embarrassment, the shame, the frustration.

Lynette stopped her scan of the numbers long enough to say, "I'm sorry, Suze. I didn't mean to hurt your feelings. It's just that I know we have more money than that. I've been keeping a mental tally, and it has to be at least five thousand, if not more."

The apology, which was undoubtedly meant to soothe her feelings, fell short of the mark, and Susan crossed her arms over her chest. "It's all inside the envelope, every last dollar."

"I'm sure it is." Lynette tossed another smile Susan's way, which didn't work any better than the last at making up for her remark. Then she went back to scanning the numbers. "Uh-oh. Here's a nineteen instead of a ninety-one."

Susan's cheeks flushed warm with embarrassment. "Maybe you should forget the math and my notes on the front, Lynette. Just take it out of the envelope and count it."

"All right, I will." Lynette, who Susan imagined was only too happy to get her tight little paws on the cash, dumped it on the table and proceeded to add it up.

The fact that she'd been right, that they'd had more money than Susan had thought, didn't matter one little bit. Not while she was still stinging from the comments made.

A part of her wanted to retaliate by bringing up the fact that the only one focused on the money was Lynette, who'd always been tightfisted in spite of having a slew of it herself.

No wonder she'd been keeping a mental note of all their winnings.

Finally Lynette looked up and smiled—a little too smugly. "We have over six thousand dollars."

"And more than enough for that trip to Laughlin," Maggie said. "Have you given any thought to ways in which you can give to those in need this Christmas?"

"We don't have to give money," Lynette said. "Right? Giving of our time helps."

Susan gave a little *humph,* reminded again of Lynette's tightfisted flaw, which wasn't one she'd been born with, like a learning disability. Rather it was one that had developed over time and nurtured by selfishness.

"It's true that you don't have to spend money in order to help others," Maggie agreed, "but if you run across someone who has a real need, I hope you'll be generous."

"Of course," Lynette said, as she recounted the money and placed it in neat little stacks.

Susan couldn't help but doubt that Lynette would actually spend a dime of her money on anyone else, but she supposed that wasn't any of her business. She could only speak for herself. And she had someone in mind already. "While I was helping out at the soup kitchen, I noticed a single mother and her children who could use some help, as well as an elderly couple whose car isn't working."

There was that homeless man and his dog, too, she realized.

"See?" Maggie said. "If you keep your eyes open, you'll find people you can bless one way or another. Sometimes taking time to smile and talk to someone who is down and out will do wonders."

"You're right. We've seen it ourselves at the soup kitchen, although there are lots of needs in the community." Rosa turned to Susan. "Since you're going to help out at Lydia's House, why don't you see if there's something special they need? Maybe we can donate it to them."

"I can do that," Susan said, although just thinking about joining Barbie and her parents at the home for developmentally disabled adults caused her to sigh.

"What's wrong?" Rosa asked.

"Oh, nothing. It's just that my sister-in-law asked me to make brownies and a coffee cake for the holiday party."

"That'll be a nice and easy contribution," Maggie said.

"Maybe, but I'd . . ." She'd meant to say that she'd rather not go at all, but she was already feeling bruised and a little stupid, thanks to Lynette's hurtful comments and insistence upon counting the money herself. So why risk any more criticism?

"But Susan," Maggie said, "I thought you liked to bake. That cake you made the other day was out of this world. And so were those chocolate chip cookies."

"I do, but . . ." Susan clamped her mouth shut, again reminding herself that she'd already been chastised for a learning disability she hadn't asked to be born with.

Why mention that she tended to get the ingredients mixed up whenever she tried her hand at a new recipe? Or tell them that whenever there'd been a potluck at Hank's mother's house, she would hire a woman from the church to make a dish for her so her in-laws wouldn't find out about her shortcomings?

It was only sheer determination that had caused her to continue baking and throwing out numerous batches of the mango-coconut cake or those chocolate chip cookies until she'd memorized every last ingredient and could make either in her sleep.

"But *what?*" Rosa asked.

"It's just that I'd rather . . . do something more."

They grew silent, probably lost in thought as they each considered people they could somehow bless, when Susan realized she'd already done so today.

"You know," she admitted, "I performed a good deed before I arrived here."

Maggie leaned forward, clearly intent upon hearing more. "That's wonderful. What did you do?"

"I purchased an outdoor Christmas decoration for one of Helen's neighbors and gave it to him. The poor guy doesn't have anything up at all, and the lighted snowman is going to look darling in his yard."

"You told me that earlier," Lynette said, "but the more I

think about it, the more I doubt that Grant will actually use that snowman."

"What makes you say that?" Susan asked, irritation lacing her voice. "He thanked me and smiled when he placed it in his house."

"Yes, but Grant hasn't decorated his yard since moving into this neighborhood several years ago. And truthfully, don't you think a snowman might be a little too . . . well, a little too feminine for a guy like him?"

Susan gave another little *humph,* although she didn't think anyone heard this one, either. If they had, they might have realized that she'd like to clobber Lynette.

"And speaking of Grant," Lynette added, "I did a good deed, too."

At that, Susan perked up. Had Lynette actually been matchmaking, like Susan had hoped that she would?

Biting back a splash of excitement and deciding she'd overreacted, that she ought to forgive the woman for the thoughtless comments she'd made earlier, Susan asked, "What did you do?"

"I introduced him to my hairdresser. She's a single mom with two kids and is really struggling financially. They hit it off and are going out on Saturday night. I'm even going to watch the kids." All of a sudden, Lynette laughed. "Actually, that should count as two good deeds since I know very little about children and have never babysat before."

A sense of betrayal slammed into Susan. Lynette couldn't have surprised or hurt her more if she'd jumped over the table and slapped her in the face.

Surely Lynette had known that Susan had wanted to go out with Grant, so how could she set him up with someone else?

The mounting frustration and anger, fueled by the earlier implication that Susan was too stupid to count, built to the point that she couldn't help herself from blurting out, "How *could* you?"

Susan scooted back her chair and got to her feet. As she grabbed her purse, she aimed a frown at the woman she'd once thought of as a friend.

Confusion splashed across Lynette's face, leaving her to appear as lost and oblivious as a masked kid playing Pin the Tail on the Donkey.

But Susan didn't give a rip about that. Instead, she strode through the house, almost stomping as she went.

In the background she heard Lynette ask, "What did I do?"

Well, Susan was done talking. The selfish blond bimbo was going to have to figure it out on her own, although she'd probably need Rosa and Maggie to explain what should have been obvious to anyone with a heart.

When Susan blew up and stormed out of Helen's house, Lynette had been too stunned to speak.

What had she done wrong?

In silent awe, she turned to the other women, hoping they had a clue as to what had just happened.

"Apparently, she has a crush on Grant," Rosa said.

She *did?* Why hadn't she said something earlier? If Lynette would have known that, she wouldn't have introduced Grant to Carly.

Although, come to think of it, Susan really wasn't the man's type. She was more . . .

Well, Lynette couldn't put her finger on what had caused her to come to that conclusion, but suffice it to say the two weren't suited.

Still, in her own defense, Lynette said, "A few weeks back, Susan mentioned something about being ready to start dating. And she asked us to be on the lookout for her, but she never said anything about setting her sights on anyone in particular."

"I think your comment about her math skills might have made her a little testy," Rosa said. "I knew what you meant, but it's difficult to have someone point out your faults in a group."

Gosh, was that what Lynette had done? She certainly hadn't meant to. If anyone knew how it felt to deal with insecurities and fears that someone would uncover hidden flaws, it was her.

Was that what had set Susan off?

If so, she couldn't blame her.

"I feel really badly about hurting her feelings and making her angry," Lynette admitted. "I'm going to have to apologize."

No one said anything one way or the other. Instead, they continued to chat about inconsequential things. Lynette gave it another fifteen minutes or so, then excused herself.

"I've got an appointment," she said, as she carried her cup and plate to the sink. "So I've got to run."

It wasn't true, but she'd never had a lot of friends growing up, so she valued the ones she had now and didn't like the thought of losing one.

After telling Rosa and Maggie good-bye, she let herself out and walked down the sidewalk, still struggling with guilt over the hasty comments she'd made.

At the sound of an approaching vehicle, she looked up and spotted Grant returning home with a surfboard attached to a rack on the top of his car.

Surely he hadn't gone out in the ocean in this weather. The water had to be freezing cold.

Unable to pretend she hadn't seen him, she headed toward his house.

Sure enough, as he got out of his vehicle, his hair was wet. He was wearing khaki-colored board shorts and a black hoodie, but his skin appeared damp, and his lips held a bluish tint.

"Don't tell me you went surfing today," she said.

He tossed her a grin. "Yep. The waves were awesome."

"But it's so cold."

"I have a wet suit, so it wasn't too bad."

She glanced down at her feet, not wanting to leave, yet still bothered by Susan's angry departure. When she glanced up, she caught Grant's gaze. "I'm not sure if you know this, but Carly isn't the only one interested in you."

Grant's eyes glimmered, and as he crossed his arms and leaned his weight onto one foot, he grinned. "Oh, *yeah?*"

She nodded. "Susan's interested in you, too."

The smile drifted from his face.

"I'm not trying to complicate your life," she added.

"By telling me about Susan?" He slowly shook his head and chuffed. "It's not like you're trying to set us up." Then he grew serious. "You're *not*, are you?"

"Oh, no. I mean . . . Well, if you feel the least bit attracted to her, that's great. She's a nice woman. And she's lonely."

"Whoa. Let's back up. Carly is more my type than Susan is, so let's not even go there."

Lynette had felt the same way, but at least she could tell Susan she'd gone to bat for her. Maybe knowing that would help her to accept the apology Lynette intended to make.

"Listen," Grant said, "if you have any influence on Susan, please ask her to back off."

"What do you mean?"

"She's been stopping by to chat with me every chance she gets, and not just on Thursdays. For some reason, she seems to be finding a lot of other reasons to be in the neighborhood."

"You mean she's stalking you?"

"No, it's not that bad. But even though I've tried to tell her nicely that I'm not in the Christmas spirit this year, she won't listen. And to make matters worse, she came by on Tuesday and brought me the driest, most awful fruitcake ever made. If I didn't know better, I'd think it was left over from last year. I actually took a bite and nearly choked. What's with that woman?"

"She's dyslexic, and it must have been a new recipe."

Grant chuffed. "So why did she have to practice on me?"

Lynette didn't want Grant to think badly of Susan, even if he wasn't interested in dating her. So she said, "She's really good-hearted."

"I'm sure she is. But she seems to have adopted me as some kind of pet project, and I have to say that I don't really like it."

Lynette couldn't help but grin. "You mean I'm not the only one of Helen's friends trying to butt into your life?"

Grant lobbed a smile right back at her. Then he reached out and ran a couple of cold knuckles along her cheek. "No, you're *not* the only one."

For a moment, she found it hard to breathe. But not because of the chill of his touch. His icy fingers had some wild, inexplicable way of warming her from the inside out.

She couldn't help but look at Grant, *really* look. And as she noticed the blue tinge around his lips, the damp hair, the intensity in his gaze, she found herself wondering if she might be the tiniest bit interested in him, too.

But she couldn't let that happen. She had to get out of here, but for some reason, the words wouldn't form and her feet wouldn't move.

They stood like that for a couple of beats, even though the poor man was turning into an icicle out here.

So why hadn't she shooed him off, telling him to take a hot shower before he caught pneumonia?

Because she actually liked the guy, more than she would admit. She liked talking to him, looking at him. . . .

Of course, she wasn't falling for him. Goodness, she couldn't do that.

But rather than spinning her wheels, trying to figure out all the internal confusion she was experiencing while he was standing just inches away, she said, "I'd better let you go inside before you can claim that Helen's friends are going to be the death of you, either by fruitcake poisoning or by freezing."

He laughed, and the way his eyes glimmered like warm

embers in the fire, the way her heart flip-flopped, had her scurrying for some kind of explanation for it all.

Lynette didn't need a man; *Carly* did.

To think otherwise made her feel a little like a home wrecker, and Grant had yet to take Carly out on their first date. But things wouldn't go any further than this. Lynette couldn't—and *wouldn't*—let it, even if Grant asked her out. Because now she had a good reason to tell him no.

She didn't date men she was attracted to.

Chapter 13

Carly left the salon early on Thursday, right after Donna Ferris, her last client, walked out with a smile and a fresh new perm.

It was only half past three, so on any other day, she would have stuck around, hoping for a walk-in client to request a service, but with Max coming over for dinner, she needed to get home and start cooking.

She told herself that the two hundred dollars he was paying her for reading his manuscript would cover any services she might have missed out on by leaving before five this afternoon.

Hopefully, by the end of the weekend, she'd have those three hundred pages read and his check deposited into her account. She owed her landlord a payment on Monday, and by giving him a little extra than she'd planned, he might let them stay in the house through Christmas.

The two hundred dollars from Max wasn't quite the miracle she'd been praying for, but she was grateful to have it just the same.

On her way home, she stopped at the market and picked up the fixings for tacos, something she hadn't made in months. Knowing she ought to provide some kind of dessert for her guest, she also purchased a generic brand of vanilla ice cream and a jar of chocolate syrup.

When she finally arrived home, she parked in the garage, then entered the house through the kitchen, where she set down the bag of groceries on the table. She could hear the TV blasting in the living room, so before doing anything else, she went in search of her sons.

Sure enough, Mikey was sitting on the sofa, watching *SpongeBob SquarePants* on television, while Josh, whose open backpack rested beside him, was seated on the floor using the coffee table as a desk. His open math book and several papers were spread before him as he did his homework.

"I'm home," she said, realizing she'd better use some window cleaner on the glass-top coffee table before Max arrived.

Mikey gave her a glad-to-see-you smile and a "Hi, Mom," then went right back to watching SpongeBob and his under-the-sea friends.

Josh, on the other hand, continued to solve a long-division problem. She supposed she ought to admire his focus, but she would have felt better if he'd at least greeted her.

Deciding to let it go, she asked, "Did I tell you guys that we're having company for dinner?"

At that, Josh looked up from his work, breaking his concentration. "No, you didn't. Who's coming over?"

"Mr. Tolliver."

"Why's *he* coming *here*?"

Even Mikey grabbed the TV remote and turned down the volume at the news. "Is he *mad* at us again?"

"No, it's nothing like that. Mr. Tolliver and I met at the grocery store the other night, and since we're kind of neighbors, I invited him to dinner."

Mikey's eyes grew wide, even without the help of the new glasses that she was supposed to pick up at the optometrist's office next week. "He's not going to yell at us about something, is he?"

"No, he won't do that."

Mikey turned to his brother. "Hey, Josh. I wonder if he'll

come over in his robe and slippers. That's all he ever seems to wear."

Both boys laughed.

"Actually," Carly said, "Mr. Tolliver asked me to do a favor for him, and he's coming over to talk to me about it."

Josh leaned back from the table, resting against the sofa. "What did he ask you to do?"

"He's writing a book, and he wants me to help with the editing."

Surprise splashed across her oldest son's face. "No kidding?"

What did he find so hard to believe? That Mr. Tolliver had created a work of fiction? Or that his mother had the ability to edit something literary?

"I can't believe that guy is writing a book," Josh added. "What kind is it? A murder mystery in a haunted house?" He chuckled to himself. "I bet it's a horror story about a zombie who eats kids."

"It's an action/adventure novel," Carly said.

Mike scrunched his face. "What's that?"

"It's the kind of book that has a bunch of ticking bombs that are about to go off in a city," Josh explained. "And a lot of guys get shot and killed trying to find them before they blow up."

Carly supposed he was close to being right, but rather than agree, she added, "Best of all, he's paying me to do it."

"Cool." Josh lit up at that bit of news, reminding her of the child he'd been just months ago. "Does that mean that, if you do a good job, he'll hire you full-time to edit all his books? And then you can stay home and not work at the salon anymore?"

"No, I'm sure this is just a one-shot deal."

Disappointment slid across his face, wiping away all evidence of the little boy who'd once liked holding her hand when they were out in public.

She couldn't help wondering if there was any other way she could support the family while working from home, but there really wasn't.

"That's cool about you helping with his book," Mikey said. "Maybe he'll hire you to do other stuff for him. I think he's super rich."

That was an interesting thing for him to surmise. "Where would you get an idea like that?"

"Because he's weird and stays in his house all day." Mikey turned to his brother. "Hey, Josh, remember that show we watched about that guy who got stuck in his house?"

"The hoarder?" Josh grinned and nodded, then turned to Carly. "It was really cool, Mom. You should have seen it. This old man had so much junk in his house that he was practically buried alive with books and boxes and garbage. And when the firemen finally broke in and found him, they had to take him to the hospital. Then, when his kids came to clean out the house, they found about a million dollars stuffed in coffee cans and boxes and stuff."

"I doubt that Mr. Tolliver is a hoarder. And I've seen him outside of his house. He was definitely wearing street clothes and not a bathrobe." Carly did have to admit that she really knew very little about the man.

"Well, he's gotta be rich, though. He doesn't have to work at a job, and he can stay home all day writing books. A poor guy couldn't do that."

She supposed her son had a point. Some rich people preferred to live a simple life and not flaunt their wealth.

"By the way," she added, "I told Mr. Tolliver to bring his dog when he comes over tonight."

At that, Mikey shot up from his seat, nearly dislodging the cushions on the sofa. "He's going to bring Hemingway with him? Did you hear that, Josh?"

"Yeah, I heard." Josh shot a look of disbelief at Carly. "You invited a *dog* to dinner?"

Carly could understand why he'd think that was an odd thing for her to do, and she wasn't really sure why she'd mentioned it to Max.

Before she could try and explain her reason, which had something to do with making an awkward situation easier on the kids, Josh began to chuckle. "Actually, I think that's kind of cool, Mom."

She was both relieved—and glad—to know he was on board with the idea, so she tossed him a playful smile. "Well, it's not *that* cool. The dog isn't going to sit at the table with us and eat tacos."

"We know that," Mikey said. "But thanks for inviting Hemingway, too. We like him a whole lot better than we like Mr. Tolliver."

She'd figured as much. "I thought you boys might like to play with the dog while Mr. Tolliver and I talk about his book."

"Sure, we can do that," Mikey said. "We'll take Hemingway out in the backyard to play. Can we eat our dinner out there, too?"

"No, the humans will eat inside."

Josh shrugged, then returned to his homework, while Mikey turned up the sound on the television.

Carly couldn't very well remain in the living room, wasting time when she had a meal to prepare.

And a house to straighten up.

Not that it was messy. It's just that it wasn't ready for company, even if she had no intention of giving Max Tolliver—or his dog—the red carpet treatment.

Max had spent a little more time than usual in the bathroom, shaving, splashing on a bit of his favorite cologne, and getting ready to go to Carly's for dinner.

He could make a lot of excuses as to why that might be, but the truth was, he was actually looking forward to seeing her again.

She'd told him he could bring the dog with him, but he'd decided against that. He might have grown fond of the crazy mutt over the last few months, but he wasn't what you'd call an animal lover, if that's what she'd been thinking. So why go overboard on that sort of thing?

He removed his car keys from the small table near the front door, turned on the porch light, then exited the house. As he locked up, he heard footsteps and glanced over his shoulder to see Maggie heading up his sidewalk with a small paper sack in her hand.

"I hoped that I'd catch you before you left," she said. "I have something I wanted to give you."

Max wasn't sure how she'd known that he had plans for the evening, but even more surprising was the fact that she'd brought something to him. "What is it?"

She opened the bag, reached inside, and whipped out a red-and-green knit dog collar. "It's a gift for Butch."

If the dog hadn't responded so many times to that name, Max might have corrected her. Of course, he wouldn't put it past Maggie to toss doggie treats over the fence, training Hemingway to answer to Butch.

But why would she do that? She couldn't be that loony, could she?

He watched as she fiddled with the collar for a moment, turning on a little switch. The next thing he knew, the thing lit up and started blinking.

"It's a battery-operated Christmas collar," she said. "Isn't it great? The boys ought to get a kick out of that."

The woman was either psychic or a basket case. How had she known he was going to see any children tonight?

He chuffed. "What kids are you talking about?"

"Joshua and Michael. Aren't you going to their house for dinner?"

If he asked how she'd known where he was going, she'd probably tell him Hemingway had told her—which wasn't possible, since Max hadn't uttered a word to the dog, as crazy as that would have been.

More likely, she'd probably talked to one of the West-brook boys earlier today. Or maybe she'd chatted with Lynette, who could have found out from Carly. Either way, Max would almost prefer to believe that the dog *had* told her rather than think he was becoming the subject of idle feminine chatter and gossip.

Still, he went ahead and took the collar from Maggie and thanked her.

"You're welcome." Her eyes, the color of the wild blue yonder, glimmered with apparent delight. "Have a great time this evening."

He stood on the porch for a moment, watching her head back to Helen's house.

The woman was nice enough, he supposed. She was also related to his neighbor, who seemed completely sane.

So what was the deal with cousin Maggie? He still hadn't decided if she was a dog whisperer, a psychic, or a snoop.

Shaking his head, unable to decide which, Max returned to the house, planning to put the collar away until he began to have second thoughts.

He only pondered the decision for a moment or two.

"Why not?" he muttered. Hemingway would probably be a good icebreaker this evening. He'd also keep the kids occupied while the adults had some time to themselves.

So he went to the back door and called the dog in.

"Do you want to go play with your friends?" he asked.

The wooly mutt responded with a little bark and a wagging tail.

"Okay, then. Let's put this on you. We can't very well go without looking our best, huh?"

For a moment, Max's thoughts took a romantic turn, but not for long. He wasn't about to compete with another man for a woman's affection. He'd been in that position once before and had refused to play the game. Instead, he would talk to Carly about the manuscript.

He'd dropped it off at her house Tuesday morning. Of course, she probably hadn't had time to read it yet, but he was looking forward to talking to her about it anyway.

Five minutes later, with Hemingway in the backseat, Max arrived at the Westbrook house, a single-story tract home on Canyon Drive.

"I probably ought to have my head examined for bringing you along," he told the dog, as he got out of the car and opened the passenger door.

He grabbed Hemingway by the Christmas collar, with its battery-operated lights blinking and twinkling, and snapped on the leash. Then, after locking up his vehicle, he walked the dog to the front door and rang the bell.

Hemingway stood at his side, wagging his tail like crazy, undoubtedly hearing the kids inside.

As the door swung open, Max was greeted by both boys, who appeared a little apprehensive upon seeing him—until they laid eyes on Hemingway.

"Hey, look at his collar," Josh said. "It lights up and everything."

The boys bent over the happy dog, scratching his back and stroking his ears. Hemingway, it seemed, was in heaven with all the attention.

"Can he come and play with us?" the younger boy asked, as he looked up at Max with wide-eyed wonder.

"It's okay with me," Max said, "but maybe it would be best if you took him outside to do that."

"Okay," Mikey said, "but can he come into our room first so we can show him our toys and stuff?"

"He's housebroken, so it's all right with me, but you'll have to ask your mom."

"She won't mind." The little guy dropped to his knees and greeted Hemingway like a long-lost friend.

The dog, his tail wagging across the floor like an automatic whisk broom, wasn't any less excited to see the boys, which convinced Max that it had been a good idea to bring him after all.

He hated to admit that Maggie might have been right—and not just earlier this evening.

You know, she'd told him, *your dog would be much happier if he had kids to play with on a regular basis.*

Max couldn't argue that. Hemingway probably would prefer to live with Carly and her sons, rather than with him.

The boys would be better off, too. At least, if they had a four-legged playmate around all the time, they might be more apt to stick around the house and stay out of trouble.

The same could be said for Hemingway, who wouldn't need to roam the neighborhood looking for excitement any longer.

Of course, if Max were to make an offer like that, he'd miss the crazy mutt.

There was also another reason to hang on to the dog, one that wasn't selfish.

Pets were both time consuming and expensive, so it was safe to assume that Carly couldn't afford the extra expense of dog food, vet bills, or an occasional new shirt for a neighbor.

On top of that, if she was forced to move to an apartment, she wouldn't be allowed to have animals, especially a big one that could be loud and clumsy at times.

No, giving Hemingway to the Westbrooks would only end up dumping more problems on Carly, something Max wouldn't do.

As footsteps sounded an approach, he looked up and spotted her coming his way, just as pretty as he'd remembered.

Maybe more so.

She had on a pair of snug-fitting denim jeans that could entice a man, as well as an oversized sweatshirt with a colorful Mother Goose appliqué that insisted she hadn't given flirtation a single thought.

After aiming a welcoming smile at Max, she placed her hand on the oldest son's shoulder and asked, "What are you boys doing?"

"Playing with the dog," the little one said.

"But you're making Max—I mean, Mr. Tolliver—stand out in the cold."

"Oops. Excuse me." Josh took the dog by the collar and led him through the living room. "Come on, Hemingway."

The boys didn't need the leash—or even the collar, for that matter. Hemingway would have followed them anywhere.

Now, as the two adults stood in the open doorway, Max returned his gaze to Carly, whose cheeks were flushed a pretty shade of pink.

"I'm sorry," she said, stepping aside to let him in, "I really have tried to teach them manners."

He was sure that she had. "Don't worry about it. I haven't forgotten what it's like to be a kid—even if the boys might have told you otherwise."

She flashed him a grin, her green eyes sparkling, then closed the door.

As Max entered the cozy living room, with its hardwood floors, green walls, and overstuffed furniture with brightly colored decorator pillows, he spotted an antique rocking chair next to the brick fireplace, its white mantel laden with picture frames.

A forest green throw draped along the back of the old chair hid most of the wooden spindles, but it was similar to one he remembered seeing at his grandparents' house when he'd been a boy.

"I like your rocker," he said. "My grandma used to have one like that."

"I wish I could say that it's a family heirloom, but I picked it up at a garage sale a few years back."

"You made a good purchase," he said, deciding the only thing missing in the room was a fire in the hearth. "It looks good in your living room."

She smiled. "Thanks."

They continued to stand in the center of the room, with him making more out of her décor than he would have normally done, but for a writer, he found himself at a loss for words this evening.

"In fact," he added, trying to shake the awkwardness, "you've got a nice house."

"Thank you. I'm going to miss living here when we move, but that's life. God must have another home in mind for us."

Max didn't know about that.

"Can I take your coat?" she asked.

"Sure." He removed the fleece-lined jacket and handed it to her.

As she hung it up on an antique coat tree by the door, he noted a plaque on the wall—one of several—entitled "Footsteps in the Sand." On the other side of the entry, he spotted one of a couple of cherubs.

The simple artwork added to the warm and cozy feeling he had the minute he stepped into her house.

As he inhaled the spicy aroma of whatever she'd been cooking, he said, "Something sure smells good."

"I made tacos tonight. I hope that's okay with you."

"It's more than okay. I love Mexican food, so this is a treat. Thanks for inviting me to dinner."

"You're welcome." She led him to the overstuffed sofa, with a beige-green-and-brown plaid print. "I just need a few more minutes in the kitchen. Why don't you have a seat?"

"Can I help with something?"

"No, I've got everything under control."

As he settled onto the sofa, he said, "Did you get a chance to look at my manuscript yet?"

"I've just read the first two chapters. When I started getting tired, I set it aside. I didn't want to miss anything."

"I appreciate that." He hated to quiz her, but since she didn't offer up any comments, he couldn't help pressing her just a little. "So what do you think so far?"

"You're a good writer, Max. The story opens with action, which was intriguing."

Max had hoped the readers would feel that way. And knowing that Carly had been hooked from the start meant a lot, although he wasn't sure why he valued her opinion so much.

Still, since she hadn't gotten to Priscilla's introductory scene yet, there wasn't much they could discuss tonight.

"Would you rather have the kids play outside with the dog?" he asked. "I think they went into the bedroom."

"No, it's getting cold, so they really need to stay in the house."

He nodded, then struggled to come up with something more to say. They really had very little in common, although he wished that wasn't the case.

"Speaking of the kids," he said, "I'm willing to talk to Josh. How do you want me to go about that?"

"I'm not sure. I was hoping you'd have some idea how to broach the subject."

Max thought on it for a moment, then said, "I'll check on Hemingway, then try to strike up a conversation with him."

"That should work. And while you're gone, I'll put the food on the table."

As Max got to his feet and started in the direction the boys had taken his dog, he realized he had a lot more experience talking to hardened defendants who'd broken the law than twelve-year-old boys.

Hopefully, he wouldn't blow it and let Carly down.

Josh thought it was pretty cool that his mom would invite a dog over for dinner, even if Hemingway wasn't sitting next to them at the table, munching on tacos and dipping tortilla chips into salsa.

It was also nice to see how excited Mikey was to have Hemingway in their room. For a kid who'd been scared of the dog at first—and scared of his own shadow most of the time—Mikey sure had taken to the big, hairy mutt.

Of course, Josh couldn't blame him for that. Hemingway had grown on both of them.

Too bad they didn't have a dog of their own. If they did, Mikey would have a watchdog to protect him and wouldn't need Josh to sleep in the same room with him anymore. Then Josh could have a place where he could hang out alone, just like he used to before their dad moved out.

A light *rap-rap-rap* sounded on the doorjamb, and Josh looked up to see Mr. Tolliver.

"Come in," he said.

It was weird having the man at their house tonight, just like he was a regular visitor. But if he was going to be their mom's boss, at least while she edited his book, he and Mikey would have to get used to seeing him around.

But that meant they could probably see Hemingway, too.

"How's it going?" Mr. Tolliver asked.

"Okay."

"Mind if I take a seat?"

"No, go ahead." Instead of looking at him as he sat on the edge of the mattress, just a couple of feet away, Josh studied his little brother and the dog.

"Has that bully been bothering you anymore?"

"Not really. I know how to stay out of his way." Josh expected the man to try and talk him into tattling on Ross "the Boss," like his mom kept doing.

"I'm glad to hear that."

They just sat like that for a while, and Josh decided it was nice not to have an adult insist you do something you didn't want to do, like snitching on someone and setting yourself up to be called a crybaby for the rest of your life.

"Of course," Mr. Tolliver said, "it's wrong to let that guy get away with bullying kids. Some of them might not be as tough as you are."

He was right about Ross picking on other people, but Josh

didn't feel that much tougher than anyone else. Of course, he wouldn't let Tolliver know that, so he said, "That guy isn't all that scary."

If Mr. Tolliver thought Josh was lying, he didn't say anything. Instead, he glanced at the dog and chuckled. "Hemingway sure seems to like you and your brother."

"Yeah, I know."

They watched the dog and Mikey for a while, and it was kind of funny. Mikey set up his *Star Wars* figures, told Hemingway he could be Chewbacca, then stuck the plastic character in the dog's mouth.

"Do you think he'll chew up that toy?" Mr. Tolliver asked.

"Mikey probably won't care if he does."

"I have a feeling you're right."

Josh hadn't planned on talking to the man, but for some reason, he couldn't help adding, "Me and my brother were afraid of your dog at first. We thought he was mean when we heard him bark. Then, when we actually saw him, we thought he looked like a Yeti or a werewolf, know what I mean?"

Josh stole a glance at the man, saw him smile and nod.

"I thought the same thing when I found him on my porch," he said.

For a minute, it almost seemed like they had something in common, which was impossible.

Still, they watched in silence as Mikey showed Hemingway his Millennium Falcon and pointed out how the doors opened, how the control panel lit up. You'd think that the dog was another kid who cared about stuff like that.

But maybe he did. Hemingway seemed to be amazed at everything Mikey said or did.

Josh shot another peek at Mr. Tolliver. He'd never really liked the guy, never trusted him, but he didn't seem so bad now.

When the man turned and caught Josh's eye, he said, "You look kind of . . . troubled."

Josh shrugged. He had a lot on his mind these days, and not just because Ross "the Boss" was a jerk. But he wasn't going to open his mouth and start whining about it.

"Is something bothering you?" Mr. Tolliver asked point-blank.

Josh shrugged again.

"Is it me? Are you sorry that I came over tonight?"

"No, it's not that."

The silence seemed to grow into this big, dark, hulking shadow that was sucking all the air out of the room, but Josh did his best to ignore it.

"Are you mad at your mom?" he asked.

"Why would you think *that*?"

"Well, you said it wasn't me. And I doubt that it's your brother or the dog. So that only leaves one other person in the house to bug you."

Josh loved his mom; he really did. It's just that . . . Well, he didn't want to talk about it with anyone.

"It's not her," he said.

"Then who is it?"

Like Josh was going to answer that question. "What makes you think something's bothering me?"

"Sometimes you have a scowl on your face, like your dog died, and you don't even have one."

He shrugged. "Yeah, well, it's no big deal. I can handle it."

"I know you can, but just so you know, your mom's worried about you."

She was? Sometimes Josh figured that she didn't think about him at all.

The silence came back, and when Josh turned to Mr. Tolliver, the guy was looking at him like he could see right through him.

So what was he? A psychic or something?

Yet for some reason—maybe because he was the one who'd come to his rescue when he'd chased off Ross "the

Boss"—Josh found himself admitting what was really bothering him. "Okay, so I do get a little mad at her sometimes."

"Why's that?"

"I don't know. I guess it's the stuff she does."

"Like what?"

Josh looked at his brother, who was so wound up showing the dog all of his *Star Wars* characters that he wasn't paying any attention to the man talk going on around him.

Still, Josh lowered his voice anyway. "She treats me like a little kid sometimes, and then like an adult two seconds later."

"And you don't like that?"

"Would you? Sometimes, when I just want to be a kid, she treats me like an adult, asking me to do all kinds of things, like babysit, put laundry in the washer, clean up the living room. . . . Then, when I want to go out with my friends and hang out, she forgets all the chores I do and treats me like a baby. She forgets that I'm almost a teenager."

"I can understand why that would bother you."

Could he?

"You need to level with her," he said. "Not when you're angry with her, of course, but when you're both in a good mood. You might be surprised at how well she takes it."

Josh wasn't sure if he believed that or not.

It was weird having a man-to-man chat with a guy like Mr. Tolliver, but it was also kind of cool.

"Communication is the key to a good relationship," he added.

"Sometimes it's hard to talk about stuff you're thinking about, especially if you don't want to fight."

"Yeah, I know. But if a man really cares about a woman, he's got to bite the bullet and open up."

"Oh yeah?" Josh turned to the man seated beside him, only to notice a weird look on his face, like he was eating something that didn't taste very good.

When he caught Josh studying him, he gave a little shrug. "Well, I guess that's what a man ought to do."

Josh wondered if Mr. Tolliver used to get mad at his mother, too. And if he remembered not talking to her about it.

If that was the case, then maybe they had a lot more in common than he'd thought.

Chapter 14

Carly hadn't cooked dinner for a man in years, but she knew they usually had hearty appetites, something she hadn't considered until she'd looked into the pan of hamburger that cooked on the stove.

Worried that there might not be enough meat, she'd taken a raw potato and peeled it, then using the large side of the cheese grater, she'd shred it into the hamburger to stretch the taco filling. It had been a trick her mom had used on occasion, and Carly was glad she'd paid attention.

After taking a bite of the finished product, which was pretty tasty even before she'd added tomato sauce and spices, she'd decided that Max would never suspect that she'd added the potato so there'd be plenty for him to eat this evening.

If he mentioned anything about the ingredients or the taste, she'd tell him it was an old family recipe—and, in a sense, it was.

Now, looking over the meal she'd prepared and realizing that everything was done, she was at a bit of a loss. The table was already set. She'd also grated the cheese and chopped the tomatoes and lettuce, which were now in three separate bowls and ready for everyone to fill their own tacos.

Earlier, before Max had arrived, she'd made Spanish rice and refried beans, both of which simmered in pots on the stove. So there wasn't much left for her to do, other than fill the serving bowls.

She glanced at the clock on the oven, noting that Max had been with the boys for a while. Did that mean that Josh was opening up to him? She sure hoped so.

With nothing else to do, she fried a dozen corn tortillas, bending them in the middle so they'd be easier to fill when they were crisp. Then she called everyone to dinner—whether their talk had ended or not.

As Mikey entered the kitchen with the dog on his heels, he asked, "What about Hemingway? Where's he supposed to eat?"

"He had dinner before we came," Max said. "Why don't I put him out into the backyard until we finish eating?"

Mikey agreed, although reluctantly, and moments later, they were all seated around the kitchen table.

With the boys in the room, the conversation seemed to flow much easier than it had when Max had first arrived and Carly hadn't known quite what to say to him. Yet that didn't mean she felt compelled to join in their chats about the Chargers or television shows they'd seen recently.

She was more interested in the talk that had gone on between Max and Josh earlier, but no matter how eager she was for answers, she couldn't bring up that subject while the boys were present. So she waited until after dinner, when everyone had eaten their ice cream and the kids had taken Hemingway back to their room.

After serving Max a cup of coffee and pouring one for herself, Carly finally asked, "Did you and Josh get a chance to talk?"

"Yes, we did, but he's pretty tight-lipped." Max added a single spoonful of sugar into his mug, then took a sip. "That's probably because he doesn't trust me yet."

"So you weren't able to find out what's bothering him?"

"Not exactly, but I do know he's feeling as though he's doing more than his share to help out around the house."

Carly wasn't sure whether she wanted to defend herself or admit she'd been wrong.

Neither, she supposed.

"Do you agree?" she asked. "Do you think I've asked too much of him?"

"There's a big difference between reality and a person's perception of it. So it's hard to say." Max returned his cup to the table, then wrapped both hands around it, appearing to be giving the situation some thought. After a beat, he looked up and caught her gaze. "I still think the bully might be part of the problem."

"Why do you say that?"

"When I asked him about the boy, he insisted that he wasn't worried."

"And you don't believe him?"

"It's difficult for a guy to admit that he's afraid or that he's vulnerable, no matter what his age. It's easier to pretend he's tough and that nothing bothers him, even when it does."

Before Carly could comment, Max grew silent. Tearing his gaze from hers, he peered into his cup.

Was he thinking about Josh? Or was he merely as pensive and cryptic as her son seemed to be lately?

Desperate for answers and a solution to whatever was bothering Josh, she prodded for more details. "Did he tell you anything else?"

"Not really, but it's kind of weird." Max looked up from his cup, and their eyes met. "While I was talking to him, I found myself offering a little advice I probably should have taken myself in the past."

"What do you mean?"

He slowly shook his head, shutting her out, it seemed. "Nothing, I guess. It's too late to beat myself up about it now."

She wasn't sure if he'd been thinking about an issue he'd had with his own mother or something else entirely. But either way, he clearly didn't want to talk about it, and she had no way of connecting dots that weren't there.

Max Tolliver wasn't an easy man to read.

Speaking of reading . . .

"I should be finished with your manuscript by Sunday," she said, deciding to change the subject. "Do you want to meet and talk about it then?"

"Sure. Should we meet at a coffee shop? Or do you want me to come by here?"

"That's up to you. I'll probably take the kids to the early service at church, but we're usually out by ten."

"Then I'll come over about eleven," he said, "if that's okay with you."

She offered him a smile. "I'll have a pot of coffee brewing."

"Well," he said, getting to his feet. "I probably ought to take off. I don't want to keep you from whatever you do in the evenings."

What *did* she normally do? After fixing dinner for the boys, she washed the dishes. She usually put a batch of clothes in the washing machine and stewed over the check register more often than was healthy.

Still, as she pushed her own chair back and stood, she didn't dare admit that his visit tonight—and having his manuscript to read—were the highlight of her week.

Max gathered his cup and saucer, then reached for hers. "I'll help you with the dishes."

"No, you don't have to do that. I've got the kitchen clean already. It's just a matter of filling the dishwasher."

"Are you sure you don't need any help?"

Just talking to him about Josh had been helpful enough, so she offered him another smile. "Absolutely. It'll only take me a couple of minutes."

"All right then."

She followed him to the boys' room, where the dog was

sitting with Mikey in the midst of the *Star Wars* toys, and Josh was lying on his bed, thumbing through a book.

"Hemingway, it's time to go," Max said.

Mikey glanced up and frowned. "Aw, does he have to go?"

"I'm afraid so," Max said. "Your mom would shoot me if I left her with the dishes *and* a dog who can be more trouble than he's worth."

"He wasn't any trouble for me," Mikey said.

Max chuckled. "I can see that."

"Maybe Mr. Tolliver will bring his dog back when he comes over on Sunday," Carly said.

"I'd be happy to." Max turned to Carly and shot her a crooked grin. "At least, as long as your mom doesn't mind."

"She doesn't care." Mikey shot a hope-filled glance at Carly. "Do you, Mom?"

"Actually," she said, crossing her arms and turning to Max with a smile. "Having Hemingway come over to play is the next best thing to owning a pet of our own. We can have some of the fun and none of the work."

"Then I'm glad we could be of help."

Moments later, Max had the dog on a leash. After he'd said good-bye to the boys, Carly walked him to the door and out onto the front porch. As their gazes met and locked, that same sense of awkwardness that had buzzed between them when he'd arrived this evening, started up all over again, although she didn't know why it would.

"Thanks again for dinner," he said. "It was a real treat. I haven't had a home-cooked meal in a long time."

It was only tacos, she wanted to say. *Wait until you try my pot roast.*

Instead, she said, "You're welcome. I'll see you on Sunday."

He nodded, then led his dog to his car.

At that point, Carly could have returned to the house, but for some reason, she waited until he got into his car and started the engine.

It seemed that she'd had an ally tonight—albeit an unlikely one.

And she hated to see him go.

Feeling more melancholy than she had in ages, Lynette sat in the comfort of her living room, a red cashmere throw draped over her legs. It was quiet and peaceful tonight—no music playing on the stereo, no wind blowing in the trees.

As she sipped a cup of chamomile tea, she found herself almost mesmerized as she stared at the fireplace, where gas flames blazed over artificial logs.

Breaking her concentration yet again, she glanced at the telephone that lay on the cushion beside her, tempted to pick it up.

Three different times she'd initiated a call to Susan this evening, only to reach for the receiver, dial the first few numbers, and then disconnect the line.

Without a doubt, she owed her friend an apology, which would be easier to make over the phone than in person, yet she still couldn't seem to follow through with it.

Not that she didn't want to make things right with Susan—she did. She just found it difficult to open her heart and apologize, then risk having the attempt thrown back in her face.

It's not that she couldn't acknowledge making a mistake. Goodness, she'd made plenty of them in her life—and would undoubtedly make many more before it was all said and done—but asking for someone's forgiveness had always been a struggle.

Well, not always.

One wintery December, when Lynette had been about seven or eight, she and her mother had to spend a couple of days in a homeless shelter, thanks to her stepdad, who'd run out on them the month before and had taken the rent money with him.

Desperate to provide a better option for shelter, Mama had placed a call to her great-aunt, a wealthy widow who'd agreed to let them move in with her temporarily.

"But just until you get back on your feet," Aunt Pauline had said. "I'm not used to having children underfoot, and I value my privacy."

Mama had assured Pauline that Lynette was a good little girl, that she wouldn't be a problem. So they'd packed up what few belongings they had and moved into the upscale, two-bedroom condo in Point Loma.

At first, having a warm bed in which to sleep had been a godsend, and Great-Aunt Pauline had been their savior. But it wasn't long before the older woman, who wore long acrylic nails and had steel gray hair, revealed a harsh and selfish side that Lynette had seen firsthand.

She could still recall that cold afternoon, just days before Christmas, when everything had changed, when she'd made a mistake that had triggered the end of their stay in paradise.

Pauline had insisted upon keeping her bedroom door closed, but on that fateful day the cleaning lady had left it wide open.

Lynette, who'd been on her way to the bathroom down the hall, had peered into the pink and frilly retreat. To a poor child who'd spent most of her life wearing hand-me-downs, the room seemed to be suited to royalty.

A dressing table, with its oval mirror and satin-padded chair, displayed a vast assortment of creams, lotions, and beauty supplies—each in a colorful container.

Mama had never been able to afford those kinds of luxuries, so, being a curious child, Lynette had wandered into the room, drawn to the table that she could imagine belonging to a princess.

Intrigued by a delicate lavender perfume bottle and unable to help herself, she'd lifted the lid to take a sniff of the floral scent. In her wide-eyed wonder, her fingers had trembled, and she accidentally dropped the glass bottle onto the floor, where the expensive liquid spilled onto the light-colored carpet.

Mortified and guilt-ridden, Lynette had tried her best to clean it up, although the fragrance seemed to permeate the walls, drapes, and bedding, reminding her that she'd never be able to make things right.

When Aunt Pauline got home, she'd been on her hands and knees, sopping up what she could with a fluffy white bath towel. The woman had swept into the room and shrieked, "How *could* you? After all I've done for you and your mother."

Lynette had wanted to seep into the carpet, along with the perfume, but all she could do was apologize. "I'm *so* sorry, Aunt Pauline."

But the woman, who'd been glaring at her as though she wanted to slap her to the moon and back, had hurtled a far more painful blow. "Don't expect me to accept your apology, you stupid child. You never should have touched my belongings in the first place."

At that, Lynette, who'd been on her way to the bathroom for a good reason before being sidetracked, had done something horrid, something she'd never forget.

She'd wet herself.

"*Betsy!*" Aunt Pauline had shrieked. "Come in here right this instant and get your little brat before I throw you both back out on the street!"

At least she hadn't kicked them out at that moment, but the very next morning, Lynette and her mom had returned to the shelter.

From then on, Lynette had kept to herself a lot of the time, which meant she didn't step on anyone's toes very often.

Of course, she could handle making mistakes. After all, no one was perfect. But the subsequent apologies were another story.

It was only after she'd begun to date Peter Tidball that she'd started to socialize, at least on a small scale. With Peter at her side, she felt as though she could handle just about anything.

And then she'd met Helen, who'd invited her to play poker with the Lils.

Now here she was, back at square one.

She might be seated in the lap of luxury, so to speak, yet she still hated the idea of humbling herself and fearing that her words, no matter how sincere, wouldn't be enough.

If Susan had merely grumbled about her displeasure this afternoon, Lynette would have just pretended that nothing had happened—a successful ploy she'd used with Peter when she'd inadvertently said or done the wrong thing. And then she would have invited her to lunch in an effort to put things to right.

But Susan hadn't been a *little* upset, she'd been furious.

"How *could* you?" she'd shrieked, her face distorted with emotion.

You stupid child could have just as easily rolled off the tip of her tongue, although she'd shown enough class to stomp off in a huff instead.

Still, there'd been no question about it. Susan was undoubtedly enraged. And while she wasn't at all like Aunt Pauline, she probably wasn't likely to accept an apology and let bygones be bygones.

In fact, reminding Susan of the thoughtless comments Lynette had made might only make matters worse. What if she didn't want to be friends anymore? Or more devastating than that, what if the other Lils took sides and sympathized with the woman who'd been hurt?

For that reason, Lynette would give it another day or so, allowing Susan to blow off a little steam.

On Saturday night, before Lynette came to babysit, Carly stopped by the market to pick up a few things for the boys' dinner.

She had several boxes of macaroni and cheese in the pantry,

since that particular dish had become a low-cost staple at her house over the past six months, but she couldn't very well expect Lynette to make a meal out of it. So she'd decided to splurge again this evening by picking up a pound of chicken to bake, as well as lettuce and tomatoes for a simple green salad.

Now, as Carly pushed the cart through the aisles, she couldn't help wishing she hadn't agreed to go out with Grant tonight. The last thing the boys needed was for her to bring a man into their lives, especially when she and Josh were experiencing a strain in their relationship.

Things did seem to be a little better between the two of them since Max's talk with the boy, although that could also be the result of her making a conscious effort not to ask too much of him.

It was a fine line to draw, though. How much was too much?

After picking up a package of drumsticks and thighs, which had been the advertised special this week, she made her way to the produce aisle and grabbed a head of iceberg lettuce and a single tomato. She was tempted to buy a cucumber, too, since it was easy to see Lynette had been used to the good life, but Carly didn't have much spare cash.

She could, of course, use her credit card, something she didn't mind doing since Max's check would be coming. But she hadn't finished critiquing his manuscript yet, so she hated to spend money she hadn't even earned.

If all went according to plan, she'd see the money soon. She'd read several more chapters last night, and four more this morning. Unless something unexpected came up, she would finish before Max came over for coffee on Sunday.

To be honest, she didn't particularly care for the action/adventure genre, but she had to admit that the writing was clean and strong.

That didn't mean she hadn't found a few problems with

the characters or the story, but she'd talk to Max about it tomorrow. Hopefully, he'd take her criticism well.

After making one last glance at her cart, she headed for the checkout lines, only to stop short when she nearly ran into another cart.

"Excuse me," she said, glancing up to see none other than Max Tolliver himself.

He seemed just as surprised to see her as she was to see him, until a slow smile stretched across his face.

"Out of cold medicine again?" he asked.

"No, this time, I'm here for food."

They just stood there a moment, caught up in something that didn't matter. Not when she had to get home so she could get ready for her date—what had possessed her to say yes?

Shaking off thoughts of dinner with Grant, she asked, "How about you? Another bout of writer's block?"

"This time it's by choice. I'm taking a break until I talk to you." He shrugged, then tossed her a you-know-how-it-is grin. "So how's the reading going?"

"I'm almost finished."

"Good."

She glanced down at his cart, planning to take inventory again, but it was empty. He'd obviously just entered the market.

He had a tight grip on the handle, though, as if he wasn't sure whether to move one way or the other.

To be honest, she wasn't too sure where to go, either.

"I guess we can talk more about it on Sunday," he said.

She nodded, yet continued to block the aisle with her cart.

"Don't you have a date tonight?" he asked.

"Yes, I do." And that meant she really needed to go.

So why wasn't she moving on?

"Then I'd better let you go," he said. "Have fun."

"Thanks." She offered him an upbeat smile, even though

she'd been having second thoughts about going out with Grant. But she couldn't back out this late in the game.

"I'll see you on Sunday," he said, moving his cart so she could get around it.

As she made her way to the checkout lanes, she couldn't help glancing over her shoulder, taking a peek to see if Max was anywhere nearby.

He wasn't, of course, and she really hadn't expected him to be. So what was with the whisper of disappointment?

For some reason, she found herself even more attracted to the man, even though he really wasn't her type.

She and her boys were the proverbial package deal, and she had no reason to believe that Max Tolliver had a paternal bone in his body. Up until their discussions about his book, Josh and Mikey had been driving him crazy. So any interest in Max Tolliver was completely misplaced.

Of course, getting involved with Grant Barrows wouldn't be any different. Carly didn't have anything to offer either of the men. Her financial situation was so precarious right now that she'd be embarrassed to share all of that with anyone, let alone someone she was dating.

After paying for her purchase, she carried the bag to her car, climbed in, and started the engine. But instead of rushing home to get ready, she found herself making a leisurely drive instead.

Why had she agreed to have dinner with a man she hardly knew? She certainly didn't need that kind of pressure at a time like this.

Minutes later, when she arrived at the house, she parked the car and reached for her groceries. Even when she pushed LOCK on the remote, she found herself heading for the mailbox instead of the house.

There probably wasn't anything in there that couldn't wait until later tonight or tomorrow morning, but it would only take a minute or so to get it. So she reached inside and removed a handful of mail—mostly advertisements aimed at those who still had Christmas shopping to do.

On her way to the front door, she thumbed through the rest of it—mostly junk that would end up in the recycle bin—and spotted a card. When she recognized Sharon Garvey's familiar script, her heart warmed. She couldn't wait to get inside and see what her friend had to say.

The last envelope, which was from the bank that had financed her car, looked . . . important. *Way* too important.

Unable to help herself, she opened it on the spot, pulled out the official letter, and scanned the words.

What?

No way. She couldn't be more than two months behind on her payments. There had to be a mistake. She'd paid them something on the first.

Or had she?

She'd been robbing from Peter to pay Paul for so long, she could have slipped up.

No, no. That wasn't possible. She'd sent them a check two weeks ago. Their letter and her payment must have crossed in the mail, and with the holidays, the post office was probably backed up.

Momentarily relieved, she entered the house and carried the grocery bag into the kitchen. All she needed was to risk having her car repossessed. Without wheels, she couldn't get to work. And without a job . . . ?

Well, she wouldn't think about that right now. If she did, she might end up stewing about all of her troubles until they threatened to drag her under for the count.

Instead, she had a date on which to focus. And for the first time since agreeing to go out with Grant Barrows, she wondered if it might turn out to be a welcome diversion after all.

Chapter 15

Lynette rang Carly's doorbell at a quarter to six on Saturday night, wishing the butterflies in her stomach would ease up and give her a break.

Who would have thought that being a matchmaker would be so stressful? Or was it the babysitting gig that had her tummy a mess?

Before she could give it any more thought, the door swung open and Carly invited her in.

"You look great," Lynette said, noting the classic black dress Carly had on, as well as the fresh application of lipstick, mascara, and eye shadow.

Carly tugged at her hemline. "It's not too short, is it? I haven't worn this in years. . . ."

"It's perfect." And so was her hair, which had a glossy sheen and curled at the shoulders.

Carly sighed, then looked down at her bare feet, the nails polished a Christmas shade of red. "I'm almost ready. I just have to slip on a pair of heels."

"Even your toes look nice," Lynette said. "New pedicure?"

"Everyone at the salon trades services. And when Monique, the manicurist, heard I was going out tonight, she insisted I come in early so she could do my nails and toes. But to tell you the truth, I'm not even sure why I agreed to go to dinner with Grant tonight. I'm really nervous."

"Don't be. He's a great guy, and you two are going to have a good time."

"Maybe so, but I haven't had a date in . . . Well, before I married Derek. So fifteen years, I guess."

While Carly seemed to ponder the passage of time, Lynette scanned the living room. When she saw that the coast was clear, she lowered her voice to a whisper. "As long as we're making confessions, I've got to admit that I'm nervous, too."

"Really? Why's that?"

"Because I've never babysat before, so I have no idea what I'm doing here."

"No kidding?" Carly furrowed her brow.

Uh-oh. Lynette wondered if Carly was merely surprised by the admission or taken aback by it. Had she expected someone with experience would be looking after her sons?

"Are you okay with that?" Lynette asked.

"The boys can pretty much take care of themselves. All you need to do is referee if they have a squabble or be a voice of reason if they want to do something that isn't safe or could upset the neighbors." Her laugh, which was more of a jittery giggle, suggested she hadn't been blowing smoke when she'd admitted to being nervous.

Lynette couldn't blame her for that. If she'd been the one waiting for Grant to arrive, she'd probably be a jumble of nerves, too.

That thought was a little unsettling, though. She'd actually grown comfortable around the man and liked to think that they'd struck up a friendship, but if he could evoke a case of the jitters . . . ?

Shaking off the possibility that she might actually be attracted to him, she said, "I'll do my best to keep them out of trouble."

"If you find something on television that they're interested in, the evening should pass quickly."

Lynette would keep that in mind. The sooner this night was over and she could go home, the better.

She wondered if Carly was thinking the same thing.

Probably.

"By the way," Carly said, "dinner's almost ready. I assumed you'd be hungry, too, so there's plenty. I've got chicken baking in the oven and a green salad in the fridge. There's a package of macaroni and cheese on the counter. You can whip that up, too—if you'd like to. There's also ice cream in the freezer for dessert."

"Sounds good." Lynette made another scan of her surroundings, this time taking in the décor of Carly's living room, with its pale green walls, hardwood floor, and overstuffed furniture.

The addition of a few antiques, as well as the plaques and prints that had been added here and there, were nice touches. All in all, Carly had a cozy place—nothing fancy, yet warm and inviting.

A couple of stockings hung from the mantel, and a few other Christmas decorations adorned the tabletops. But she wasn't quite ready for Christmas.

"Where are you going to put your tree?" Lynette asked.

"We're not going to have one this year. I'd rather use the money to buy the boys each a present."

Lynette had known that Carly was going through a rough time financially, and while she and her mother had rarely celebrated a traditional Christmas as a child, she knew that wasn't the norm for most kids, and she couldn't help feeling sorry for Carly and her sons.

The doorbell rang, and Carly froze in her steps, her eyes growing wide and panicky. "Oh, no. That must be Grant. Will you please get it? I need to get my shoes on."

If Lynette hadn't been suffering from another burst of tummy flutters herself, she might have gotten a chuckle out of the other woman's reaction. As it was, she answered the door.

It was Grant, all right. Gorgeous as he was, with his

shorter hair and those big blue eyes, she hardly recognized him without his trademark Tommy Bahama style.

Tonight he was dressed *GQ* casual in dark slacks, a sports jacket, and . . . oh, wow . . . a killer cologne that made her want to relish a second whiff and then a third.

Okay, so she'd seen him decked out in his suit that day he'd gone on the job interview, but she hadn't realized he might actually have a variety of clothing in his closet.

What other secrets had she yet to uncover about him?

For a long, stretched-out moment, their gazes met and locked. Neither of them spoke or moved until Lynette shook off the momentary blip in her radar and gained control of her senses.

"Carly's almost ready," she said, stepping aside to let Grant into the house. "She'll be out in just a minute. Come on in."

Before Lynette could suggest that Grant take a seat, Carly came out looking even better in black spiky heels than she had in her bare feet.

"Wow," he said. "You look nice."

"Thanks, so do you."

Lynette had never liked awkward moments like this, but she had to admit she was thinking the same thing. The two really did make a sharp-looking couple, and for some reason, just knowing that caused Lynette to realize she was standing on the outside looking in, much as she'd done all through those geeky high school years.

"Are you ready to go?" Grant asked Carly.

"As soon as I introduce Lynette to the boys. It'll just take a minute."

Carly slipped off down the hall, leaving Lynette to feel like the proverbial third wheel when there were only two people in the room.

"I'm not sure what I'm going to do with the boys for the next couple of hours," she admitted, those butterflies in her stomach all fired up again. "I'm not used to being around kids."

"Don't you like children?"

"It's not that. It's just that . . . Well, I'm not sure I'll be able to relate to them."

"Did you forget what it was like to be a kid yourself?"

No, and that's what seemed to plague her adult years, if she'd let it. Instead she said, "I wasn't all that social growing up."

"What about babysitters? Did you ever have a good one you can try and emulate?"

No, she'd been left to fend for herself more often than not. "Not that I can remember."

Grant reached out and placed a hand on her shoulder, warming her from the inside out. "Just ask them if they'd like to play a game or watch television. You'll do fine."

She sure hoped so. She managed an appreciative smile. "You make it sound easy."

"It'll be a piece of cake."

Again, their gazes zeroed in on each other. And for a moment, she wished he was going to stay here with her. The kids would really like a guy like Grant, and with him around, watching them *would* be a piece of cake.

Before either of them could say anything else, Carly returned to the living room with both boys in tow.

The youngest was a cute little guy who appeared to be as nervous and awkward about the situation as Lynette was. The older boy seemed a little . . . grumpy.

Great. This was going to be tougher than she'd thought.

As Carly made the introductions, Lynette realized there wasn't a single person in the room who wasn't uncomfortable or unbalanced.

Other than Grant, maybe.

When she stole a peek at him, he winked at her, and her heart soared. Funny how a little nonverbal you-can-do-it seemed to settle her right down.

"Do you have my cell phone number?" Carly asked Lynette.

"Yes, but don't worry. The boys and I will be just fine."

Lynette, who still had plenty of doubts in spite of Grant's unwavering support, wondered if her words had actually convinced anyone that they'd all make it through the evening unscathed.

She sure hoped so.

And if her luck held out, Carly would return before the boys saw through her bluff.

Carly had never eaten at Maestro's, one of the newest restaurants in Fairbrook, but she passed it on her way home from the salon each day. So when Grant had asked if she'd like to eat there tonight, she'd been eager to try it.

Now, as they sat at a white linen-draped table, with a single red rose and flickering candlelight providing more ambiance than she'd expected, she still couldn't believe she'd agreed to go out with him—or with anyone else for that matter.

"So what do you think of the place?" he asked.

Carly gave the dining room another once-over, noting the white plaster walls, the dark wood beams, and the lush green plants hanging throughout. "I like the décor. It's got an old world charm, don't you think?"

He nodded. "And the food's good, too."

"Mine's even better than good." She'd ordered the pasta primavera, which was especially tasty and loaded with vegetables. She'd been hungry, but the portions were so generous that there was no way she'd be able to finish it all in one sitting.

"Then we made a good choice."

In coming to Maestro's? Maybe so, but Carly still wasn't convinced she should have agreed to go out with Grant in the first place. Not that he wasn't nice, respectful, charming, attractive. . . .

"Have you known Lynette very long?" he asked.

"Not really. I've been doing her hair for a couple of months now."

Grant lifted his wineglass and took a sip of the Chianti he'd ordered. "So you're not actually friends?"

Not really.

Had Lynette told him that they were?

Carly, who didn't want to contradict something Lynette might have said, lifted her napkin and blotted her lips. "We're becoming friends, though. Why do you ask?"

"No reason, I guess." He glanced down at his lasagna, his expression thoughtful.

Did he find it odd that one of Carly's new clients would take it upon herself to try and set them up? She had to admit, it was a little unusual.

When Grant finally looked up, he asked, "What do you know about her?"

"Lynette? Just that she's a widow in her thirties." For some reason, Carly felt a little disloyal, so she added, "She seems to be a nice person with a good heart."

He nodded as though he thought so, too, then asked, "Is she dating anyone herself?"

"Not that I know of. At least, she's never said one way or the other. To be honest, we've talked more in the past week than ever. I guess that's because of her trying to . . ."

"Play matchmaker with us?"

Carly believed that honesty was always the best policy, especially in this case, so she nodded. "I'm not sure why she thinks I need to have a man in my life. With work and my kids, I have very little free time. And on top of that, I'm having a few financial problems, which limits what I can afford to do. So it's not in anyone's best interest if I get romantically involved right now—no matter who that person is."

Grant tilted his head to the side, as if he was trying to figure out why, that being the case, that Carly had agreed to have dinner with him. She supposed she couldn't blame him, and if he asked her, she'd be hard-pressed to give him an answer.

So how was she going to get out of the corner in which she'd just backed herself?

"I'm not sure why I agreed to all of this," she admitted, hoping that an explanation of some kind would come to mind, although it didn't.

Grant smiled, then reached across the table and placed his hand over hers. "If it makes you feel better, I feel as though I sort of got roped into this, too. I'm not opposed to romance or a relationship right now, but I'm not looking for one. And for the record, I'm having some financial issues, too."

In one way it helped Carly to know that Grant understood just where she was coming from, yet in another, it made it all worse.

Should she offer to pay for her own meal? And if so, with what? Her credit card was getting dangerously close to being maxed out.

No, she couldn't afford dinner at a place like this without jeopardizing her rent money or her plan to buy the kids a little something for Christmas.

"Don't worry about it," he said.

About what? Had he sensed what she'd been stressing over? She sought out his gaze, hoping to read something in it, only to find a ray of compassion shining back at her.

His fingertips trailed across the top of her knuckles as he removed his hand from the top of hers. "You're a beautiful woman who's personable and a pleasure to be around. So if something works out between us, then so be it. And if not, no problem. Let's just enjoy the rest of the evening, okay?"

"Thanks, Grant. I feel the same way. You're a great guy— or at least, you seem to be." She managed a smile. "And someone is going to be lucky to date you—whether it's me or not."

"Then we're on the same page."

She sure hoped so. She really didn't need any more complications in her life right now, and with the way Josh was eyeing poor Grant when she'd introduced them earlier, a Christmas romance was sure to blow up in her face.

When Carly and Grant left, Lynette had stood on the porch and sent them off with her best wishes. But as she'd watched them get into Grant's car, she'd suffered an unexpected pang of regret.

She'd tried to shake it off and tell herself that she didn't need a man in her life, yet as Grant and Carly drove away, she wasn't so sure about that.

Unfortunately, even if she were to have a complete change of heart, there wasn't anything she could do about it at this point, because even if Carly didn't want to date Grant, Susan had next dibs on him. And Lynette wasn't about to do anything that would further jeopardize her friendship with the Lils—any of them.

Since Susan had gotten so upset about Lynette doing a little matchmaking, there was no telling what she'd do if she were to learn that Lynette actually wanted to date the guy herself. And what if the other Lils were to decide that Lynette had broken some kind of BFF code of honor?

Why, she'd lose the best friends she'd ever had, and she'd never risk doing something like that. Life was lonely enough.

So she'd closed the door and turned to face the troops, only to see the oldest boy scowling at her.

"What's the matter?" she asked.

He crossed his arms and shifted his weight. "I don't need a babysitter."

Her first inclination was to either scowl back at him, or to break into tears of frustration. Instead, she blew out an exaggerated sigh and popped off with a little tongue-in-cheek sarcasm. "That's a relief. You have no idea how glad I am to hear that."

Are you serious? his morphing expression seemed to ask.

As serious as a heart attack, she was tempted to respond, but she wouldn't admit to that.

Instead, she shrugged. "I'm really not a babysitter, but it's probably best if you don't tell your mom that. I'm just here to hang out with you guys, maybe watch a little TV if we can find something cool, and play a game or two—if you have something in mind."

Before either boy could respond, an idea sparked, and she added, "I don't suppose you guys have a deck of cards we can use."

The older boy—Joshua—rolled his eyes. "If you're thinking about something like Go Fish, you can play with Mikey. I'm not into baby games."

"Neither am I," Lynette said. "The only card game I know is poker, but maybe that's too grown-up for you."

At that, the older boy brightened, straightened his shoulders, and stood a little taller. "Not for me. I'd be up for that."

"Okay, then." Lynette wasn't sure how Carly would feel about her boys playing poker, but she was glad to have found some common ground with them. Besides, someone must have taught them the ropes long before she came along.

"So where'd you learn to play poker?" she asked.

"Well," Josh said, losing some of his bluster, "I don't actually know the rules or anything, but I heard it was fun. And I've wanted to learn, so would you teach me?"

Before she could agree, the little one chimed in, "Will you teach *both* of us?"

She vacillated a moment between right and wrong, between adult and child, but not for long. What else was she going to do with them tonight?

So she gave in. "It's not hard to learn."

"There's a problem, though." Josh shoved his hands in his pockets and pulled out a couple of dollars and some change. "This is all the money we have, and since we're saving it to get our mom a Christmas gift, would it be okay if we played for baseball cards or marbles or something else?"

Teaching the kids to play poker was one thing, but gambling put a completely different spin on it. Maybe she'd better give this some thought. If she were to go so far as to teach them how to wager, even with something other than money, she'd be contributing to the delinquency of a minor, wouldn't she? And if so, what kind of babysitter would that make her?

Still, she could either go back to the awkward glances and scowls or come up with a better idea. And right now, she was at a loss when it came to options.

At least, bending the rules a little, she had their attention—and maybe even their respect. So she would just have to deal with any repercussions later.

"We don't have to play for money," she said. "I learned with matchsticks."

"Good." Josh glanced at the wadded-up cash and change in his hand. "It took a long time for us to collect this much, and we've already found every recyclable bottle and can there was in the canyon."

Touched that they'd go to that kind of trouble to buy their mom a present, Lynette smiled. "What are you going to get her?"

"We don't know yet. Maybe some lotion or something. She likes smelling good."

It might not sound like much to a lot of people, compared to the kinds of gifts Peter had bought Lynette while he was alive, but it was sure to please a mom.

In fact, it would certainly please Lynette, if she were their mother.

Maybe she could even chip in and help them buy something a little bigger, a little better.

She thought about the open, tissue-lined box that lay on her dining room table right now, bearing a present she'd just received in the mail from Peter's elderly aunt Mable.

It was a beautiful silk scarf that Lynette planned to return to Saks. She might have actually worn it if the color hadn't made her look a little green around the gills.

That shade of yellow would, however, look nice on Carly.

"Guess what?" she told the boys. "I have a perfect solution. I just received a gift today, and I was going to return it to the store because I don't have anything to wear it with. We could go to my house, you guys could look at it, and if you like it, I'll let you have it to give your mom."

"What is it?" Josh asked.

"A yellow scarf. And it will look great with that dress your mom wore tonight."

The boys looked at each other and shrugged.

"How much do you want for it?" Josh asked.

"Oh, no, you don't have to pay me. I'm just going to give it to you. It'll save me a trip to the Fashion Valley Mall."

"Cool." Josh tossed her an appreciative grin. "Thanks, Lynette. Should we go and get it now? While she's gone?"

"Well, since dinner is ready, let's eat first. Then we'll run to my house, pick it up, and be back in a snap."

Josh bit down on his bottom lip. "But what about poker?"

Lynette couldn't help but smile. "Don't worry about that. We'll still have plenty of time to play a few hands before your mom gets home."

And she'd been right. An hour later, the scarf, which the boys had marveled over, had been wrapped in gold foil paper that had been left over from several Christmases ago, adorned with a bow, brought back to the house, and hidden in the closet.

Now they were seated at Carly's kitchen table, holding the cards Josh had just dealt.

Babysitting, Lynette had decided over dinner, wasn't so tough after all. In fact, she'd be willing to do it again sometime—if Carly wanted her to.

The kids were really cute, although Josh would put up a real squawk if she was to tell him that to his face. Just being around them, listening to them talk, made her wish she'd had brothers when she'd been a girl.

"Poker's a lot of fun," Josh said, looking up from his cards. "No wonder my friend likes to play."

Lynette thought so, too.

"It's easier than I thought it would be," Mikey added. "Thanks for teaching us."

"You're welcome." Lynette smiled at the younger boy. "I can't believe how quick you guys caught on."

In fact, they'd picked up on the basics a lot faster than Lynette had when Helen had taken her under wing. And Mikey, who'd racked up a big stack of checkers, which they'd been using as poker chips, seemed to be a natural.

"I bet two chips," Mikey said, removing them from his stack.

Josh scrunched up his face as he studied his cards.

Lynette sure hoped Carly was okay with the entertainment she'd chosen for the evening.

And speaking of Carly . . . Lynette glanced at the clock on the wall, noting that the couple should have been home by now—especially if things hadn't gone well and they'd wanted a quick ending to the night.

In fact, even if they'd taken a leisurely dinner, they should be here by now. Had they extended their date?

She didn't know if she should be happy things were working out, saddened by it, or worried about their safety.

"I call you," Josh said, drawing Lynette's mind back to the game and to the pair of threes she held.

"I'll fold." She laid down her cards on the table, preferring to let the boys win.

It seemed weird now that she'd actually worried that she would be in over her head and that babysitting might be an awful chore, but she'd done all right—at least, if Carly didn't flip out about her sons learning a game some people might consider a vice.

At the sound of a car outside, Lynette began to gather the cards together. "That's probably your mom. Let's pick up our mess before she comes inside."

The boys made fast work of the cleanup, then while they took the checkers into the bedroom and put them away, Lynette went to greet their mother.

"You're back," she said, as a smiling Carly entered the living room and closed the door.

From the look on her face, the date must have gone well.

"Were the boys good for you?" Carly asked.

"They're great kids. It was fun spending time with them."

"I'm glad to hear that." Carly dropped her purse onto the sofa and kicked off her shoes.

"So how about you?" Lynette asked. "Did you have a good time?"

Carly nodded. "It did me a world of good to dress up and get out of the house for a while. Grant's a nice guy."

Lynette thought so, too, although she'd come to realize that it would have been okay with her if Carly hadn't agreed. "Did he ask you out again?"

"He wants to do something next weekend, although I'm not sure what that will be. He even said we could include the boys."

It sounded as though the man might actually be nicer than Lynette had thought he was, and once again, she felt a tremor of regret. But what was she going to do now? Wrestle Carly for him?

"Thanks so much for babysitting," Carly said. "I couldn't have gone out if you hadn't."

"Uh, yeah, about that . . ." Lynette glanced around the room, noting that the boys still hadn't returned, and lowered her voice. "It'd probably be best if they continue to think that I'm not a sitter. I told them that I came here to hang out with them until you got back. They . . . well, Josh . . . thinks he's old enough to take care of himself. You'd know whether he's right about that or not. But he's a good kid, and it would make him feel better if he was treated like a grown-up."

Carly's brow furrowed as though she was surprised by

Lynette's suggestion and maybe giving it some serious thought.

"I'll try to remember that," she said.

Lynette reached for her purse, which she'd left on the floor near the hearth. "I probably ought to get going. But if you ever need someone to hang out with them again, and if I'm free, which I usually am in the evenings, give me a call."

"Thanks. I'll do that."

Lynette headed for the door, but before she could place a hand on the knob, Carly stopped her. "Would you like to come over for dinner sometime? Maybe even watch a movie or something?"

Lynette turned, and her lips parted. "You mean just for fun?"

Carly gave a little shrug.

Were they actually going to become friends?

Lynette smiled. "Sure, Carly. And I'll bring the popcorn."

"You got it."

As Lynette stepped onto the porch, Carly said, "Good night."

Lynette flashed her one last smile.

Yes, it had been a really good night. She wasn't sure how Grant was going to play into all of this, what with the attraction she was feeling for him, but something told her she was going to need a new friend.

Especially when she might have lost one of the few she'd had.

Chapter 16

After leaving Helen's house on Thursday, when Lynette had been so hurtful and mean, Susan had gone home and eaten several helpings of chocolate ice cream, which had always been her comfort food of choice.

It had been soothing for a while—until the guilt had kicked in and she'd realized how many calories and grams of fat she'd consumed.

Two days had passed, and she'd yet to hear an apology, which left her still annoyed beyond measure. But last night, while she'd been tossing and turning and praying for sleep, she'd given some thought to the various conversations they'd had over the past several months.

If push came to shove, she had to admit that she wasn't entirely sure that she'd actually come right out and told Lynette that she wanted to date Grant—or Max, either, for that matter. She'd just implied that she'd been interested in both men. But how hard was it to notice someone's enthusiasm, especially when she was delivering cookies and Christmas ornaments?

Of course, Susan was still hurt over the comments Lynette had made about her mixing up numbers, especially now, while she had all the ingredients for brownies spread upon her kitchen counter and a recipe she'd never followed before.

She'd been praying that she'd get it right, that she'd measure everything as directed.

Since Barbie had specifically asked her to bring brownies to Lydia's House for the party on Monday afternoon, she'd decided to make a practice batch or two. Just in case she screwed up, she had a backup plan. She would make a couple dozen chocolate chip cookies, which were sure to turn out perfectly. That way, she would have gotten at least one thing right.

She was still stressing about attending that party, though. And feeling a little guilty at the same time.

Maggie had been right when she'd said, *They're just like you in a lot of ways, vulnerable, loving, kind . . . They cry when they're hurt.*

At this very moment, that statement rang true for Susan, too. She always tried to do the right thing, but her best-laid plans didn't always turn out the way she wanted them to, whether it was reading and following a recipe, keeping a running total of poker winnings, or finding a new husband. And like the residents of Lydia's House, she, too, hurt when someone pointed out her flaws.

She wouldn't feel so sad and vulnerable, though, if she had a husband and a family of her own. She'd be too caught up in the Christmas rush—shopping, wrapping gifts, decorating the house—to stew about anything else for very long.

Instead, she was merely going through the motions, hoping no one could see how very lonely she was.

But God knew what was going on inside, and He was the only one who could make things right. So standing in the kitchen, with a dusting of flour on her hands and an ache in her heart, she bowed her head.

Lord, I'm hurting something awful. You know how badly I want to have a baby, and time is running out. Please don't let me spend another holiday alone, without the one thing that would make me whole.

You've blessed me in other ways, and I'm grateful for that.

I also realize that I don't deserve anything You've given me or even this request I'm making. But please make the pain go away, Lord—or at least make it tolerable.

Just as she was going to wrap up her prayer with an Amen, an unexpected thought came to mind, chasing away all the others.

Are you forgetting something? it asked.

She didn't think so.

How do you expect to find joy amidst the anger and bitterness in your heart?

Anger and bitterness? The only one who'd annoyed her, at least recently, had been Lynette, but those feelings hadn't had a chance to take root yet. Had they?

Even so, she couldn't very well forgive the woman she'd considered a friend and forget those hurtful comments she'd made until Lynette actually apologized. And so far, Lynette had yet to utter a single word of remorse.

Why wait?

Well, because, as far as Susan was concerned, the ball was in Lynette's court.

It all seemed logical, fair, and just. But as Susan held fast to that belief, it grew a little hard and unwieldy in her grip.

Okay, so I'm being a little stubborn, she thought. *No one's perfect.*

As she raised her head and opened her eyes, she studied the ingredients that lay before her, waiting to be measured, whipped into a batter, and baked in the oven.

Flour, cocoa, eggs, butter . . .

They aren't very tasty in and of themselves, are they?

No, other than the sugar, they'd be dry, bitter, slimy, or greasy in the mouth.

But in the hands of a baker, just imagine what they could become.

True, she thought. When blended together, heated to a certain temperature for just the right amount of time, the mix would become a rich, chocolaty treat.

You need a Master Baker in your life.

Susan's thoughts, it seemed, were running away with her. And that was just plain crazy.

Of course, it wasn't crazy to let God take charge of her life, but thinking that He might actually be talking to her was. So she shook it off and tried to focus on the recipe.

Yet even as she studied the words, she couldn't help wondering if God could actually work in her life like that. Could He take the ugly ingredients—the disappointments, the bruised feelings, the broken dreams—and create something beautiful?

It would be amazing if He could.

If He *would*.

Susan had no idea how long she'd stood there, staring at the clutter of ingredients on her counter, thinking about life and the unexpected messes she'd either created on her own or stumbled into.

Would God do something remarkable with her life, if she'd let Him?

She'd certainly like Him to, so she took it a step further.

"Make something out of my mess, Lord." Then, as though He was standing right beside her, rather than in the throne room of Heaven, she added, "If there's anything I can do to help things along, just let me know."

As she returned her gaze on the recipe, another thought sprung to mind. *Then feed My sheep.*

She'd gone to Sunday school as a child and knew who the Good Shepherd was. And she supposed you could say that she'd fed His sheep when she'd helped Rosa at the soup kitchen last week.

If truth be told, she'd come home that day feeling better about herself than she had in a long, long time.

She supposed Maggie had been right when she'd suggested that the Lils share their time and money with others this holiday season. Maybe Susan ought to talk to Dawn Randolph and ask if she could volunteer at the kitchen on a regular basis.

Again she glanced at the recipe she was trying to follow, one Barbie had suggested she make and take to Lydia's House on Monday afternoon. She supposed attending the party and providing goodies was another way to help the less fortunate this season.

"All right," she said out loud, as if God was actually standing beside her in the kitchen. "I'm going to put on a happy face when I go to that party and make the best of it."

She waited for a response, one of those out-of-the-blue thoughts, but she didn't get one. Of course, she wasn't about to worry about that. At least she had some direction and a game plan now: She would go above and beyond for others this Christmas, and in doing so, maybe she would turn the tide of blessings in her favor.

And if it didn't work out the way in which she hoped it would?

Then so be it. She'd be content knowing that she'd done something to make life a little better for someone else.

On Sunday morning, Max woke earlier than usual—at least in his world nine thirty was early.

He'd fixed a pot of coffee and drank his usual two cups. But then he'd gotten a wild hair, and for some crazy reason he'd climbed into the attic and pulled out several strings of multicolored Christmas lights he'd been storing since the year before last.

Even as he took them down, leaving the other holiday decorations where they were, he wondered why he was giving in to neighborhood pressure.

Or was it more than that?

Maybe Carly had something to do with it.

On Friday night, when he'd gone to Carly's for dinner, he'd spotted the stockings hung on the mantel and noticed the way in which she'd adorned her house with Christmas knickknacks and the kids' artwork. As he'd taken it all in, he'd felt a sense of home and hearth he hadn't otherwise experienced in ages.

For some reason, Carly's holiday spirit had been contagious, and he'd been compelled to drag out the lights this morning.

Of course, he wasn't going to go all out, like some of the other neighbors did, by putting up all the other stuff Karen had once used to spruce up the house and yard. But it wouldn't hurt to decorate that big tree in the front.

After stretching the lights across the lawn, he took the plug to the nearest outlet, which happened to be on the porch, and checked for burned-out bulbs.

As he studied the sparkling display of colors blinking on and off, he slowly shook his head and grinned. How about that? After two years of collecting dust, they still worked.

"Hey," a voice called from across the street.

Max turned to see Grant cracking a grin as he approached. "It looks like you're caving in to community pressure, too."

Although it hadn't been the neighbors who'd sparked Max's climb into the attic this morning, he gave a little shrug, implying that Grant had it all figured out, before changing the subject to one he'd much rather talk about.

"How was your date last night?" he asked.

"It was all right."

Max didn't pick up any enthusiastic vibes, which he took to be a good sign that he'd been right, that the two weren't suited.

"So there wasn't much to shout about?" he prodded.

"Well, I wouldn't say that. It was a pleasant evening."

Max wouldn't mind spending an evening with Carly, either, but Grant still wasn't giving him much to go on. "So are you going to take her out again, or was it just a one-shot deal?"

"I wasn't so sure at first, and I don't think she was, either.

So I left the option of a repeat date open. But by the time dessert rolled around, and we had a chance to talk a little more, I realized she was a nice woman and figured, why not?"

"Because she has kids." Shouldn't that be reason enough to cause a guy used to setting his own hours at work and taking off to the beach anytime he felt the urge to have second thoughts about dating a single mother?

"I've considered that," Grant said. "And for that reason, I suggested we include the boys next time. It'll give me a chance to see how things go."

"Where are you taking them?"

"I'm not sure. Since it's probably best if we wait until after Christmas, I have time to think of someplace we'd all enjoy."

Max hadn't especially liked the idea of Grant and Carly going out to dinner, but for some reason the idea of a family-style date wasn't any more appealing.

Instead of looking Grant in the eye, which might make the guy think Max was more interested in the budding relationship than he ought to be, he focused on the colorful blinking lights stretched across the lawn and said, "So Carly being a package deal doesn't bother you?"

"I thought it would." Grant shoved his hands in the pouch pocket of his sweatshirt. "Maybe there's something about the holiday season that makes a ready-made family a little more appealing."

Max hadn't thought about it that way. When he'd felt all warm and fuzzy inside while at Carly's house the other night, he'd figured it was because he'd finally gotten a clue as to what might be missing in his life.

Still, when he thought about Grant dating Carly, his gut twisted into a knot and tightened to the point where he found it hard to feign indifference.

So why was that?

He had no idea—unless he was interested in Carly himself. But he wasn't about to go there. Not with Grant—and certainly not out in the front yard, where everyone and their brother might pass by and quiz him about his sudden holiday spirit, which was now fading fast.

"Well," he said, still focused on the stupid lights, "it looks like they all check out."

"Where you going to put them?"

"On the tree, I guess." Max glanced at his watch. "But I'm going to do that later this afternoon."

By the time he got the lights hung up, especially if Grant continued to shoot the breeze and slow him down, he'd be late to Carly's house. And he had a stop he needed to make before he got there.

So, while Grant took the hint and headed back to his own place, Max rolled up the lights and took them inside.

Twenty minutes later, he parked in front of Carly's house, then glanced at the pink box that sat on the passenger seat. He'd picked up an assortment of every donut and Danish the baker had to offer. Max couldn't imagine a kid who didn't have a sweet tooth, and he suspected Carly's boys would have a difficult time choosing the one they'd most like to eat.

Hemingway, who was wearing his flashing, battery-operated collar and sitting in the backseat, barked as though he knew exactly where they were and what they were up to.

"Take it easy," Max said, as he reached for the donuts, then got the dog out of the car.

He could have told himself to settle down, too. For some reason, as he led Hemingway to Carly's front door, his pulse had kicked up a beat.

The unexpected rush of nervousness had nothing to do with seeing her again and everything to do with what she had to say about his novel. He'd believed that to be the case, too—until she opened the door, wearing a pair of black denim jeans, a cream-colored sweater, and a breezy smile.

That's when his heartbeat really went whacky.

And when he realized that he'd arrived ten minutes early.

Did that make him appear too eager?

"I hope we're not too early," he said, wishing he would have remained in the bakery parking lot a little longer.

"No, not at all. Come on in."

As he stepped into the living room, the aroma of fresh brewed coffee filled the air, and he was again caught up in that same warm, cozy swirl of coming home.

Before he could ponder a comment, the boys came bounding into the room to greet the dog.

"I brought donuts," he said, hoping that his efforts would earn him a welcome and a few brownie points.

"Cool," Josh said. "Thanks, Mr. Tolliver."

Should he tell the boys to call him Max? Or had Carly taught them to be formal when addressing adults?

Deciding to let it go for now, he handed the leash to Mikey and the box to Josh. "Why don't you and your brother have first pick?"

Several minutes later, when the boys had each chosen a donut and taken the dog out to play in the backyard, Max took a seat at Carly's kitchen table, where his manuscript rested next to the donut box like a big white elephant in the room.

Yet for the first time since he'd taken the leave of absence from the probation department, his focus wasn't on the story he was writing. It was on the pretty hairdresser who was pouring him a cup of coffee.

"How'd your date go?" he asked.

"It was okay."

Grant had pretty much responded the same way, which further convinced Max the two weren't going to make a good match.

"Just okay?" he asked.

"Grant's a nice guy."

So was Max. But what good had that done him? Even Karen, his ex-wife, hadn't seen the value in that. And in their case, the old adage had proven true: Nice guys finished last.

Carly carried two red mugs—adorned with snow-tinged

Christmas trees—to the table, placed one in front of him, then took a seat. "Before we get started, I'd like to ask you a question."

"Sure." He settled back in his chair. "What's that?"

"Last time you were here, you said that you gave Josh some advice that you wished you'd taken in the past. You don't have to explain the circumstances, but I was curious about just what that advice was."

The question took him aback, not because he couldn't remember the conversation he'd had with her son, but because he wasn't sure how he wanted to respond, what he wanted to reveal to her.

Opting for disclosure, which had never been easy for him, he said, "I was divorced about a year ago. And I probably could have done something to prevent it, but I didn't."

"What could you have done?"

"I might have been a better listener."

Carly placed both hands on her mug. "You mean you tuned her out?"

More often than not, he supposed, and as much as he hated to admit it, his marriage had started to unravel years before Karen had actually left.

"I guess I've reached that post-divorce state that allows a person to admit they might have been at fault, too," he confessed.

She smiled, nodding. "It's easier when there's a villain to blame."

"It's taken me nearly a year to come to grips with that." He wondered if she took any of the blame for her own divorce, but he didn't ask.

Still, if he had to guess, he'd say the guy had been an absolute fool to let her get away.

"So," she said, placing a manicured hand on the top page of the manuscript. "Let's talk about your book."

"Okay." Max braced himself for the critique, hoping she

had something valid to say, something that would free his muse to finish the last two chapters.

"You're a talented writer, Max. Your dialogue is sharp, and the action scenes are very well done."

So far, so good, he thought.

"But you're lacking the emotion to make this book great. Logan isn't fully fleshed out."

"What do you mean?"

"He could be so much more if you'd let him show his feelings."

Max bristled. "Have you ever read an action/adventure novel?"

"No, but I've seen a couple of movies."

"Which ones?"

"I don't remember the names. One was about a guy who went to a party at a new high-rise in the city. His ex-wife was working for a big corporation, and these terrorists came in and took everyone hostage. The guy, who was a cop, was the only one who knew they were trouble, the only one who could save them."

"Are you talking about *Die Hard*?" he asked.

"Maybe. I really don't remember the name, but it was a good movie. And even though it had too much shoot-'em-up stuff for me, I loved the romance."

"If you're talking about *Die Hard*, you're right. It *was* a great movie. Bruce Willis ended up saving the day and kissing Bonnie Bedelia at the end, but it wasn't a romance. It was an action flick. You're probably thinking about another movie."

"No, I remember now. That's the one. And in spite of all the blood, bullets, twisted metal, and broken glass, it was a romance."

"Bruce and Bonnie were hardly together the entire movie."

"But it was his love for her that kept him going, wasn't it?"

Max supposed so.

"Bruce's character wasn't just trying to save the day, he

was trying to salvage his marriage. It was his love that refused to die."

Max tried not to roll his eyes, although he had to admit that she had a point.

Carly took a sip of coffee, then smiled. "It's every woman's dream to have a man love her that much. And if you can show Logan really struggling with his failures as a husband and his feelings for Priscilla, you'll have a much bigger audience for your book."

She might be right, but she was suggesting a massive rewrite. And even if Max wanted to put that much work into a revision, he didn't have the time.

"Do you just want to see your name on the cover of a book?" she asked. "Or do you want to have a best seller?"

Truthfully? "Both."

"Then why not try to appeal to male *and* female readers? I'm not saying that you need to make this a full-on romance. But Logan has never failed at anything in his life, and just as he's about to solve the biggest case of his career, bring down the bad cops, and prove the naysayers wrong, he finds himself losing on the home front."

It was a dilemma Max himself had faced, but on a much smaller scale.

"Can't you see it?" Carly asked. "If Logan goes after Priscilla, he'll fail at the job. And if he puts his job first, he'll lose his wife. It would be a hard choice for him to make, and the reader will enjoy seeing his struggle. Then all you need to do is find a way for him to win both battles in the end."

"And just how am I supposed to do that without compromising the story?"

"I'm just a reader. You're the author. But the action will mean a whole lot more when there are human emotions at stake."

Max was still trying to wrap his mind around what she was suggesting when she added, "There's something else missing."

"What's that?"

"Faith."

"Why would you say that's missing? Logan's got faith in himself, in his partner."

"Yes, but you made it clear early in the story that Logan had given up his faith in God. And that he didn't believe that good would ultimately trump evil—at least, somewhere down the road."

What was she trying to do to his book?

"I'll pray that the plot comes together for you," she said, "even if you don't take my advice."

She was going to *pray* about his book? What made her think God even cared about things like that? Prayers were best left for the big stuff—like life-and-death situations.

God didn't care about minor things, like books—or even Max, who was just an insignificant little blip on the heavenly radar, if he was even that.

"I'll also pray that you get a publishing contract soon," she added.

Now that would be nice. But when push came to shove, Max was skeptical—of her suggestions, of her faith. . . .

. . . and if truth be told, of his ability to pull off something of the magnitude she was suggesting.

Chapter 17

After Max left Carly's house, he wasn't any closer to solving his literary problems than before. In fact, he'd had so much to think about that his muse had gone even deeper into hiding.

Carly's comments about increasing the emotion and adding a faith element in his story had merit, but making changes like that would take his book and his characters in a different direction than he'd planned. Worse yet, it would require a complex revision that would take more of his time than he had available—unless he wanted to deplete his savings completely, which would be foolhardy.

So he'd allowed himself another day off from writing, hoping to give his imagination a break.

Or so he thought. In spite of his best intentions to forget everything Carly had said for the rest of the afternoon and evening, her critique had simmered in his mind for hours.

When he'd gotten home and saw that Grant's car was gone, he'd thought about dragging the lights back to the front yard, along with a ladder, so he could put them up without having his neighbor see what he was doing. But once he'd stepped into the house and saw the rolled strands on the coffee table where he'd left them earlier, he'd stopped short.

For some reason, whatever holiday spirit he'd had earlier in the day had completely disappeared, leaving him with a bah-humbug attitude to rival any Charles Dickens had ever imagined. And he had nothing to blame except Carly's critique.

Trouble was, it was more than the thought of revision that bothered him, it was her pointing out Logan's flaws and shortcomings. Because in spite of the character being a figment of Max's imagination, Logan Sinclair and Max Tolliver had a lot more in common than he wanted to admit. And, according to Carly, Logan was not only lacking emotion and a commitment to his marriage, he was lacking faith in something bigger than himself.

I'll pray that the plot comes together for you, she'd said.

She might as well have said that she'd be praying for his life to come together, too.

But none of it made sense anymore—the plot of his novel, or the direction his life had either taken or failed to take.

Now, as he stood in front of his open refrigerator, feeling the cold vapor on his face and looking for lunch meat to make a sandwich, something . . . clicked.

While his physical movements froze, his mind took off like a shot, and a scene began to roll in his mind.

Afraid to lose the dialogue that was unfolding, he shut the fridge and hurried to the computer. As he waited for his Mac to boot up, he realized the scene that was coming to him like a gift was pivotal to the story, to the climax.

Why hadn't he seen the big picture before?

Somehow, even without a game plan like this, he'd set the seeds in play early in the manuscript.

Even Carly had noticed it. *You made it clear early in the story that Logan had given up his faith in God,* she'd said. *He doesn't believe that good will ultimately trump evil—at least, somewhere down the road.*

Yes, Max had set the seeds, but he hadn't allowed them to bear fruit.

He'd even written a scene in one of the first chapters, where Logan had been holed up in the church, hiding in the confessional. He'd had opportunities to add more introspection there and had missed it.

There'd been other scenes, too, when a teenager had darted out in front of the getaway car. The kid had lay dying in the street, and Logan had been the first one to come upon the scene. He'd had a real dilemma then, too. And Max had missed an opportunity to lay more groundwork.

While he waited for the document to load, he was half-tempted to call Carly and share his literary epiphany, but he didn't dare do anything that might slow the story flowing in his mind. Instead, he placed his hands on the keyboard and let his returning muse take flight.

> *The perp raised his Glock, aiming it at Logan's heart. "Say your prayers, tough guy."*
>
> *"I always do." Logan stood firm, looking death in the eye without flinching.*
>
> *Faith did that to a man, he supposed. Faith in something bigger than himself.*

Now Logan would need to pull a rabbit out of his hat to get out of the mess Max had put him in. And he would, thanks to the church he'd been holed up in earlier, a scene Max would go back and tweak after he'd finished writing this one.

And write, he did.

The sun went down that evening with Max sitting at the desk, and it rose again the next day with him in the same place.

Sure, he'd taken an occasional bathroom break, as well as some time to stretch his back and to work out the crick in his neck and shoulders. But other than that, he'd continued to work, polishing the new scene, revising others, adding lines of introspection, and tweaking dialogue to match the story's new direction.

At a quarter to nine, with the sun burning through the slats in the shutters, Max typed *"The End."*

Staring at the screen, exhausted, amazed, and still bursting with the kind of energy one felt after a job well done, he was too wound up to sleep. So why even fight it?

He went to the kitchen, put on a pot of coffee, then relished a cup of the fresh morning brew as he reread his ending scene.

Wow, he thought as he sat back in his chair. Even with a red pen in hand to edit the hard copy, he'd only found a couple of typos and a word out of place.

It was good—*very good*—and he couldn't wait to tell Carly that he'd taken her comments and run with them.

But first . . . ?

He got online and composed an e-mail to the agent who'd requested the manuscript months before. After writing a short note as a cover letter, he attached the document. With his hand over the mouse, ready to click on SEND, he caught himself.

How much of all of this had to do with his skill as an author? And how much had to do with Carly's critique?

What about her prayer?

There was no need to risk a bolt of lightning for not giving credit where it was due.

"Thanks for letting this come together for me," he said.

Again he gripped the mouse.

That's not all that's coming together for you.

What else was working out? A relationship with Carly?

The thought seemed to come out of the blue, although Max knew what had happened. His brain was so numb from his work that stray pieces of dialogue continued to flow out of his subconscious.

Still, maybe there was some truth to that. Maybe something was happening between him and Carly—a friendship for sure. And maybe even a professional relationship. He would certainly value her opinion on any other manuscript he might write in the future.

"Thanks for Carly," he said.

It wasn't exactly a prayer, he supposed. At least, not the Our-Father-Who-Art-in-Heaven kind he'd been taught in his youth. But it had been directed to God, even if it was a little on the casual side. He supposed looking to and talking to the Almighty didn't come easy for a guy who'd been relying on himself for so long.

With that aside, he clicked on the mouse, sending his manuscript hurtling through cyberspace to an office in Manhattan. Then he sat back in his seat, and blew out a weary sigh.

Carly would be pleased to know what he'd done, but she deserved more than a phone call.

Shear Magic buzzed with activity, as the clients filed in and out of the salon in an attempt to get their hair cut or styled before the holiday, and Carly's appointment book was full. She'd started early and had already completed a color, highlights, and a haircut by ten thirty.

Unless someone canceled, she'd be working through lunch again, but she'd much rather be busy than not, so she wouldn't complain about having to steal bites of a peanut butter sandwich between clients.

Twyla Helfrich, who worked in the station next to hers, had taken the morning off to go shopping, and Carly couldn't help feeling a little envious. Fortunately, she'd managed to pick up two small gifts for the boys on her way to work this morning, and she'd hidden them in the trunk of her car.

Now, as she blew-dry Lori Barton's hair, she found herself praying again that God would come through with enough cash to get her caught up on her rent and her car payments.

She knew He could work a miracle. And she truly believed that He would, but as the time drew nearer, her faith was getting a little sketchy.

"Do you think I should have had a touch-up instead of just a cut?" Lori asked over the drone of the dryer.

Carly studied her client's roots, which were just beginning to show a gray fringe underneath the dark brown color. "I know you're on a tight schedule today, and it's not too bad. You can wait another week or two."

"I know, but John and I are going to an open house at his boss's house this evening, and I wanted to make a good impression."

"You're going to look great, Lori. Don't give it another thought." Carly brushed a wet strand of hair, lifting it and rolling it under as she aimed the hot air on the ends.

Out of the corner of her eye, she caught sight of someone approaching her station. She turned to get a better look and spotted Max.

What was he doing here? He didn't have an appointment. Had he come by to talk to her?

A boyish grin suggested that he had, and her heart did a little swan dive in her chest.

"Hey," he said as he reached her side. "I know you're working, so I won't keep you. I just wanted to thank you again for reading my manuscript."

"You already thanked me," she said, forcing her hands to keep moving as she tried to wrap her mind around his surprise visit. "And you paid me, too."

"I know, but . . ." He glanced at the client in Carly's chair, then back to her. "I'm sorry to just drop in like this, but is there any chance I could talk to you for a second or two when you're finished?"

As much as she'd have liked to take an early lunch break and talk to him at length, she had an eleven o'clock appointment coming in, so she gave a little nod toward the empty station to her right. "Sure, I can take a minute. Why don't you have a seat? I won't be much longer."

"Great." He folded his large frame into Twyla's chair and

spun it a few degrees so he could face her while she finished Lori's hair.

Trouble was, Carly was more interested in making eye contact with Max and trying to read his expression than she was in minding her work.

Curiosity nagged her while she continued to blow-dry Lori's hair, and when she finally finished, she walked her client to the front of the salon so they could take care of the payment and make another appointment for a touch-up. Then Carly went back to her station.

Upon her approach, Max got to his feet and tossed her yet another crooked grin. "I'll make this quick. You were right about the lack of emotion in my novel, as well as Logan's lost faith. If I wouldn't have addressed those issues, they would have been loose strings I hadn't tied up, and the book would have fallen flat."

"I'm glad I was able to help. After you left yesterday, I worried that I'd upset you."

"In a way, you did, but you were right. So besides thanking you again—this time from the bottom of my heart—I also want to tell you that I'm sorry if I came across as hard-headed and unappreciative yesterday."

"You don't have to apologize."

"Yeah, well, something tells me that I do. Logan wasn't the only one making a character arc last night." Max tossed her another grin, but this one wrapped itself around her heart and gave it a breath-stealing squeeze. "I also have some good news to share with you. While I was writing last night, the story took a turn neither of us expected. And now it's done."

"You finished the book?"

A full-on smile splashed across his face, crinkling his eyes and setting off an I-struck-it-rich spark in his eyes. "I sure did. And it's already in New York."

"That's great."

"Well, the agent probably won't read it for months, but at

least I met my goal. I'd told the guy he'd have it by the end of the year, and thanks to you, I was able to pull it off."

"I don't know what to say."

"You don't have to say anything, but right now, as far as I'm concerned, you're a genius."

His praise went a little over the top, yet it touched something deep inside of her, making her feel as though she wasn't a complete failure after all, something that seemed to be a Christmas miracle in and of itself.

Before she'd divorced Derek and he'd taken off for parts unknown, she'd had a healthy sense of self-esteem. But over the past six months, her inability to get her checking account back into the black and a son who was making her question her mothering skills had given her confidence a couple of good, hard kicks.

"Thanks, Max, but I wouldn't go that far."

"Either way, I have something for you." He reached into his pocket, pulled out what appeared to be two one-hundred-dollar bills that had been folded in half, and then reached for her hand. As he pressed the money into her palm, warming her from the inside out, he held on for a moment longer than necessary.

Could he feel her pulse throbbing in her wrist?

Shaking it off, she asked, "What's this for? You already paid me."

"I know, but this is a bonus. You have no idea how good it feels to have that manuscript done and gone. I might even go home and string some Christmas lights in celebration."

At that, she returned his smile. "I guess there's nothing like success to make a person feel festive."

"You're right, and since you played such a big role in helping me get past my writing slump, I'd like to take you to dinner. I'm probably going to go home and crash this afternoon since I've been up all night working, but are you free tomorrow?"

"That's the twenty-fourth, and I'm taking the boys to

Mulberry Park for the Christmas Under the Stars program the church is sponsoring."

"Oh, yeah. I've seen those flyers around town. Well, we could make it tonight, if you can get a sitter."

"I'm sorry. That's not going to work, either. I can't ask Lynette to watch the kids again so soon. But why don't you join us at the park tomorrow?"

"I'm really not into church events."

"But this isn't anything like sitting in a pew and listening to a sermon."

He didn't appear convinced, but for some reason, she really wanted him to go.

"Everyone bundles up in jackets and winter clothes. We hold candles, sing carols, listen to the Christmas story, then have hot cocoa and cookies. I think you'll be surprised at how much fun you'll have."

He seemed to give it some thought, then shook his head again. "I think I'll pass. But thanks for asking."

"Okay." As she stood there, a sense of awkwardness settled over her, and she glanced at the cash he'd given her, then returned her gaze to his. "You really don't need to pay me anything extra."

"I know, but I want you to have it. Use it to buy a tree and get your kids a few presents."

"Actually, as much as I'd like the boys to have a Christmas to remember, I'm going to give this to my landlord. It'll get me current for the month, which is a real blessing."

His brow furrowed, and his left eye twitched. "I'm sorry. You mentioned having some financial trouble, but I didn't realize it was that bad."

"Things are looking up now," she admitted. "And this extra two hundred dollars is an answer to my prayers."

His head tilted slightly to the side, and a whisper of confusion crossed his face. "So do you pray regularly?"

She used to be better at it, but she tried to make prayer a part of her daily routine, so she nodded.

"I know you said you would, but did you actually pray about my manuscript coming together for me?"

"Yes, right after you left my house. And again last night before I went to bed." She tucked a strand of hair behind her ear and smiled. "I guess you have Someone else to thank, too."

"Maybe so."

"Carly?" another stylist said. "Your eleven o'clock is here."

"Thanks, Jennelle. Tell her I'll be right there."

"Well," Max said, "I won't keep you any longer."

On impulse, Carly lifted her arms for a parting embrace.

He hesitated briefly, and for a moment, she thought he might bolt out of the door, but he stepped into a hug. As they came together, she caught the scent of soap laced with his woodsy cologne, felt the warmth of his touch, the strength of his arms.

When had she last experienced a heart-stirring embrace like that?

She had no idea, yet in spite of the temptation to hold on to him as long as she could, she let him go. "Thanks again for the bonus."

"I wish it was more."

Reluctant to see him leave, she said, "If you change your mind about going to the park with us on Christmas Eve, just let me know."

He nodded, then headed toward the front of the salon.

In spite of having a client waiting for her, she remained rooted to the spot, watching him go.

He'd only taken a couple of steps when he turned to face her again. "You know, maybe I'll take you up on that invitation after all."

"To go to the park with us tomorrow night?"

He gave a single shoulder shrug. "To be honest, I really don't have anything better to do."

A smile spread across her face. "It starts at six. I've got lawn chairs for us to sit on."

"Okay. I'll pick you and the boys up at five thirty."

"We'll be ready."

She waited a moment before heading to the front of the salon herself to get her eleven o'clock appointment, savoring a buzz of excitement.

Inviting Max to attend Christmas Under the Stars had seemed like the most natural thing in the world to do. And something she realized she'd never even considered asking Grant to do. She supposed that was because she'd been thinking more about Max in terms of friendship—or whatever.

Trouble was, with her situation, she had no business thinking of anyone other than her sons or anything other than making a home for them.

And even though the extra cash meant that she could catch up on her December rent, January was closing in on her, so she wasn't out of the woods yet.

Lynette had spent more money in the last two hours than she had in ages, which was quite a feat for a woman who pinched her pennies, even when she had plenty of them to spare. Yet that wasn't all she'd done. She'd actually paid the department store to wrap all of her gifts, which was another first.

However, if she'd taken them home, she would have had to scrounge around the house for paper, tape, and ribbon, so it had been easier this way.

Besides, she'd been eager to see Carly's expression when she walked into the salon with Christmas presents for her and the boys.

Now, with her arms loaded down with bags and feeling like one of Santa's elves, she strode across the tiled floor on a natural high she hadn't expected.

Maggie had been right about giving freely to those in need this year. And for the first time in her life, Lynette understood what people meant when they said it was more blessed to give than to receive.

As she made her way to Carly's station, her heart and spirits soared.

"Wow," Carly said, spotting Lynette. "Someone's done some major shopping today."

"You're right." Lynette set the bags on the floor and rubbed the reddened crease lines the weight of the bags had made on her arms and fingers. "And every last one of these is for you."

Carly, who'd been trimming a teenage boy's hair, froze in mid-snip. "They're for *me?*"

"Well, one is for you, but the rest are for Josh and Mikey."

"But why . . . ?" Carly stared at the bags, clearly surprised, then she looked up at Lynette, the question still splashed upon her face.

"Because I wanted to." Lynette had missed out on enough Christmases in her life to know what it felt like to be the only kid in school to return from winter break without having one single new item to wear or a toy or game to talk about.

Carly's eyes filled with tears, as she set down the scissors and embraced Lynette, who didn't know what else to do, other than to hug her right back and to relish the feel of friendship.

"I don't know how to thank you," Carly said.

"You don't have to."

"Yes, I do." Carly slowly released her new friend. As she stepped back, she wiped the tears from her eyes. "You've given my kids the Christmas I'd been praying they'd have."

Lynnette, who was choking up, too, liked thinking that she'd been a part of God's plan, but she knew better than that. She'd always felt more like a divine afterthought in the scheme of things, so she tried to make light of what she'd done by asking, "Where do you want me to put the presents?"

"I guess in the trunk of my car—if they'll fit."

"I'm sure they will," Lynette said, "but since you're working, why don't I take them out for you?"

"That would be great." Carly reached for her purse, then dug inside until she pulled out a heart-shaped key ring. "Here you go. It's the white Toyota Celica parked in back of the salon."

"You've got it. I'll be back in a snap."

Before Lynette could pick up the bags, Carly gripped her arm and gazed at her with unshakable appreciation. "You have no idea what a blessing this is. God is awesome. He really does answer prayer."

Yeah, well, who was Lynette to question God's plan, especially since she found it hard to imagine herself being a part of anything like that.

Minutes later, after she'd locked the packages in Carly's trunk and returned the keys, Lynette wished her hairstylist-turned-friend a merry Christmas, then left the salon and headed to her own car.

As a cool breeze whipped around her, she pulled her sweater closed, wishing she'd worn a jacket. It wasn't supposed to rain today, but it wouldn't be the first time the weather forecasters had been mistaken.

She'd no more than clicked on the remote, unlocking the driver's door of her vehicle, when she spotted Maggie walking away from the church parking lot, rubbing her arms as though chilled to the bone.

When Lynette called her name, the blonde broke into a warm smile and strode toward the car.

"What are you up to?" Lynette asked.

"I was helping out at the soup kitchen today, but Carlos and Rosa showed up. Carlos insisted that they take over the cleanup, so I'm walking home."

"It's getting pretty cold and wintry out for that. Why don't you let me give you a ride?"

"Okay, thanks. I'd appreciate that."

Moments later, the women were seated in the car and headed down the street. As Lynette adjusted the heater vent, she said, "You'll never guess what I did today."

"What's that?"

"I bought Christmas presents for a family in need, and you were right. It's a great feeling to know that I made a difference in someone's life—just like Adam, the guy who had the chest of coins that never emptied."

Maggie smiled, a light sparking those remarkable blue eyes.

As Lynette pulled in front of Helen's house, Maggie thanked her for the ride, then climbed from the car. But rather than drive off, Lynette waited to make sure she got inside.

While Maggie unlocked Helen's door, the roar of a diesel engine sounded, as a FedEx truck parked in front of Grant's house. Moments later, the courier carried an envelope to the front door.

Grant's car wasn't in the driveway, so he probably wasn't home. And since the guy seemed to be leaving a note, she realized it required a signature.

Should she step in and tell the courier that she would accept it on his behalf?

She waited for a moment longer, watching the FedEx guy head back to his truck with the envelope still in his hand, then climbed out of her car. "Excuse me. Grant Barrows is a friend of mine, so if you need a signature, I can do that for you."

"Thanks, ma'am." He handed her an electronic device to sign. After she scratched out her name, he gave her the envelope, hopped into the truck, and drove away.

She was just about to write a note for Grant and leave her phone number, when she heard his car drive up.

"I hope you don't mind," she told him, "but I signed for this delivery. If I hadn't stopped the courier, he would have taken it back to his station."

"I don't mind at all. Thanks." Grant took the envelope, glanced at the return address, then tossed her a smile. "I'm glad you're here. I've wanted to ask you something."

"What's that?"

"Would you like to have dinner with me one of these evenings—and maybe take in a movie?"

The question nearly sucked all the words she'd ever learned right out of her.

"What about Carly?" she finally asked.

"What about her? It's not like we have a commitment to each other." Grant's gaze locked on hers, and her heart spun dangerously out of control.

"But that would be awkward," she said.

"Not for me."

Lynette didn't know how to respond, especially since she couldn't quite form the word no.

"If I had my choice in the matter," he added, "I'd rather go out with you. So what do you say?"

Yes came to mind, but so did thoughts of both Susan and Carly. Opting for time to think, she said, "I really hadn't planned on dating anyone."

"Why's that?"

She didn't want to tell him that she'd made bad choices when listening to her heart, and that her marriage to Peter had been more of a business decision based upon a trusted friendship. But she doubted that he would understand, and she feared he'd realize that she still harbored a few too many insecurities than a woman ought to.

So instead of answering, she nodded at the FedEx envelope in his arms. "Important papers?"

If he thought it was odd that she'd bypassed his question completely, he didn't mention it. Instead, he said, "I sold a piece of property out of state, and the agent's scanner is on the blink. He had to overnight the paperwork instead of e-mailing it to me. So time is of the essence."

"You mean you could miss out on the deal?"

"No, but I need to sign the settlement statement and get it back to him so the deal will close before the end of the year."

"The tax stuff can be such a headache, especially capital gains and that sort of thing." Fortunately, Peter's CPA took good care of her so she didn't have to worry too much.

"Actually," Grant said, "I had a couple of bad investments earlier in the year, which left me in a jam. So I need the cash to turn things around for myself."

He was having financial problems?

That in and of itself was a good reason not to go out with him. What if he went broke? Or worse yet, what if he thought Lynette ought to bail him out, risking her nest egg?

"What's the matter?" he asked.

Had he read her reaction in her face? If so, she tried to feign indifference. "Nothing's wrong. I just realized that I was supposed to . . . go to the bank and sign some papers myself. I can't believe that I nearly forgot." She was lying, of course, but hopefully he wouldn't come to that conclusion.

As she turned to go, clutching her purse close to her side, he called out, "Lynette, wait a minute."

"I really can't." She didn't dare stick around any longer. Not while Grant was turning her heart on end.

Goodness, he was the kind of man she was growing more and more attracted to, which meant that she could decide to ride off into the sunset with him, only to find herself parked in front of the poorhouse.

About the time she reached for the door handle of her car, Maggie stepped out on Helen's porch and called her name.

"Can it wait?" Lynette asked, feeling as though both Grant and Maggie had it in for her.

"I'm afraid not," Maggie said. "Dawn Randolph just called. Rosa collapsed while washing dishes at the soup kitchen. She's in an ambulance and on her way to the hospital."

"Oh, no."

"Do you mind giving me a lift to Pacifica General?" Without waiting for an answer, Maggie was heading down the sidewalk with her purse.

"Of course not." As Lynette slid behind the wheel, her heart pounding with real fear instead of that which might only have been imagined, she looked over the hood at Grant.

"Let me know if there's anything I can do to help," he said.

"You can pray," Maggie told him, as she climbed into the passenger seat.

Lynette barely waited for the woman to close the door, then she put the car in Drive, her fear growing by leaps and bounds.

If Maggie suggested that Grant pray, then things must not look at all good for Rosa.

Chapter 18

Before entering Lydia's House, Susan sat a while in her car, studying the estate that had once belonged to Alejandro Montoya, the patriarch of Fairbrook's most successful pioneer family.

The grand, three-story brick mansion sat on a hilltop overlooking Mulberry Park on one side, and providing an impressive view of the Pacific Ocean on the other.

According to what Barbie had told her, the ornate house had been custom-built during the World War I era and modernized over the years to provide handicap access. But it had always been surrounded by lush, park-like grounds encircled with a black wrought-iron fence.

Both Lydia's House—the building itself, as well as the foundation that had been created to benefit adults with developmental disabilities—had been named after Alejandro and Josefina Montoya's youngest daughter, who'd been twelve years old when she suffered a serious head injury after being thrown from a horse.

Lydia had lived, thanks to the best surgeons and medical care available at the time, but the bright and effervescent young girl who'd dreamed of owning a stable full of Thoroughbreds when she grew up would never be the same again. And the Montoyas had to accept the hard fact that their beloved child would need constant care the rest of her life.

Doctors had advised the parents to find a suitable institution in which to place her, and while they'd gone so far as to check out several, they'd refused to send the girl to live with strangers in settings like the ones they'd seen.

In the early sixties, Alejandro suffered a debilitating stroke. At that time, the family began to worry about what would happen to Lydia when her siblings and her parents passed away. So they'd created a charitable foundation that would provide housing and training for other adults like her—whether their disabilities were genetic birth disorders or conditions acquired later in life.

From then on, Lydia's House filled that special need within the community.

In the early eighties, Lydia Montoya passed away in the only home she'd ever known, but the foundation named in her honor continued to provide the same loving care to all the other residents.

Deciding that she'd taken enough time to brace herself for the afternoon's festivities, Susan slid out from behind the wheel of her car, reached for the plate of brownies she'd baked earlier, and started for the house.

As she made her way from the parking lot to the lawn, she thought about the twenty-three people who lived on the property, one of whom was Ronnie Ferris, Hank's brother. Unlike Lydia Montoya, Ronnie had been born with his challenges.

Susan had met him a time or two, when Stan and Donna Ferris had brought him home for a weekend, but it hadn't gone well. Ronnie had been agitated and noticeably troubled, which had made Susan uneasy. Eventually, the Ferris family had realized that Ronnie was happier with his friends and caretakers at Lydia's House, in the surroundings he'd become accustomed to over the years.

It was then that Susan had realized that Hank was even more uncomfortable around his older brother than she'd been.

She tried to reassure herself that Ronnie would be comfortable, that he wouldn't cry or strike out at people here, but she had no idea what to expect from the other residents.

It's only for an hour or so, she told herself. She'd make an excuse to leave, and it would soon be over.

When she reached the front door, which had been adorned with a holiday wreath hung by a big red bow, she raised her fist to knock, then spotted the bell and rang instead.

Moments later, a stocky young woman with Down syndrome opened the door. Her dark hair had been woven in a French braid and tied with a green ribbon that matched her green velvet dress.

"Merry Christmas," she said with a bright-eyed smile. "Come to the party."

Susan stepped inside the estate, which had been decked out in holiday splendor. People milled about, but it was easy to differentiate the residents from the guests.

They're just like you, Maggie had said.

Still not convinced, yet wishing it was true, Susan followed the woman into the house, where holiday music played softly.

Without warning, the woman stopped short and turned. "Do you have a friend who lives here? I can take you to them."

"I'm a . . . Well, I'm a friend of Ronnie Ferris."

"I know him." The girl bit down on her lip. "I think he's upstairs. He can't come down yet."

Was he throwing another fit? Agitated like before?

Susan glanced at her watch, making note of when she arrived and when she could make her excuse to leave.

"What's your name?" the woman asked.

"Susan. How about you?"

"I'm Stephanie. I live here. And I helped make the sugar cookies."

Susan reached out her hand. "It's nice to meet you. Thank you for being such a good hostess."

Stephanie beamed at the praise.

Just like you . . .

"That's a pretty dress you're wearing," Susan said.

Stephanie gave a little curtsy. "Edna made it for me. My daddy and my sister bought the . . ." She glanced down at the green velvet, then tugged at it.

"The fabric?"

Stephanie nodded. "Yes, and she made my slip, too. Do you want to see it?"

Susan smiled. "No, you better not show me here. But I'll bet it's pretty, too."

"And it's soft." Stephanie bent over, lifted the hem of her dress anyway, and revealed a white satin slip trimmed in lace. "See?"

"Very nice. I wish I had a pretty dress and slip like that."

"I can ask Edna. She's going to be here today. So is my daddy and my sister."

"I'd like to meet them."

Stephanie beamed. "They aren't here yet. That's why I'm waiting by the door. My sister is going to play the music, and we're going to sing."

"Cool."

Stephanie nodded, then brightened. "Want me to show you where to put the cookies?"

"That would be nice."

Moments later, after being led to a large dining room, Susan was instructed to hand her plate of brownies to a woman wearing a Christmas apron. She introduced herself as Tanya Sullivan, the mother of one of the young men who lived at Lydia's House.

"Don't these look yummy?" Tanya said. "My son is going to love these."

While Susan looked over the spread of goodies on the dessert table, Barbie joined her and slipped an arm around her. "I'm so glad you came, Susie. Come on, I want to show you around."

As Barbie gave Susan a tour of the kitchen, the library, and the classrooms where the "kids" learned life skills, she took time to introduce various residents along the way, each one decked out in holiday attire, their smiles as bright as Stephanie's had been.

Maggie had been right; those who lived here *were* just like the Lils in many ways, but they had a childlike innocence and honesty that Susan had lost years ago.

Instead of taking a seat in an out-of-the-way place and waiting for the time she could make an early escape, Susan found herself glad that she came to visit and looking forward to the party.

Of course, she'd yet to see Ronnie Ferris.

A bit curious about why he hadn't joined the party, Susan said, "Stephanie, the woman who answered the door when I arrived, told me that Ronnie hasn't come downstairs yet."

"We thought it would be best if he rested until the party got underway."

"Is something wrong?"

"He's been diagnosed with heart failure and tires easily," Barbie said. "In fact, we're afraid this might be his last Christmas."

"I'm sorry."

"So are we. He's been a special part of our family for a long time, although some people might not understand that."

Hank certainly hadn't.

And as a result, neither had Susan. Sadly, for the first time since their marriage, she felt remiss by that and decided an apology was due. "I'm also sorry that Hank and I weren't more . . ." She wasn't quite sure how to phrase it. She wasn't sure that "compassionate" was the word she was looking for, since Hank had always been generous with his checks to the foundation, something Susan had never minded.

"Hank had a difficult time accepting Ronnie's limitations," Barbie said.

"Do you think he was embarrassed by his brother?"

"Somewhat. And then . . ." Barbie paused. "Well, after his engagement to Brittany, it became even more of an issue."

"His *engagement*?"

"You didn't know that he'd been engaged to someone else before the two of you were married?"

No, he'd never mentioned it to her.

The stunned look on Susan's face must have been a dead giveaway to her utter surprise, because Barbie went on to explain. "Hank was in his third year at college when he met Brittany, and he fell fast and hard. By the time Christmas rolled around, he'd given her a ring and had invited her to Fairbrook to meet the family. I'm not exactly sure what happened while she was in town, but she broke up with him and flew home earlier than she'd planned."

"Did Ronnie have something to do with their split?"

Barbie glanced around as if checking to see that their conversation was private. It was, but she lowered her voice anyway. "Hank never actually said, but that's when I noticed him distancing himself from Ronnie—and from the rest of us, for that matter. My folks and I can't help thinking that Brittany was afraid that she and Hank would have a baby with genetic imperfections, although we don't know that for sure."

Barbie looked to Susan, as though seeking some kind of confirmation. But even though she'd suspected that Hank was afraid to have a child for that very reason, he'd never come out and actually said it. So she kept that to herself and just listened.

"About the time Hank and Brittany broke up, he began to insist that Mom and Dad find a home for Ronnie."

"Is that why your brother's here? Because Hank pushed your parents to place him in a home?"

"Not really. They knew that there was only so much they could do for him, and they also knew that they were getting older and wouldn't be alive forever. So they started checking out various facilities. But when they toured Lydia's House and saw all they had to offer, as well as how happy the residents were, they knew it was the right place for Ronnie."

From what Susan had seen so far, she suspected that they'd been right.

Barbie glanced at her wristwatch. "I'd better check and see what's keeping Ronnie's caregiver. He's supposed to be bringing him downstairs in a wheelchair."

"Where should I wait?" Susan asked.

"Mom and Dad are out on the lawn, so that's a good place to meet. I know it's a little chilly outside, but Ronnie likes to walk the grounds with us whenever we come to visit."

Before either Susan or Barbie could make a move, one of the residents, a young man, cried out, "Look what I found!"

Susan turned to see him stooped over and picking up a coin that had been lying on the floor. When he straightened and lifted up a penny, he burst into a grin. "It's a lucky day."

She thought of the ditty she'd learned as a child: *Find a penny, pick it up, and all the day you'll have good luck.*

"Congratulations," she said with a smile.

The young man glanced at the penny in his hand, bit down on his bottom lip, then looked at Susan and grinned. "Here, you can have it."

"Oh, no." Susan wasn't about to take away his joy or his treasure. "You're the one who found it."

"But it's Christmas. And it's good to share."

Barbie slipped her arm around the young man and gave him a hug. "I'm so proud of you, Joseph. And you're right. When you give love or share your blessings with others, there's always enough to go around."

Susan thought about Maggie's magic treasure story. How strange that someone who might be considered mentally challenged understood a concept she was just now grasping.

"If you'll excuse me," Barbie said, "I think I'll go get Ronnie myself."

Minutes later, Susan found Stan and Donna Ferris outside, seated on a concrete park bench near a fountain. As they greeted each other, Donna thanked her for coming. "It will mean so much to Ronnie to have you here today."

Susan didn't think that was possible. She'd only been around the man a few times.

Moments later, Barbie approached them, pushing her brother's wheelchair. Ronnie, who was in his late fifties and balding, wore a bright red vest, a white T-shirt, and dark sweatpants. Susan hadn't seen him in years, but she would recognize him anywhere.

She reached out and patted his arm. "Hi, Ronnie. You probably don't remember me, but my name's Susan."

"I know you," he said. "I have pictures."

"We gave him a photo album one year for Christmas," Donna said, "and we bring him pictures of the family to add to it."

So her in-laws had been keeping Ronnie abreast of his brother and sister-in-law, even if they hadn't taken time to visit him themselves. The thought—or worse, the reality—was heartbreaking, and tears welled in Susan's eyes.

"He asks each year who'll come to the party," Stan said, "so we were happy when you told Barbie you'd come."

One tear slipped down Susan's cheek, followed by another, and she swiped them away with her fingers. "Well, I promise not to miss any more parties from now on."

"Guess what," Barbie told her brother. "Susan brought brownies. And she made your favorite recipe—the ones with the chocolate fudge icing."

At that, the man smiled. "I like brownies."

Susan's cell phone rang, and as she tried to silence the ringtone, she glanced at the display. It was Rosa.

She probably ought to ignore the call, but Rosa wasn't one to chat. So Susan said, "Excuse me. I'll just be a moment, then I'll shut off my phone completely."

As she flipped open the lid, she spoke into the receiver. "Hi, Rosa. This isn't a good time for me. Can I call you back later this evening?"

"Susan, this isn't Rosa. It's Carlos."

That was odd, Susan thought. "What's up?"

"Rosa . . ." Carlos's voice cracked, and it seemed to take him a moment to continue. "She's unconscious and on her way to the hospital in an ambulance. I have no idea what's wrong with her, but I thought you and her other friends should know."

Susan's heart dropped to the pit of her stomach. "I'll be right there."

Then she turned to provide the Ferris family with a real excuse to leave, one that was far better than any she could have imagined when she'd first arrived—a reason she no longer wanted to have, yet couldn't ignore.

"One of my dearest friends is being rushed to the hospital," she explained. "I'm sorry, but I need to be with her. Please forgive me for leaving. I've had a wonderful time. And I'd love to come back and visit again soon."

"I understand," Barbie said.

Tears welled in Susan's eyes to the point of overflowing again, and as emotion balled up in her throat, she responded with a nod, then headed for the door.

On the way out, she spotted the elderly couple she'd met at the soup kitchen—Stan and Edna Grainger—coming toward the house.

They moved slowly to accommodate Edna's walker, as did the people accompanying them, a tall, rather attractive man and a red-haired girl who carried a guitar.

Susan stopped briefly to say hello, then quickly excused herself and hurried to the car.

"Dear God," she prayed. "Please don't let Rosa's illness be serious."

The thought that it might be critical, that her friend might actually die, was too scary to comprehend.

Maggie and Lynette entered the double doors to the Pacifica General Hospital ER, which was filled with a hodgepodge of people waiting to be seen or for patients they'd brought in. As the women hurried to the reception desk, Lynette's heart was pounding so hard she could feel the pulsation in her head.

Thank goodness she hadn't needed to make this trip alone.

Before Peter had passed away, he'd spent two days in the ICU, which had left Lynette feeling uneasy in a hospital setting. The day he'd died, she'd sworn she would avoid medical centers unless she was a patient and had no other choice. But that was before she learned of Rosa's collapse.

"Excuse me," Maggie said to the receptionist behind the desk. "A friend of ours was brought in by an ambulance. Her name is Rosa Alvarado. Can you tell me if she's still here or if she's been admitted?"

"Let me check."

It felt as though they'd waited for hours, but it was only a matter of minutes when the receptionist said, "Her husband has been taken to a private waiting room. I can show you where he is."

Moments later, the women were led through a security door and down a hall to a small waiting room, where Carlos sat, his face pale, his eyes wide.

"What happened?" Lynette asked.

"I don't know. We were at the soup kitchen, and she was washing dishes. I was talking to her about Christmas Under the Stars and told her that I wanted to have another meeting. She argued with me, but I'd insisted. And . . ." The man who'd been leaning forward, with his forearms resting on his thighs, began to tear up. "It wasn't a big fight. . . . I didn't raise my voice . . . But she . . . gripped her chest . . . and . . . crumpled to the ground."

"Was it a heart attack?" Lynette asked.

"I'm not sure. They won't let me in the room with her." Carlos lifted his head, yet his shoulders remained slumped. "I always thought that I'd be the first of us to go, but if she . . ."

He focused a tear-filled gaze on Lynette, then turned to Maggie. "What am I going to do without her?"

Lynette didn't know how to answer him. She'd lost Peter, and while she'd grieved his passing, they hadn't been together as long as Carlos and Rosa had. And they probably hadn't loved each other as much, either.

"I can't believe this." Carlos slowly shook his head. "After all the time we've spent on the less fortunate and the time we've given to charity . . . Well, it's just not fair."

In a sense, Lynette felt the same way Carlos did. The Alvarados did more in a week for the community and the church than Lynette, Helen, or Susan did all year. Rosa still had work to do on earth. Why would God let this happen? Or if worse came to worst, why would He take her away?

Maggie eased forward and placed a hand on the anguished man's shoulder. "It sounds to me as though you think you made a deal with God, and that He didn't hold up His end of the bargain."

"It's not as though we entered into any kind of covenant," Carlos said, "but I followed the rules and obeyed His commandments. That should be enough. . . ."

"To earn a ticket to Heaven?" Maggie asked.

Lynette's heart dropped to the pit of her stomach. Was Maggie suggesting that Rosa was going to die, that she was receiving her just reward?

She certainly deserved it, but what about those who loved her? Those left behind? And what about all the people she'd helped—the homeless, the poor, the downtrodden? Surely her work on earth wasn't finished.

"Heaven is a gift of grace," Maggie said. "You can't earn your way there."

"Maybe you're right," Carlos said. "But didn't Jesus say, 'Whatever you do unto the least of these, you do unto Me'?"

"Yes, He did. And we do that out of love for Him and obedience to His Word, not as a means to secure our place in

Heaven." Maggie took the chair next to Carlos. "I don't know why this happened or what the outcome will be. But you need to slow down on your volunteerism. All the work took a toll on Rosa's health."

Carlos seemed to ponder her words, then ran a hand through his hair. "You're right. I pushed her too hard. And earlier, at the soup kitchen, I argued with her. She was telling me that she was tired, that she didn't think another meeting was necessary, and I refused to listen."

"Rosa has been breathing hard and dragging herself from one event to another for months. And while she didn't complain—"

"She shouldn't have had to," Carlos said. "I should have seen the signs, and I failed her."

Before either Maggie or Lynette could say anything else, a man wearing a white lab coat entered the room. "Mr. Alvarado?"

Carlos got to his feet. "Yes?"

"I'm Dr. Jacobi. I'm afraid your wife has had a heart attack."

"Is she going to . . . be okay?" Carlos asked.

"It was very serious, and we still have more tests to run, but she's stabilized for the time being."

"Can I see her?"

"For a few minutes."

As Carlos followed the doctor out of the room, the women took a seat. Lynette's thoughts were on Rosa, but she couldn't help being a little confused about what Maggie had told Carlos. So she turned in her seat to question the woman who seemed to have her spiritual ducks in a row, wondering if she actually did. "I'm a little confused. You've been telling Susan and me that we need to be doing more for others, yet you just told Carlos that he and Rosa needed to do less. It seems to be a contradiction, unless there's a fine line between not enough and too much."

"It's more complicated than that," Maggie said. "A person

can't earn God's favor. It's impossible for anyone to be good enough. And it was for that very reason that God, in a loving act of grace, sent His Son to die for anyone willing to accept His gift."

"I get that part. Those who accept His Son are assured of their place in Heaven. And doing for others is a good thing for us to do. But . . . ?"

"When a person becomes a child of God, he seeks to do the will of the Father—which is to feed the hungry, care for the sick, and provide for the poor. And he rejoices in doing those things because he's experienced God's love and grace himself."

Lynette still wasn't sure she understood the point Maggie was trying to make. "You mean, when I learned that my hairdresser had fallen upon hard times, and I went out and bought her and her children Christmas presents, I was doing the will of the Father?"

"How did you feel while you were shopping for the gifts? And when you gave them to your hairdresser?"

"Pretty awesome, actually. It was as though I'd somehow done something special and made the world a better place."

"There you go. It's all in the motivation."

Lynette thought about that for a while. "So you're saying that Carlos wasn't trying to make the world a better place?"

"I'm sure he was, to an extent. But in his overzealous push to impress God with his good deeds, he failed to see how he was hurting Rosa in the process. And as a husband, he vowed before God and man to love, honor, and cherish his wife."

Lynette wasn't sure how Maggie, who barely knew them, had come to that conclusion, yet it seemed to be a reasonable assumption.

While she considered all she'd heard, Maggie got to her feet, walked across the small room to the open doorway, and peered into the hall. "Here she comes now."

"Who?" Lynette asked.

"Susan."

For a moment, Lynette had completely forgotten about the fact that Susan would be coming to the hospital—and that she was still angry and hurt. Lynette wished she would have apologized sooner, but she hadn't. And now it was long overdue.

Still, in the scheme of things, the hurt her words had caused and making it right seemed pretty minor now.

Would Susan feel the same way?

Maggie stepped away from the doorway, and Susan walked in dressed in black pants, a white blouse, and a red silky Christmas vest.

"What happened?" she asked. "How's Rosa?"

As Maggie filled her in on the details, Lynette struggled to come up with the words that needed to be said, hoping and praying that they'd come to her.

And that when they did, she could handle Susan's reaction—whatever that might be.

Chapter 19

As Susan stood in the center of the small waiting room, with its stark white walls and cold gray chairs, she couldn't believe that Rosa had suffered a serious heart attack.

Still caught up in the innocent, childlike faith she'd just witnessed in some of the residents of Lydia's House earlier, she tried to find a ray of hope in the situation. "If the doctor said she was stable, that means she's going to pull through, don't you think?"

"I'm not sure," Maggie said. "They're still running tests, so she's probably not out of the woods yet."

As the hope Susan had tried to hang on to wavered, she released the breath she'd been holding.

It was hard to believe that the woman who'd given so much of herself to her family, friends, and the community might die. Just the thought of never seeing Rosa's smiling face or hearing her laugh again was too much to bear.

"She's going to be okay," Susan said. "I'm going to hold on to that belief. She's too good and too young to die."

Maggie placed her hand on Susan's shoulder. "Life is a journey, and no one knows just how long each one will be."

"Then I'll pray that Rosa's journey isn't finished yet." It was all Susan could do, all she could hang on to.

Feeling more helpless than her words had indicated, she slipped her hands into the pockets of her Christmas vest, only to finger something hard and round—the copper penny Joseph had given her at the party.

It's a lucky day, he'd said.

At the time, she'd been touched that he'd shared his good fortune with her, but Susan wasn't feeling very lucky anymore. She pulled the coin from her pocket and looked at it, remembering the disabled man's words.

It's good to share, he'd said.

That was true, but Susan had very little to offer anyone. Even her hope-filled thoughts hadn't convinced Maggie that things would turn out all right.

She glanced to the corner of the room, where Lynette sat in silence, her expression one of fear and grief.

Was she letting go of hope before they had reason to?

"I suppose it's a good time for us to pray," Susan said.

"Prayer always helps," Maggie said, "although it should never be considered a last resort. God likes to hear from His children on a regular basis."

"You're probably right, but my prayers don't seem to be very effective." Susan thought about her nightly pleas, about begging God not to let her spend another holiday alone, without the one thing that would make her whole.

"Maybe you've been praying for something you've had all along." Maggie's blue eyes flashed with something akin to understanding, although that wasn't possible.

Or had she been suggesting that Barbie, Stan, and Donna Ferris were her family? And maybe even Ronnie, too?

Before her visit to Lydia's House, Susan wouldn't have even considered the possibility, let alone been encouraged by it. Yet even if she felt closer to her in-laws now than she had in ages, they weren't the family she'd been praying for, the one in which she'd have a child of her own to hold and love.

At that moment, Lynette, who'd been sitting in a corner of the room, got to her feet and approached Susan.

"I know this is a bad time," Lynette said, "but I want you to know how sorry I am that I hurt your feelings the other day. You're one of the most honest, trustworthy, well-meaning women I know. And you were the perfect choice to hold on to our poker money. Anyone could have made a mistake in addition. And I shouldn't have pointed it out in front of anyone."

Right now, none of that seemed to matter anymore. But Susan couldn't quite bring herself to tell Lynette there'd been no harm done.

"I'm also sorry about trying to set up Grant with Carly," Lynette added. "I truly didn't realize you were interested in him."

"Maybe not, but you knew I would've liked having a matchmaker of my own. You even teased me about being on a manhunt."

"Yes, that's true. But you never mentioned the name of the man you were hunting."

If truth be told, his name hadn't mattered all that much. She'd just wanted to have a special man in her life this Christmas, and hope for a family in the coming year.

And right now, as Susan stood to lose one friend to death, she didn't want to risk losing another to anger or stubbornness.

"I'm sorry, too," Susan said. "I suppose I've been a little jealous of you."

"Of me?" Surprise splashed upon Lynette's pretty young face. "Why?"

"Because you're rich and beautiful. And you have everything it takes to attract a husband. You've also got plenty of time to bear a houseful of children, if you want to."

Lynette seemed to ponder that for a moment, then slowly shook her head. "For what it's worth, I don't *feel* all that lucky. And I doubt that all the money in Fort Knox would make any difference in the way I've always seen myself."

Susan fingered Joseph's penny, then reached for Lynette's hand and pressed the coin into her palm. "This was freely given to me in love, and I'm giving it to you. If you lose every bit of that inheritance Peter left you, there's enough love in that single penny to see you through anything life throws your way."

Lynette studied the copper coin as though she'd been given a diamond. And maybe, in a way, she had been given a priceless gem. When she looked up, she said, "Thank you, but I'm not sure I should take this from you."

"Why not?"

Lynette took in a deep breath, then slowly let it out. "Because you're not the only one feeling badly about Grant going out with Carly."

Susan wasn't following her.

"I . . ." Lynette looked at Maggie, as though needing a little moral support, then continued. "I'm attracted to Grant, and he asked me to go out with him, too. If I accept, which I'd really like to do, I could end up hurting Carly or you. And it seems as if I'd be breaking some kind of BFF code. Know what I mean?"

"So you'd miss out on a chance at happiness just for me?"

"You're my friend, Susan. And the Lils are the sisters I never had."

Susan wrapped her arms around Lynette. "Right this moment, with Rosa in there fighting for her life, your love and friendship mean a lot more to me than having a man in my life."

Before Lynette could respond, Carlos entered the waiting room.

"How's Rosa doing?" Susan asked.

"She's still alive, but she doesn't look good." A tear slipped down the man's cheek. "Why didn't I realize how sick she was before? Why didn't I insist that she take it easy? Or that she see a doctor?"

Susan didn't know what to say. As it was, she could only tell Carlos that she'd be there for him—and hopefully, for Rosa, if God allowed her journey to continue.

* * *

Even though his mom had told him and Mikey that there wouldn't be a tree or presents this year, Josh was still excited about it being Christmas Eve and was sure it would be a good one. Thanks to Lynette, he and his brother had a really cool gift to give their mother this year, and he couldn't wait to see the look on her face when she opened the box and found that pretty scarf.

They might not have a tree, but that didn't matter, either. They'd be going to Mulberry Park for the Christmas program, and if it was anything like last year's event, there'd be plenty of trees lit up and decorated. So who needed to have one in the house?

"Hey, guys," Mom said, as she entered the living room wearing a pair of jeans and a long-sleeved sweater. "Max will be here in a few minutes, and I need to talk to you guys before he comes."

She probably wanted to tell them the rules, like how to act and what to eat, and while that might have bothered Josh before, he didn't care so much about it now.

After talking to Mr. Tolliver the night he'd come over for dinner, Josh had done some thinking about the things he'd said. And he figured that mothers couldn't help bossing their kids around. It was how they showed their love.

"I thought it might be nice if we prayed together before we went," Mom said.

Josh wasn't sure why she'd suggest something like that, but he guessed it was okay.

As his mom reached out her hands for the boys to take hold, Josh stepped forward. And there, in the middle of the living room, they came together in a circle and bowed their heads.

"Heavenly Father," Mom said, "we just want to thank You for seeing us through a difficult year. We thank You for the blessings You've given us—even those we haven't yet seen. Help us to be a blessing to others, not just tonight, but always."

She paused as if waiting for either Josh or Mikey to chime in with words of their own, but Josh didn't have anything to say—at least, not out loud. He liked to keep his talks with God private.

"Lord," Mikey finally said, "I know You can do anything, so would You please let it snow tomorrow? Lots of kids have white Christmases, and I've never had one before. Besides, when I told Nick Hastings all about You, he said You weren't real. And I told him that I would prove that You were by asking You to make it snow tomorrow. Please do it so that Nick can believe in You. Amen."

Josh couldn't help but roll his eyes. Why would Mikey go out on a limb like that? It *never* snowed in Fairbrook.

"Honey," Mom said, "it's not a good idea to put God to a test like that."

"But didn't He turn water into wine?" Mikey asked. "And walk on water? And part the Red Sea? God does miracles all the time, Mom, so making it snow in Fairbrook ought to be easy for Him."

Josh couldn't help but grin. How was their mom going to answer *that* one?

Mikey crossed his arms and shifted his weight to one leg. "All we got to do is believe, Mom."

"I *do* believe. And while I don't mean to place limits on what God can do, we live on the coast in San Diego County, and the last time it snowed at sea level was . . . Well, it was before I was even born, and it didn't last very long."

"Are you forgetting that God can do anything?"

"No," Mom said, "but He also set natural laws into effect, which means there are certain climates that are prone to snow and others that aren't. So I don't want to see you disappointed tomorrow."

"Maybe I won't be," he said.

At that moment, the doorbell rang, and his mom let the whole thing go.

"It's not going to snow," Josh told his brother. "So you

might as well think of something to tell that kid when you see him at school in January."

Mikey just scrunched his nose and made a face.

"Hi, Max," Mom said, as she let Mr. Tolliver and Hemingway into the house. "Come on in."

"Are you ready?" the man asked.

"We just need to grab our jackets and the lawn chairs."

Minutes later, they all piled into Mr. Tolliver's car and drove to Mulberry Park, which was already filling up with people and families spreading out blankets and setting up folding chairs.

The trees at the far end of the park were covered in white blinking lights, and a stage had been set up for the band that would play Christmas carols.

After getting out of the car, they crossed the lawn, making their way through the park. Josh and Mr. Tolliver carried the chairs, while his mom walked beside them and Mikey led Hemingway by his leash.

It was weird, Josh thought. For the first time since his dad had walked out on them, it seemed as though he was part of a family again.

He stole a glance at Mr. Tolliver, who'd said he could call him Max, but Josh didn't know about that. As much as he'd like to have a man to look up to, he wasn't sure Mr. Tolliver was that guy.

It'd be cool to have a stepdad, though—at least, for his mom's sake—but something like that would be too good to be true. After all, his own dad hadn't wanted him or Mikey, so what made him think that a guy who didn't even have a blood connection to them would want to step in and be there for them?

And one divorce was enough for a family to go through.

About the time Josh figured the evening was going to be a nice one anyway, he spotted Ross "the Boss" walking toward him, and his whole world exploded.

Oh, crap. Why did that guy have to go and ruin everyone's Christmas?

Ross glared at Josh as though he would rush over and kick his butt right now—if there weren't a couple of adults with him. And Josh didn't doubt that he would.

So there went any possibility of drinking hot cocoa or anything else tonight. No way did Josh want to risk a trip to the bathroom, where Ross might find him without anyone to protect him.

But then again, he realized Ross was with an adult, too, this evening—a man who must be his dad.

It seemed unfair that a jerk like Ross would have a father, when guys like Josh didn't.

As he gave the man a once-over, Josh saw that he was looking at Mr. Tolliver with a funny expression—kind of like he recognized him and wasn't all that happy about it. Or maybe he just wasn't happy to be walking in the park with his son. Josh sure wouldn't be if he felt responsible for raising a mean kid like that.

Uh-oh. Mr. Tolliver turned in the Shurlocks' direction, which meant the men really did know each other. As he reached out a hand to Ross's dad, Josh wanted to melt into the damp grass.

"Hey, Frank," Mr. Tolliver said. "How's it going?"

Aw, man. He wasn't going to invite them to all sit together, was he?

"All right," the man said.

"You got a minute?" Mr. Tolliver asked.

"Sure."

Mr. Tolliver nodded his head to the left, and the men stepped away, out of earshot, leaving Ross to glare at Josh with beady little eyes that seemed to say, "I think you're pond scum."

So much for God working miracles in this day and age—or answering prayers at all for that matter.

* * *

Max hadn't expected to run into one of his former defendants at the park, and under normal circumstances, they would have silently acknowledged each other and gone about their own ways. But that was before he'd realized that Frank Shurlock's son—and who else could it be when they looked enough alike to be brothers?—was the kid who'd been bullying Josh.

So he'd asked Frank to speak in private.

"What's up?" the man asked. "You're not my PO anymore."

"I know. I'd heard you were doing well, and that your probation would be up at the end of the year."

"Yeah. I've been going to AA and following the program. I'm also trying to right a few wrongs, which hasn't been easy. My wife and I split up after the trial, so I've been trying to convince her to let me see my son."

"Is that him?" Max asked, glancing at the bully.

"Yeah. He's got a lot of anger built up inside of him, all of it aimed at me. But I'm trying to make up for all I put him and his mom through. I guess it's just going to take some time."

"I'm glad things are on an uphill swing," Max said. "And I'm even happier to know that you're trying to make amends with your boy, but I think his anger has been directed at more people than just you."

"What do you mean?"

"I saw him bullying a smaller kid the other day in front of my house. I stopped the fight, and he took off. I had no idea he was your son until I spotted him with you this evening. I tried to get Josh, the boy I'm with, to tell me his name, but he refused to snitch."

Frank glanced down at his feet, then back at Max. "I guess I'll be paying for my mistakes for a long time."

"Not necessarily. By joining AA, making new friends, and trying to right things with your family, you're off to a good start. You also might want to check into some counseling to help you work on a better relationship with your son." Max reached into his back pocket, pulled out his wallet, and searched for one of several business cards he always kept on hand.

When he found the one he'd been looking for, he handed it to Frank. "Here you go. Arlene Soto is a great counselor. Tell her that I referred you."

"Thanks, but I can't afford it."

"Arlene works on a sliding scale. She's also been given a federal grant to help keep the costs down for people who've been on probation or parole. You really ought to check into it."

"Okay, I will."

Max continued to thumb through his cards and pulled out one belonging to Ramon Gonzales. "Here's someone else who might be able to help. Ramon is involved in a special sports program for kids who have one or more parents incarcerated. I know you're out of jail now, but your son is still eligible to participate. You'd be surprised at how good Ramon is with those kids."

Frank took Ramon's card. "It might do Ross some good to learn teamwork."

"And it'll probably help him channel some of his energy."

"I'll talk to him about it."

Max nodded, then added, "I hope you'll handle the bullying issue discreetly. Josh refused to tattle, and if your son thinks he had anything to do with our talk, it could backfire, and I don't want Josh caught in the backlash."

"I'll keep Josh out of it, and I'll see what I can do to put a stop to the bullying."

"I'd appreciate that, Frank. I'd hate to see your son go down the wrong path and end up in trouble."

"You and me both."

When the men returned to the others, Max introduced Frank as a friend of his. Then he placed a hand on Ross's shoulder. "I spotted your son in front of my house the other day. I had no idea that you two were related. It's a small world, isn't it?"

"Sure is," Frank said. "And thanks for the advice. I'll be giving both Arlene and Ramon a call first thing after Christmas."

As Frank and his son walked away, Ross glanced over his shoulder. But this time, instead of that surly expression he'd been wearing on his approach, he wore one of disbelief.

"Is Frank an old friend?" Carly asked.

Max didn't want to lie, yet he didn't want to claim the guy had once been on his caseload. "I worked with him last year."

She nodded, probably assuming that they'd been coworkers.

"So where do you want to sit?" he asked.

"Anywhere you like."

"Then this is as good a place as any," he said.

So they set up the chairs and took a seat, waiting for the event to start.

It felt a little surreal to be watching a Christmas program at Mulberry Park with a beautiful woman and her two sons, which was a first for him—and a nice one at that.

As it neared six o'clock, a couple of teenage girls began passing out unlit candles to everyone in the audience. As they offered them to Max, he took four, keeping one for himself and giving Carly and the boys the other three, just as if they were a family unit.

You'd think he'd be feeling uneasy about that, which was why he'd initially told Carly that he hadn't wanted to attend the Christmas program with her. But he wasn't the least bit uncomfortable now and was actually glad that he'd come.

After all, she could have invited Grant, and she hadn't.

Okay, so for all he knew, maybe she had asked Grant, and he'd turned her down. Either way, Max liked thinking that she'd chosen him over the other guy.

If truth be told, Max wasn't sure if he should be happy

about that or worried. It could mean competing with Grant for Carly's affection, he supposed, which was something he'd refused to do when Karen had left him.

As Craig Houston, the pastor at Parkside Community Church, welcomed the community to the fifth annual Christmas Under the Stars event, Max turned to look at Carly, who was gazing back at him. Her eyes shimmered with something he hadn't seen in a long time—if ever—and her smile reached deep inside of him, applying a balm on whatever might have been hurt or broken in the past.

Yes, he was going to have to tell Grant that he was dating Carly, too. And if that meant a competition, so be it. Max and his character, Logan Sinclair, had been through a lot these past few days, and like Logan had decided during the course of the book, there were some women a man shouldn't let walk away.

Before long, a few people in the front lit their candles, using one flame to light another, and by the time the fire came their way, the event got underway.

A man read Luke's version of the Christmas story, then a woman led them in singing carols, including a couple Max had once considered his favorites, "Silent Night" and "The First Noel."

When the evening was over, and they'd had their fill of hot cocoa and goodies, Max and Carly rounded up the kids and the dog, then headed for his car.

He'd never felt like a part of a family before, and while he'd reminded himself that he'd warned Grant about Carly's "baggage," the fact that she had kids didn't seem to be a big deal. In fact, it almost made her even more appealing.

The trip back to Carly's house took only a couple of minutes, and Max found himself driving slower than usual, wanting to stretch out the time they were together.

Would she invite him in? He sure hoped so. He wasn't in any hurry to go home to an empty house after the night he'd just had.

As he pulled up in front of her house, she let out a gasp. "Oh, no!"

"What's the matter?" he asked.

"My . . . car. It's . . . gone."

Stolen? That was terrible.

"Let's call the police," he said. "The sooner we report it, the better chance there is that they'll recover it."

While he reached for his cell phone, he glanced across the console and saw her face in the streetlight, the tears in her eyes.

"It'll be okay," he said, turning on the interior lights and flipping open his phone.

She dug through her purse, then handed her keys to Josh. "Take your brother in the house, will you? I'll be there in a minute."

Assuming that she didn't want the kids to hear the phone call to the police, Max waited until Mikey gave Hemingway a good-night hug and the boys climbed out of the car. Then, as they headed to the front door, he began to dial the number from memory.

Before he could finish, Carly reached across the console and gripped his arm. "Wait a minute, Max. That might not be necessary. I don't think it was stolen."

"What makes you say that?"

"Because . . ." A tear slid down her cheek, and her bottom lip began to quiver. "I'm behind on the payments, and I think it was repossessed."

Oh, no. And on Christmas Eve? Of all the nights for something like that to happen. Didn't those repo guys have families—or a heart?

"It'll be okay," he told Carly, knowing he'd do what he could to get her car out of hock once the holiday had passed.

"No, it won't be." A second tear slipped down her cheek, followed by one after another. "The trunk was full of presents for the boys, thanks to the generosity of one of my clients. So now those gifts are gone, too."

Max glanced at his wristwatch. He was guessing the stores were all closed, so he couldn't even go shopping for the kids himself.

"Thanks for a nice evening," she said, her voice breaking as she reached for the door handle.

What did he say to that? How did he end the night when he knew how devastating it must be for her?

"Is there something I can do to help?" he asked.

"No." She managed a broken smile. "I'm afraid not. But don't worry. We'll be okay."

So she said, but he didn't believe her. Still, he walked her to the door, hoping she'd invite him in and suspecting that she wouldn't.

When it became clear that she was going to enter the house alone, he placed a hand on her cheek and kissed her brow, wishing he could do more, knowing that he couldn't.

As she went inside, closed the door, and clicked the dead bolt, Max returned to his car, feeling as helpless as he'd ever felt in his life.

"Carly deserves a Christmas miracle," he said in a lame attempt to pray. "I know that her prayers are more apt to reach You than mine, but can You please give her a break—at least, for the kids' sake?"

Then he started up the engine, trying to have faith when there wasn't any to be found.

Chapter 20

Susan stood behind the lit dessert table in Mulberry Park, serving goodies to those who'd just participated in Christmas Under the Stars.

Carlos and Rosa, who'd been the committee chairs for the event, hadn't been able to attend since Rosa was still in the hospital and Carlos refused to leave her side. So Susan had volunteered to do whatever she could to help out this evening. And thanks to all the work the Alvarados had put in ahead of time, everything had gone according to plan.

She would suggest that they ask the volunteers to make more of the frosted sugar cookies next year. They'd gone over especially well with the children and were gone before the singing had ended. Of course, they'd had a bigger turnout than they'd anticipated this evening, according to what Susan had been told. In fact there were still a lot of people milling about, laughing and chatting with each other.

Yet even though Susan had found herself surrounded by children and families this evening, she'd kept busy enough that she hadn't felt too awfully sorry for herself.

As she rearranged a couple of platters, a male voice asked, "How's it going?"

Susan looked up to see Pastor Craig Houston, who'd emceed tonight's event, standing before her table. She smiled at the nice-looking young man and said, "No problems whatsoever. Are you ready for a cup of coffee yet? Or maybe some hot cocoa? The drinks are to your left, and all the goodies are right here."

"Thanks." The fair-haired minister reached for a Snickerdoodle. "Carlos will be happy to know that everything ran like clockwork tonight."

"Speaking of Carlos, have you been to the hospital today?"

"I stopped by this afternoon, and Rosa's condition still hasn't been upgraded."

"That's the word I got this morning. The heart attack caused a lot of damage, and she's still critical."

Craig's expression grew somber. "Carlos asked me to find someone to fill his and Rosa's positions for a while. He's talking about taking some time off. He even promised to take her to Belize after she's able to have surgery."

Neither of them mentioned the fact that doctors were unable to perform a bypass due to complications from her other health issues.

"It's too bad that it takes a crisis for some people to get their priorities straight," Susan said. "Rosa has wanted to take a cruise for a long time. I just hope she'll be able to do that."

"She's on the church prayer chain, so we'll just have to have faith that she'll pull through."

"I hope so." Still, Susan couldn't help thinking about what Maggie had said. *Life is a journey, and no one knows just how long each one will be.*

Or what to expect along the way, she supposed.

"Hmm," Craig said, as he munched on one of the chewy cookies. "These are really good."

"Aren't they?" Susan inadvertently placed a hand on her stomach, which was always the first thing to expand when she put on weight. "I've had several already, but I'll worry about the extra calories after Christmas."

"If there's one thing to say for the congregants at Parkside

Community—we always have plenty of food at our potlucks, not to mention the best desserts you'll ever eat." Craig tossed her a smile. "So you're going to have to start coming around more often."

Susan's church attendance, as Craig obviously knew, had dwindled to almost nothing in the weeks after Hank's death, but instead of making an excuse when there really wasn't one, she said, "I'll make a point of it, Pastor. Don't be surprised if you see me on Sunday."

"Good." He popped the last of the cookie into his mouth, then reached for one of the brownies Susan had made for the event, just as Kristy, Craig's wife, approached the table with their eight-year-old son, Jason.

The minister slipped one arm around the beautiful brunette and stroked the back of the boy's hair. "Did you guys get enough to eat?"

"More than enough," Kristy said. "Do you want us to wait for you?"

"I'm sure Jason's tired, honey. And he's probably going to be up before dawn. So why don't you take him home and put him to bed? I shouldn't be too much longer."

Kristy nodded, then after telling Susan good night and blessing Craig with a love-you-honey kiss, she took her son's hand and led him to the spot on the lawn where they'd left their blanket.

That, Susan realized, was exactly what she'd been missing. Or at least, it was what she'd thought she was missing. For some reason, her longing for a family seemed to have decreased over the past few days, even though Christmas morning loomed on the horizon.

"Well, I'd better get back to work and help with the teardown and cleanup." Craig reached for two more cookies, tucked them into his jacket pocket, then grinned at Susan. "I'll just take a couple of these for the road."

As Susan watched the man go, she looked forward to attending church services on Sunday and hearing him preach.

"Excuse me," a young voice said, drawing Susan's attention to an eleven- or twelve-year-old girl standing in front of the table. "Is it okay if I take some of these cookies home?"

The leftovers were supposed to be wrapped up and taken to the soup kitchen, but Susan hated to say no to the copper-haired girl with a knit scarf and mittens. "Sure. How many do you want?"

"At least two, but as many as you can spare, I guess." The girl looked a little familiar, and Susan tried to remember where she'd seen her.

"They're for our neighbors," a dark-haired man behind the child said. "Stan and Edna are members of the church, but the cold weather bothers their arthritis, so they couldn't attend tonight. My daughter thought it would be a nice gesture."

Now she knew why the girl looked familiar. "I saw you pick them up at the soup kitchen when their car was on the blink. And you were also with them at Lydia's House."

The man smiled and nodded. "I'm Adam Barfield, and this is my daughter, Penny."

Adam and Penny? Even their names sounded familiar, although Susan couldn't say why.

Had the Graingers introduced them?

No, she didn't think so. She did, however, remember what the elderly woman had said about her neighbor.

He lost his wife in a car accident nearly a year ago, but he's a good father and is trying to make the best of things this Christmas. Stan and I would like to help, but there's not much we can do. I did knit the girl a muffler and mittens with scraps of yarn I had.

"It's nice to meet you," Susan said, reaching out her hand to the girl's father as she introduced herself.

Her hands, which were chilly from the night air, relished the warmth of his touch, as well as his firm grip. And while she found herself wanting to study him a bit longer, she turned her attention to the girl. "That's a pretty scarf, Penny."

"Thank you. Edna made it for me. She's teaching me how to knit, although I'm not very good at it."

"Penny's pretty talented, especially when it comes to music," her father said, "so I'm sure she'll catch on before we know it."

"Do you play the guitar?" Susan asked, remembering that she'd carried one the day she'd been at Lydia's House.

Penny nodded. "Music is a lot easier than knitting, though."

She was a sweet girl, Susan decided. And with that pretty hair color, the name suited her.

"Well, we'd better get going," Adam said. "Stan and Edna usually go to bed early, and we want to take the cookies to them before they turn in for the night."

Susan went right to work, filling a plate with goodies, then placing a piece of foil over the top. "How's this?"

"It's great," Penny said. "Thanks so much."

"No problem." Susan studied the man for a moment. He wasn't what you'd call handsome, but she found him appealing just the same. And he clearly adored his daughter.

"Stan and Edna are lucky to have you two as neighbors," she said.

"We're the lucky ones." Adam placed a hand on Penny's shoulder. "We don't have any family around here, and neither do they. So we've kind of adopted each other, which makes it nice."

"It sounds like a win/win."

"It is." Adam's gaze seemed to linger on Susan.

Or had she only imagined it?

"Maybe we'll see you at church sometime," Penny said.

That would be nice. So she said, "I'll be there this coming Sunday at the ten o'clock service."

"We'll be there, too." Adam tossed her a smile. "Merry Christmas, Susan."

"Same to you." As Susan watched the man and his daughter walk off, she couldn't help thinking that there was something almost . . . magical . . . about this night . . .

Carly had fought her tears and heartache as long as the kids were around, but once she'd gone into her bedroom, she'd broken down and cried.

"Why?" she'd asked between sobs. "I don't understand why You would let this happen, especially tonight."

But as far as prayers went, that was all she could muster. Anything more seemed like a lost cause.

Sure, she still believed that God was in control, that He'd help her work through her financial mess, that He'd somehow make all things right. But He certainly didn't seem to be very hard at work—or to see her prayers as having any kind of priority.

Feeling a bit betrayed—not to mention frustrated and a little angry—she had to admit that she really did have a lot to be thankful for—her children, their health.

So who needed a present when they had that?

But the car? Now that was a problem. How was she going to get back and forth to work?

The bus came to mind, but it wasn't a comforting thought.

Oh, well. There wasn't any use crying over spilled milk, so she cuddled beneath the warmth of the quilt her mom had made years ago and eventually fell asleep.

Minutes—or maybe hours?—later, she dreamed of glass clinking on glass.

Or was she actually being awakened by the sound?

As her eyes opened, she tried to focus in the morning light, only to hear the sound again—something hard hitting her windowpane.

What could it be?

She threw off the covers, rolled out of bed, and padded to the window. When she pulled back the curtains and peered outside, she spotted Max lifting his arm and preparing to pitch something.

A little stone?

She unlocked the window and slid it open, only to feel a blast of the cold morning air on her face. As she peered out into the gray dawn, she called out to Max, who was wearing a ski jacket and boots. "What are you doing?"

"Trying to get your attention without ringing the doorbell and waking the kids."

She rubbed the tops of her arms, attempting to chase away the chill to no avail. "Why?"

"Because I brought Christmas to you." He nodded toward the street. "Unlock your front door so I can bring it inside."

She didn't know if she should laugh or cry. What had he done?

And better yet, why had he done it?

Unable to wrap her mind around an answer, she decided that the only thing that mattered was that he had. So she shut the window, hurried to the closet, and pulled out her robe. Then after slipping it on, she tiptoed to the boys' bedroom, closed the door quietly, then went to let Max in.

As she watched him untie a tree of some kind from the top of his car, her breath caught. She took a step onto the porch, planning to help him somehow, but as her bare feet touched the cold concrete, she had a change of heart and returned to the house.

Goodness, it was cold out—gray and dreary, too.

What time was it? She had no way of knowing without looking at a clock.

As Max removed the tree from the car, her heart swelled to the bursting point. How sweet of him to do this for the boys, for her.

Realizing she should have included him as one of the blessings she'd counted last night, she whispered a follow-up thank-You for Max.

As he carried in the ugliest, scrawniest tree she'd ever seen before—a tree that might not even be a pine—into the house, she asked, "Where did you get this?"

"From my backyard. I cut it down last night." His cheeks were flushed from the cold, his eyes twinkled with excitement. "I even strung the lights on it already. All we need is a plug and something to lean it against."

Tears welled in her eyes, this time the happy kind that sprang forth when she laughed herself silly—something she couldn't remember doing in a long time. "This is so sweet of you."

"Yeah, maybe. But I don't think my neighbors appreciated my grunts and groans at midnight. I came away with a couple of scrapes on my knuckles and a respect for loggers." He smiled, revealing a pair of dimples that creased his cheeks. "So what do you have to put this in?"

"I'll get the stand out of the garage."

"While you do that, I'll bring in the presents."

"You got the boys gifts, too?"

"Well, nothing new. But I had some stuff around the house and garage that I figured would make them both happy. We'll see if I was right."

There, in the center of the living room, with a rush of cold air still wafting in from the open front door, Carly went up on tiptoes and wrapped her arms around the sweetest man she'd ever met. "How can I ever thank you?"

"Well," he said, chuckling. "This is a good start. But it would be nicer if you hugged me again when I have both arms free."

"I'd be happy to."

Then she took off to the garage, in search of a tree stand, and the angel that had been in her family for years.

When she returned, Max stood in the living room, with Hemingway at his side. The dog wore a big red bow on his collar, and Max held an armful of aluminum-foil-wrapped gifts. One was at least six feet long and skinny. "What in the world is that?"

He lowered his voice to a whisper. "It's a fishing pole. I'm also giving Josh a gift certificate for a fishing trip."

The tears struck again, blurring her vision. "He's going to love that."

"I hope so." He set the gifts down near the hearth. "I also wrapped a tackle box, which I've only used a couple of times."

Max had outdone himself, and she was speechless.

"There's only one problem," he said.

She certainly hadn't seen one yet. "What's that?"

"I hope you don't mind, but I'm giving Mikey the dog."

Her lips parted, and even though she wanted to object, she couldn't bring herself to do it. Her youngest son adored that dog.

"I know it's not cheap to have a pet," Max said, "but we can share custody, and I'll foot the bills for food and the vet. Besides, Hemingway loves the kids, and he'll be happier living with them."

It might be way too soon to ponder the possibility, but for this very moment in time, she loved Max Tolliver with all her heart.

Finally, she said, "I don't know what to say."

"You don't have to say anything—especially any comments about the Charlie Brown Christmas tree. It really was the best I could do at the last minute."

"The tree, the gifts . . . It's a miracle as far as I'm concerned."

And last night, while she'd been crying and—yes, even blaming God for not answering her prayers in the way she'd wanted Him to—He'd been answering them all along.

And in a wonderful, unexpected way.

* * *

Lynette had been so worried about Rosa that she hadn't slept very well last night. She'd finally gotten up at a little after six, then put on a pot of coffee.

As the water began to gurgle in the carafe, and the aroma began to fill the room, the phone rang.

She had no idea who it could be, and the thought that it might be Carlos, calling with bad news, made her stomach knot. Still, she snatched the receiver from its cradle and answered.

"Hello?"

"Hi, Lynnie. It's Helen. I called to wish you a Merry Christmas."

Lynette blew out a ragged sigh of relief. "Where are you?"

"We just got into port in New York. We'll stay two days in Manhattan, then I'll fly home on the twenty-seventh."

"Did you have a good time?"

"The best ever. Wait until you see all of my pictures."

Lynette hated to have to be the one to tell her, but Helen needed to know about Rosa. So she relayed the bad news, trying to make a positive outcome a little more possible than it actually might be.

"Oh, no. That's terrible. Will you please keep me posted? I'll keep my cell phone charged and handy."

"I'll let you know if there's any change. We sure missed you, Helen. But we enjoyed having a chance to meet Maggie."

"Maggie?"

"Your cousin."

There was a beat of silence, then Helen said, "I don't have a cousin named Maggie."

Of course, Lynette had forgotten. Maggie was only a nickname. "I mean Mary-Margaret Di Angelo. You e-mailed us about her, saying she would house-sit for you while you were gone and asking us to introduce ourselves to her."

"I didn't e-mail anyone," Helen said. "And I don't know a

woman by that name. In fact, I asked Grant and Max to look after my house for me."

Lynette blinked several times, trying to sort through the information she'd been given.

"What are you saying?" Helen asked, her voice rising an octave. "Has someone been staying in my house?"

"Yes, I'm afraid so."

"Oh, no. It must be a drifter . . . Or a homeless person trying to stay out of the cold. Or maybe a criminal hiding out from the law . . ."

"She's actually very nice, so I'm sure there's a mistake." Lynette couldn't imagine what it would be, though. "Don't worry, Helen. I'll check on your house right now."

"Thanks, Lynnie. Call me as soon as you know something."

"I will."

As Lynette hung up the telephone, she wondered what she was getting herself into.

And just who Mary-Margaret Di Angelo, aka Maggie, really was.

Chapter 21

Twenty minutes later, Lynette had showered, thrown on some clothes, as well as her jacket, and driven over to Helen's.

As difficult as it was for her to believe that Maggie, who was one of the sweetest, gentlest women she'd ever met, had lied or was up to no good, she had to admit that something wasn't right.

After parking at the curb, she surveyed the exterior of the old Victorian, as well as the yard. She couldn't see anything amiss. Even the sidewalk had been swept free of leaves, the lawn newly mowed.

Still, Helen said she didn't know Maggie and hadn't asked her to stay at the house. What if Maggie really had been hiding out from the law? And what if she had a partner in crime?

Okay, so Lynette's imagination was running amok, but either way, it probably wasn't a good idea for her to confront Maggie alone. For that reason, she would ask Grant to go with her.

As Lynette climbed from the car, she clicked on the key remote to lock the vehicle, then strode to Grant's front door and rang the bell.

When he answered, wearing a pair of black sweats, his hair tousled from sleep, her heart lurched.

What was it about the man that, even when he was hanging out at home or working in the yard, he had a way of turning her inside out?

He lit up when he spotted her on the porch. "Hey. Merry Christmas. You're sure out and about early."

After she explained why, he said, "Wow. I always thought there was something weird about that woman. Hang on for a minute. I'll get the key to Helen's house—just in case Maggie's not there to answer."

"Why wouldn't she be?"

"Yesterday, I saw her in the yard talking to a shaggy-haired man with a beard. When I approached them, she told me that Helen would be coming home soon, so she'd be leaving. She wasn't sure if she'd see me again, so she said good-bye."

"Who was the guy with her?"

"She introduced him as Jesse. He was middle age, average height. Other than having shabby clothes and needing a shave, he seemed friendly."

"I'm a little uneasy about confronting them," she admitted.

"It's not like we have to bust in like a SWAT team. I have Helen's key. If Maggie doesn't answer, we'll let ourselves in. And if she's inside, sleeping or something, I'll tell her that I assumed she was already gone." Grant reached for her hand and gave it a gentle squeeze. "Don't worry. I'll be with you."

His support meant the world to her, but she didn't comment. Instead, she waited for him to get the key.

Ten minutes later, they'd searched Helen's house from top to bottom, only to find no sign of anyone having been there. The furniture had been dusted, the kitchen sink scoured. The countertops were clean, too.

Upstairs, the beds had been made—no rumpled spreads or comforters, every pillow in its place. Even all the bathroom towels, which appeared to be freshly laundered, hung straight.

"I guess she's gone," Lynette said. "But who was she? And why was she here?"

"I have no idea."

Both clearly awed and bewildered, they stood in the center of the living room with more questions than ever.

"I'll have a locksmith come out tomorrow and change all the locks on the doors," Grant said, "just to be sure Helen's secure. But I can't see that there was any harm done while Maggie was here."

Lynette furrowed her brow, still at a loss.

Grant reached for her hand again. "Are you ready to go? I can't see any reason to stay here any longer. Why don't you come back to my place and have a cup of coffee? I just put on a fresh pot, and I've got a fire blazing in the hearth. It'll be a good place to stay warm and dry."

It *was* really chilly this morning. And she didn't have anything else to do but to go back to an empty house. "Sure. That sounds like a wonderful idea."

And it really did. It would also give her a chance to call Helen and let her know that everything was okay.

After locking Helen's door, they returned to Grant's house hand-in-hand. Lynette supposed she could have let go of him, but she kind of liked having a physical connection to someone, especially on Christmas.

"You never did tell me whether you'd go out with me or not," Grant said, as they entered his living room.

Lynette still wasn't sure if she should, although she'd already come to the conclusion that he wasn't the kind of man who'd be abusive. But she had to admit being concerned about his job prospects and financial situation, which had her uneasy and reluctant to throw caution to the wind and trust her heart. As a result, she kept quiet for a couple of beats.

Finally, she asked, "What about Carly?"

"I told you before, neither of us even broached the subject

of a commitment. We just went out to dinner—*once*. If I never call her again, I doubt she'll be disappointed."

On the other hand, if Lynette didn't say yes, if she let Grant go without giving their friendship or whatever it was a chance, she might always wonder what she'd missed. And it might even be a whole lot.

She had half a notion to tug on his hand, to pull him closer, but some old habits were hard to break.

In an attempt to fight temptation, she slipped her hands into the empty pockets of her jacket, only to find a bit of lint and the coin Susan had given her the other day.

If you lose every bit of that inheritance Peter left you, Susan had said, *there's enough love in that single penny to see you through anything life throws your way.*

Something told her that was true, so how could she not take a chance?

"Okay, Grant. I'll go out with you."

A boyish grin spread across his face. "Then how about today?"

The suggestion took her aback. "But it's Christmas."

"A lot of restaurants offer a brunch. Why don't we take a drive and see what we can find?"

As his eyes searched hers, as their gazes locked, her heart skipped a beat.

Why not *today?* she thought. *Why* not *now?*

For once in Lynette's adult life, she realized that she had nothing to lose and everything to gain.

Carly's sons had yet to wake up, but the tree, which tilted a bit to the left, was up, the colorful lights blinking on and off.

Together, Max and Carly had placed the presents he'd brought beneath the bottom branches, then they'd perched the angel on the top.

Proud of a job well done, they'd gone into the kitchen to plan a Christmas breakfast.

"How about pancakes?" Max asked. "If you've got flour, eggs, and milk, we can whip up a batch."

"That sounds great, and I've got everything that we need to make them, but I'm out of syrup."

"Do you have jam or jelly?"

She smiled. "I'm afraid that's a staple around here, along with peanut butter."

"Good, then we're set." He tossed her a smile, surprised at how good it felt to be part of a team, especially on a day like this.

As they set about mixing the batter, Max said, "You know, I've been thinking. I'm going to call the county HR department tomorrow and tell them I want to go back to work."

"But what about your book?"

"There's not much I can do now but wait to hear from the agent, which might be months. I could work on proposals for the next books in the series, I suppose. But I can do that on a part-time basis, too. I . . ." He paused, wondering why he found it so easy to share his thoughts and plans with Carly, when he hadn't opened up with Karen all that much.

There was no rhyme or reason for it, he supposed, other than it just felt right.

"After talking to Frank Shurlock at the park," he continued, "I realized that my work at the probation department was more than a job. With the right attitude and a little faith, I might actually be able to help people, to make a difference in their lives."

"You've certainly made a difference in mine."

Max gazed at the woman who stood next to him, and all the walls he'd ever built to protect himself began to crack and tumble.

As he reached for Carly's cheek, running his knuckles along her soft skin, his heart pounded like crazy, racing to escape all the old scars and baggage, no doubt.

Would she pull away and let him know that he was way

off base? That he'd taken her appreciation and made it something she'd never meant it to be?

When she turned to face him, her lips parted, and he knew they were on the same page. He was going to kiss her—and she was going to let him.

As their lips met, and Carly leaned into his embrace, wrapping her arms around him, their kiss blossomed with innocence and awe, with the promise of a future together.

How about that?

Max had been given an unexpected gift this Christmas, too—an incredible blessing he didn't deserve.

But one he would cherish from this day forward.

Josh couldn't believe how incredible Christmas had turned out to be—or what a surprise it had been to wake up and find Max and the dog at their house.

The guy had even given him a fishing pole and gear, which was cool by itself. But what made it even better was that Max planned to take Josh to Lake Jennings tomorrow.

How cool was that?

Then Max had given his dog to Mikey, something his little brother had gone nuts over.

"For *real?*" he'd asked, looking first at Max, then at Mom, and back again. "I get to *keep* him?"

They'd both assured him the dog was his. So now maybe Mikey wouldn't expect Josh to entertain him so much, which meant babysitting him wouldn't be such a chore. And the dog could even sleep with him, so Josh could have a room to himself again.

His mom had loved her scarf, too. She'd put it on as soon as she opened it up, even though she wasn't going anywhere.

Now, as the adults took a seat on the sofa, looking kind of lovey-dovey, Josh figured it would be best to let them have some privacy. Maybe, if he was lucky, they'd fall in love and Max would start coming around more often.

"Hey, Josh," Mikey said. "Do you want to go with me and Hemingway?"

"Where to?"

"For a walk."

Josh glanced at the adults one last time and saw that they still wore those goofy smiles. So he said, "Sure. I'll go with you."

"Bundle up," Mom said. "It's looking pretty cold and nasty outside."

After putting on their jackets, they headed outdoors, then turned down the street toward the path that led to the canyon.

"Want to take Hemingway on the Bushman Trail?" Mikey asked.

"I guess so."

They'd barely made it as far as the creek, when Mikey glanced up in the sky at some little white fluffs of nothing coming down like fairy dust. "What's that stuff?"

It wasn't rain. Or hail, either. It was too soft for that.

Oh, man. Was it *snow*? In *Fairbrook*?

"I could be wrong," Josh said, "but I think it might be snowing."

Mikey let out a wild *whoop-de-doo* that caused the dog to jump. "He *did* it. He *really* did it. I told you God could do anything. You just gotta believe that He can. Wait until Nick sees *this*."

"Yeah, but it'll probably melt as soon as it hits the ground."

"But it's still *snow*," Mikey said. "You gotta admit that."

Josh supposed there was no argument there.

As they stood in the center of the canyon for a while, they watched the snow fall and tried to catch it on their tongues. They probably looked kind of dorky doing that, but Josh didn't care. Kids around here didn't see this kind of thing every day.

"Hey, dude," a boy's voice called—and not very nice.

Josh turned to see Ross "the Boss" standing near the

creek, holding a shiny black skateboard and wearing what looked like brand-new clothes—shoes, jeans, a white sweat-shirt.

Ross might have gotten more presents, but Josh had gotten a much better deal for Christmas.

"What are you doing out here?" Ross asked, his voice not the least bit friendly.

Before Josh could answer, Mikey popped off with, "We're walking our dog. He used to work for the military, sniffing out bombs and eating bad guys. His name's Killer, so you better not get too close."

A grin tugged at Josh's lips. His baby brother was getting kind of smart these days.

Unfortunately, Josh didn't think Ross would fall for the killer-dog story, which was too bad.

Him being here right now was also lousy timing. Josh had been all happy and thanking God for the snow, then dumb ol' Ross had to show up and ruin a totally cool miracle.

"Yeah, well, you guys need to get out of here," Ross said. "And take your wimpy dog with you. The Bushman Trail is part of my backyard, and you're trespassing."

He was full of it. The canyon was city property—and it backed up to a lot of people's yards. But Josh wasn't going to challenge Ross.

"Whatever," he said. "Come on, Mikey."

About that time, Ross bent over and picked up a rock, no doubt planning to throw it at them. But as he wound his arm, his foot slipped. And just like in the cartoons, his legs went out from under him, landing him right on the muddy slope of the stream.

The look on his face was worth a hundred bucks, especially when he slid into the cold, muddy water.

Josh wanted to laugh and tease him in the worst way, which would probably be suicide, no matter how funny it was—or how badly he deserved it.

Instead, he turned to Mikey. "Come on. Let's go home."

As they trudged up the snow-littered path to the street, trying not to slip like Ross had, Mikey asked, "Do you know what I think?"

"What's that?"

"His guardian angel probably got sick and tired of watching him pick on people and gave him a big push."

Actually, Josh wasn't so sure guys like Ross had a guardian angel. But if they did, angels probably weren't in the habit of pushing anyone around. Of course, he didn't know that for sure.

By the time they got home, the snow had stayed on the ground long enough to turn it a frosty white. Josh was going to call his mom and Max to the window, but before he got a chance, Mikey shouted out the good news.

At that, the adults went to check it out.

"I can't believe this," Mom said. "Mikey prayed that it would snow. And while I knew it wasn't completely impossible, I really didn't expect it."

"It probably won't last long," Max said, "but it sure makes for a perfect Christmas, doesn't it?"

"I couldn't agree more." Mom leaned into Max just a little, like they were good friends sharing a secret or some really good news.

"And you know what else?" Mikey said. "Ross 'the Boss' was giving Josh a hard time out in the canyon, but right before he could chuck a rock at us, he slipped and fell into the creek."

At that, Mom stiffened as though she was going to run outside and check on him. "Is he okay?"

"He's fine," Mikey said. "I think it was God's way of giving him a spanking."

"His fall was just a coincidence," Mom said. "But are you sure he's all right?"

"Yeah, but when his mother gets a look at how wet and dirty he is, he'll be in plenty of trouble with her."

"Well, speaking of getting in trouble with Moms, you guys

need to take off those dirty shoes and leave them by the door. Then wash up. Max and I are making hot cocoa and opening a box of graham crackers."

It wasn't exactly a special treat, but it was the kind of thing a normal family might do.

How cool was that?

Boy, things really seemed to be coming together. God had answered every one of Josh's prayers, although not in the way he'd imagined.

So even if his mom and Max didn't get married, even if they had to move out of this house, and Ross never did become a decent kid instead of a jerk, everything was going to be okay.

As Josh was kicking off his shoes, he heard his mom say to Max, "I received the Christmas miracle I'd been praying for—happy kids, loving hearts, good friends . . ."

"I know what you mean." Max gave her hand a squeeze. "Some of us even received a miracle we hadn't been praying for."

Ain't that the truth, Josh thought. And he had a feeling that a lot of those kinds of miracles were still in the works.